Also by Jonah Buck

Substratum (A Jasper O'Malley Novel)

CESSPOOL

A JASPER O'MALLEY NOVEL

CESSPOOL

A JASPER O'MALLEY NOVEL

Jonah Buck

A
Grinning Skull Press
Publication
Bridgewater, MA 02324

The Skull logo with stylized lettering was created for Grinning Skull Press by Dan Moran, http://dan-moran-art.com/.
Cover designed by Jeffrey Kosh, http://jeffreykosh.wix.com/jeffreykoshgraphics.
Published by Grinning Skull Press, PO Box 67, Bridgewater, MA 02324

ISBN: 1-947227-34-3 (paperback)
ISBN-13: 978-1-947227-34-7 (paperback)
ISBN: 978-1-947227-35-4 (ebook)

DEDICATION

For Mom and Dad

CONTENTS

"The silver light of the moon struck a half-reclining figure, snowy white… something dark stood behind the seat where the white figure shone, and bent over it. What it was, whether man or beast, I could not tell."

–Bram Stoker, *Dracula*

"A hundred times have I thought New York is a catastrophe, and fifty times: It is a beautiful catastrophe."

–Le Corbusier

"New York has a trip-hammer vitality which drives you insane with restlessness, if you have no inner stabilizer... In New York I have always felt lonely, the loneliness of the caged animal, which brings on crime, sex, alcohol and other madnesses."

–Henry Miller

Chapter 1
Cell Out

November 7ᵗʰ, 1925

Jasper O'Malley lay on the lumpy jail mattress, his hat covering his eyes. His gray suit was streaked nearly black with soot, and he reeked of kerosene and ash. More grime covered his face and hands. The guards had confiscated his pistol and collection of tools, but left him with his clothes.

Tall and wiry, Jasper's lanky frame took up the full length of the jail cot. Some superficial first-degree burns had turned his pale skin an angry red in places. His left ear was missing, but that injury was old and scarred over. Normally, he kept his hat tilted so it hid the worst of the damage, but the brim had partially burned away.

His long, delicate fingers were laced together over his chest as he rested. His chest moved up and down in a slow, steady rhythm, the only indication that he wasn't lying in state like some deceased totalitarian leader.

The cell was hardly peaceful, though. Jasper's cellmate jabbered incessantly. He sat on the opposite cot, muttering half to himself and half to Jasper. His eyes were glassy and bloodshot, and his pupils had a hard time tracking movement. The man sat because he was still too drunk to stand without wobbling.

Jasper had learned the man's name was Claude. His breath puffed the smell of cheap alcohol, the ghosts of bottles past, into the cell to mingle with the scent of fire and accelerant. They'd been processed at the same time and stuck in the cell together all morning.

Claude was bulky and short where Jasper was thin and tall. Thick, curly hair ran down Claude's arms all the way to his calloused knuckles. Bushy eyebrows loomed over his face like angry caterpillars. His pushed-in nose and meaty lips made him look like a shaved Sasquatch secretly living in Chicago's urban jungle.

Currently, he was explaining for the third time about how he just *knew* his wife was cheating on him, and *by golly* he was going to teach her a lesson, and she *deserved* that thrashing, and no he couldn't *prove* anything, but he was going to nip any thoughts of unfaithfulness in the bud *goddammit*, and the police had *no right* to interfere with a man asserting his prerogative, the damn Paddies.

Jasper was trying to tune out Claude by mentally reciting as much of *Hamlet* as he could from memory. He'd made it into Act II, minus a few hazily remembered soliloquies, when he heard the footsteps.

Somewhere at the end of the hall, a door squealed open, and Jasper recognized the soft, plodding footsteps of a guard's leather shoes. However, there was a second set of footsteps, a harsher *clack clack clack* against the polished cement floor that Jasper recognized as a pair of woman's heels.

A few seconds later, his suspicions were confirmed when a loud wolf whistle cut through the hushed conversations and muttered invectives that filtered out of the cells. Jasper didn't bother to raise his hat off his eyes as the footsteps approached, but he could hear prisoners in nearby cells moving closer to the bars to get a look at what was coming. More catcalls echoed down the jail's corridors.

Claude pushed his way to his feet and walked over to the cell door. He moved like a man fighting rough seas. He steadied himself against the bars and leaned his face close to the metal.

"Knock it off," Jasper heard the guard shout as the footsteps moved closer and closer. "Nobody wants to see that."

Finally, the footsteps stopped directly in front of Jasper's cell. He tipped his hat back on his head, revealing a set of unearthly green eyes beneath a shock of red hair. A few freckles stood around the base of his large, aquiline nose like campers contemplating a difficult summit. His features were sharp, but not unhandsome.

"Hello, Jasper," Amelia said. She stood a few feet back from the bars, her lips quirked into the beginnings of a smile. She was dressed in a trench coat and a man's black fedora. She looked good.

"Heya, sugar tits, don't bother with that bum. Why don't you come over here and talk to a real man," Claude said. He reached his arms through the bars and beckoned Amelia closer. Several nearby inmates hooted their approval, and the cell block buzzed with chatter.

Amelia's lips opened wider into something that could have been mistaken for a full smile. She stepped closer, and Claude's face broke open in a big, dopey grin. The guard started to reach out to stop her, but it was too late.

Amelia lifted her arm, and Claude reached out to take her hand. Before he could react, her fingers shot out and wrapped around his wrist, clamping down hard.

"Whoa, hey, what gives?" Claude said. "What are you ARGH JE-SUS THAT HURTS!" He lurched backward, trying to break her grip. She wrapped her other hand around his wrist as he retracted his arm as far as he could.

Amelia gave a sharp, vicious yank, and Claude shot forward. His forehead met the metal bars with a crack that reverberated all the way down the cell block, from one end to the other and echoing back a few times. Claude slumped to the ground in an unconscious heap. The jail's hall fell suddenly silent, the astonished inmates staring in a mixture of surprise and horror.

"I'm keeping the arm of the next one of you that calls me 'sugar tits'," she said, just loud enough for everyone to hear. Jasper could hear the other prisoners moving slowly away from the bars.

Amelia Rio was not a woman to be trifled with. Actually, she was usually the one doing the trifling, and she trifled hard. Before she met Jasper, she'd worked in the Detroit underworld. Now she was his partner at the Attican Detective Agency.

Her dark, curly hair was clipped into a short bob under her hat, framing her face. She was quite pretty by any standard, an asset that came in handy sometimes. More than one mark had spilled his guts to the friendly lady with the big brown *hey-there-handsome* eyes.

The Agency kept her around for more than her looks, though. She had been a getaway driver in her previous employment, and she was absolute hell on wheels. When things got rough, she also knew how to use her hands to keep herself safe.

Amelia frequently wore dainty, white driving gloves on her jobs, not because she was worried her fingerprints would be found where they shouldn't, but because her hands were rough and often splotched with stubborn oil stains. Hands that could field strip an engine and punch out a donkey didn't match well when she needed to work under-cover.

Jasper lifted himself up, unfurling his full height. "We can't take you anywhere." His voice was dry, but his eyes flashed amusement.

"Oh, is that so?" Amelia dug into one of the inside flaps of her trench coat and pulled out a folded edition of the day's newspaper. She snapped the paper open to the front page. "Nice to meet you, Pot. I'm Kettle."

The top story, highlighted in full-size screamer font, read:

Chicago's Milk Supplies Threatened

It continued with several alarming sub-headers.

"That?" Jasper asked. "I can explain that."

"Uh-huh. Start talking, O'Malley."

"I told you I had a lead on that opium smuggling ring. They were using an old farmhouse and barn south of town as their center of operations. Somebody paved a section of the field out in the middle of nothing so it would be hard to see without hopping some fences. Once a shipment was ready, they cleared the cows into another pasture and landed a plane on the asphalt. Everything stayed in the barn until they could bring it into town mixed in with trucks of farm goods. It was a pretty slick operation, really. I was canvassing the area, pretending to be a door-to-door salesman."

"What were you selling?"

"Encyclopedias."

"I bet you made a lot of friends doing that."

"Let's just say that I'm happy to be a detective instead of a sales-man. I think I'd starve to death in short order."

"So, what happened?"

"It took some snooping, but I found the smugglers' airfield."

"How did you spot it if they'd concealed it all the way out in a pasture?"

"I saw one of their planes land."

"Jasper O'Malley: super sleuth."

"I managed to sneak over and check out the barn as they unloaded. They had enough opium to supply morphine for a major war. Crates and crates of the stuff."

"I may not have been with the Agency all that long, but even I know you should have brought in the cops at that point."

"Somebody spotted me, and I needed a distraction."

"A distraction?"

"I might have set the barn on fire at that point."

"And I'm the one we can't take anywhere?"

"It could have been worse."

"Yes, it could have been," Amelia held up the paper again. "You sent a gigantic opium cloud billowing across half the state. Every cow from here to Wisconsin is over the moon right now, drugged out of their minds. Nobody can drink their milk without falling into a morphine high. You're just lucky the wind didn't blow the smoke over the city."

"Whoops."

"So what about the smugglers?"

"Some of the ones on the ground got away. They scrambled out of there once the police started to show up. The cops caught most of them, I think. They're on another floor in this jail, actually."

"What about the ringleaders?"

"They took off in the plane."

"So they got away? They're just going to collect another crew of lowlifes and set up shop somewhere else. They'll probably be back in business inside a month."

"I would be very surprised. I used most of the fuel from their plane to start the fire. They left in kind of a hurry, so they must not have done a preflight check. They didn't get real far."

"All right, then. Let's review. You burned down a barn, so that's arson and property damage, caused a plane crash, and sent a cloud of drugs drifting across half of Illinois."

"Don't forget trespassing. I wasn't supposed to be on that property in the first place."

"You're incorrigible." Amelia turned to the guard and nodded. He removed a hefty collection of keys from his belt and thumbed through them until he reached the correct one. He punched it into the lock, and the door clanked open with a groan of protest.

"C'mon out of there, son," he said. "The district attorney is declining the case. Let's get you out of here."

Amelia tossed him his Attican Detective Agency badge, and he snatched it out of the air. The badge disappeared into his jacket pocket, and he smoothed his rumpled suit. This was hardly the first time he'd seen the inside of Chicago's jail system, but the Agency had accumulated a lot of chips with the police, the district attorney, and the mayor's office over the years. Just last week he had picked up Amelia from the Women's Correctional Facility after she sank a gangland lawyer's yacht on Lake Michigan.

Jasper stepped over Claude's crumpled form and out of the cell. Baleful gazes met him from several nearby occupants. They directed their stares elsewhere when Jasper turned his liquid green eyes on them.

"Can I pick up my things?" Jasper asked the guard.

"We left them bagged at intake, as usual."

"Excellent. I'll need to pick up some fresh clothes, and then we can pay a visit to our client to settle out payment for this last job."

"Carlson's already been sent to close tabs with the client. You and I have a new client," Amelia said.

"That's a fast turnaround. What's the rush?"

"Special assignment. A client out of New York requested you specifically."

"There's an Attican branch office in New York. They can hire one of the local agents."

"They wanted you specifically. Barsymes sent me to tell you. Looks like I'm along for the ride."

"What do they need me for?"

"The client's letter said you might be able to track somebody down. They're looking for somebody named Ray Armstrong."

Even under the layer of soot and ash covering Jasper's skin, Amelia watched his face grow suddenly paler.

Chapter 2
No Business Like Sewer Business

Gordon Belmont moved down the narrow ladder one step at a time. His bulky boots and thick rubber gloves made it difficult to maneuver in the narrow manhole shaft, so he moved with an abundance of caution. The last thing he wanted was to slip on one of the slimy rungs and plunge ten feet into the sewer tunnel or get a leg caught in the ladder and snap an ankle.

Above, on the surface, a chill was beginning to settle over New York City. It wasn't the icy grip of winter yet, but that would come soon.

Down here in the darkness, it was still nice and warm. The water and insulating earth helped keep the sewers beneath the metropolis a stable temperature. It would have been pleasant but for the dankness, the rats, and the lingering smells. But honestly, that simply meant it was a damper version of any given back alley in the city.

He reached the bottom of the ladder and planted his feet on firm masonry. Cement ledges lined either side of the large central shaft. More ladders up to the street level lined the catwalk at regular intervals on either side of the tunnel. A few pinpricks of sunlight illuminated each ladder from holes in the manhole covers above, but most of the shaft sat in gloomy darkness.

Gordon reached up and flipped on his headlamp. A beam of light shot out and illuminated his immediate surroundings, revealing brickwork, lichen, and graffiti. Several brown glass bottles lay near the base of the ladder. Prohibition had driven booze underground, more here—literally—than in most places, but it hadn't eliminated it. Several gangs operated distilleries and speakeasies throughout the city, and others imported the stuff from Canada and Europe.

Gordon tapped one of the bottles with a foot, and it tipped over with a sharp jangle that echoed down the entire tunnel. The bottle rolled to the edge of the catwalk and dropped over the side. A few feet down, it splashed into the sluggish gray river below.

When he first started in this job years ago, Gordon wore a full beard. On his second day of work surveying the tunnels, he'd slipped on a patch of green slime and tumbled headfirst into the water below. He'd come up with candy wrappers, a half-rotten shoelace, and a decaying, severed duck's foot stuck in his beard. He chose to go clean shaven ever since.

The water below was hardly a stream of bubbling filth; the sewer system was too well maintained to produce any truly awful buildups, but it wasn't exactly clean either. Storm drains and other less-savory sources all emptied into tunnels like these before it all ultimately flowed into the river and sea.

During a hard rain, the tunnels might flood until the water rose up over the catwalk. A big storm would send leaves, trash, and rat carcasses shooting down the tunnel in an unstoppable tidal wave. Part of Gordon's job as a sewer inspector was to check for damage and structural instability before the really bad rains hit. If certain walls were breached, it could flood the subway system or even undermine the structural stability of certain buildings on the surface. A typhoon of raw sewage had a way of negatively affecting property values in the city, and so a select group of urban spelunkers like Gordon patrolled the tunnels with plat maps and headlamps to mark problem areas for repair.

It was a fine job, and for the most part, he enjoyed it. He was given plenty of time alone with his thoughts, away from the constant droning bustle of the city above. In a lot of ways, it was like exploring the lost ruins of some ancient civilization.

He had another duty around this time of year: rousting the homeless who inevitably gathered underground. The warmth below made the sewers a surprisingly hospitable environment during the harsher winter months. Sometimes little communities sprang up in the larger tunnels, odd little villages full of individuals and sometimes families.

Gordon didn't particularly enjoy kicking them out of the tunnels, and even less so when he needed to lead a few police officers down here for the occasional stubborn hothead. Ultimately it was for the best, though. Every year, one or two people were caught in the tunnels when the water crested. People drowned in the rising tide of icy filth or were swept away until the tunnels spat them out or they became a blockage somewhere deeper in the system. Neither option was a death Gordon would wish on any living soul, not even the rats that called the underground labyrinth home.

He examined his tunnel map, preserved under a sheet of clear plastic, and oriented himself. By the end of the day, he needed to check this entire grid.

Moving down the narrow walkway, he swept his headlamp from side to side. He checked where he was putting his feet, lest he trip and plunge into the stream below. Some lessons were never forgotten.

In a few places, heavy metal doors were recessed into the walls. Most of the airtight, submarine-style doors led to a connecting tunnel, either for the subway or some other utility. Others led to control rooms where wheels and levels could be operated to manually control some of the flow in the sewers.

Some of the newer doors didn't even appear on Gordon's plat map, and he had no idea where they went. The map didn't show where some of the doors went either because they opened up to the basements of some of the city's older buildings. Basically, the map was worthless, but Gordon didn't trouble himself with where the doors went, though. He just checked to make sure they were dogged shut and all the seals were intact.

In several places, he stopped and examined areas of crumbling masonry. One overflow tunnel appeared to be clogged. He wrote it all down, marking the coordinates on his map. Hopefully, the city engineers could get down here and repair the inevitable wear and tear before another wet season further eroded the damage.

Rounding a corner where the tunnel split, he finally saw what he had been expecting all along. A pair of legs sat stretched out from an alcove beneath another manhole cover. The legs were wrapped in a pair of stained, raggedy pants that might have been fashionable at some point, but were now only fit for a scarecrow. The pants terminated at a pair of cheap boots, the kind that couldn't keep water out and fell apart after a few months.

Some bum was sitting in the alcove, taking advantage of the thin streamers of sunlight that fell through the manhole cover above. Gordon sighed to himself.

Most of the folks down here were basically good-natured about moving along, especially once he explained that the tunnels flooded this time of year. A few were pieces of work, though. True of humanity as a whole, he supposed.

"Hey, buddy," he called as he walked closer.

His feet crunched on something. Shining his flashlight down to look, he saw... *What the hell was that?* He almost dismissed it as a clump of trash.

It was a thin, brittle sheath of some sort. Whatever it was, it reminded him of old paint chips that had fallen off the side of a house, except much larger. The debris was about the size of a watermelon, or it had been before he stepped on it. The weight of his foot had shattered it, but it had clearly been shaped into some complex form when it was whole.

A pair of odd divots had been punched into the cement near the curious mess. They looked like someone had been at the surface with a hammer. Little chips of concrete rested in a spray pattern around the imprints. The twin gashes were purely superficial, so Gordon didn't bother to write them down, but they were odd.

The pair of legs didn't stir. Gordon took his clipboard and whapped it on the brickwork to get the bum's attention. The legs still didn't move, and Gordon hoped the man wasn't drunk off his ass. Trying to drag drunks up one of the ladders was an ordeal for a younger man who still had a good back. Gordon was well past those days.

He walked all the way up to the alcove and stood directly in front of the legs. "Listen, Mack, I'm going to have to ask you to..." His voice trailed off as he saw what lay before him.

The man was dead. Very thoroughly dead.

His body looked like it had been mummified. The skin was wrapped tight around his bones and had the texture of a crumpled paper bag. His mouth gaped open in a silent scream, his shriveled lips tight against his teeth. Two festering balls of maggots writhed in the man's sunken eye sockets, staring back at Gordon. His arms were locked across his chest, desperately trying to fend off some unknown assailant.

Gordon had no idea what killed the man. It looked like his entire body had been drained of fluids. In several spots, blotches of blood stained his tattered clothing.

Had he been shot? No, the patches of blood weren't big enough. These looked more like deep puncture wounds. But even a knife would leave far more blood than Gordon could account for here.

Gordon stumbled backward. This wasn't the first time he'd seen a body in the tunnels. One way or another, a few people met their ends through some misadventure down here every year, but this was different. This man had obviously not died a good death. His face was locked into a final moment of fear and profound anguish. There was no sign of what or who killed him.

Gordon felt his arms break out in gooseflesh, He needed to reach the surface and find his supervisor and some police officers.

The corpse was propped half against the ladder leading up to the manhole above. Gordon dared not try to clamber over the body and scurry up the rungs. He might contaminate the crime scene and smear his fingerprints over valuable evidence.

At least, that's what he told himself. Somewhere deeper down in his mind, though, he could imagine one of the figure's skeletal, claw-like hands reaching out and latching onto his ankle as he tried to ascend, the corpse's dry, yellow teeth clacking together.

He shook the image out of his mind. The unexpected discovery of a body always made him skittish. *Perfectly understandable response*, he told himself.

Turning around, he started back the way he had come. He resisted the urge to break into a trot. His headlamp illuminated a cone around him, piercing through the gloom ahead.

The darkness, which he hardly noticed before, now seemed like a physical entity looming over his shoulder. His heart galloped around in his chest like an excited dog chasing after a ball, and he was suddenly aware of every trickle and drip in the tunnel. Every alcove was a pool of shadow that could be hiding anything. Immediately overhead, a truck trundled across a manhole cover. The noise rumbled down into the earth, and the shaft distorted the sound into a low growl.

Gordon licked his lips as he forced himself to walk at a steady pace toward the next ladder that would take him to the surface. A cold sweat formed on his brow in the warm, humid tunnel.

A soft thud sounded from somewhere behind him in the tunnel. Gordon spun around, half convinced the dead man would be up on his feet and shambling down the walkway.

His light spun crazy shadows across the tunnels as he darted his head back and forth, looking for the source of the noise. The dead hobo was still propped up in his alcove, his legs poking out like a couple of dried sticks.

Running his tongue along the roof of his mouth to work up some saliva, Gordon stood perfectly still. He knew the sounds of an active sewer, from the creaking pipes to the fetid trickles of outflow pipes.

This was not an ordinary sewer sound. Someone was down here with him, moving somewhere beyond the beam of his headlamp.

"Hello?" His voice rang down the shaft and echoed back as a hollow pantomime. There was no answer except for the gurgle of water.

He kept watching the darkness. Most likely, it was just another homeless person somewhere deeper down in the tunnel. He was torn. On the one hand, he desperately wanted out of here. On the other, whoever was down here might desperately need his help. He couldn't just leave them down here if there was…

Holy shit, what was that?

A shadow detached itself from the rest of the darkness in the tunnel and swept toward Gordon with horrible, freakish speed. He screamed, turned, and ran, his feet pounding on the cement.

Something thudded behind him, and heavy footsteps pounded out from the shadows. The echo chamber effect of the tunnel made it impossible to tell just how far back the footsteps were, but Gordon could tell they were gaining.

His rubber boots slowed him down, forcing him into a bandy-legged duck sprint. He flailed down the tunnel, the sounds of footsteps loud in his ear. He'd only caught a glimpse of the thing in the shadows, but the memory was now seared into his mind like the Titanic disaster.

Rounding the corner, one of his boots slipped in something moist. He flailed his arms as his legs spilled out from under him. Smacking into the brickwork, he thought he felt his ribs crack as the air was forced from of his lungs. Pushing his arms under himself, he scraped the skin off his palms as he hurtled back to his feet.

Black, oozing muck clung to the front of his clothes, but he didn't care. The footsteps were right on top of him.

He tossed a desperate glance backward as he started moving again, and his headlamp illuminated the thing right behind him. Gordon shrieked as the artificial light lit up a cruel, inhuman face.

A claw reached out and snagged Gordon by the shoulder, ripping him off his feet and nearly wrenching his arm out of its socket. He wailed as he was spun around to face his attacker.

Gordon had just enough time for a final, lingering scream before the horrible mouth clamped down over his throat. The last thing he heard before his vision faded out was the echoes of his own screams mixed with inhuman sucking sounds.

Chapter 3
If They Try to Execute Me Again

The cream-colored Peerless slid through New York's traffic like a shark gliding through the surf. When they reached their destination, Amelia slid the Agency car into a spot in front of the Shandor Building apartments. The Attican Detective Agency came into possession of the luxury sedan after its prior owners, a succession of jumped up gangsters, met various grisly ends.

Since the Agency purchased it at a police auction, Amelia had tinkered with the engine and worked it into peak condition. The car was fast and as nimble as a magician's fingers. The engine gave a final growl before she removed the keys, and it subsided into moody silence.

Jasper stepped out of the passenger door and waved off a valet. He'd changed into a fresh gray suit, with a white shirt and blue tie. His closet contained a row of identical suits, all tailored to his spindly frame.

Walking into the structure's lobby, the first thing Amelia noticed was the dark wooden floor. She thought it might be teak, but she wasn't sure. Someone had polished it into a nearly frictionless surface, and it looked so clean the Pope could probably eat off it without complaint. Various pieces of expensive-looking Bauhaus furniture filled the lobby, inviting residents to sit and read or chat in the sunlit lobby. A fire lit up the space, banishing the November chill outside like a surly bouncer ejecting undesirables.

A concierge smiled at Jasper from the front desk, but his eyes watched the two new arrivals to see what they would do. His smile looked like it was surgically affixed to his face.

"Can I help you?"

Their client's name was Laramie Resweber. Neither Jasper nor Amelia knew anything else about the man, why he wanted to find Ray Armstrong, or why he needed Jasper to do it. All they had was a name and an address for where to meet.

"I'm here to speak with Mister Resweber," Jasper said. Amelia didn't say anything. She was still new to the Attican Detective Agency, and she was nominally under Jasper's tutelage. Maybe that wasn't the best idea, given that Jasper tended to handle cases the way he wanted rather than the way the Agency wanted.

"Ah, you must be the detectives he sent for. I'll buzz him and inform him you've arrived." The deskman turned to a row of speakers and pressed one.

Amelia frowned to herself. Apparently, the clerk knew to expect them. He might very well know more than them about the investigation at this point.

"Thank you," Jasper said.

She could tell he was feeling the same twinge of irritation over being the least-informed person in the room. He tapped a long, spidery finger on the surface of the desk and looked around.

This was a nice building. Certainly not the Ritz, but upscale. That boded well. Occasionally, customers tried to stiff the Agency and refused to cough up for services rendered. They usually paid in the end. It was never wise to annoy people in a position to dig up all your dirtiest secrets and air them to the world

The clerk turned away from the wall-mounted speaker and nodded, that same obsequious smile plastered over his face. Amelia wondered how long the clerk could keep his face like that. "Mister Resweber will see you now. He's in room 517. The elevators are to your left."

Jasper nodded politely and turned around. Amelia stood near the fire, her hands shoved deep into the pockets of her trench coat. She watched the crowds pass by outside, a roiling mass of faces and jostling bodies. She was watching to see if they'd been followed.

Walking straight past the elevators, Jasper headed for the stairs. Amelia knew he didn't like confined spaces. They'd both had some bad experiences with a mine elevator not too long ago. She fell in behind him.

"Any idea why this Laramie Resweber character wants you specifically for this job?" she asked. Jasper had been silent almost the whole trip out here. Something was obviously eating at him, but she didn't want to push him. Now that they might be walking into the hornet's nest, she wanted to know at least some of what she might be getting into.

"I grew up in New York. I still have some family here. Resweber's looking for Ray Armstrong, and I used to run with Ray before I joined the army and flew recon planes over France. Ray and I never got back in touch, and I ended up in Chicago afterward."

"Went your separate ways?"

"In more ways than one."

"How does Resweber know about any of this?"

"I have no idea."

"I honestly didn't know you had any family," Amelia said. She knew Jasper used to have a brother, Percy, who had been his partner at the Agency before her. Percy had died some years ago, though Jasper had never bothered to share the details of that incident and she chose not to ask.

"A couple of younger sisters," Jasper said.

They reached the fifth floor, and Jasper marched out into the hallway. Plush, red carpeting covered the floor, and the walls were covered in a tastefully understated floral design. Through a window on the far end of the hall, Amelia could just see some of Central Park's taller trees peeking out from down the street.

They walked down the hall until he found room 517. Normally, clients came to them. This was their first time making a house call.

Raising a fist, Jasper rapped on the door one, two, three times. *Tap. Tap. Tap.* The heavy wood absorbed his blows. Amelia heard movement behind the closed door, soft, padded footsteps.

Next came the sound of a series of locks disengaging, one after the other. Amelia could tell what kind of mechanism each of the locks used based on the noise they made as they unlatched. There were five bolts, enough that someone would practically need explosives to break into the apartment.

Finally, a chain bolt scraped free, and the door slid open an inch. Unless he was badly mistaken, this was not Laramie Resweber.

"Hello. We're with the Attican Detective Agency. We have an

appointment with Mister Resweber," Amelia said to the pretty blonde nurse standing in the narrow crack of the doorway.

Jasper lifted his hat politely with his left hand to draw attention away from the fact that his right hand had reached into his jacket.

"Do you have ID?" She looked at the pair of private eyes through a crack in the door, not opening the door any wider.

"Of course," Amelia said, showing the woman her badge. Jasper held his badge up as well, and the nurse scrutinized them through the narrow opening. After a moment, she nodded and opened the door wide enough to allow them inside.

"I'm afraid Mister Resweber is very particular about security," she said a bit sheepishly. "He's in the living room. Please, come with me."

Amelia had already drawn some conclusions. Working with the Detroit underworld, she'd learned the rackets. Resweber was scared of something, but not the most sophisticated security expert. The front desk man had allowed them upstairs without fuss. Even a door with multiple locks could be battered down with relative ease using the right equipment, and a lone nurse made for a poor bodyguard. These defenses might turn away an assassin if that assassin was an asthmatic six-year-old, but more formidable opponents would not be so easily dissuaded.

The apartment was nice, like the rest of the building, but it was spartan. She didn't see any pictures hanging from the hall's walls. There wasn't much furniture, and the scattered pieces Amelia could see were new. Some still bore their price tags. Resweber had apparently blown into this apartment and left most of his past behind. She didn't see any personal touches or sign that this was anything but a newly furnished model apartment.

After a few feet, the hall opened up into a larger room, and Amelia caught her first glimpse of Laramie Resweber. Resweber was a black man who had probably once been as tall as Jasper, though it was difficult to gauge his full height because he sat in a wheelchair.

Figuring out the man's age was harder still, given the extensive burns on his face. In several places along the hairline, the skin was fused smooth in concentric patches. No hair grew in the burned spots, leaving his scalp with a blotchy pattern.

A crazy network of scar tissue covered his face and stretched down to his neck. In places, it looked like he'd been bombarded with tiny meteorites, with little craters blown out of his face. His skin had a strange glazed quality, as if his entire face might shatter if someone punched him in the nose.

Resweber's eyes looked like peeled grapes, blank, veiny orbs. Amelia moved slightly to the right, but Resweber's eyes didn't track her. The man was obviously blind.

"The detectives you called for are here," the nurse said.

"Thank you." Resweber's voice sounded like he'd been gargling gravel. "Please, please sit down." He gestured in the general direction of a couch.

Walking over, Jasper sat down and sank into the soft cushions. Amelia plopped down beside him. They glanced at each other. Neither one of them had expected anything like this.

Amelia cleared her throat. Resweber cocked his head. "That's a woman's voice. Mister O'Malley, did you bring a secretary?"

"I'm Amelia. We're partners." Amelia kept the tone of her voice plain and level. It was true. There were very few female private eyes in the business. Most of the large organizations, like the Pinkertons, didn't hire lady detectives. People constantly mistook her for a secretary or Jasper's girlfriend.

Occasionally, she wanted to strangle those people with their own intestines, but she wasn't above using it to her advantage either. No one expected a woman to be working as a private investigator. She could easily befriend suspects' wives, and tight-lipped men turned into braggarts when a pretty face hung on to their every word.

"Sure, sure. Yeah," Resweber waved the explanation away.

"You wanted help finding someone. Ray Armstrong," Jasper tried to jumpstart the conversation.

"Yes, that's why I enlisted your help. You know Armstrong. That makes you uniquely valuable to me." Resweber spoke in a quick, jaunty fashion, but Amelia sensed an underlying nervousness. She'd heard men who weren't sure if they were going to leave the room with their knee-caps intact or not speak with the same, rushed joviality. *We're all buddies here, right?*

"You've done some research," Jasper said, "but Ray and I haven't talked in a long, long time. What makes you think I'll be of any use to you?"

"I did some homework, yeah. Everyone said you were the best, and I want the best."

Jasper leaned back into the couch. "Perhaps you better explain just why you're looking for Mister Armstrong. Maybe I'd as soon not find him."

Amelia was itching to find out what this was all about, but she didn't say anything. She didn't want to butt in until she knew a little more about the monkey on her partner's back.

Resweber smiled at that. It was a ghastly expression. The smile grew so wide that the thin, brittle skin on his cheeks cracked slightly. Blood started to trickle down the sides of his face.

The smile faded from his lips like a dead star collapsing. The nurse reappeared to daub the blood from his cheeks. A few seconds later, his face was bandaged up.

"Do you know how I got here?" Resweber gestured to encompass the new apartment around them.

"Can't say that I do," Jasper said.

"I used to be a fixer. Grew up in Harlem, but branched out, you know? I had contacts. If you needed to get rid of an item without attracting attention, you came to me. If you needed an item of, shall we say dubious ownership, you came to me."

"You were a fence," Amelia said. She knew how the underworld worked, knew more than she wanted to know, actually. This was her language.

"Just one of my many talents," Resweber said. He looked like he was about to smile again, but suddenly thought better of it. Little roses of red had appeared on the bandages on either side of his face, like a macabre blush.

"You had dealings with Armstrong?" Jasper rubbed his chin.

"Yeah. Not often, but I knew who he was. He'd come by every once in a while looking for things, but never selling. Guns, usually. He wasn't an independent like me, though. I gathered he always worked for somebody else, but he never said who. We didn't ask too many questions of each other. One day, he came in and asked if I could set up a meeting."

"He wanted to meet somebody from another organization?"

"Sorta. I didn't know who the guy he wanted to meet was. He wasn't the sort who traveled in my circles, but I have contacts. It took me a while, but eventually I managed to get an ear to the guy Armstrong was looking for."

"Who was it?"

"Some professor type. Doctor Duncan Horvath. He worked over at Colombia, definitely not part of my usual social circle. Taught Old Church Slavonic in their languages department or some damn thing. Involved with some archeological preservation and stuff out in Eastern Europe, too. Transylvania. Bulgaria. Whatever. Like I said, not my turf."

"Doesn't sound like Armstrong's area of expertise, either. Any idea why he wanted to meet this Doctor Horvath?"

"I don't ask questions. It's part of the reason people come to me. Well, came to me. I don't exactly get many visitors in my current state. Not asking questions came back to bite me, as it turns out. I thought maybe this Doctor Horvath character might be looking to offload some stolen artifacts or something, and Armstrong was hoping to jump to the front of the line. All sorts of stuff have been smuggled out of that part of the world since the Czars fell. A lot of the stuff I pass along was pried out of the hands of some Russian noble or another." Resweber gave a little shrug.

"So how did you convince Horvath to meet with Armstrong?"

"That's the thing. He wanted to meet. Seemed to know who Armstrong was and wanted to set up a contact. He was edgy, though. He didn't volunteer much of his business, and I didn't want to know. Not all the stuff getting carried out of Russia is *things*, exactly. You get people. Girls. Some things not even I'll trade in. He wanted me to accompany him, though. Didn't have his own protection and didn't know where to get it. Thought having a third party along would keep things from dropping out of control, I guess."

"It sounds like he guessed wrong. Would he be interested in finding Armstrong as well?"

"He was the wrongest sack of turds you ever laid eyes on. You won't be able to hear his side of things either, because he's dead. Dead on toast, in fact. Armstrong shot him."

Jasper mentally tried to add everything up, but he was still missing a lot of pieces. "I'm still not seeing why you want to find Armstrong, though. It sounds like your business with him ended when he shot Horvath."

"Normally, it would have. I set the meeting up at an abandoned brownstone. It's been torn down since, but it was a drop point I'd used a couple of times before. I showed up with Horvath. When Armstrong arrived, they went inside together. I stayed outside to keep a lookout on the area. A black man just sitting on the stairs of a run-down building is pretty much invisible in some parts of this city."

"So what happened? What went wrong?" Amelia had seen gang-land deals go bad before, sometimes to catastrophic effect. Usually, the problem centered on money, but ego was also a big factor. A lot of people from her past strutted around like angry little game roosters, and sometimes they didn't mix well. Even when there were deals to be made, you might end up watching a cockfight.

"I have no idea," Resweber said. He shook his head. "They weren't in there five minutes before I heard a shot. Hell, the whole neighborhood heard the shot. As my luck would have it, there was a patrol car a block away. A black man sitting on an old porch may be invisible, but one booking it in the opposite direction of gunshots might as well glow in the dark. I was in the back of that prowler less than two minutes after I heard the shot."

"Where was Armstrong?"

"Gone. Poof. Horvath was still there, though. They found him dead on the floor, a bullet straight between the eyes. The gun was still there. I'd sold the thing to Armstrong not two weeks before. Sold him the rope he used to hang me. A couple of my prints were still on it. Armstrong must have used gloves, though, because it turned up clean on him. Not a trace. Slicker than shit through a goose, am I right?"

"So Armstrong framed you?"

"I'd say I was more of a convenient scapegoat. I don't think it was any sort of personal vendetta against me. Armstrong saw the bus coming, and he threw me under it as soon as I'd outlasted my usefulness."

"Mister Armstrong is not a particularly pleasant person," Jasper said.

"Keen observation, Sherlock. Here's a gold star. The evidence wasn't exactly airtight, especially given that I didn't do it, but the jury saw what they wanted to see. Cops find me. Fleeing the scene of a murder. Leaving behind a gun with my prints. And no sign of anybody else. The trial wasn't exactly pretty."

"You seem, ah, less incarcerated than most people convicted of murder."

"Give the man a cigar for his powers of observation and deduction. It goes a little further than that, buddy. The jury came back with a death sentence."

"So what are you doing here? How'd you go from death row to a wheelchair and a nice apartment near Central Park?"

"Aye, there's the kicker. I spent six months in Sing Sing, waiting for them to kill me. Do you have any idea what a strange feeling that is? You're sitting there every day, counting off the hours until you die, if you're so inclined, and you can't do a thing about it. You're surrounded by people who *will* kill you, and all you care about is what they're serving for lunch that day because you don't want to think any further ahead than that.

"Well, finally the day came. They use an electric chair at Sing Sing, and it's a mean bastard. Everybody—guards and prisoners alike—calls it Old Sparky. Not exactly gallows humor if it's a chair, but you get the idea." Resweber's mouth cracked open in another smile. His nurse stepped over and checked the IV bag hooked to his arm.

"They took me out of my cell just past midnight. Standard practice. They take you over on your appointed day as soon as they possibly can. That way, if there's some problem, they have a full twenty-four hours to fix it. Besides, nobody likes being left waiting, right? It was almost a relief when the guards came and got me for the last time. The waiting, the anticipation, is what really cuts into you if you let it. After all, we're all going to die someday, but most of us get to pretend it's never going to happen and live our lives like normal. We'd all go insane if we just marked each day off as another step on our shuffle toward the grave.

"They strapped me in. They have to make sure you don't squirm away obviously, but they also don't want you bolting upright and start doing the 2,000-volt mambo. There was this one guy, a big guy with a Polish name, who they executed around the time I arrived in Sing Sing. The current caused him to twitch so violently that his legs broke against the straps.

"You get your eyes taped shut, too. Turns out that much electricity pretty much cooks you from the inside out. A man's guts might be two hundred degrees by the time they declare you dead. People's eyes tend to melt when they get that hot. Sometimes they explode, if the stories I heard are true. They tape your eyes shut so the janitor doesn't have to hose your peepers off the floor.

"To make sure the connection is good. They have to shave your head and one of your legs. They attach the electrodes, one to your head and one to your calf, and you're ready to go. The electrode for your head is a sort of helmet thing with a wet sponge inside to help fry you up good.

"The part that actually kills you isn't having your brain cooked, though. I read up on it. Sort of morbid fascination, I guess. The voltage makes your heart go crazy and shuts it down. If you're lucky, it'll blast the consciousness right out of your skull, and you'll just stop breathing. Your muscles twitch and jive whether you're awake or not. Really, the only way they know how long you're alive is if you manage to scream. They tell me I was a screamer, but I don't really remember that well. I just remember my vision under the bandages going from black to all white when they threw the switch."

"You mean to tell me you…survived…your execution?"

"I wouldn't have if they kept at it, but they were never supposed to take me there in the first place. The governor had signed a commutation to life in prison half an hour before. Thought the evidence was a little too shaky to want my death on his conscious, but didn't particularly care if I rotted in prison for the rest of my life, I guess."

"So why did they start the execution?" Amelia felt odd realizing she was talking to a man who had been executed.

"The commutation got there late. They drove it over and got stuck in traffic. The governor's man stormed into the room about ten seconds after they hit me with the first jolt. Started shouting at them to stop. Security almost tackled him, thinking he was some nut. Can you believe that? Stuck in traffic. A minute earlier, and I'd have been in the clear. Ten seconds late, and it took somebody most of the next day to scrape all the burnt skin off the electrodes.

"After that, they gave me a full commutation and a stipend, enough to set up here. As far as they're concerned, the great state of New York has done its duty to justice in punishing Horvath's killer. It's not that much more expensive to set me up here, and it's a lot cheaper than gearing up for the Supreme Court fight I'd put up if they try to execute me again."

"I think I know where to start, but first I need to make sure I understand why you want to find Armstrong. We're not a hatchet squad. We can turn down any case we don't like. If you're just doing this hoping we'll kill him, or if you will just send people after him once we find him…"

"I don't want a hit put out on him. Not in so many words, anyway. My name is still on the books for Horvath's murder, and Armstrong's out free. He set me up to take the fall. I want the police on his tail. I want him in Sing Sing. I want to be in the observation room when they lock him into that chair and pull the lever."

Resweber smiled too wide thinking about Armstrong frying, and his charred lips ripped open.

Chapter 4
Reunion

The Peerless rolled to a stop in front of the docks. Its sleek contours stood out among the harbor's work trucks and honking traffic. Black Fords buzzed up and down the street like ill-tempered ants. A single yellow cab worked its way through the pack, the driver periodically waving his fist at slower vehicles or pedestrians.

Amelia parked illegally near some dock front warehouses. The smell of salt water and oil was strong in the air. Seagulls wheeled through the deceptively sunny sky, shrieking at each other like the other New Yorkers.

"I'm surprised your contacts are still good here, Jasper. If you've been gone for most of a decade, a lot of people will be out of the game."

"That's why we're starting here. I would have heard if this one went out of business. Some contacts are like that."

Amelia shrugged. If anything, she'd learned that her partner was a very private individual. Sometimes it struck her that she really didn't know Jasper very well despite spending so much time with him. He didn't give away much, even off the job.

Jasper pointed toward one of the larger warehouses, a ramshackle condemnation paper magnet that looked like it was ready to fall into the ocean. The corrugated tin roof was covered in such a thick layer of gull droppings that it looked like an early snow had come to New

York City. The parts that weren't covered with guano were covered in rust, and the wooden support beams looked like they might collapse if anyone leaned on them. Just looking at the structure almost gave Amelia's eyeballs tetanus.

He started off, and Amelia followed. The warehouse had a big rolling door for receiving bulky shipments and a normal door wedged next to it. Jasper walked up to the human-sized door and raised a fist to knock.

Before his knuckles could rap against the streaked metal, the door flew open on well-oiled hinges. Amelia's hand instinctually dropped to the Luger tucked away in her trench coat, but she didn't need it.

"Jasper O'Malley!" A man built like a tugboat barreled out of the open doorway and wrapped his arms around Jasper in a gigantic bear hug. He lifted Jasper off the ground and spun him around like a child.

Amelia had seen people greet Jasper by throwing things at him, shouting, or discharging various calibers of firearms in his general direction, but this was a first. Their job often involved sticking their noses where they didn't belong, and people usually responded in a less than amicable manner.

"Hi, Rocky," Jasper said as he was put back down.

"We knew you were in New York."

"Word travels fast."

"But we didn't know if you would actually stop in."

"I need information."

"Who doesn't?"

Amelia eased her hand away from the butt of the Luger. "I'm Am—"

"Amelia Rio. Out of Detroit. We know," Rocky said.

Amelia's teeth clacked together as her mouth snapped shut. What in the blazing blue hell was this? They hadn't told anyone save Resweber they were coming to New York.

Jasper must have noticed her look of consternation. "This is an information brokerage. It's what they do." He shrugged.

"Ever given any thought to quitting the Atticans, Jasper?"

"You know I'd be second fiddle around here. It would be… stressful."

"Well, come in anyway. If you're not here to sign up, we can at least help. C'mon. The boss will want to know you're here." Rocky disappeared inside the doorway. His wide shoulders barely fit through the doorframe. Jasper followed him inside. Amelia stepped through the rectangular portal and blinked.

The floor was smooth glass. Not just any glass, though. It was cut into individual squares and reinforced to give a better view of the water just inches below. Someone had turned the floor into the most amazing aquarium she had ever seen.

Several small sharks circled the length of the building. One of them swam straight toward Amelia, and she had to resist the urge to step out of its way. It tilted its eyes upward as it swam under her shoes, examining her. She kept her combat boots planted firmly on the floor and let the predator pass her by.

Other sea life also filled the miniature biome. Small schools of colorful fish darted about, seeking shelter amidst clusters of rocks when the sharks drew too close. Clownfish sat amid clumps of anemones.

The effect of the floor was at once mesmerizing and disorienting. Each step made her think she would plunge into the water.

Nor was the floor the only curiosity in the strange warehouse. Along one wall was a fully stocked wet bar. Prohibition didn't outlaw the possession of alcohol, but it did ban its manufacture and importation. Judging from the labels, a lot of the beverages had come from Europe and were definitely not legal. She spotted German beers, Italian wines, and French champagne. There was also a stockpile of pre-Prohibition American whiskey.

A couple of men stood around the bar. They glanced at Amelia with a mixture of suspicion and professional interest. They seemed to recognize Jasper, though. A flurry of hushed conversation passed between them.

The building's interior walls had been done over with regular drywall. The inside bore none of the signs of disuse and rot evident on the outside. Impressionist paintings hung from several of the walls.

Rocky led them toward the back of the warehouse. Jasper walked along behind Rocky without any apparent interest in his surroundings.

Amelia knew his eyes would be crawling over everything and cataloging it all. She, on the other hand, wasn't above a little straightforward gawping. She'd seen her fair share of fancy digs during her time in Detroit. Her boss, an ex-German army officer who took some former elite stormtroopers and carved out a major criminal fiefdom, had lived in a veritable villa near Lake Michigan. This blew his set out of the water.

What sort of contacts did Jasper have here? Obviously, this place wasn't on the level. She suspected there were enough hidden security measures in place to keep the place safe from anything but a battleship. Just keeping the joint a secret would require greasing a lot of palms, some of them fairly powerful.

Rocky led them toward a pair of imposing oak doors, intricately carved from top to bottom and probably worth more than most people's yearly salary. Rocky knocked and opened the doors without waiting for a response.

The doors swung open to reveal a single, large office. A spacious desk stood in the center of the room. This place practically exuded quiet power and authority, and it was obviously the organization's sanctum sanctorum.

What really caught Amelia's attention was the woman standing behind the desk. She was tall and gorgeous, with flowing red hair that fell down past her shoulders. A dark blue dress clung to her figure as she picked at her unpainted nails with a bone-handled knife.

She glanced at them, and Amelia noticed one last thing. She had spooky green eyes.

Oh shit.

"Hello, Jasper," the woman said. She nodded, cool but polite.

"Hello, Iris," Jasper responded. He turned to Amelia. "This is my sister, Iris O'Malley."

Chapter 5
Knowledge is Power

"You must be Amelia," Iris O'Malley said. "Hmph."

Jasper sat down in one of the chairs in front of the desk without waiting for permission. He looked at his younger sister, marveling at the fact that he hadn't seen her in the better part of a decade. The years hadn't changed her much. Meanwhile, he had quite the collection of scars, not all of them necessarily visible, to show for his years.

"I need information, Iris."

She sat down behind her desk. A single, small fish approached the pile of rocks under her desk. A tentacle shot out from a gap in the rocks, and the fish disappeared in a flash of scales and a spurt of blood.

"Information is my business," she purred. "Who do you need dirt on? I can dig it up. Or plant it, if that's what you want. I'd have to charge you the usual rate though, of course."

"It's not that kind of job, and it's not that kind of information I'm after."

"But this is more than just a social call, isn't it?" She flashed a winsome smile. Jasper had to remind himself of the reasons he'd left New York in the first place. He knew some dangerous people, but Iris knew all his weaknesses. Right now, she still didn't know what he needed, so he was being appraised. He wished he had some other contacts to go to, but Iris was his best bet.

"I'm looking for Ray. I don't see him around."

"Ray left the organization. He doesn't work for me anymore."

Jasper blinked, the only sign that showed his surprise.

Amelia looked back and forth between the two O'Malleys. She didn't like being left in the dark. She really didn't like that Jasper had been so coy with what he knew, but now she could see some of the reason he was trying to keep as much as possible under his hat. There was an electric undercurrent in the conversation, the tide of suppressed history threatening to overflow its dam and come cascading out.

"You've got a deer-in-the-headlights look on your face, dearie." Iris turned to Amelia. "Didn't my dear brother tell you what he was getting you into? He does that. I don't think Percy really knew what he was getting into, either."

"Leave Percy out of this," Jasper said. His voice was flat and hollow in his own ears. He'd never told Amelia the painful details, but Percy O'Malley had been Jasper's partner before her. He died when a job went bad. Jasper had worked alone for a long time after that.

In a lot of ways, Amelia reminded him of his brother. They were both comfortable around other people, whereas he was an increasingly solitary creature. Quick on their feet and shorter tempered than his own unflappable manner, they made up for some of his defects.

Iris was still focused on Amelia. "Let me ask you this. Do you know why you're looking for Ray?"

"We have a client who wants him found." Amelia gave a perfect non-answer, revealing exactly zero information about Laramie Res-weber or his motives.

Jasper was pleased. He'd personally recruited Amelia, and she was shaping up well.

"No, no, no. You misunderstand. Do you know why *you* are looking for Ray? Why not some local boys? There are other Atticans in New York. The city is practically crawling with Pinkertons and other sleuths. But somebody must have come to you specifically asking for Jasper, didn't they? Why else would they have pulled you all the way from Chicago?"

Amelia sat in silence.

"Poor, dearie. My brother's left another partner in the dark. Let me tell you a little about Ray and Jasper."

"She doesn't need to hear this," Jasper said. But it was too late. The ship was already pulling out of the harbor, and there was nothing he could do short of setting the building on fire to stop it.

"Knowledge is power," Iris said, completely ignoring Jasper now. Her eyes stayed on Amelia. "You must know that better than most people. You're being trained to ferret out secrets, after all. Lots of people have dirty little secrets that could ruin them. From the mightiest politician all the way down to the lowliest unfaithful husband. A lot of them would pay dearly to keep those secrets under wraps. On the other side of the equation, there's plenty of people who would love to get their grubby little paws on that information. From political rivals all the way down to suspicious wives. Even businesses will fight tooth and claw to protect their trade secrets.

"What I run is an information brokerage. There's always disparities in how people value information. An employee might have information that his much-despised boss is doing something illegal, which he might be willing to sell for a quick hundred dollars. But maybe we have a dossier on that employee from one of his co-workers. We come to the boss, and he buys information for five hundred dollars that the employee is embezzling money."

"Iris runs New York City's preeminent blackmail clearinghouse," Jasper said.

His sister tapped a thin cigarette out of an ivory case. Jasper held out a lighter, and the smell of rich Virginia tobacco began to fill the room. Iris blew a puff of pungent smoke at Jasper, and he waved it away. The tiny cloud dissipated.

"Please. We're not so different from the stock exchange. People value information differently, and we merely facilitate bringing those needs together. Someone wants to buy. Someone else wants to sell. Nowadays, we sell bundles of secrets by the thousands to the highest bidder. They dig through the information themselves, and if they want to use it for blackmail, that's their business. Just so long as we get a cut, of course. "

"Oh. Well, that changes everything, then. Pardon me," Jasper said. He tried to ignore the noxious cigarette odor.

"Come off your high horse, Jasper. You and Ray built this place. You were the one who recruited me, actually. Remember that? I was only seventeen when you and Ray asked me to join, just a couple of kids yourselves." She snorted.

"Things were different then. The whole place worked a lot more like a detective agency. We tried to solve problems for people. We forwarded most of the criminal information to the police."

"Most? Not all?" Iris smiled. There were a lot of teeth in her smile.

"I've always used my discretion. I still do. It doesn't mean I'm always right, but I do what I think needs to be done. We used to help people."

"Uh-huh. That's really beautiful, Jasper. Just peachy," Iris let the smoke waft across the desk. "We still help people. People come to us for information, and we provide it. We're just using a better business model than you. Everything is worth what people will pay for it. If someone isn't willing to pony up to buy information or to keep it suppressed, it must not be worth very much to them.

"Our organization provides dirt on demand instead of waiting for clients to walk in our door. We already have information when they come in our door because we're constantly collecting it. If we don't have what they want to know, only then do we send somebody out on a specialized job. People get exactly what they want without the wait. Quick and clean.

"We're always looking for good talent. We would take you back with open arms if you wanted to be here, Jasper. I can go look up how much you earned last year. I guarantee we can double it."

"I'm not looking for work, Iris. Where's Ray? We need to speak with him."

"Hmm. A pity. How about you, Amelia? We're always looking for fresh blood. The protégé of one of our organization's founders would be quite a catch."

Amelia opened her mouth to politely decline, but she had to admit that she recognized just a tiny bit of herself in Iris. She knew what it was like working in the boys' club outside the law, an outsider among the outsiders. There was something oddly comforting in seeing that Iris O'Malley had made it in that world and thrived.

"Off the table. We just need to find Ray, and then we're going back to Chicago," Jasper said.

Amelia looked at Jasper and closed her mouth. A frown creased her face for half a second before she wiped it away. She didn't like having answers given for her. Iris smiled again, her red lipstick accentuating her sparkling white teeth.

"Very well, brother. I'll cut you a deal. I don't know exactly where Ray is right this second, obviously, but I'll tell you a place where he'll come around."

"Has he shacked up with one of the gangs? If he's not working for you anymore, he'll have gone somewhere else where he can cause trouble."

"No, he's gone straight."

"I somehow doubt that," Jasper said. He thought back to Resweber's account of Ray shooting Dr. Horvath in an abandoned building.

"Well, straighter, at least. This is Ray we're talking about."

Jasper sighed. "All right, what's your offer?"

Iris sucked the remainder of her cigarette down to the nub and stubbed it out in an ashtray. Another small fish was approaching the pile of rocks near her desk in the aquarium. "I'll tell you where to find him, but I want something in exchange. Anything you find out in your investigation, you hand over to me."

Jasper looked at her for a moment. "Deal."

Chapter 6
Security Breach

Amelia parked the Peerless directly in front of a "Parking Permit Required" sign, got out, and slammed the door. Jasper unfolded his wiry frame from the passenger seat and shut the door with a gentle push.

He looked up at the glass-and-steel structure that served as Yersinia Bioresearch's New York headquarters. The medical company performed all sorts of cutting-edge research and had done some impressive work with vaccines. They had a fairly famous international outreach program that worked to bring medicines to remote parts of the world and provide basic medical training.

Jasper didn't know much about them beyond their sterling reputation, which made it all the more surprising they would hire the likes of Ray Armstrong as their head of security. He was surprised they would hire him as a janitor, let alone a senior position. Ray was liability incarnate, and his methods didn't exactly fit with Yersinia's warm, fuzzy public image.

But what Iris had said made a certain amount of sense. If the company were working on something big, really big, they wouldn't want corporate poachers stealing it. The people who had the best chance of stealing the information from Yersinia were Iris and Ray, insiders who knew how to find information leaks and plug them. Yersinia must have offered Ray a wheelbarrow full of money to get him to leave the information brokerage. Maybe several wheelbarrows.

This was why Iris agreed to help in exchange for information. Anything that warranted such extensive measures had to be worth having. If Jasper could get it for her, she wouldn't mind burning Ray. So much the better, actually. Ray wasn't an asset anymore, and he was standing in her way.

He could tell Amelia wasn't happy he was playing his cards so close to his vest on this job, but there were private matters to be dealt with. A lot of history he would have preferred buried risked being disinterred. She would just have to deal with it. Now that they knew where Ray worked, it was only a matter of time until they got what they wanted and went back to Chicago. He would just ride this out and then smooth things over later. Eventually, they needed to grab Ray, but first, they needed information.

"How do you want to handle this?" Amelia looked at the building, too, squinting against the sunlight reflecting off its glass exterior. She chewed on her lip a second. "There's no point in trying to do a smash and grab. We don't even know if he's in right now. Resweber wants us to sic the cops on your old pal. Even if we got our hands on him, he's not wanted for anything right now. The police sure won't hold him, and we'll just look like kidnappers."

"Right. We need something that'll let the police nab him. If we can just link him to the Horvath murder, or a few other things for that matter, they'll get their hooks in him, and Resweber will get what he wants. Then we can pack up and ship out of this town."

"What sort of other things has Armstrong been involved with?"

"Not now."

"You mentioned other things. Is this tied in with the information brokerage?"

"Let's keep focused. I say we scout the place out. We need dirt on Ray, but he'll be good at hiding it. He won't keep many records, but there's a lot of bureaucracy tied up in a corporation this size. He won't be able to operate with total free reign. If we can find something, anything, incriminating, we'll bring in the cops, and they'll put him on ice."

"Fine," Amelia said. "How are we going to get in there? They're not going to just let us wander around."

"I'm glad you asked, Miz Cruz." Jasper ducked his hand into his jacket and emerged with a bulging billfold. He flipped it open to reveal a New York driver's license with a picture of Amelia beneath a description of her appearance. The name on the license read "Penelope Cruz."

He removed another fake ID from among the several dozens clustered in the billfold. This one featured a picture of Jasper. It was a hospital badge identifying him as Dr. Gary Silverstein of Boston.

"I'm here for a meeting, and you're my personal assistant. We better hurry, or we'll be late to our appointment." Jasper began walking toward the imposing structure, marching straight up to its revolving glass doors. Amelia scampered to catch up.

Jasper shoved his way into the revolving door, walking at a brisk pace. When he emerged inside the building, he was wearing a pair of thick glasses, and a slouch had lowered his frame considerably. A few subtle changes had rendered his profile almost unrecognizable.

He sidled toward the front desk. A directory placard hung nearby, and he picked a name at random. The secretary at the desk smiled at him.

Near the elevator, a janitor in a spiffy blue uniform pushed a mop across the sparkling tiled floor. A giant chrome sculpture that looked like a twisted, inverted wind chime towered over the desk in front of them.

"Ah, yes. Hello. Sorry I'm running late. Doctor Silverstein. I'm here to see Doctor Forrester. Could you point me in the right direction?" Jasper adjusted his glasses by pushing them up the bridge of his nose.

"I'm sorry, but you're…?"

"Doctor Silverstein. I really mustn't keep Doctor Forrester. This is my assistant, Miz Cruz." Jasper eyed the laminated ID badge pinned to the greeter's lapel.

"I'm sorry. I don't have any record of—"

"Never mind, he's expecting me. I'll just head up and see him." Jasper headed toward the elevators, moving at a fast clip. Amelia started to follow him.

The secretary all but leaped out from behind her desk and charged after Jasper. She ran up to him and grabbed him by the elbow. Jasper spun around in her grip, and they bumped into each other.

Near the giant sculpture, the janitor dropped his mop to the floor and appeared next to them in a blue flash. He piled in next to Jasper.

"Whoa, hey. What's all this? Get your grubby hands off me, you insignificant little non-entity." Jasper stopped and whipped his arms free. The secretary and janitor both released him.

"Sir, you're going to need to check in with security in the basement before you go anywhere," the janitor said, his voice all steel. "Ernest Hives" was stitched across the breast of his uniform. He brushed his hands off on his stainless jumpsuit as if Jasper was encrusted in excrement from diseased farm animals.

"Doctor Silverstein, please," Amelia said. "It will be okay if we're late. I'm sure Doctor Forrester will understand."

"Fine. Fine. Fine." Jasper crossed his arms.

"C'mon, you two," Ernest said. "I'll escort you down to the security office." He turned around to lead them to the elevators. The janitor wasn't what he appeared to be. Mr. Hives was clearly part of Yersinia's security team.

Jasper had planned to dart into the building under the pretense of a meeting, but he could make this work as well. It would be even better if they had let him wander around without supervision, but this would allow him a chance to check out their security apparatus up close.

"Very well," Jasper said. With the disguised guard's back turned, he slipped something into Amelia's hand. It disappeared into her pocket in a single, fluid movement.

The janitor moved to a bay of elevators and pressed the down button. A low hum filled the alcove as the elevator descended from the heights above.

Their escort had dropped all pretense that he was here for any reason but to oversee the entrance. It wasn't a bad ruse. Yersinia's lobby looked like it was completely unguarded and open, but Ray had a pair of eyes watching.

With a ding, the elevator doors slid open. Ernest shuffled them inside, and the doors closed shut behind them with a slow finality. Jasper watched the view of the lobby compress to a mere slit and then disappear completely.

"Unfortunately," the janitor said, "there are some very sensitive research projects at this facility. Given that you almost breached security, we'll have to perform our standard protocol consisting of a brief questioning, inspecting your possessions, and a strip and full body cavity search. The process should only take a few hours."

Jasper felt it in his gut as the elevator began a swift descent down into the building's basement. They seemed to descend for a very long time.

"That seems a bit…excessive," Jasper said. "I'm sure if you just check with Doctor Forrester you'll find that we scheduled this meeting months ago. I'm here to discuss my new centrifuge design for blood transfusions. There must be some mistake. I'm sure if you just look at Doctor Forrester's schedule, we can clear this whole thing up."

Dr. Forrester obviously didn't know any Gary Silverstein of Boston and certainly wasn't expecting them, but Jasper had to play the part. Hives was taking them right to the security floor, exactly where they wanted to go.

"And we will, doctor. Believe me, we will. Hopefully, we can clear this whole thing up in just a few hours. That would be nice. But if you really did speak with Doctor Forrester, he should have warned you about how seriously we take security here. We'll still have to follow the usual protocol, though. Probably best to just sit back and relax. You're going to be here for a while once we get you checked in."

Hives spoke like he was talking to a child standing near a broken vase. Maybe a particularly dim child. There was an undertone of anticipation, though. Jasper decided that he didn't much care for Ray's new lackey.

The elevator shuddered to a stop with a groan.

Jasper stood rod stiff. Partly, he wanted to play the part of the mortally offended researcher, but he was also tense about the prospect of possibly seeing Ray Armstrong again. It had been a long time since they last saw each other, and the circumstances had not been pleasant.

"All right, you two, processing is just down this hall. It'll be off to the interrogation cells from there."

"I…I don't want to be here," Jasper mumbled. "You can't treat us like this."

"New boss. New policies around here. Nobody gets to just waltz in here. These projects are too valuable."

Ernest reached into a pocket in his jumpsuit, and his hand emerged holding a small metal object. The artificial light gleamed off the tube's tapered surface. With a flick of his wrist, he transformed the small cylinder into an extendable baton. The full truncheon gleamed much more evilly now that its deadly length was exposed.

"Too bad. You shouldn't have tried to come barging in here. Now get moving."

Shuffling his feet, Jasper moved out of the elevator into the well-lit, unfurnished hallway. Doorways led off from either side of the hallway, but no one else seemed to be occupying the hall. Amelia followed him out of the elevator, and the guard brought up the rear. He smacked the tip of his cudgel into the palm of his hand in a steady rhythm.

With a little whimpering noise deep in the back of his throat, Jasper proceeded down the hall, Amelia walking next to him. Their captor walked with a swagger, maybe not consciously enjoying himself, but certainly feeling the balance of power in his favor.

They passed a door on the left. A little placard read "Supplies." The door was some sort of cheap particle board fixed to look like something much fancier. However, the doorframe was made of thin, tapered metal.

Good enough.

Jasper stopped in his tracks.

"Hey, keep moving," the blue-clad guard ordered.

Jasper didn't move except to raise his hands. "You're making a mistake. I'm not supposed to be down here."

"I said, keep moving." The guard came up from behind with the truncheon. He laid his free hand on Jasper's shoulder. Jasper spun around in the opposite direction, breaking the man's grip and simultaneously bringing one of his own arms around. Using the momentum from his spin, Jasper reached out and planted his hand on the side of the man's head. He followed through with the swing, shoving the guard to the side and smashing his skull against the metal doorframe.

The man staggered, any sensible thought pounded straight out of his mind. "Bluh," he said, his eyes trying to focus on Jasper. He raised his baton, but Jasper dug his hand into the man's hair for leverage.

He bashed the man's head against the doorframe again. This time, the man's knees buckled. The truncheon flashed out, and Jasper used his free hand to grab the man by his wrist. The weapon flailed uselessly for a second before Jasper bounced the man's head against the doorframe a final time.

The guard's legs fell out from beneath him completely, and he slumped to the ground in an unconscious heap. Three little dents lined the door's metal frame.

"You're making a mistake. I'm not supposed to be down here," Jasper muttered. "Didn't even bother to frisk us," he said to Amelia as he pulled a lockpick out of his jacket.

"Won't be making that mistake again," Amelia observed as Jasper picked his way into the supply closet. A second later, and he pulled the door open. Checking both ways in the corridor, he dragged the unconscious guard inside, kicking the baton in as well.

Jasper stripped off the janitor outfit and put it on over his suit. The fit was rather snug and too short in the arms and legs, but it looked acceptable. As the finishing touch, he took the man's ID badge, which bore a red ring around the periphery, and clipped it to the front of his new outfit. His disguise wouldn't withstand prolonged scrutiny, but it would stand up from a distance.

Taking the man's undershirt and socks, he fashioned a crude gag and bound his hands together. Once he woke up, he'd probably wriggle his way free in a half hour, but Jasper intended to be gone by then.

The guard had a Colt 1911 tucked into his jumpsuit, the same kind of sidearm used by the US military. It was a bigger, blockier pistol than the FN Model 1922 that Jasper kept hidden in a shoulder holster. The FN Model 1922 was an updated version of the gun used to assassinate Archduke Franz Ferdinand, a handy little tool in a pinch.

Jasper dropped the man's Colt into a bucket of sudsy water. The truncheon he compressed back into a cylinder and tucked in his own pocket.

Amelia took the item Jasper had slipped her earlier and examined it. It was the front desk secretary's ID badge, which lacked the red band around the edges. By itself, it was hardly a disguise, but it would give her a few seconds of bluffing space and add some initial confusion if anyone tried to stop them.

"We're in," Amelia said as Jasper shut the door to the supply closet. Their former captor hadn't stirred.

"What we need to do is find Ray's office. It should be down here somewhere. If we can just find something worthwhile, we can get out of here and hand it over to police."

He briefly wondered what the cops would think of Yersinia's private security operation here. This looked more like a secret police apparatus than a corporate security office.

Jasper shut the door to the supply closet. He glanced down the hallway in the direction the guard had been walking them. It split in a T intersection ahead.

"Walk in front of me like I'm escorting you somewhere. Hopefully, we don't bump into anybody, and if we do, let's try not to look lost." He had no idea where Ray's office might be. It wasn't as if they could just walk up and ask someone.

"Ooh, my own private escort. I didn't know you cared, Jasper."

"Later we can role play guard with an authority complex and mouthy detective, but right now, we should keep moving."

When they reached the T intersection, they went left. Several of the doors in that direction had placards with what appeared to be names, maybe those of Ray and his top lieutenants. The hallway ended in a dead end, but Jasper hoped this would be easy.

As they drew nearer, it became obvious that this was not what they were looking for. The cheap particle board doors had been replaced with steel. An applique over the metal made the doors look like they were made of the same cheap wood from a distance, but they were more akin to the doors of a mental asylum.

There were names next to the doors. Or more accurately, a string of code numbers that Jasper couldn't make heads or tails out of. There was a slat at eye level on each of the doors.

Walking up to the first door, Jasper thumbed the slat open and pressed his eye to the peephole. "Well, this is certainly a start," he said. He gestured for Amelia to look inside.

She pressed her face to the slot and gazed inside. The room behind the door was completely padded. There wasn't any furniture to speak of except for a chair and a cot, both bolted to the ground.

A gaunt, bearded man dressed in little better than rags sat huddled in the corner, his legs pressed up close against his body. He had his head between his knees, and he wasn't moving except to breathe. He looked like he'd been living on New York's streets when he was brought here. That, or he had been here a very long time. Maybe both.

"This might just be our ticket," Jasper said. He checked a few other doors and found that they all had occupants, none of them doing much.

"We've got what we need. Let's get out of here," Amelia said. "This clearly isn't normal."

"I don't think we can leave yet," Jasper responded. "You're right. This isn't normal, but we need something that links Ray directly into this. If the cops storm down here and it turns out these people signed up for some sort of sensory deprivation experiment, or they're under company quarantine, we'll have lost all credibility with the police and played our hand. Plus, there's probably some assault charges in it for me."

"Eh, a little jail time builds character. Let's see if we can't find

Ray's office anyway."

They set off in the opposite direction, checking several rooms along the way. The basement was used for more than just security apparently. There were rooms filled with ductwork and furnace parts, while others presented mazes of mothballed medical equipment hidden under canvas tarps. Jasper wiped down each surface and doorknob he touched with a piece of cloth to remove any fingerprints.

Rounding another corner, they came face to face with a man in a lab coat, checking things off on a clipboard. Their pace stuttered for a second before resuming as normal. The man looked up from his notes, and Jasper gave a friendly but bored nod.

The scientist looked back down at his clipboard and scurried off in the direction of the steel doors, ready to note the hell out of whatever today's results were. Apparently, even Yersinia staff didn't like dealing with internal security personnel.

Understandable, given Jasper's introduction to the security roster. In several places, they passed checkpoints, none of them manned, where new arrivals must go through the various stages of intake. Apparently, they didn't get enough unauthorized visitors to man the stations all the time, but Jasper noticed an intercom system where backup could be summoned for more difficult detainees.

What on earth was Yersinia doing here that they needed such an elaborate security apparatus? Jasper could more easily picture this sort of operation in the basement of a Soviet government building than a pharmaceutical company.

"What have you gotten yourself into, Ray?" Jasper whispered to himself.

Finally, they reached what appeared to be the security center. They passed a locker room and break area, the scent of stale coffee strong in the air. Several men in more official-looking guard uniforms sat around, laughing at something. Jasper gave a friendly wave as he passed the doorway, and a few of them returned the gesture half-heartedly without looking up.

One of the great secrets to life: Walk around like you belong somewhere, and people assume it's true.

Jasper walked up to a suite of offices. The frosted glass window of each one bore someone's a name, stenciled in large, white capital letters. Ray's office was at the end of the hall. A quick knock on the door confirmed that no one was inside, and Jasper's lockpicks reappeared. After a second, the door swung open and they stepped inside.

The room was large but workmanlike. The office didn't hold a candle to Iris's back on the docks. The room was ringed with filing cabinets, and a large desk sat in the center of the room. Jasper was struck by the monk-like austerity of the decorations. There were no pictures on the desk, no potted plants, no sign of a life outside of work. It reminded him of his office back in Chicago.

"Start checking the filing cabinets. I'll start with the desk," Jasper said. Amelia was already opening the first drawer and rummaging through the file folders.

The desk was covered with several large rolls of paper, dense with schematic drawings. What were they? Patent applications? Blueprints?

Upon closer inspection, Jasper realized that they were maps, maps of New York City's sewer system and subway tunnels. He stared at the mess of lines and numbers overlaid with streets and pipe systems.

Big red X's had been drawn all over the maps, sometimes in little clusters and sometimes by themselves. They were scattered all over the place, seemingly at random. He looked to see if Ray had made any sort of map key to indicate what the X's meant.

He hadn't. The city maps came with their own complex notation system, though. He noticed a series of black squares interspersed over the grid system by the mapmakers themselves. Most of them connected parts of the sewer to parts of the subway, but some of them appeared to connect both systems to various buildings around town, some of them municipal and others not.

They appeared to be access doors of some sort. Most likely, they were for in case either system suffered a collapse. If a subway tunnel underwent some sort of catastrophic structural failure, the series of access doors gave rescuers a better chance of saving stranded survivors quickly rather than trying to burrow through the rubble.

Jasper noticed that one of the doors connected with the basement of the Yersinia building in the furnace room. A series of red X's had been slashed onto the map all around that door.

There was only one other item on the desk that Jasper saw, and it had nothing to do with the maps. It was a diagram of statistics regarding Spanish Flu. The pandemic struck near the end of the Great War, probably spread by soldiers in the trenches mobilizing and returning home. It extended all around the world, infecting at least five hundred million people and spreading from pole to pole.

Of the infected, at least fifty million, and maybe more depending on whose records were used, succumbed to the illness. In the end, the disease killed more people than the war that allowed it to spread. The Great War's engineers had nothing on Mother Nature, the murderous old hag.

The flu was especially feared because it seemed most likely to kill off the young and healthy, often leaving children and the elderly alive in its wake. Jasper never contracted it, but he knew plenty of people who did. One of the pilots from his squadron died just before the end of the war from Spanish Flu. Jasper had seen his body stacked in a pile of other corpses that died from the disease that day.

Spanish Flu seemed like exactly the sort of topic Yersinia might be interested in, but why Ray? He was clever and devious, certainly, but he had a ninth grade education. He was hardly a doctor. Jasper wasn't sure why the numbers would interest him.

Suddenly, Jasper heard voices out in the hallway. A key slid into the lock, and the door pushed open.

Chapter 7
Side Tracked

Ray Armstrong walked in and stopped dead when he saw Jasper standing over his desk. The head of Yersinia's security had thick black hair swept straight back in a carefully combed mane. A neatly trimmed beard covered his round cheeks. He was wearing a tweed jacket with elbow patches that made him look like a well-heeled college professor just back from his poetry class. The only thing that spoiled the effect was the pistol holstered in his belt.

His eyes locked with Jasper's and everyone stood perfectly still for a second that lasted approximately four weeks.

"Jasper," Armstrong said in a warm, jovial voice. At the same time, his hand lunged for the pistol at his hip.

At that point, Amelia sprang out from behind the door. She kicked the edge and sent it swinging into Armstrong. He twisted around in surprise and grunted as the door smacked into his side. Jasper vaulted straight over the desk, kicking maps in every direction, and charged Armstrong.

Lowering his shoulder, he augured into Yersinia's security boss at a full run. Already off balance, Armstrong fell on his butt with an outraged roar. Jasper reached down and grabbed the pistol out of Ray's hand.

Several doors opened up, and heads poked out to see what the commotion was. Eyes widened when they saw Jasper and Amelia struggling with Armstrong.

"Run," Jasper shouted to Amelia. She took off down the hall. He fired a shot from Ray's pistol into the ceiling, and everyone ducked their heads back into their offices. Following Amelia, he took off down the suddenly empty hall.

If Armstrong's security team captured them now, they were well and truly screwed. Knowing Armstrong, they wouldn't be turned over to the police. They'd be lucky if he decided to just throw them in one of his padded cells and keep them there.

As Jasper turned the corner, a gunshot whizzed down the hallway behind him. It was followed up with the angry *BraaAAAaaap!* of a submachine gun. Chips of plaster and concrete exploded away from the wall a split second after Jasper rounded the corner and disappeared out of range.

He caught up to Amelia. She started to turn a corner.

"No, this way," he pointed straight ahead.

"But the elevators are this way," she protested.

"They're going to block them off in a minute, if they haven't already."

Ray's voice crackled out of one of the speakers overhead. "Attention all personnel. We have two intruders in the facility. Lock down all exits immediately. They should be considered extremely dangerous. Shoot to kill. I repeat: shoot to kill."

"That's not good," Amelia said. "What's the plan?"

A guard dashed out from a door in front of them, shrugging an ammo vest over his shoulders as he cradled a Tommy gun in his free hand. He turned and saw the two detectives running straight for him with a look of almost-comical surprise on his face. Jasper shot over the man's head, and he dove back into the room. Jasper heard the snick of a lock sliding into place as they passed by.

Most of Yersinia's security staff would be upstairs, going about their usual duties. The only guards down here were either on break or part of the skeleton crew that kept their basement headquarters running. None of them expected a group to breach their security section rather than the valuable intellectual property and medical research on the upper floors. The offices and break rooms down here simply weren't worth manning most of the time. Who wanted to guard some old storage space and ductwork?

Jasper tore down the hall, making another turn. He was navigating by memory, remembering what he saw on the map and the building's blueprints. He headed for the main furnace room.

"There," he shouted. He pointed to a door midway down the hall as the sound of pounding boots began to converge from several directions at once.

Jasper tried the door. It was locked. He pulled one of the lock-picks out of his jacket.

Before he could touch the knob, Amelia blew it apart with several well-placed shots from her Luger. The door swung open of its own accord.

"Right," Jasper said, tucking his picks back into his jacket. The thud of boots was just around the corner as they darted inside the furnace room.

A row of dim, flickering fluorescents provided the only light in the room. The ductwork hissed and groaned as the heating unit struggled to keep the early November chill out of the building. Jasper ducked behind some pipes and moved toward the rear of the room.

"Jasper, where are we going? We're cornered in here." Amelia followed him, ducking under rat-chewed insulation and cobwebs large enough to ensnare large tropical bats.

"There should be a door back here," Jasper said.

"To what? We're in a basement."

The room's main entrance burst open. "Come out with your hands up," a voice boomed. "We have you surrounded. No harm will come to you if you surrender now."

"There they are," an excited voice shouted. A gunshot rang out and thudded into a pipe a few feet from Jasper's head. Steam shot out in an angry tea kettle whistle, obscuring the path between them and their attackers.

"You idiot," a third voice yelled. "Now they know we're going to shoot them."

Jasper continued to work his way toward the back of the room, hoping the map had been accurate or that the door hadn't been sealed over with brickwork.

"You two," Armstrong's voice rang out even above the hiss of the ruptured pipe. "Go in there and flush them out.

"Uh, yes sir."

Jasper burst through the last of the maze of pipes like a man stumbling out of the jungle into a clearing. He looked around at the plain, blank brick wall. He didn't see a door.

Oh crap.

"There." Amelia pointed. He followed her finger deep into the darkest pool of shadow, far in the corner of the room. There was a thickset metal door that looked like it belonged on a submarine. A wheel at the center sealed and unsealed the door.

Scampering over, he laid his hands on the wheel and twisted. The wheel gave half an inch and then stopped with a loud grating noise. He strained, but nothing more happened.

"A little help here."

Amelia threw herself in beside him, grunting with effort as they both worked at the stuck door. It gave a little more, then froze again.

"Okay, on three. Ready?" Amelia asked. "One."

"I see them," a voice shouted from back in the labyrinth of heating equipment.

"Screw it. THREE!"

Amelia and Jasper heaved together, and the wheel gave with a mechanical scream. With a few quick twists, they unsealed the door and pulled it open. They scampered inside and pulled the door shut behind them. The door didn't have a wheel on the inside, probably so people in the tunnels couldn't break into buildings on the surface, but that also meant they couldn't seal it up from this side.

They had emerged in a narrow concrete alcove in a pitch black tunnel. The walls were redolent of rat urine and wino vomit, two bad smells that went worse together. Jasper and Amelia moved forward as fast as they dared in the darkness. As they emerged from the alcove, a few anemic beams of light from further down the tunnel revealed a small drop with rails at the bottom.

This must be part of New York's subway system. Mercury vapor arc lights lined the tunnel at regular intervals, but too far apart to cast any significant light on the whole of the tunnel. They just created individual islands of light separated by vast seas of darkness.

Jasper hopped down onto the tracks. "Watch out for the third rail," he said to Amelia as she joined him. The electrified third rail kept trains running down here, but it would fry anyone who touched it to a black, twitching crisp.

Jasper walked in the center, between the railroad ties. If a train came along the tracks, they'd be able to skitter off to the side and press tight against the walls. Hopefully, they wouldn't get creamed into a red gruel down the length of the tunnel if that happened.

There were more immediate concerns to worry about, though. Behind them, Jasper heard the door from the Yersinia building screech open, and the hushed voices echoed down the tunnels.

"Do you see them anywhere?"

"I don't think so. Wait, look down there. There they go."

Running into the shadows, Jasper and Amelia scurried into the deep darkness. Soon, they couldn't even see each other as they moved into the shadows between two of the weak light sources.

Jasper reached out a hand and took Amelia's so they wouldn't become separated in the darkness. Her hands were rough but warm. His long, spidery fingers enveloped hers, and they both held on tight.

He could hear the two guards breathing hard behind them. It didn't sound like their colleagues were following them, so it was either taking them a long time to navigate the mass of pipes back in the Yersinia building or these two were on their own.

From further back in the tunnel, Jasper heard the sound of the metal door slamming shut. Even from a distance, he could hear the squealing of the gears as the door was dogged closed, sealed from the inside. There was no going back for the two men who had been sent in. Armstrong knew the tunnels from his maps. He was no doubt sending men to other access points to head them off, but it would take a while to dispatch so many Yersinia guards without raising suspicion. Time was of the essence if they were going to get out of here alive.

The darkness was their ally, though. The pursuing guards couldn't shoot what they couldn't see.

"Hey, what the hell is that?" one of the men shouted from behind them.

"Oh my God! They're in the tunnel with us!" Suddenly, gunfire lit up the tunnel in a rapid-fire strobe effect.

"Run!"

Suddenly, a high-pitched squealing noise reached Jasper's ears. Amid the distorted soundscape of the subway tunnel, the noise sounded like a cat caught in an industrial washing machine. He didn't turn around. He wouldn't be able to see anything even if he did.

"It's got my leg! Gerald, help me! Hel—" The guard's voice cut off with a wet puncturing noise and a deep gasp. Jasper could hear the thrashing of limbs and a series of grunts, but the noise that held his attention, the noise that chilled his soul, was the loud slurping sound the echoed down the tunnel.

Okay, maybe the darkness wasn't their ally. Maybe the darkness had double-crossed them and allied with something else entirely. Jasper held his pistol in his free hand as he clung to Amelia with his other. Out of the frying pan and into the fire.

Far off in the distance, Jasper could see what must be a subway station. There wasn't so much a light at the end of the tunnel as a more pastel black. He had no idea if they could outrun whatever was in the tunnel with them, but they were going to try.

He heard the second guard breathing hard behind them. "No! Stay away; stay away, you goddamn bloodsucker!" A blast of submachine gun fire tore up the tunnel, away from Jasper and Amelia. The muzzle flashes lit their way forward for a brief moment before leaving their eyes dazzled and robbed of much of their night vision.

Another burst of panicky gunfire shot in a completely different direction. The frightened guard had no idea where his target was, and he was shooting at shadows.

Suddenly, Jasper heard an odd *thud* behind them, like something landing from a great height. The guard screamed, and his weapon let loose with a long, sustained burst before clicking dry. "Oh God. Get back!"

A series of clicks sounded down the tunnel, the sound of a new clip being fumbled into the gun by shaky hands. Then there was a different series of clicks that Jasper couldn't identify.

"No!" The scream was followed by a wet ripping noise. More screaming followed, but not articulate words this time, just animal howls of pain and fear. Above it all, Jasper heard that same horrible sucking noise again. The sound went on and on, and the screams died away. The sound of thrashing limbs ceased. But that dreadful sucking noise continued for several more seconds.

There was the sound of something heavy thumping to the ground, and then all Jasper could hear was his own pounding footsteps and heavy breathing.

Wait, there was another noise, too. Something much deeper in the tunnel. A low rumble that Jasper felt more than heard. Somewhere down the line, a train was coming.

He wondered if they could hide in the shadows until whatever was in here with them gave up and went away. No, he decided. Whatever it was had found the two guards without any additional light, and it had dispatched them with the ease of a leopard springing from the underbrush to snap a gazelle's neck. There was no safety in the shadows that ringed the tunnel.

That odd clicking noise reached Jasper's ears again, and he suddenly realized what it was. Something hard was clacking against the railroad ties behind them, moving with its own steady rhythm. Jasper realized that what he was hearing was the tread of heavy footsteps.

The gray blob ahead of them had resolved itself into a proper light at the end of their tunnel. It must be a station. If they could just reach the light, they could escape from this hell hole.

The sound of the approaching train grew louder. If the thing in the tunnels didn't kill them, the locomotive might very well run them over.

Jasper listened intently for the sound of the clicking footsteps. They were his only indication of where the darkness-cloaked entity was in the tunnel. It was hard to hear over the sound of his heart pounding in his ears. The footsteps were quite a bit farther back in the tunnels. Maybe the killer was satisfied with the guards alone.

The footsteps stopped altogether. Jasper strained his ears, but he could hear no sign of the tunnel entity.

Good. It must have—

There was a heavy thud not thirty feet behind them. Impossible! The footsteps had been far back in the tunnel, fading with distance. No one could make up the distance that quickly, not unless they were shot out of a cannon.

The footsteps resumed again, each heavy footfall loud behind them as the killer followed them at an awkward gait. Without slowing down to aim or look, Jasper pointed his pistol behind him and squeezed the trigger. The gunshot was horrifically loud in the close space of the tunnel, but the randomly aimed shot didn't seem to deter their hunter.

There was enough light now that Jasper could make out the rail ties he was stepping on as he ran. His own feet slapped against the ground as the humping footsteps drew closer behind them.

Jasper's grip tightened on his pistol. They were so close to the station, only a couple hundred yards away, but they weren't going to make it to the platform in time. Whatever this thing was, they couldn't outrun it. One of them might be able to make it, though. He dropped Amelia's hand and spun around just as the tunnel suddenly grew brighter.

He caught a glimpse of something as he raised his pistol. It was just a glimpse, but the brief flash was…all wrong. Whatever it was, it moved incredibly fast, unnaturally fast. The shape disappeared into the darkness as if catapulted down the tunnel.

The impression of movement he did see didn't even have time gel in his mind, as he realized why the tunnel had grown suddenly brighter. Behind them, the train had rounded the bend and was bearing down fast.

The train engineer caught sight of them and laid on the train's horn. The man probably thought they were a homeless couple.

They scampered the last hundred yards to the subway platform and clambered up onto the cement surface. The crowd stared at them, but no one wanted to lose their place in line by trying to interfere with them.

A few seconds later, the train arrived at the station with a whoosh of air and whining brakes. The crowds on the platform moved forward as soon as the doors opened and a scrum developed between those trying to exit the train and those trying to board.

Through some sort of osmosis, the dense crowd eventually sorted itself out. The mass of people who had just disembarked set off toward the stairs to the street level, and Jasper and Amelia joined them, mixing in.

They stepped out into the daylight just as a throng of Armstrong's security force arrived and charged pell-mell down the stairs to secure the site. In their haste, they blew right past Jasper and Amelia.

Chapter 8
Maybe It Runs in the Family

"…and then we escaped into the tunnel system," Jasper said. He and Amelia had already told Laramie Resweber about their little expedition. Their client had been pleased with their initial success in locating Armstrong, but disappointed they couldn't find anything to directly tie him to the murder of Dr. Horvath or any other serious crime.

Now, they were at the information brokerage, telling the same story to Iris. Jasper didn't like sharing his information with anyone, let alone his sister; however, he had cut a deal: she would give them Armstrong's location, and he would share any information he gathered.

Of course, he hadn't mentioned to either of them what he'd seen in the tunnels because he had no idea what he'd seen. None at all. If he didn't know what it was, it wasn't information he could disclose. Loophole.

Iris had watched the entire recitation with the expression of a cat that had spotted a bird outside its window but couldn't get outside to get it. Her eyes were slitted and intense. Even after almost ten years, Jasper recognized that expression. She knew, or at least suspected, that he was holding out on her.

After a moment of reflection, she leaned back in her chair. The springs creaked under the rich red leather. It was the only sound in the office. The light reflecting off the aquarium flooring sent odd shadows rippling across the room. A medium-sized shark, maybe three feet long, drifted into the room, but stayed well clear of the pile of stones near Iris's desk.

"Sewer maps," Iris said, mostly to herself.

"And the subway system," Amelia added.

"Why would he have maps of the area below New York?" Iris asked herself. Jasper couldn't say for certain, but he suspected it had something to do with the thing in the tunnels. If it was moving freely through the underground, the city had something a lot more dangerous than alligators to worry about down there.

Jasper suspected he knew what the little red X's all over the map were, too. Odds were, there were now two more drawn onto the map of the subway system near the Yersinia building to mark where the guards died.

Armstrong's men would have figured out what happened to their two colleagues based on the fact that they didn't return. Now the only question was, were they were still looking for Jasper and Amelia? Armstrong had to at least consider the notion that they had perished in the tunnels with the Yersinia guards.

"That fact that Armstrong knows you're interested in him makes your job a lot harder, you realize." Iris cracked her knuckles.

"Oh, I realize, all right," Jasper said. He had spent all day trying to figure out which cards he had left to play. It was a damnably poor hand.

Armstrong could assume they were dead, but he wouldn't. His suspicious little mind wouldn't be satisfied until he saw their bodies with his own eyes, a trait Jasper had always admired in his old colleague. But now it was going to be a continuing problem.

Ray had plenty of contacts through the information brokerage, many of them with the less-savory elements not only of New York City, but beyond. Even if he and Amelia returned to Chicago empty-handed, someone would come for them. Maybe not right away. Maybe not for years. But it would happen. Their names had been filed away in Armstrong's Rolodex of spite, and nothing on earth would scrub that grudge away. Jasper knew how Armstrong worked. They had come for him on his own turf, so he would come for him on theirs.

Their one main advantage was that Armstrong had no idea what they wanted from him. He might think someone had hired them to make off with the company's secrets and pure chance had set them on a crash collision. Alternatively, he might think that Jasper had come to settle some old scores.

"You're going to have to act fast, Jasper," Iris said. "He has your scent. You two had your little truce for years, but Armstrong won't let this stand. He might not even let you leave New York alive. Reservations at the Pine Box Motel for both of you."

"You always knew how to cheer a guy up, Iris."

"I'm still not sure what happened between you and Armstrong," Amelia said. "You've had your hackles up ever since I told you what the job is. What's the deal?"

Iris threw back her head and barked harsh laughter. She drew out a cigarette as the laughter faded into a throaty chuckle. "Oh, Jasper. You always were a bastard and a half to work with. You still haven't told this poor thing about why you and Ray want each other's heads on a platter?"

Jasper realized he'd gone stiff in his chair. He looked down and saw that his hands had formed into claws on the armrests, his fingers white where they gripped the wood. Before answering, he stopped to pick an invisible fleck of dust off his tie. "Some things are best left in the past."

"For Pete's sake. I'll tell her then. Listen up, Dearie."

"You'll do no such thing."

"And what makes you think you can stop me?"

"We can leave. There's planning to do, and we have to discuss the situation. We don't need to waste any more time here." Jasper stood up.

"Tsk. Tsk. Tsk. Jasper, you can leave. Sure. But you're speaking for the lady, too. I think she gets to decide if she stays. What do you say, Amelia? Mind if I bend your ear?"

Amelia looked back and forth between Iris and Jasper. Jasper's already pale face had gone cadaverously white. Iris was smiling like a Jack O' Lantern.

"If this concerns our current job and working with you, I really think I ought to know," she finally said. Jasper collapsed back into his chair.

"Well, it goes a little something like this," Iris said, clearly enjoying her brother's discomfort.

"No, I'll tell the story," Jasper said, waving Iris off. "I at least get that."

Iris sat back and puffed on her cigarette, waiting for Jasper to start. A contented look parked itself on her face. It was her job to drag facts kicking and screaming into the light, and she'd done an admirable job on this one.

"Ray and I used to be good friends," Jasper began. "We started this enterprise together when we were just a couple of kids, fresh out of college and looking for something to do with ourselves. He was always the wild one, taking risks, making the wrong people angry.

"And we both know you've never made the wrong people angry, Jasper," Iris baited him.

"But I don't do it for fun. Ray liked to cause trouble; it was in his blood. Someone has to spend a lot of time pushing just the right buttons to make me go after them. There's not many people who can do it." Jasper looked pointedly at Iris. "But there's a few."

"I'm flattered," Iris said.

"We ran our little partnership together for almost a year, and things went well. We brought in new people. Iris here. My brother, Percy. Rocky." Jasper pointed in the general direction of the office's doors to indicate the building's hulking doorman. "A few others who are still around.

"Ray and I knew how to cover for each other, though. It was like we knew what the other was thinking. We were a hot commodity in those days. Did a little of everything. Investigations. Bounty hunting. Security. The both of us thought we could lick the world. We could turn down any case we didn't like, and three more would be lined up behind it."

"Any case *you* didn't like, Jasper. Any case you didn't like. You turned down a lot of cases with lots of money on the line because you didn't like the person offering the work."

"Some of them were crooked. Others were in the wrong and trying to use us as a way out. I went into this line of work so I could have some say over what I worked on. I always want to have the discretion to refuse a job if I disagreed with it. You'll work with anyone, Iris."

"You're a gumshoe, Jasper. You deal with details. I run an information trading business. I deal with details. We basically operate in the same line of work."

"The devil is in the details. You of all people ought to appreciate that one, Iris."

"Sanctimonious prick," she mumbled under her breath.

Jasper ignored the comment. "Ray wanted to take the company in a different direction. He saw opportunities where I saw troubles."

"Different sides of the same coin," Iris said.

"Not when you lose track of what you wanted in the first place. Anyhow, eventually a bank consortium came to us. Hot diggity, right? Someone had been committing robberies all over the city. Plugged two guards and one teller across five hold-ups. Very thorough. Very professional. The police hadn't been able to make much headway.

"I agreed to do the job. Ray didn't want to, which struck me as odd at the time. There was money involved, and we'd never done a bank robbery case before. It was tough work. Whoever was responsible was good. It was a one-man outfit, and he was ruthless. There were three more robberies and another death in the next month, spread out all over the city.

"Eventually, I worked out something of a pattern. The locations of the robberies didn't make much sense when you laid them out on a map. They seemed pretty randomly distributed across the city. Of course, that meant they were carefully chosen. There was no way to discern a base of operations from the scattering of dots, something the robber had to know. The fact that they were all over the city as opposed to an area the robber frequented also meant the locations would have to be scouted out beforehand. Random patterns of crime are rarely truly random. There's almost always some method behind the madness.

"In this case, it didn't become clear until after some other patterns were laid over the map. When you marked off all the police stations in the city, it became obvious that the robberies were only occurring at banks that fell the maximum distance from the areas where police could respond quickly. It required some fairly clever geometry work and a lot of forethought. Someone had been systematically exploiting the weakest points in the in the city's police network.

"Placing all the remaining banks in the city on the grid, it became pretty obvious that there were only so many prime targets left. Most of the banks were clustered in a few areas, generally with a matching police presence. There were just a few stragglers left. Our robber had been picking off the weakest of the herd.

"I decided to stake out a few of the remaining banks. I left first thing in the morning the next day without telling anyone what I had planned. I was still excited from my discovery on the map the night before, and I wanted to make sure it still made sense in the morning."

"I think I see where this is going," Amelia said.

"Yes, you probably can at this point. I'd been there a few hours, parked outside, when a car roared up and a man in a mask and gloves jumped out and ran into the bank. He fired a few shots into the ceiling. He was ordering everyone onto the floor when I walked in.

"He spun around, but I already had a weapon beaded in on his head. That's when I saw his eyes go wide. You can tell a lot about what someone's thinking by their eyes, especially if you know them. When someone's eyes widen in surprise, it's different from when their eyes widen from recognition. I'm not sure I could articulate exactly how, but you can tell."

"It was Ray all along, wasn't it?"

"It was him all right, and I imagine he saw an expression on my face very much like the one he was wearing. We both just froze for a minute. Neither of us moved or said anything. Then, he just sort of left."

"I remember it a little differently," Iris said. "There were shots fired. About one hundred thousand dollars in property damage. You spent three days in the hospital. Ray had a concussion, but drove away anyway."

"We didn't exactly part on good terms, no."

"But why was he robbing banks in the first place? You said you were doing good work and making money."

"Some people cannot be satisfied. The money was fine by Ray, but it was never enough. It could never be enough. I didn't discover until too late that Ray lives for the challenge. He is a creature of very loud and demanding needs, and that often creates very ugly results. If he doesn't test himself, those needs simply fester until they explode.

"First he practiced against the smaller criminal elements our company was hired to look into. When that didn't prove enough, he decided to test himself against the police. After I left, he changed this place into the information brokerage. A lot of his clients were near the top of the criminal food chain, organized mafia-types of pretty much every stripe, but that's also who he harvests secrets from as often as not. He'd reached the big leagues there.

"He always needed something more. Instead of diminishing, his needs just grew more powerful each time he indulged them. He just wanted to move another rung up the ladder each time. It's like he became desensitized to what he'd done before, and he needed bigger and bigger jolts each time to sustain himself. That's part of the reason I'm so surprised he would leave the brokerage. I always thought this was the fiercest game in town. Although, I suppose it makes some sense. Now he can pit himself against the very organization he helped build."

And trying to hunt down that thing in the tunnels would be a challenge, too. Whatever it was, it wasn't entirely natural. Jasper thought of all those red X's on Armstrong's map. Maybe the man had finally met his match.

"And now he has a new challenge," Iris said. "You two. He must be loving that."

"I'm sure he is."

"Wait," Amelia said, holding up a hand. "If you knew he was responsible, why didn't you have him arrested?" Amelia thought back to her own imperfect past and briefly wondered why Jasper had agreed to take her on as a partner. It occurred to her again that she really knew very little about how his mind worked.

"I might have been able to figure out how to ignore the robberies. Maybe. There was nothing I could do about the deaths, though. Three people had died over the course of that crime spree. I came back to the company and laid out everything I knew. Ray had gone into hiding at that point."

"So what happened?"

"We didn't want to get rid of Ray," Iris said. "He was our friend. He was like another brother to me."

"And you were just a little bit in love with him."

"Shut up, Jasper."

"So I laid down an ultimatum. It was a simple one, one I thought would force everyone's hand. Either we turned Ray over to the police, or I left."

"You overplayed your cards on that one, brother dearest."

"Yes, yes I did. Percy was the only one who sided with me. Everyone else wanted to leave it for the police to figure out for themselves. So Percy and I left. Left New York entirely. Wandered the land for a while. Ended up in the military. I flew reconnaissance airplanes over France for a stint. Eventually ended up in Chicago working for the Atticans."

"Percy left with you. Now Percy's dead, you're back, and you're here with a new partner who you've thrust headfirst into danger. You were always so determined to do things your way that you forgot about the consequences. You've really done yourself proud on this one, Jasper," Iris said, bitterness straining her voice.

"Leaving was a mistake. I should have just turned everything over to the police. I was knocked off my feet, first by Ray, and then by you. I just left and hoped things would work themselves out for the best. Obviously, that didn't happen. Laramie Resweber wouldn't need to hire us if I'd just done what I thought was right ten years ago. People have paid for that mistake. This job is my chance to correct a decade-long error."

"That's what I wanted you to hear, Dearie," Iris turned to Amelia. "You're mentor here has a couple of previous partners. One of them is dead, and the other wants to kill him. You sure you wouldn't rather work for me?"

Amelia had never known much of Jasper's past, and now she knew why. It rattled her a bit to hear that she'd stuck her hand in the grinder without knowing why. Joining the Attican Detective Agency and going straight with the law…had been mostly good for her… mostly.

At least part of her was mad as hell that Jasper hadn't told her this before. She'd gone in blind, and Yersinia's security team nearly shot them. Not to mention that whatever was living in the subway tunnels nearly took them. She liked Jasper, but she didn't want to end up dead in a ditch with him because of his pride. She wasn't going to jump ship because of this, but it put a dent in her trust.

"I'm fine where I am," Amelia said.

Iris blew out a puff of smoke. Jasper relaxed slightly in his chair.

Iris sighed. "Very well, but you know where to find me if you change your mind. You've been standing in the path of a regular shit tsunami, and you didn't even know it because someone refused to tell you. At least now you know. My brother thinks I don't play straight because I work for a different kind of clientele than he does. I think maybe it runs in the family."

Jasper looked resolutely sour.

"Well, we're on the same team now whether we like it or not," Iris continued. "So I have something that you may find interesting."

She reached into a drawer of her desk. Iris's hands had the same spindly fingers as Jasper. They were the hands of a concert pianist or a surgeon. Her hand emerged a second later clutching an envelope. She slit the seal open with her bright red thumbnail and pulled out two pieces of thick cardstock paper. Handing one to Jasper and the other to Amelia, she smiled.

Eyeballing the card, Jasper flipped it over. *You are hereby invited to Yersinia's Annual Charity Dinner and Ball*, it read in gilt letters. The font had so many swooshes and fancy curves that the script was almost unreadable. The cards were dated for tomorrow.

"Ray may have a scheming mind, but he'll expect you to go to cover now that your first attempt has failed. He won't be looking for you at Yersinia's biggest event of the year. All of New York's high society will be there, turning out to be seen at the charity ball. It's tomorrow evening. You and your date better get ready."

Chapter 9
Charity Wrecking Ball

Jasper adjusted the cufflinks on his tuxedo. He preferred his usual gray suit over the unfamiliar jacket and bowtie. Fortunately, the tailor Iris hired knew his work and asked no questions. The black jacket was fitted to conceal his shoulder holster, leaving not so much as a bulge where his weapon rested comfortably. He'd had a few extra pockets installed within the lining to make room for some of his other tools.

Running a finger along the brim of his new top hat, he waited for Amelia to emerge from the dressing room. He checked all his pockets one more time. Everything was in a slightly different place from where he kept it in his normal clothes. He didn't like not being able to grab things through pure muscle memory.

Finally, the door to the dressing room creaked open, and Amelia stepped out. Jasper stopped fiddling with his pockets.

She'd chosen a pale blue dress that ended a few inches above her ankles. The sleeveless garment wrapped around her like a living thing. Amelia walked toward him in flat shoes, something she could run in if necessary, and Jasper noticed she'd applied a dusting of makeup and red lipstick.

"You look, uh, nice," Jasper said, trying not to sound like an idiot.

She reached out and adjusted his bowtie so it was no longer crooked. "You almost sound surprised."

"No, I've just never seen you dressed up before."

"Yeah, I can tell. You sound like you just experienced massive head trauma and haven't recovered yet."

"Noted."

"You look…acceptable."

"Gee. Thanks. Ready to go?"

In response, Amelia hiked up one side of her dress, baring her leg. Jasper chose to very pointedly stare at a nearby lamp for a second as Amelia dug her Luger out of its thigh holster. She spun the weapon on her finger and checked the action. Satisfied, she re-holstered the weapon. "Ready," she said.

They had spent all day preparing, and Jasper had watched the weather grow steadily worse the entire time. The radio said that the storm would only grow worse. It was part of winter's initial assault on the city, and the season had already established a major beachhead.

Rain pattered down on the sidewalk and ran in streams through the gutters as they stepped outside. Night had fallen over the Big Apple, but street lights and neon signs lit up much of the city.

Rocky pulled around the corner in a Rolls Royce Silver Ghost. His massive form took up most of the vehicle's front section, making the car look smaller than it really was. Jasper didn't dare take the Peerless to the Yersinia building. They were taking enough of a risk just by showing their faces.

They hoped Armstrong's men would primarily be interested in anyone skulking around the building, not the guests themselves. Their fancy clothes and invitations were the best disguises available. Act like you belong somewhere and people tend to believe it. It was a strategy that had already gotten them into the building's basement once.

Jasper and Amelia rushed from the front door to the car and hurled themselves in to avoid getting their finery wet. A minute later, they were on the move, leaving the docks behind.

Water sluiced up from the tires as Rocky tore down the streets. Lights flashed at them, and Jasper observed that New Yorkers still tended to use their horns interchangeably with their brakes. Rocky kept up a steady banter the entire time.

"So New York has changed quite a bit since you WHERE THE HELL ARE YOU GOING? Anyway, so the city's grown a fair amount since you left, Jasper. They completely tore down the old LOOK AT THIS IMBECILE! GET OFF THE ROAD!"

After a few minutes of terrifying, hair-raising driving, Rocky pulled up in front of the Yersinia building. Jasper stepped out of the Silver Ghost, followed by Amelia. A soaked valet in a red jacket scurried over and held an umbrella over them as they walked up the stairs to the medical giant's headquarters. Jasper caught his reflection in the building's glass doors and fixed his bowtie again.

The valet opened the door for them after Jasper flashed their invitations, and he slipped the man a dollar. It was a charity ball after all.

Jasper stepped inside and was blasted by a gale of music and the tinkling of glass. Laughter and loud voices washed over him in a wave. A waiter in a white jacket walked up to them and offered them flutes of something fizzy. Amelia took one and slugged it back without looking at the contents. Jasper waved off the waiter and examined the crowd.

The charity ball was a mess of suits, tuxedos, gowns, and flashing earrings. A band played on a platform set up in front of the odd wind chime sculpture at the center of the lobby. Tables of food had been set up at one end of the massive room. Jasper spotted caviar, a mound of cheeses, and platters of boiled shrimp. An eight-foot-tall ice sculpture of a swan presided over the entire spread. Waiters milled about the crowd, offering hors d'oeuvres and drinks. Jasper wondered how much money would actually be left over for charity at the end of the night.

Socialites and New York's glitterati mingled near the tables or jittered around on the dance floor to the band's jazzy beat. Silver-haired gentlemen stood around with one or more blondes on their arms. Matronly figures with feather boas and long-stemmed cigarettes eyed each other disdainfully. Jasper suspected this environment was much more carnivorous than appearances would imply.

A large banner hung over the lobby. "Welcome to the 14th Annual Yersinia Charity Ball," it read. Then, in smaller letters, "Your donations are the blood of the community."

After a few seconds, he spotted what he was expecting. Some of the waiters weren't offering food or interacting with the crowd. Several stood with their hands behind their backs at key positions near the elevators and stairs. Those would be Armstrong's guards, dressed to the nines. They were meant to be unobtrusive, but they stood out like crows among a flock of pigeons. This event was meant for mingling, accreting social points that would eventually aggregate into future deals and connections. The guards' stiff appearance marked them as outsiders. No doubt, their main task tonight was to find ways to politely separate any of Yersinia's benefactors who might happen to become involved in drunken fist fights. Jasper knew that more than a few of the old families here couldn't stand each other. Some of them couldn't even stand their own kin. And they'd also be on the lookout for any trouble of a more serious nature. After his and Amelia's explorations earlier today, the guards would be on alert.

Suddenly, Jasper spotted something he'd been hoping not to see. Armstrong himself was working the crowd, laughing and shaking hands. He trailed behind a couple of Yersinia executives who were similarly glad-handing. Most of the guards would only have a description of him, not a firm mental image. Armstrong would recognize him immediately. If Ray spotted them, they would just have to slip away as quickly as possible.

Ray was heading in their direction, so Jasper took Amelia's hand and whisked her toward the opposite side of the massive lobby. "Eleven o'clock. Ray's here. That's going to make things more difficult."

"Three o'clock. One of the guards is coming this way," she responded.

Jasper changed course in the only direction still available, straight onto the dance floor. The band was playing a slower song, and they fell into motion along the edge of the crowd.

They watched over each other's shoulders, their faces close. The guard kept walking, moving right past them without so much as a glance. Behind them, Armstrong socialized his way to the opposite side of the room, all smiles and warm welcomes. Most of the guests probably thought he was a Yersinia executive, but Jasper knew he was working his way through the crowd, memorizing faces.

"Huh. You actually know how to dance," Amelia said.

"I'm a man of many talents." The song ended, and they spun out of the crowd's orbit. The coast was clear. Back to business.

The plan was to sneak up to the executive floors and see if they could find anything on Ray or his activities up there. His office below would be under lockdown, and they hadn't found anything to use against him down there in the first place. Just maps and Spanish Flu statistics. Somehow, Ray was involved with the thing underground, which might be their ticket to nailing him. They weren't going to find that information downstairs, though.

Jasper eyed the elevators. Only one guard was manning them, and he seemed more interested in the nearby table of food and the cluster of buxom young women standing nearby than the elevators.

They would still need a way to avoid the guard, though. Jasper looked around the room until his eye fell on the banner hanging above the dance floor. It was secured with ropes on either side of the room, their leads tied down near the buffet tables along the walls.

Amelia followed his gaze.

"Are you thinking what I'm thinking?" he asked.

"Give me your lighter," she said.

The chromed lighter appeared between his fingers, and he dropped it in her open hand. She palmed the lighter and began picking her way across the room, cutting directly through the mob. Jasper moved toward one of the tables and made like he was trying to select which of the many fragrant kinds of cheese he wished to partake of next.

Amelia made her way to the far side of the room and milled around the opposite table. She popped a grape into her mouth with one hand and held Jasper's lighter up to the rope securing the banner with the other. After a few seconds, the rope began to smolder. Moving one of the candelabras closer to belay suspicion of trickery, she worked her way back toward Jasper.

She walked, deflecting three offers to dance along the way. One suitor proved particularly insistent and tried to follow her over. Turning around to confront him, she bumped into one of the waiters, shoving him directly into the young man's path. A tray of seltzer waters crashed to the ground and all over the suddenly sputtering man. The waiter began to apologize profusely and tried to dry off his victim with a handkerchief, but the man simply stalked off. Amelia had already disappeared back into the crowd before the tray even hit the ground.

As she reached Jasper, the rope on the opposite side of the room burned through, and the banner fluttered down to the ground on one side. The canvas material engulfed several revelers with squawks of surprise and indignation. Partiers shifted from their positions to watch their fellows struggle out from under the fallen banner while waiters and guards alike scrambled over to tie the smoking end of the rope back onto its cleat.

But the guard near the elevators hadn't moved far. He'd made it to the buffet tables when he decided that the situation was being cared for and therefore not his problem. Before moving back to his post, he grabbed a handful of prawns and began munching on them.

People were still gawping at the fallen banner, chattering among themselves as Jasper moved toward the guard. He was watching his co-horts clean up the banner, a bemused expression on his lips. The band began to play again, trying to entice people back onto the dance floor.

As Jasper stepped close, the man caught the movement and turned to look. It was the same guard who had been dressed as a janitor earlier that day, the same one who had led Jasper down to the basement. Ernest Hives. Now he had a discreet patch shaved along his temple and a row of stitches running up into his hair. Their eyes locked, and the guard opened his mouth to shout a warning.

Jasper pistoned his arm straight into the unlucky man's stomach. Instead of a yell, a large gob of half-chewed prawn was ejected from his mouth, landing on the floor with a *splat*. The breath billowed out of Ernest's lungs, and he doubled over. Moving with feral swiftness, Jasper drove his knee into the man's face.

Ernest slumped to the ground, pummeled into unconsciousness for the second time in as many days. The women he had been ogling noticed the commotion and looked over.

Waving them over, Jasper gestured to the downed guard. "He was choking on that," Jasper pointed to the lumped of severely masticated prawn on the floor nearby. "I think he fell and knocked it out of himself. Here, you girls set him up in this chair and make sure nobody bothers him. He might have a concussion."

The women murmured concern and did as Jasper asked. They set Ernest up in a chair and gathered around, blocking the unconscious man from view.

"Smooth," Amelia said as Jasper punched the button to summon the elevator.

Jasper smiled as the elevator doors dinged open, and they stepped inside unnoticed.

Chapter 10
The Sound of Gunfire

Stepping out of the elevator on the executive floor, Jasper looked around. The wide glass windows offered a stunning view of the New York night. Signs and street lamps lit up the sidewalks twenty stories below. People and vehicles bustled through the streets despite the rain and darkness. Jasper could hear the whistling wind of the storm mixed with the ubiquitous honking and street noise below.

The city itself was lit up, too. From tenement slums to looming office buildings, windows burned with lamps and neon. Even from here, Jasper could see the glow of Times Square a few blocks away, like a false sunrise. The city that never slept apparently couldn't be forced into restfulness by bad weather, either.

They moved past the window, listening for any sounds of movement from elsewhere in the office. If they were caught up here, it would be trouble. There was no escape hatch on the side of the building here. Well, there was. It was called a window, but that wouldn't really help if they were cornered. A twenty-story plunge to the pavement below was not a viable escape plan.

However, as far as he could tell, the office was still. Everyone must be downstairs, keeping tabs on the shindig below. Of course, that wouldn't last forever. If they were going to find anything, they better find it fast.

Jasper moved down a row of offices, looking for a promising one.

Each of the doors had a small placard bearing the name and title of its occupant, and each one was locked, but that didn't keep Jasper out for long. His lockpick made quick work of the tumblers, popping the pins open with practiced ease. The locks were meant to keep secretaries and underlings from wandering in at inopportune times, not keeping out determined detectives. Another item for Armstrong's to-do list around here.

Most of the offices were the same. Expensive paintings on the walls. Chairs for meetings with subordinates. Sometimes a scattering of unfinished paperwork and unread memos sitting in tidy piles on the desks.

Jasper picked a few banal items and memorized their gist. He wasn't about to dig around just to find things he'd have to tell Iris. She could have a few token tax papers to make it less obvious he was holding out on her.

Even if the offices would have been a treasure trove for Iris, Jasper wasn't interested in the vast majority of information he found. Moving from office to office, it quickly became apparent that it was going to be very difficult to find anything at all on Ray, let alone exactly what he wanted. Not that they knew what they were looking for in the first place. Before they could find the needle, they first had to find the haystack.

Jasper moved toward the office of the head of research and development. His feet were silent along the building's plush carpeting. He picked his way into the R&D deputy director's office. It was more disorderly than the rest. Papers from other departments littered every available surface. Jasper saw reams of paper from Yersinia's in-house lawyers detailing an ongoing legal battle over one of their patents. File folders were stacked up in the chair, and the desk looked like wild ferrets had been using the papers there for bedding.

For a moment, Jasper thought he found something with a map of an island in the Indian Ocean and details for security personnel, but it turned out to be nothing. He slid the map back in its folder.

A prototype of a new heart pump sat on a low counter. Wires stuck out of the contraption's guts, and its partially disassembled pieces lay nearby. The device looked like it had been carted through Verdun and then run over with a pickup truck a couple of times.

Something stood out on a desk, though. It was a memo from Ray. Jasper might not have noticed it at all but for the *SHRED THIS* written in red pen at the bottom of the memo. He picked up the paper.

"Leonard, we had a security breach in the basement today. We're taking care of the matter internally, no police. Obvious reasons. The intruders are a private outfit, but I don't know who they work for yet. We lost two men in the tunnels pursuing them. It's possible they're still alive, so we're scrubbing your control group subjects from the facility. If they're working for Horvath's people, this whole thing could blow up on us in a hurry. P.S. Clean your goddamn office. I don't want this or anything else about the rest of the inoculation project floating in that swamp."

Horvath's people? This was it. This was a big part of what he'd been looking for. Here was something that directly tied Armstrong to Dr. Horvath, if only tangentially. Not exactly a smoking gun, but it was a start. Jasper silently thanked the research and development head and his horrible office-keeping habits.

What did Horvath have to do with Yersinia? Resweber said the man was a professor of Old Church Slavonic, not biology or medicine. There was no obvious connection between his field and the company's interests.

And what did Ray mean by "Horvath's people"? It could just be an oblique reference to Resweber and the Attican Detective Agency, but Jasper didn't think so. The phrasing implied that Horvath belonged to some group, that he had confederates. Jasper realized that he might be looking at this case from the wrong angle.

He'd been focused on Armstrong, pouring all his energies down that channel in the hopes that they would trickle down to Horvath. But there were oh so many ways to skin a cat. Jasper still had no idea why Horvath had agreed to meet with Armstrong in the first place or why Ray killed the man. If he could start at Horvath's murder and work his way back by figuring out why Horvath and Ray had crossed paths in the first place, it might be easier than banging his head against the wall up here looking for clues that didn't exist.

The scrap of paper raised more questions than it answered, though. What in the world was the inoculation project?

Inoculations generally involved vaccines. The basic idea was that by introducing a small amount of a weakened virus or bacteria into the body, the immune system could attack the hostile organism, steal its lunch money, and annihilate it. That way, the body had a basic familiarity with the disease when it encountered the real thing. Antibodies could swarm the disease and tear it apart before it could sicken the host.

The widespread use of vaccines had probably proven the most significant advance in medicine in the past hundred years. When everyone was vaccinated, diseases that once wiped out whole populations were banished to the far reaches of the globe. Hundreds of thousands of lives had been saved thanks to widespread inoculation programs.

Was the charity ball the inoculation project? Certainly, one of the ball's stated purposes was to raise funds so Yersinia could send doctors to the far-flung reaches of the globe to provide basic medical care, including bevies of shots for long lines of wailing children.

Jasper dug through the stacks of papers sitting everywhere. They were in roughly chronological order, so it was like excavating through strata of rock looking for fossils. He found plenty of information on Yersinia's projects dating back several years, but he saw nothing else from Ray.

There were a large number of papers regarding Spanish Flu, though. Yersinia's researchers had been hard at work trying to develop a vaccine during the height of the outbreak. It looked like they still had a variety of projects running regarding the disease. There was also a surprising amount of money flowing into them, given that the plague had subsided and largely disappeared from the public imagination.

He folded up the sheet of paper mentioning Horvath and tucked it into his jacket. So far, it was his only genuine clue. Amelia walked in and saw him place the paper in his pocket.

"Find something? You look like you're ready to throw on a deerstalker cap."

"A bunch more questions, mostly. I do have something that shows Armstrong knew Horvath, so that's a start. Not exactly enough to lay the whole murder at Ray's feet, though. It does give me some ideas, though. How about you?"

"Yersinia's chief accountant is having an affair with his secretary, and they like to write each other dirty poetry. Really dirty. Not exactly going to crack the case with that."

"No, but I think we're making headway," Jasper said as the first chatter of automatic weapons sounded from down on the first floor.

Chapter 11
Party Crashers

Jasper bolted down the stairs, taking them three at a time. He had his FN Model 1922 in his hand, covering the way down as he charged toward the ground floor. He and Amelia leapfrogged between landings. She'd taken her Luger from its thigh holster and looked like she was ready for another world war, which might be just what they were walking into. Weapons continued to bark down below. Jasper could hear the *pop pop pop* of pistols, probably Armstrong's men. However, whoever they were fighting had them severely outgunned. The roar of Tommy guns and the occasional heavy rifle shot echoed up the staircase and smote Jasper's ears.

Who on earth would attack a charity ball? Just as pressing, why would they do it? Maybe gangsters hoping to rob the rich partiers of all their worldly possessions would try it. There would probably be a big take from such a job, but it would bring down the full fury of the New York Police Department upon anyone who even attempted it.

Besides, anyone who knew about the ball would also know about Armstrong's security presence. Criminals were generally lazy creatures, seeking the path of least resistance. Demanding protection money from helpless shopkeepers was a much easier revenue stream, and it was a lot less likely to provoke a massively armed response.

Whoever was responsible, they must want something very particular, something they couldn't get anywhere else. And they had come in force to get it.

A man came up the stairs from below. He had a swarthy, Mediterranean complexion and dark, thinning hair combed straight back. A mole that looked like happy deer tick clung to his cheek near his lips, and he wore dark clothes and a heavy leather jacket. The man was out of breath from having just run up several flights of stairs.

What struck Jasper immediately, though, was that the man seemed to be wearing some sort of modified neck brace; the thick material was pared down to give him unrestricted head movement. A large gold cross hung from a chain around his neck.

He spotted Jasper and Amelia running down the stairs and waved his Tommy gun at them. "Stop! Get on the ground. Right now," he ordered in a heavily accented voice. Evidently, he saw their clothes and assumed they were a pair of guests trying to flee the scene.

Jasper neither stopped nor got on the ground. They were close enough to the strange intruder that he didn't have time to notice that they were packing weapons of their own. Jasper didn't even bother to raise his. He simply vaulted the short distance down to the landing and crashed directly into the man.

Gravity added to his momentum, smashing the black-clad man back into the staircase's concrete wall. Jasper stripped the Tommy gun out of his surprised attacker's grip and tossed it over the banister, where it clattered to the ground several stories below.

The air went out of the man with an *oof*, and Jasper squeezed the rest out by jamming his fist into the pit of his opponent's stomach. Jasper pinned him hard against the concrete, and he pressed his face in close. He wanted answers, and he wanted them quick.

"Who are you? What are you doing here?"

"No! Be gone," the man wheezed. He tried to wave his crucifix in Jasper's face, but he swatted the man's hand away.

"First question: Who are you?" He pressed the man a little harder against the wall for emphasis.

"You are one of their agents! I'll never betray my brethren. Never," the man said. Well, this was going nowhere.

"Why are you here?" Jasper had his hands on the man's lapels and thumped him against the wall again. His prisoner tried to push back, and Amelia thumped him on the side of the head.

"We will destroy you and your foul masters alike. We will purge this city of your presence. Your day of reckoning is nigh." The sound of battle continued below, but it was tapering off. The pistol shots of Armstrong's men became more sporadic. They were simply outgunned.

"Oh, screw this," Amelia said. "You're coming with us, jerkoff. Jasper, cuff him. Maybe we can sneak out the back and see what he knows back at your sister's place."

"No," the man wailed. "I shall never be one of your thralls." As Jasper reached for the pair of handcuffs stowed away in one of his custom pockets, the man's face contorted, and he bit down on something.

Jasper recognized what was happening and smashed his hand down on the man's chin, trying to wrench his mouth open. But it was too late. Within a couple of seconds, foam began to dribble from the corner of the man's mouth, and the light left his eyes. He went stiff in Jasper's grip and started convulsing.

Reaching his fingers inside the man's mouth, Jasper removed a small wad of rubber. The material had been punctured, releasing its contents into the man's mouth. Cyanide, most likely. Jasper flung the wad of chewed rubber to the ground.

He let the man slump to the floor, still convulsing. Already, he was unconscious, and he'd be dead within three minutes at the outside. The poison was in his bloodstream, destroying his cells' ability to receive oxygen. By now, the individual molecules were bonding in his brain, killing them off in vast swathes. There was absolutely nothing they could do for him.

The man made garbled noises as he twitched on the ground. Jasper left him there and continued down the stairwell. Below, the sounds of gunfire had died away into a brooding stillness. He liked the silence even less than the gunfire. At least when there was shooting going on, he knew the attackers were occupied in their task. When it was quiet, he had no idea where people were or what they were doing.

Only a couple of minutes had passed since the gunfire erupted, but the police would be here soon, and they would be here in force. Jasper hoped they could make it out of the building before the boys in blue arrived. Their arrival might spark another gunfight, and even if it didn't, there would be lots of awkward questions that needed answering.

Sneaking down the last leg of the stairs, Jasper paused at the door to ground level. He pressed his ear to the wall and listened.

There was movement in the lobby. Using his lightest touch, he pressed on the door's exit bar. It opened a crack, and Jasper stuck his eye to the gap.

He saw more men and a few women, all of them dressed similarly to the one they had met in the stairwell. Each one wore black clothing and a throat guard. Most of them had similar golden crosses dangling from their necks as well.

They were in the process of leaving, retreating from the lobby in haste. Ray was walking with them, but not voluntarily. His hands were in cuffs, and two burly men to either side of him held onto his arms. He was resisting, dragging his heels along the floor and trying to lash out, but his large captors simply carried him along despite his best attempts to break free.

Jasper knew what he needed to do. The enemy of his enemy wasn't always his friend. Sometimes they were actually much worse.

These clowns might be dragging Armstrong off to put a bullet in his head and dump his body in the river. Case closed. Collect expenses and return to Chicago. Jasper could quibble with their methods, but Laramie Resweber's plan wasn't much more than a legalistic path to the same destination.

There was also the very real possibility that these people, whoever the hell they were, wanted Armstrong for something else entirely. Ray had once had his fingers in every pie in the city, and they might be here to abduct him for purposes worse than anything he was doing now. They were clearly kooks of some sort, albeit highly organized, well-armed kooks with an agenda.

Much as he didn't like to admit it, there was another factor Jasper had to consider. He'd finally been close to acquiring some closure for the failures of his past. He had come to confront Ray and maybe, possibly, put an end to an issue that had clawed at his thoughts for close to ten years. If he lost Ray now and the man disappeared off the face of the earth, Jasper would always wonder what happened to him and if he was still out there somewhere.

No, he had to deal with this matter himself. And that meant he had to rescue Ray. Why couldn't things ever be simple?

The black-clad goons schlepped out of the lobby, Ray in their grip. Jasper pushed the door open wider and snuck through the remains of Yersinia's charity ball. Many of the company's security team lay dead across the room. Several guests had been caught in the cross-fire as well, and they lay in untidy heaps of bloodstained finery.

Tables of food had been overturned, and one of the guards lay sprawled in the smorgasbord. His brains were dripping onto a platter of cheese cubes. The head of the giant ice swan lay nearby, where it had been shot off the sculpture. Jasper didn't see a sign of any living soul as he crept through the debris. The welcome banner had fallen down again during the fracas and lay across the dance floor. A couple of unmoving shapes lay beneath it.

Jasper spied the corpse of one of the assailants. A line of bullets had blown most of the man's face across a nearby wall. A few of the other bodies wore black and came outfitted with heavy golden crucifixes. Odd that they wouldn't collect their own dead. When the police arrived, they would use fingerprints and dental records to identify the stiffs, and that would point them toward the identity of the group.

Speaking of police, Jasper could hear mounting sirens in the distance. In a matter of minutes, half the force was going to come crashing down on the Yersinia building from every direction. They'd probably roused the chief of police from whatever speakeasy he was curled up in to come help with the situation.

Watching through the shattered glass of the revolving door, Jasper saw the thirty or so men preparing to leave. They had a convoy of vehicles that Jasper recognized. Each one was an old wartime ambulance, probably bought off one of the bankrupt European nations for a song and shipped over cheap.

Someone had painted the bulky ambulances dull black. The automobiles no longer looked like the clunky, bustling vehicles of mercy Jasper remembered from the war years. Now, they looked like hearses that had been injected with rhino testosterone. Engines rattled as the drivers started their lumbering, mutated transports.

The storm was picking up steam, and rain lashed the attackers in sheets. Some of them entered the passenger compartment of each vehicle while others clambered into the back. The two men carrying Armstrong lifted up his kicking, screaming form and tossed him into the rear of one of the middle vehicles like he was a sack of peat moss. They climbed in after him and slammed the doors shut.

"I don't think we can handle this on our own," Amelia whispered.

Jasper agreed with her.

There was no way he could stop them. Most of the men still had automatic weapons slung over their shoulders. He and Amelia would be torn to quivering red gobs in a matter of seconds, even with the element of surprise if they attacked. That didn't mean they couldn't do something, though. They needed a plan and quick. The convoy of ambulances was already starting to pull away.

They needed to follow the ambulances and find out where they were going. Rocky was supposed to pull up in case of an emergency, but Jasper saw no sign of him. The platoon of heavily armed strangers storming the building no doubt convinced him it was time to bug out.

He spotted what they needed just as the last ambulance started to pull away. A lone Model T sat parked across the street.

"C'mon," he said as he darted through the broken glass and rubble and stepped out into the storm. He scurried across the street, bent low against the rain and any possible eyes from the ambulances.

Running over to the passenger side of the Model T, he jimmied the door open. Stealing a car wasn't his ideal choice, but they were out of options. Amelia moved around to the front of the car.

"Can you get this thi—" The engine gunned to life, cutting him off. Amelia hopped into the driver's seat with a smile.

"Jasper, if it has a motor, I can get it started."

"After those ambu—" Jasper's words cut off as Amelia kicked the car into reverse and went screaming backward at full speed. The tires howled against the asphalt as she steered with her left hand and punched the car into the street.

They reached an intersection and, still accelerating, she swung the Model T around so it faced forward. Jasper pinballed around the vehicle's cabin as Amelia worked the controls. The car was off and moving forward before Jasper could even grab hold of anything to steady himself. The acceleration pushed him back into his seat. The row of ambulances had already traveled several blocks.

The first police car arrived on the scene behind them, sluing into the spot the Model T had recently occupied. More vehicles arrived behind it, parking helter-skelter around the building. A police sergeant popped out of his vehicle just as the first firebomb went off.

Glass blew out of the Yersinia building in a wave of deadly hail as flames suddenly burst out of the first five floors. The police sergeant threw himself back in his vehicle just in time to avoid being pureed by the torrent of deadly shrapnel. Orange-wreathed papers fluttered out into the night through the gaping windows. Rain pelted them to the ground in short order, where they quickly turned to sodden mush.

Jasper now understood why the attackers hadn't bothered to collect their dead. The police couldn't collect evidence from the bodies if they were incinerated.

Despite the downpour, the fire immediately began to climb upward through the building. The conflagration scaled the structure like a human fly act, feeding on the dry interior. The enormous police presence converging on the office building had just been rendered almost entirely moot. Now, most of the city's fire department would need to be summoned. Regardless of how quickly they arrived, the building was going to be unsalvageable.

The world seemed to increase in temperature by about twenty degrees in the blink of an eye. Jasper thought he could feel the faintest breeze as the massive fire sucked up oxygen. The flames writhed around the building, adding a glow that surpassed even that of Times Square.

Amelia slowed down as the ambulances turned a corner and disappeared from view. She hung back several blocks. Most of the traffic and pedestrians had cleared the area when the shooting started, though now rubberneckers were beginning to emerge from their buildings to stare at the growing inferno down the street. The Yersinia building's glow reflected off the wet streets, and Jasper could feel its heat on his skin even from several blocks away.

As they turned the corner, traffic began to reemerge around them. More sirens were on the way, but the scene back at the Yersinia building was too chaotic for the police to have gotten more than a fleeting glance at the Model T or the ambulances it was stalking. Now, they were blended in among dozens of nearly identical vehicles, impossible for either the police or the ambulance drivers to keep track of. Soon traffic had returned to its normal, circus-like levels, completing their camouflage.

Muscling their way through traffic, the ambulances waddled out of central Manhattan heading east. Eventually, they crossed the East River and entered Brooklyn. Zigzagging through the streets, they eventually made their way toward the docks.

In many ways, this area wasn't so different from the waterfront where the information brokerage was located, but the roaring economy had brought a resurgence to this area. Many of the buildings were rundown, industrial dinosaurs, but others had been torn down and replaced with new facilities.

Lights burned at many of the docks as stevedores moved from ship to ship, offloading goods. Crews worked in multiple shifts, covering the docks around the clock. The work never ended for the ports in this area.

It did come to a standstill, though. Many of the workers and the crews of the ships themselves had stopped and gathered around to watch the strange, flickering glow that lit up the sky in Manhattan. The convoy of ambulances looked enough like delivery trucks that no one paid any heed to the vehicles as they trundled past.

Jasper hoped they weren't heading for one of the giant merchant ships. If they bundled Ray off onto one of those, Jasper would need the Coast Guard to get him back, and that would involve a lot of explaining.

As Jasper watched, the ambulances pulled into the lot in front of one of the docks. Amelia kept driving for a minute, then switched off her lights and doubled back.

The men clambered out of their vehicles. The rear doors of one ambulance swung open, and Jasper recognized the silhouettes of the two gorillas that had been dragging Ray. A second later, Ray himself was pulled out of the rear of the ambulance. He tried to kick at the two behemoths restraining him, but the one on the left merely cuffed him upside the head.

They all moved toward the boat docked nearby. The vessel was not what Jasper was expecting. It was a gigantic garbage scow, its flat deck heaped high with refuse.

Most of the debris appeared to be wrecked car chassis piled atop wrecked car chassis. The rusting Fords and Brewsters lay in tangled piles all the way around the ship's surface, ready for their bon voyage into the automotive hereafter. Presumably, the parts would be taken away and compacted somewhere before being disposed of. Or maybe the boat would simply float ten miles offshore and then bulldoze the entire stack into the sea.

For that matter, Armstrong might be strapped to the hood of one of the vehicles when they did it. Jasper still didn't know who this group was, let alone their intentions.

The men and women in black crossed the gangplank onto the garbage scow, carrying Ray along with them. Gradually, they filed through a narrow passage in the heaps of cars, disappearing from sight.

"We have to follow them," Jasper said.

"I'm not sure that's a good idea. These guys are clearly nuttier than a squirrel farm. They just burned down New York's premier medical research company and abducted its head of security, and we have no idea what's waiting on that boat."

"Yes, but if they set out to sea, we'll lose our only lead." Jasper stepped out of the car and disappeared into the shadows surrounding the dock. Amelia sighed and followed him. It was a lot harder to disappear in the shadows while wearing a gauzy blue evening gown.

Chapter 12
By Hook or By Crook

Jasper slipped past the ambulances, scanning for movement as he went. The men hadn't left any lookouts on the docks, which was a clear sign that they would probably be setting off soon, but two of their number patrolled the garbage scow's deck. The guards circled the great heap of broken down automobiles like industrial buzzards scavenging amongst the mechanical carrion.

The boat was quite large, with probably a good two acres of surface area on its deck. It was constructed similarly to a large raft, basically a flat plane with a stubby superstructure and a motor for steering. Its edges were covered in hookup points so that a tugboat could help push the ungainly craft in and out of the harbor.

Rain pummeled the docks. Jasper's coat soaked through in a matter of minutes, and Amelia's gown clung to her frame. The water along the docks had turned a shade of ugly brown as runoff from the city flowed into the sea. A nearby discharge pipe sent a steady jet of scuzzy water and debris into the ocean, New York emptying its bladder into the great latrine surrounding the city. It would take at least a week for the water around the beaches to clean itself out.

Jasper kept his FN pistol tight in his hand, trying to keep the weapon as dry as possible. The weather wasn't making it easy.

Up on the deck, the two guards looked perfectly miserable as they paced around the perimeter of the ship at irregular intervals. They both had flashlights, but that only made them easier to spot. The beams of light couldn't cut more than a few feet through the storm. Beyond that range, the slashing rain simply reflected the light back toward them.

One of the guards stopped near the gangplank and tried to roll a cigarette. The paper soaked through almost instantly. Cursing, the guard tried to add some sad little clumps of tobacco, but the paper merely tore. Cursing even louder, the man tossed the entire wad over the rail into the roiling sea. As he did so, he caught a glimpse of something moving toward him.

He had just enough time to unshoulder his Tommy gun before the butt of Jasper's pistol crashed into his skull. The loud crack was lost against the greater roar of the storm, and the man went limp as death.

Grabbing him by the shoulders, Jasper dragged the man over to a banged-up red Rickenbacker and stuffed him in the cabin. In the dim light of the docks, the man's unconscious body was almost invisible. Jasper fished through the man's pockets and came up with keys, extra ammo, and a little money, but no identification.

The barge rolled under Jasper's feet, and he steadied himself by keeping one hand against the boat's railing. His hands were already frigid, and he could feel the heat leeching from his body under the rain's bombardment. He wasn't dressed for this weather, and he'd surely catch hypothermia if they spent too long out in the open. Behind him, Amelia's hair was plastered to her head, and she was shivering.

Moving across the slippery deck to the boat's stern, he spotted the second guard. The man was hunched under an overhang created by a precariously balanced wrecker perched atop a small mound of similarly decaying cars. He had his collar turned up against the rain and was dutifully watching the docks.

Jasper looked at the stack of cars. If a particularly rough wave slammed the barge, he wouldn't be surprised if the whole pile tumbled down on top of the man. Jasper could probably push on the stack like a pile of blocks and cause the same result.

Instead, he repeated the process he used on the first guard. This one went down in much the same manner. Jasper hid the man's unconscious form inside the body of another automobile.

He debated rolling them both over the side and into the waves, but he wasn't a cold-blooded killer. Despite what he'd seen, he had no idea what the troupe of strangers actually wanted. They certainly weren't in New York to sightsee, but that didn't mean Jasper could start picking them off like insects. An anonymous tip to the police would settle the situation once he had Armstrong in his own clutches.

Sliding across the deck, Jasper found the passageway through the heaps of twisted metal that Armstrong's captors had used. It was a meandering, narrow path through the maze of wrecked automobiles, switching first one way for twenty feet and then the other way.

Amelia watched their backs as he crept forward. He felt like a stagecoach driver sending his horses down a blind canyon in hostile territory. He had no idea what awaited beyond the next bend.

A moment later, he found out. He had assumed that the entire deck was more or less covered with old cars. From the docks, it certainly looked like an impenetrable jungle of steel and rust, but that was just the perimeter. In reality, there were just a few rows of junked cars stacked on top of each other to create a sort of fence, blocking all views to the center of the barge.

A strange vision presented itself before Jasper. Row after row of tents had been set up on the boat's deck, the heavy canvas repelling the rain. Several larger tents had been set up around the perimeter. One appeared to be a small infirmary, with about ten beds and a medic's station. Another appeared to be a command and control post, and yet another housed an extensive array of radio equipment. A tiny cafeteria and supply dump had also been established at one end of the boat.

The entire scene looked like a highly organized military encampment of the sorts Jasper had seen during the war. Hell, this was better organized than some of the frontline camps Jasper saw in France. Half the facilities at his old aerodrome were basically mud holes with a tarp to call a roof. Someone could invade a minor nation and install themselves as president with a force like this.

Jasper estimated that there were roughly one hundred tents laid out in neat rows across the deck. Assuming there were two people per tent, this represented quite the combat force. They'd lost a few men at the Yersinia building, but not enough to make a major dent in their numbers. Forget calling the cops. He would need to call in New York's National Guard.

Where had these people come from? A lot of their equipment looked like old Austro-Hungarian surplus military gear, not that Jasper could tell much from that. When the old empire split up into a raft of fractious, minor nations after the war, a lot of its old military equipment was sold to pay off outstanding debts and fund nascent governments. A lot more of it was probably stolen outright and sold to the highest bidder when central supply chains fell apart and records were lost.

In fact, it looked like the tents and equipment came from a hodge-podge of Eastern European sources. Some of it was Romanian, other pieces Bulgarian, and still others German and Russian. Jasper even spotted a crate with the seal of the defunct Ottoman Empire's army.

Lamps burned inside many of the tents, where almost everyone had already hunkered down for the night. No one wanted to ride the storm out in the open air.

There were clusters of activity in some of the larger tents, though. Jasper saw a few people hunched over tables in the cafeteria, and several of the infirmary beds were occupied with the survivors of the assault on the Yersinia complex.

In the distance, Jasper could still see a faint glow where their handi-work continued to burn. The rain and most of the city's fire depart-ment must have dampened the flames somewhat because the glow was no longer as bright as it had been. That, or the building had all but completely burned itself out.

Jasper stared at the largest tent, which appeared to be a command post of some sort. He could see several people gathered near the open doorway. The warm glow of light spilling out onto the deck silhouetted several people, including the hulks who dragged Ray aboard. As best he could tell, the other individuals in the tent were the ones in charge of this operation.

They wore long, dark greatcoats, and they were gathered around something inside the tent. The disparity of gear and odd quarters ruled out the possibility that this was any sort of national army, but they might be professional mercenaries out of Southeastern Europe. The war and ensuing Bolshevik Revolution in Russia had left the region with a sur-plus of disaffected soldiers.

A small, black banner hung above the open doorway. It depicted a leering human skull with fangs and a dagger through the top. Some-thing was written in Cyrillic underneath. Probably not a friendly greet-ing, Jasper decided.

Why on earth would they kidnap Ray? If it was money they wanted, they could have scooped up half of New York's four hundred most elite at the party and bled their coffers dry. If they wanted Yersinia's in-formation, they could have infiltrated the building quietly, as Jasper and Amelia had done, or they could have abducted one of the company's top scientists or executives. Unless someone had one hell of a personal grudge, taking Ray didn't make much sense. Maybe these were "Horvath's people."

Cloaking himself in the night, Jasper worked his way around the camp's perimeter. The deck sawed under his feet, but the sheer size of the craft mitigated the worst of the wave action.

Jasper made his way over, slinking past the tents. A loud sneeze came from a nearby tent as he walked past, and he froze as the tent flap peeled open. Lantern light spilled out onto the deck, and a large man poked his head out. The man pressed a finger to one nostril of his twice-broken nose, made a noise like a water buffalo in heat, and spat a slimy gob onto the deck. Jasper breathed a sigh of relief as the head disappeared back into the tent without so much as looking in his direction.

Creeping forward again, he made his way to the command post. Reaching into one of his hidden pockets, he lifted a tiny mirror. Angling it in his palm so he could see what was going on inside, he saw everyone gathered around a figure slumped in a chair.

The man in the chair was Ray. His face was puffy after having sustained several blows, and he had the beginnings of a world-class black eye.

Several of the officer-types questioning Ray were women. During the war, women had worked in the factories and fulfilled plenty of roles that would have been socially forbidden before, but none of the armies had made use of women soldiers. If this was a mercenary operation, they were drawing from a wider swath of people than just the ex-armed forces.

One of the women said something in a language Jasper didn't understand. Russian maybe. Something Slavic.

A translator relayed the question to Ray. "We already know you are lying. Why is Yersinia studying vampires?"

Vampires? Jasper's mind seized on the word. As in pale, semi-human creatures that flitted across the landscape to feed on the blood of the living? No, wait. That was the Attican Detective Agency's legal department. As in *fictional,* pale, semi-human creatures that flitted across the landscape to feed on the blood of the living?

Jasper glanced up at the banner over his head. The grinning skull's fangs hung down over him like the sword of Damocles. Ray had been captured by…vampire hunters? What in the gobsmacking hell?

However, a thought suddenly occurred to Jasper. The thing in the tunnels. It had killed two men without Jasper even seeing it clearly. Hadn't one of the guards called it a "bloodsucker" before he died? And those horrible slurping noises.

It made more sense than Jasper cared to admit. He had seen some odd things in his career as a private eye; however, the idea that one of the world's most respected medical firms was using its research money to study vampires struck him as absurd.

Still, he looked around. Most of the equipment and accents of the people on this barge indicated they were from southeastern Europe, the historic heart of the vampire myth. Their gear, from the crucifixes to the neck guards, certainly implied that they took the job seriously.

Ray coughed and looked up at his captors. "You destroyed the entire building. All the notes, all the research, all of it. You have no idea what you've done."

"We've prevented this scourge from infecting the entire city," a new woman said. She seemed to be in charge. Tall, with black, frizzy hair and pale skin, she stood out among the other vampire hunters. She paced around Ray, her dark, intelligent eyes fixed on him as she moved.

Her accent was lilting and melodious, from the same general region of the world as the rest of her crew. Serbian maybe? No, Jasper had met a few Bulgarian POWs during the war, and she sounded most like them.

"Did you think no one would read the reports and draw the conclusions we did? The homeless population of New York City has plunged in the past year. Unexplained disappearances in your subways. Corpses drained of virtually all fluid found in the storm drains. Something has taken up residence in the dark underspaces beneath your city, and it did not take long for our people to draw the connection to Yersinia. That's why you were brought in, no? To help keep us at bay?"

"You don't understand the situation at all," Ray mumbled.

"My organization has been dealing with this menace for hundreds of years. We understand far better than you, Mister Armstrong. The creatures must be wiped out, not studied. Destroying the Yersinia building was the only way to ensure that the knowledge your scientists gathered was never disseminated. Our teams will flush the vampires out of the underground and destroy them in due time, but we need to know who else was involved with the project. That's why we need you. You don't understand the research. Give up the names of those who do, and we'll allow you to live."

Ray laughed. The sound was hollow and bitter. "Cute strategy. Dangle out a little hope for cooperation. Carrot and stick. I've used it myself. Killed 'em all anyway, but it got people talking. You can't bullshit a bullshitter, lady. Besides, I've already told you what you need to know, and you simply refuse to understand the situation."

"You mean we refuse to swallow your lies. Very well. You may have it your way, Mister Armstrong. We'll get what we want eventually." The woman looked to one of her subordinates. "Bring the trucks on board. We're going to set out to sea. The authorities might have acquired a description. We'll come back in a few days and start working the tunnels. We'll have names then, so we can send teams after everyone connected with this."

Jasper nudged Amelia. They weren't going to have a chance to counter-abduct Ray stealthily, as he had hoped. Frankly, he would have been happy to leave Ray to his fate, but they were clearly nowhere near the bottom of this case.

Somehow, they'd gotten sucked into the middle of a battle of corporate espionage and monster hunters. Jasper had no idea what was going on, but he suspected it would come back to bite him on the ass if he wasn't careful. That meant he needed information, and he needed it now. He needed Ray.

Jasper and Amelia stepped in front of the open tent flap, their weapons raised. He had no intention of firing, that would bring the entire camp running, and neither of them would last ten seconds under a sustained attack from that many people.

The dark-haired woman looked up and stopped pacing, mid-stride. Everyone else turned around to see what she was staring at. "Are you part of Yersinia's security team?" She looked between the two of them. Jasper hoped she wouldn't notice the way their pistols wavered as they shook from the cold.

"Private operation," Jasper said.

"Ladies and gentlemen, let me introduce Jasper O'Malley, one of my most-trusted confidants," Ray said.

"Shut up, Ray. Untie him, please. We need him."

"You are making a mistake," the woman said. "If this situation isn't put under control soon, the entire city may be overrun. We can clear it out, but there are people who can create the same conditions all over again. We need their names, and Mister Armstrong here can give them to us."

If they dumped him over the edge in the storm, Jasper could sleep soundly at night and report back to Resweber that his ultimate goal had been achieved, if by rather uncouth methods.

However, they were clearly determined to get those names from Ray. This woman's cronies just torched a major corporation's headquarters and murdered a portion of its security force to do so. A little torture probably wasn't beneath them, and they would break Ray eventually. Everyone had a snapping point, even if finding it required some creativity. They would have a lot of time to get creative alone on the seas.

Those names would mean the deaths of more people. How innocent they were, Jasper didn't know, but he was in a position to prevent them from being systematically murdered. His sleep wouldn't be nearly as pleasant if he knew their blood was on his hands. Standing by and allowing some of the world's foremost vaccination researchers to be gunned down somehow seemed like a recipe for bad karma. Like, live tigers raining out of the sky bad.

One of the men near Ray reached toward the pistol holstered at his belt. Amelia gestured at him with her own gun.

"Now, obviously, you realize that you have the two of us outnumbered. Even you can do that math and, I mean, look at you. However, you also must realize that my partner and I have the drop on you. Whichever one of you draws first dies. It's as simple as that. Odds are, we can gun down all of you before you can clear leather. Granted, your troops will come running, but that doesn't do you much good, now does it?" Amelia's teeth chattered as she spoke.

The man's hand moved away from the butt of his weapon and came to rest very deliberately on the nearby map table instead.

"Untie him," the woman in charge spat. She crossed her arms and stared at Jasper and Amelia with narrowed eyes. Her pupils flicked back and forth between them as one of her subordinates sliced through the ropes binding Ray to the chair.

Armstrong stood up and rubbed at his wrists. "Thanks, ol' buddy, ol' pal. Where would I be without you?" Ray's voice was cold and his eyes colder still. He knew as well as Jasper that this wasn't for his benefit.

"Hold out your hands, Ray."

"Why? Say, do you have a spare gun I could borrow? I feel a bit naked without mine."

"Just hold out your hands."

"Fine. Let's just do everything your way, shall we? That's been going real well so far. You know, two of my guards would still be alive if you hadn't—Whoa, whoa! Hey! JESUS."

Jasper spun a set of cuffs out from the interior of his jacket and snapped them around Ray's wrists with one hand. He cinched them tight before Ray could even react, leaving his arms chained together in front of him.

"Turn around. We're getting out of here."

Ray stood in front of them, creating a human shield. "You know, you always were an asshole, Jasper. Your whole family. Assholes. With you as the grand high patriarch of the asshole clan. How's Percy? Oh, right. Dead. Mostly because you're an asshole."

Jasper didn't say anything as they backed out of the tent and retreated toward the rear of the ship, toward the dock.

"Say, who's your new partner? Hey, sugar tits, how's it going?"

Without taking her gun off the group of vampire hunters in the tent, Amelia reached around with her other hand and punched Armstrong directly in the ear.

"Ah, that hurt. What the hell? Now my ear's ringing. Criminy, no wonder you two are working together. Assholes. I'm surrounded by assholes."

Jasper sighed. "Ray, we're going to trade you back to them if you don't shut up for five minutes."

"Fine. Let's pick up our getaway sticks and blow this popsicle stand. A pleasure meeting you, Ralitza. We really must all have brunch sometime. My people will be in touch with your people. Don't be a stranger, mmkay?" Armstrong baited the woman in charge of the vampire hunters. Her expression didn't change as she stood with her arms crossed.

She uncrossed her arms in a quick movement. It wasn't a dramatic gesture, but it was fast. Jasper's instincts pressed his head down before his conscious mind even registered anything whizzing toward him.

A long, pointed object shot through the space his eyes had occupied a half second before. It was a wooden stake, carved smooth into a tapered dowel. The woman vampire hunter must have pulled it from a hidden pocket of her own and hurled it with tremendous force. Jasper's vision could only pick up a pale streak of movement for the split second the stake was overhead, and then it disappeared into the darkness behind them.

The movement broke the spell amongst the other hunters, and they all lunged for their weapons. "Run," Jasper shouted as the first bullet cracked through the air. They stood no chance against the whole army of vampire hunters.

Instead of moving around the perimeter, the way they had come in, Jasper darted straight through the lines of tents. By dashing down through the miniature tent city, he hoped to block the hunters' aim. They wouldn't want to risk hitting their own people with a stray bullet.

At least, he hoped not. Most of the characters he dealt with weren't ruthless enough to burn down a major biomedical research facility. He pushed Ray in front of him, keeping one hand locked around the man's shoulder to prevent him from escaping in some other direction.

He still couldn't quite believe these people were vampire hunters, but they had pulled out all the stops if they were anything else. One of their number had willingly chomped down on a cyanide pill to avoid being taken alive, and their leader apparently carried stakes around with her.

But vampire hunters inherently implied vampires. Jasper didn't like the idea that his job had suddenly crashed head-on into the supernatural, but he honestly didn't have a better explanation for the thing in the tunnel.

Heads poked out of tents at the sound of the gunfire. Surprised eyes blinked at Jasper and Amelia as they darted past. People sprang out of tents, some of them in their night clothes. They grabbed rifles or tried to strap on holsters and leap into their boots at the same time. The garbage scow's entire deck erupted into sudden anarchy.

A few stray shots whizzed over their heads, but the deck was in too much disarray for anyone to draw a clear bead on them before they plunged into the passageway through the wrecked cars. Jasper lunged through the jagged switchbacks, his dress shoes fighting for traction against the deck's slick surface. He, Amelia, and Ray charged down the gangplank to the docks.

"You two planning to crash every party in town tonight? Mind dropping me off at the Waldorf Astoria?" Ray asked.

Vampire hunters came spilling out onto the dock, clearing the bottleneck through the destroyed automobiles and spoiling for a fight. Everyone ducked behind a parked ambulance as a line of automatic gunfire stitched across the dock.

Another quick dash took them to their stolen Model T. Jasper hurled Armstrong into the backseat as Amelia dove behind the steering wheel. Jasper piled in beside her as the engine howled to life. The tires spun, and the car shot off like a startled rabbit. The acceleration mashed Jasper back in his seat as he tried to turn around to see what the vampire hunters were doing.

But he didn't need to see. He could hear the sound of engines roaring to life behind them.

Chapter 13
Die Toten Reiten Schnell

Amelia jammed down on the gas, and the Model T sluiced through the rain. It was already dark, but the roiling storm clouds blocked even moonlight from infiltrating the darkness. The only light at all seemed to come from the electric lights of the city itself, and the rain blocked most of that with dazzling sheets.

Barreling down the middle of the street, Amelia tried to pull more speed out of the little Ford, but it was an older model, and its engine wasn't as fine-tuned as the Agency's Peerless. Compared to the throaty purr of the company car, the noise emanating from under the hood sounded more like a colony of sick bees. She followed the road along the docks, tearing back toward Manhattan.

"You just make friends everywhere you go, don't you, Jasper? It's a wonder they haven't given you the key to the city yet," Ray said from the backseat.

Jasper turned around, his nearly numb hand gripping his pistol. Water beaded along the barrel and dripped down to the floorboards. His body left a sodden stain on the seat where he had been sitting. Both he and Amelia were drenched, and his wet clothes chafed against his skin.

"Talk," he said. He gestured with his gun, but he was careful to hold it way back, out of range from a mad lunge.

"Well, what should we talk about? It's been ten years since you left, Jasper. There's just so much for us to discuss."

"We aren't discussing anything. You're going to explain, and I'm going to listen. Who were those people?"

"I thought they explained themselves rather well. They're vampire hunters."

"Don't avoid the question. Specifically, who are they?"

"You just met their leader, Ralitza Petkova. She's a pistol, that one. I don't know most of their names."

"What's their game? Why are they in New York?" Jasper glanced through the rear window. A collection of headlights was moving fast down the roadway behind them. The vehicles were gaining.

"I told you. They're hunting vampires."

Jasper gritted his teeth. Ray was trying to bait him, hoping to open up some opportunity to escape. The man was under no illusion that he was being rescued. He just didn't know if he was in more or less trouble yet; he was biding his time until he could wriggle away.

"We've got company coming up fast," Jasper said.

"I see them," Amelia responded.

"Why are they after you, Ray? What do they gain by snatching you?"

Armstrong threw back his head and laughed. He gave a series of high-pitched snorts and giggles. The man had deteriorated noticeably in the intervening years since they worked together, but that didn't make him any less dangerous. Maybe more so, actually. Ray had always been crazy, but it just shone through the cracks a little brighter now. A decade ago, Jasper hadn't been able to see it until it was too late.

"They think Yersinia has been doing research into vampires."

Amelia swerved around a slow-moving truck, and Jasper had to grab onto his seat to keep from sliding into her. She bounced back into their lane, an angry horn bellowing after her.

"What have they been doing research into?"

"You always were nosy, Jasper."

"Tell me about the inoculation project you've been working on." Jasper remembered Ray's comment on his message to the R&D head. It was his one card he could surprise Armstrong with.

Ray seemed to deflate a little. "Nosy, nosy, nosy."

"Cough it up, Ray."

"Yersinia has been working on a new idea for next-generation vaccination programs. It's rather clever, if I do say so myself. They wanted to develop it in case Spanish Flu ever came back. Plagues do that sometimes. One of the things I've learned since I started working here. You can get waves of outbreaks; things will calm down for a while, and then the disease comes back with a list of names and its ass-kicking boots spit shined."

"Did they have any success?"

"Yes and no. The real secret was in the vaccination method rather than the vaccine itself. The vaccine never worked, but the method produced some interesting results. You know anything about the Black Death?"

"Bubonic Plague. Wiped out about a third of Europe."

"See, I heard the plague was caused by rats, but that's not right. It's the fleas on the rats that spread the plague. Diseased rats come in on a ship or something and spread the fleas through town. The fleas hop onto people, bite them, and BOOM. Welcome to Plaguesville, baby."

"The plague hasn't been a problem in a long time. Why does Yersinia care?"

"Well, think about it. Fleas carry the plague and drill it right into your bloodstream, and then you die. But who says they have to carry plague? Why couldn't they carry something else? Like a weakened version of some other bacteria? Some egghead got pretty clever with the whole thing and realized that we could release a horde of specially modified fleas into a rural village, and they'd inoculate the place for us inside a week. No fuss. No muss."

"That's…fairly clever, actually. And this could prevent Spanish Flu from flaring up again??"

"That was the goal, but there were some problems with the formula. Some of the specimens were accidentally released into the subway system."

"Accidentally released?"

"Well, maybe we set a batch of fleas loose down there as a field test to see if they'd be fruitful and multiply on their own."

"So, if you had some troubles with the formula, you had some unwitting test subjects. What exactly are the fleas spreading when they bite people?"

"It was supposed to be some harmless hormones and a dummy virus. Things didn't really go as planned."

Jasper looked over Ray's shoulder out the back window again. The ambulances drew steadily closer. The vehicles had large, powerful engines meant to pull them through the muck of a heavy war zone. Overtaking a smaller, poorly maintained Model T would take a little time, but the results were inevitable.

"Let me guess. This dummy virus has some adverse effects, like turning people a little bloodthirsty? So Yersinia botched the experiment and accidentally created vampires in New York's subway and sewer system. How am I doing?"

"You know, Jasper, you're always so judgmental about everything. Someone makes one tiny mistake, and you're all over them. So we created some monsters. It could happen to anyone." Ray gave a big, unpleasant smile.

"All right, how did the vampire hunters become involved?"

"They have people all over the place. This one fellow, Doctor Horvath, was one of their American contacts. Taught Old Church Slavonic at Columbia or something. Can you believe that? Who the hell speaks Old Church Slavonic? I mean, other than ancient orders of vampire hunters. Seriously, who the hell speaks that? Makes Latin look like it's up and bouncing around like Fred Astaire."

"And you killed him."

"'Killed' is such a strong word. I'm all about solving problems."

"But they found out anyway."

"Yeah. Maybe a little. It really pissed them off, too. They're normally out crawling through old castles in Transylvania or what have you, but they sent almost their entire crew over here. Probably normally paid in goats and hillbilly piss vodka or something by a bunch of toothless villagers, but they assembled quite the outfit for this job."

"They must have come to bask in your enormous personal charisma. How'd they get word about the situation here?"

"Horvath must not have been their only contact here. They have people all over the place looking for disappearances and other signs that things have gone hinky. The world's a smaller place since they were founded. Global commerce. International trade routes. The whole shebang. I understand they stamped out quite the situation in Panama last year, and Ralitza was just telling me about how we almost lost Shanghai during the war."

Amelia hadn't been able to shake the trail of black ambulances yet. They were far too close for Jasper's comfort. A man poked his head out the passenger window of the lead vehicle, gauging distance.

"What have you been doing about the situation?"

"At first, we kept sending men down there to deal with it. At one point, I had actually managed to requisition some flamethrowers for the task. Do you have any idea how hard it is to get flamethrowers? It ain't easy, let me tell you."

"And how did that work out?"

"Oh, everybody died."

A bullet cracked through the rear windshield and buried itself in the seat between Jasper and Amelia. Ray flinched away from the burst of powdered glass a few inches away from his head. Amelia swerved wildly, trying to make them a harder target.

The sound of more bullets popped from behind them. It was too far past normal work hours for the dockside traffic to be very heavy. The vehicles that had chanced the wet roads scurried off onto side streets as their drivers realized that the sharp cracks weren't the sound of thunder.

"Quick, give me a gun," Ray said. Jasper completely ignored the request.

"We need to get off the main road and lose them," Jasper said.

"I'm working on it." Amelia twisted the wheel, plowing around a delivery truck poking its way into the intersection.

The traffic began to thicken, and Jasper realized she was headed in the direction of the East River. Suddenly, she swerved deeper into Brooklyn. Even at night, there was traffic, and the streets narrowed between the looming buildings that hunched over the roads. Torrents of water guzzled down storm drains. Some of the drains had backed up, creating significant pools of water. The Model T sent up twin plumes of white froth as Amelia gunned the engine through one of the small ponds forming in the middle of the street.

The ambulances behind them were forced to slow down and merge into a single file line. They nosed around slower traffic, their horns braying to the high heavens as they did so. Windows flew open, and tenement residents stuck their heads outside to see what the unholy racket was. Even for New York City, their chase was creating a stir. It was only a matter of time until the police heard about it and came to investigate, something the ambulance drivers must be keenly aware of.

Jasper had his head out the side window, his pistol steadied in his arms. He didn't want to use the weapon on the crowded streets, and it didn't look like he'd have to. On the narrower city streets, the

Model T was gaining ground over the convoy of angry vampire hunters. The smaller, nimbler car was inherently better suited to the traffic and vehicle-eating potholes of the city. The ambulances just couldn't maneuver as well. Add Amelia's skills behind the wheel and it would prove genuinely difficult for any of the large, snorting vehicles to catch up.

Suddenly, the Model T slowed, its brakes clamping down. Momentum smashed Jasper against the dashboard. He looked ahead, expecting to see some sort of insurmountable obstacle. A thirty-car pileup. A washed-out road. A traffic jam from here to Cincinnati.

The road ahead was completely clear. The Model T began to drift drunkenly toward the sidewalk at a much slower speed, and Jasper looked at Amelia to see what the problem was.

The problem was she was being strangled. While Jasper wasn't looking, Ray had taken his manacled hands and slipped them up over Amelia's head. Now he was pulling straight back, the chain between his wrists crushing her air pipe.

Amelia made a gagging noise as she tried to reach backward over the seat and claw at Ray, but it was an impossible angle, and her hands simply flailed at the air behind her. With her hands off the steering wheel, the Model T continued to drift along like a bloated hippo corpse caught in a river current. It smacked into a nearby Packard with a crunch, smashing one of the headlights against the other vehicle's fender.

The Model T came to a dead stop, and the ambulances were quick to close in. They only had a few seconds before the meat wagons were on top of them.

Jasper placed the muzzle of his FN Model 1922 directly against the skin of Armstrong's wrist, only a few scant millimeters from the fragile puzzle of bones beneath the surface, and then he pulled the trigger. The noise was cataclysmic inside of the confined space of the vehicle.

The muzzle flash sent a breath of gunpowder belching through the car. Black powder sprayed across Ray's wrist where his hand suddenly tore loose from the rest of his arm. The bullet sizzled through the skin, the flesh virtually melting against the hot metal. It sawed through the bone, spraying tiny, jagged shards across the Ford's interior. The tendons and gristle and meat were all blown apart. Taking a final exclamation point of flesh with it, it blew out the other side of Ray's wrist, punched through the side door, and embedded itself in a brick wall across the street.

A jet of blood sprayed across Amelia's face, and Ray made an inhuman shrieking noise. The only thing holding his hand to the rest of his arm was a thin string of sinew. The chain was still around Amelia's neck, but it had lost all its tension.

Cursing, Amelia grabbed the loose hand and pulled. The hand ripped entirely free with a wet tearing noise, and Ray made more noises like a branded steer. With nothing anchoring it on one side, the chain dropped away from Amelia's neck. It was still attached to Armstrong's good left hand, but it simply slid off the stump where his right hand used to be.

The severed hand fell in Amelia's lap. She bent the hand's digits and held it up to give Ray the finger with his own hand. Yowling, Ray clawed at the door handle with his remaining hand and leaped out of the stalled vehicle. Jasper didn't even try to stop him. They had bigger problems to worry about.

A bullet pinged off the asphalt near their front tire as the ambulances bore down. Amelia, her blue dress now streaked with red, punched down on the gas and turned the wheel. The Model T scraped free of the Packard, taking a substantial portion of the larger vehicle's paint with it. The cars groaned and then parted ways with a tinkle of glass.

She sped away as more gunfire erupted behind them. The car weaved across the lanes in a mad jitterbug dance, juking and never staying in one spot for too long. A few desultory pops sounded behind them as the ambulances were forced to resume their pursuit.

They were much closer now, though. The only thing keeping them from laying down a full blast of lead was the constant jinking motion of the car. Scurrying around on the road like a roach hoping to avoid being squished would only work for so long, though.

"Do you have a plan?" Jasper asked, trying not to tumble around the car's interior too much as Amelia zig-zagged down the street.

"Sort of. If we can't shake them, I'm going to drive us back into Manhattan and go straight past whatever's left of the Yersinia building. Half the cops in town are probably still there watching it burn. They might take an interest in our pals here," she said as she swerved across into oncoming traffic and hopped up onto the sidewalk. The Model T frolicked off the curb and back into the street as a couple of bullets smacked into the wall of the apartment building behind it.

Suddenly, the entire left side of Jasper's vision filled with dazzling light as they passed through an intersection. He looked over just in time to see a pair of headlights glaring at them. Amelia pushed through the intersection a few feet ahead of the larger black vehicle.

The ambulance swerved hard and bounded into the road behind them. Water sprayed from its tires as it slid sideways for a second, hydroplaning. With a lurch of metal, it lost all traction and flipped onto its side. It grated across the road on a trail of sparks before coming to a stop.

"Where did he come from?" Amelia shouted. She looked down and realized Ray's hand was still resting in her lap where she'd dropped it. She tossed it out the window without looking.

"They must have dispatch radios in the ambulances. The ones tailing us are relaying instructions to the others so they can prepare for us."

"Well, that's just peachy," Amelia said. "Let's see them prepare for this." She twisted the wheel hard to the left, and the Model T fishtailed onto a new street. Jasper held on for dear life as the little car threatened to go up on two wheels. Instead, it rounded the bend and sped off.

Behind them, the vehicles had to slow down and trundle through the curve like a troupe of elephants. Ahead of them stood the Brooklyn Bridge, pathway to Manhattan, symbol of the city. The massive steel-and-concrete structure loomed out across the East River. Its cables hung down like the vines of some mechanical jungle.

Amelia steered the rattling Ford onto the access road. The storm had driven most of the traffic from the bridge, and she zipped around the few cars braving the winds and rain. Their tires hummed on the asphalt until they hit the bridge itself.

In the distance, Manhattan glimmered like a fistful of golden coins. Street lamps and neon blinked, even at this hour. The city beckoned through the rain.

Through the rear window, Jasper saw the first black ambulance round the curve in the access road behind them. It was soon joined by several of its sisters, all of them rolling onto the bridge. They moved like a pack of feral dogs hunting a rabbit. They fanned out, taking up all the lanes as they moved forward.

The fact that there were fewer cars on the bridge actually worked to Jasper and Amelia's disadvantage. With a light frame, the little Model T had better acceleration than the hulking vehicles chasing it, but its engine wasn't as powerful. The older Ford topped out at a lower speed than its pursuers. On a flat, empty road like this, they might as well have been staring each other down across a dusty street in the Old West, just waiting for the clock to strike noon. Unfortunately, the vampire hunters had a lot more firepower at their disposal and a quicker draw.

Below, the water of the East River roiled and sprayed foam against the bridge's pilings. Silt and refuse churned up and swept in from the city had turned the water an unpleasant shade of brown.

The bridge was long. If they could just make it back to city streets, they had a chance. The vampire hunters would be forced to give up if the Model T reached an area with a high concentration of police. That, or they would be systematically chased down and cornered.

Personally, Jasper hoped they would continue their pursuit and invite the full wrath of the New York Metropolitan Police Department. Interrogations would eventually lead them to Ray and straight to Horvath. That was all Jasper needed to complete this job.

Oddly enough, the crew of vampire hunters provided exactly the link Jasper needed to stick Ray with Horvath's murder. Before, the connection hadn't made any sense, but Ray had admitted he killed the man and left Resweber with the bag to cover up the company's failed inoculation experiment.

The police might also move to investigate what was happening in the tunnels. Jasper still wasn't sure whether or not to take Armstrong's word that they were genuine vampires. Where would Yersinia even acquire the know-how to create such a thing, especially when their goal was to fight Spanish Flu? Someone needed to find out exactly what was down there and exterminate it. Jasper wasn't ready to leave the task up to a collection of Van Helsing poseurs.

Unfortunately, those were all questions for another time because Jasper realized they weren't going to make it to the end of the bridge. The ambulances were gaining too fast.

"Must go faster," he said.

"I can't," Amelia responded. "We're going as fast as we can go."

The black vehicles loomed large behind them, gaining ground every second. Their grills flashed like hungry teeth and their headlights gazed soullessly forward. Jasper could see leering faces behind the windshield of the closest ambulance as it surged ahead.

They were nearly to the end of the bridge, almost in Manhattan.

The Model T sped toward the end of the bridge, fighting its way back toward city streets. Rain washed off the bridge in thick rivulets as the vehicle tried to escape.

The front bumper of the ambulance smashed into the rear of the Model T with a crunch of metal. Jasper jerked as the ambulance bumped them forward. Their tires lost their grip on the slick road.

Amelia worked the wheel, trying to regain control, but the vehicle merely fishtailed. The tires shrieked liked startled banshees as they made futile attempts to snap back onto the road surface.

From behind, the ambulance rammed them again, harder this time. Jasper held on as he felt the vehicle hydroplaned toward the railing. Amelia no longer had any control over the steering. The car veered, and Jasper realized that they were going to go over the edge.

With a screech of metal, the Ford tore through the guardrail on the side of the bridge and sailed into the open air.

Chapter 14
Tunnel Rats

Amelia had been thinking about something the whole evening. Plunging out of the sky toward the roiling waters below really crystallized the thought, though.

They had made it almost all the way across and off the bridge. The water below was only about thirty feet down before it washed against the edge of Manhattan itself. If they'd been pushed off the road at its midpoint, they would have plunged some two hundred feet down before hitting the water, which would have been as tough as concrete from that height. The Model T would have exploded into twenty dozen crimped pieces and splattered them to chum in the process.

Thirty feet was still a long way to fall, though, and the water seemed to loom toward Amelia in slow motion as they plunged over the side of the bridge. She blinked, and the water was suddenly much closer, filling up her entire vision.

The thought that occurred to her was simple. This night, she'd been shot at, attacked by vampire hunters, frozen her butt off, nearly strangled, escaped out of a building a few minutes before its contents were incinerated, and now someone had just shoved her off a bridge.

Seriously. What the hell?

There were other things she could do with her life. She could run a roadside attraction like a poisonous snake farm. She could drive one of those clown cars for the circus and get harassed by carnies. She could take up a nice, relaxing job like working with high-voltage electrical wires. So why was she doing this for the Attican Detective Agency? Jasper was her friend. She didn't have many. She wasn't really a "friends" kind of girl. She wasn't much of a people person at all, really, but Jasper meant a lot to her. He was one of the few people willing to take a chance on her.

But was anything worth all this?

The water drew closer as she watched. She braced herself against the steering wheel. Jasper gripped the dashboard as gravity pulled the car into a swan dive position.

There were other jobs available to her. Iris O'Malley had offered her a position at the information brokerage. Before, she hadn't felt particularly tempted. That was before it felt like half the city was trying to kill her.

Somebody needed to help people like Laramie Resweber. However, it wasn't as if the Attican Detective Agency did it out of the goodness of their hearts. Somebody wired their boss a large sum of money, and then he dispatched the appropriate number of detectives until the problem went away or the money ran out. The Agency wasn't built off altruism, and in that regard, was it really so different from the information brokerage?

Iris was simply more upfront about her motives. The vast majority of people would never receive the benefits of Attican detective work, and most of the clients they worked for were fundamentally trying to screw over someone else in one form or another. Resweber's motives might be just on some level, but they were basically intended to poke Ray Armstrong in the eye.

Amelia strongly suspected that most of the work for the information brokerage wouldn't get her pushed off bridges, either. And judging from the opulent setup of their offices, there had to be some money in it, right?

The car hit the water.

Amelia's arms folded as the impact smashed through her entire body. She rocketed straightforward as the Model T's nose crashed into the waves, nearly impaling herself on the steering column. The air shot out of her lungs from the intensity of the steering wheel colliding with her sternum.

She tried to drag the air back into her lungs with a ragged gasp, but her mouth filled with seawater instead as the vehicle plunged beneath the waves. Brown, sludgy water poured in through the open windows in an icy flood. She tried to open her door, but it wouldn't budge.

So far, the water was only up to about her nose. There was still a pressure differential between the interior of the car and the outside. She couldn't see anything except brown muck through the front windshield.

The water was as cold as the grave. It tried to steal what little breath she had left. The cold seeped into her pores and bit at her muscles. It crawled over her bones with the tingle of swarming ants eating her alive. The cold physically hurt as the water rose up over her nose and she was forced to hold her breath. Her body felt like it was turning to stone, the energy sucking out of her as the water continued to rise up until she was completely submerged. She squeezed her eyes shut.

With a thud, the car came to rest on the shallow bottom of the river near the shore. Amelia popped her eyes open and immediately wished she hadn't. They stung from pollutants and silt and God alone knew what else. She could see the hazy shapes of sunken tires and the rotted pilings of a pier that had fallen into the river many years ago.

Shoving hard, she tried to work the door handle. The door still didn't want to open. Fighting back an edge of panic, she dug her feet into the floorboards and put her whole body into pushing the door open.

It gave with a lurch. The fall had jammed the mechanism, and it took a hefty application of brute force to unstick it. A couple of stray air bubbles escaped toward the surface, and she chased after them.

She surfaced with a gasp. Rain pounded down on top of her head, and she pushed her sodden hair out of her eyes. Coughing, she spat out a stream of water that tasted like dog colons.

Jasper popped up beside her and looked up. "Dive," he shouted and immediately dipped back below the waterline.

Amelia looked up as well and saw figures lining up at the edge of the bridge. The black-clad figures didn't look like friendly Samaritans gathering to help. Most Samaritans weren't nearly so well armed.

Gulping down a lungful of air, Amelia disappeared beneath the river just as the first patter of lead peppered the water's surface. She dove deep, skimming the debris field along the bottom of the river. The bullets expended most of their energy in the first few feet after hitting the water and then drifted harmlessly with the current.

One landed at the base of her neck, and she swatted it away. It was hot.

A hand grabbed her arm. The long, spidery fingers were even colder than the surrounding water. The hand started to drag her toward shallower water. Both she and Jasper had to surface to take another breath of air, but they propelled themselves right back beneath the waves as another salvo of small arms fire probed for them.

Amelia was able to see what Jasper was aiming for, though. There was a storm drain built into the embankment ahead. Obviously, they couldn't stay in the river forever. She once read that hypothermia could set in within minutes. Even if the vampire hunters simply sat up on the bridge and took occasional pot shots, both she and Jasper could very well be dead within twenty minutes as their core body temperatures plunged.

Nor could they simply clamber out of the water. There was very little cover around the retaining walls at the river's edge. They'd be gunned down before they could take ten steps. The firing squad up on the bridge didn't have the aim or trigger discipline of an army, or even one of Chicago's more competent gangs, but they could put a lot of lead in the air very quickly. Someone would get lucky with their aim sooner or later.

The large, circular drainage pipe offered the only chance of escape. It vomited water, leaves, and debris into the river like a reveler after a long night at a speakeasy. It wasn't clean. It wasn't dry. It wasn't even particularly safe, but it was their only shot out of this mess.

They made an oblique approach toward the pipe, zig-zagging to make it impossible to tell ahead of time where they would surface for breath. Whenever they did pop up for a lung load of air, they had to slip back below before the chatter of gunfire could start up again.

Finally, they reached the edge of the pipe. The water was shallow here, only a couple of feet deep. The pipe dangled a few feet above the water line, and its contents spewed out in a magnificent industrial waterfall. Jasper signaled that he would boost her up first and then follow.

They surfaced behind the gush of water, hiding from the men and women on the bridge. The roar of water was deafening. She couldn't hear sirens yet, but she had to assume that someone had reported the armed convoy parked on the Brooklyn Bridge firing Tommy guns down at swimmers below. Even for New York, that was excessive.

She shivered and hugged her arms around her body. Her entire frame shuddered against the chill air. Jasper cupped his hands together to form a step, and he boosted her up through the raging torrent. The water tried to wash her away, to scour her from the smooth walls of the concrete tunnel, but she held on and crab scuttled forward.

The tunnel was large, but not quite big enough to stand fully erect. She turned around and reached out a hand to lift up Jasper. He grabbed on to her wrist. She could really only feel his grip as a vague pressure, her entire body was so numb.

Hauling Jasper up, they both collapsed in the wash and had to scramble to their feet. On the bridge, the vampire hunters were packing it in and jumping back in their vehicles. Amelia just hoped they didn't have quick access to maps like those in Armstrong's office. If they knew where all the tunnels and pipes terminated, they could have people waiting at the other end, like someone with a shotgun just waiting for a rabbit to poke its head out of a hole.

"Let's get out of here," Jasper said. Amelia had trouble understanding him as his teeth chattered. He pulled a small flashlight out of one of his pockets. Miraculously, the water hadn't completely soaked through its seals. The light blinked to life and shone down the bore of the tunnel. Jasper's hands were shaking too badly to hold the beam steady, and the light jittered and rocked from side to side.

They trekked down the concrete tube as quickly as possible, but the going was difficult. The swift-moving water tugged at their legs, threatening to sweep them off their feet. The ground was slick with congealed slime and mats of rotting leaves. Her feet grew so numb she felt like she was walking on meat stilts.

Jasper's flashlight beam could only illuminate so much of the tunnel. It felt like the darkness was trying to swallow the meager light. Neither of them could hear anything. The solid roar of water drowned out all the other noise, save for the occasional thrum of a vehicle passing overhead.

Smaller pipes, too small for them to enter, branched off at regular intervals. Water poured down into the main channels from the smaller pipes, fresh from the streets above. Gravel, cans, and burned-out cigarettes all poured into the pipe near their feet. Amelia kicked a decomposing rat carcass out of the way and continued on.

Graffiti lined the walls in vast, colorful smears. Some of it was artful. A lot of it was just grammarless concoctions of profanity and poorly drawn dongs.

After a few hundred feet that felt like a forced march across Asia, they came to a large grate. The metal bars were set wide apart, meant to allow trash and debris to pass through unimpeded, but to prevent people from venturing further into the tunnels. Near the center, the bars had been stretched apart, creating a large gap. Some of the bars had snapped entirely under whatever pressure had been applied to them.

A large blockage had developed at the base of the grate. Jasper directed his flashlight down at the clotted mass. Slimy bones wrapped in the remains of a sewer worker's jacket lay in a disarticulated heap. The constant flow of water had stripped off most of the flesh, but decaying chunks still clung in stubborn patches. The skull screamed up at them from the floor. At a glance, it was impossible to definitively tell what killed the sewer technician, but part of his cranium had been bashed in. The interior of his skull lay open for them to see. Some muck that might or might not have been organic in nature was clotted in his brainpan. Whether the injury occurred before or after death was anyone's guess at this point.

Amelia wondered if the body had been drained of blood before it was unceremoniously swept away by the subterranean river. She stepped through the bent bars, careful to make sure she didn't stick her foot straight into the man's rat-chewed remains. Jasper followed her, his breath steaming in the flashlight's feeble beam.

They had just passed into something else's domain. The corpse left here in the tunnels was proof of that. Amelia suddenly knew what prehistoric cave painters felt like, shimmying down into the darkness with only the light of a crude torch, hoping that a saber-toothed cat hadn't chosen the base of the crevice for its den. This was something else's territory, and it wasn't friendly.

Further down, the flashlight picked out an area where the pipe was broken. Something had burst through the concrete into a chamber beyond. Chunks of debris lay strewn across the floor like river rocks.

Amelia poked her head into the chamber to see where it led. Jasper sloshed up behind her and shone the light inside. It appeared to be a connection to the sewer system, not so very different from their own tunnel except it had a catwalk above the water for maintenance workers to use.

She clambered through the hole. A number of small shapes lay clustered around the base of the hole. Pointing, she gestured for Jasper to shine the light down.

The shapes were rat corpses. They sat in little heaps, apparently piled there. All of the corpses had been completely drained of fluids, and they were little more than leathery husks of bones and scabrous fur.

There was something else on the ground as well. Amelia couldn't immediately figure out what it was. The mass was oddly shaped and flaky-looking. It looked a bit like the husk of a large insect. Maybe a gigantic sewer spider that had also fallen prey to whatever killed the rats? Or a crab that had crawled in from the East River, perhaps?

It was maybe the size of a full grown guinea pig. That was one big spider. She'd rather run into a stray alligator, personally.

Jasper stepped through the hole as well. They both dripped on the brickwork. She looked down and saw that her fingers had turned slightly blue. She tried to flex her hands, but they were all but stuck in the shape of crude claws.

Not good. Jasper was even paler than usual, and she watched his teeth rattle uncontrollably. Involuntary shivers ran through both of them. They continued walking, their shoes slapping against the ground. *Splorch, splorch, splorch.*

Ladders led up to various manholes overhead. Streetlight and rainwater dribbled down from above. Amelia could hear cars passing by. They continued on the length of several blocks, hoping to come across a cover in an area without traffic. It wouldn't do to pop up on the surface only to immediately be run over.

Another automobile passed by overhead, the rumble of its engine throatier than its companions. The vehicle stopped almost directly overhead. Heavy footfalls sounded. Suddenly, there was a loud scraping noise as the manhole cover above was ripped away with a pry bar. A pair of black-clad legs slid down the ladder.

Spinning around, Amelia and Jasper ran on stiff legs in the opposite direction. The skin on her legs pricked and tickled as she tried to move quickly. It felt like someone had pulled the muscles out of her legs and replaced them with rusty bed springs and shards of glass.

"Пажња," a female voice shouted behind them. Amelia had no idea what that meant, but it was probably something along the lines of "Hey!" or "Freeze, you no-talent ass clowns!" It didn't sound like an invitation to warm coffee and a seat by the fire.

Her Luger was still in its holster, but it had been drenched with river water. She needed to clean it inside and out before it was usable again. Even if Jasper's flashlight survived a dip in the river, his sidearm wouldn't have. Their only chance was to run.

But there was nowhere to run to. The tunnel didn't offer any easy escape routes. The cross sections were few and far between, and even then, they'd be easy to follow. It was like trying to hide inside a giant gun barrel. The only route out was the next alcove down, taking the ladder up to the surface. They couldn't make it, but they were going to try, dammit. The story of their night.

Skidding into the alcove, Amelia started up the ladder. Her hands could barely grasp the rungs, and she couldn't really tell how firm her feet were on any given step. She made it three rungs up when a bullet spanged into the brickwork next to her head. Their pursuer circled around to the front of the alcove, an outdated military carbine in her hands. She was shouting in something that sounded like Russian. The cross around her neck bounced as she gesticulated wildly with her weapon.

Amelia stepped off the ladder one rung at a time. Her legs might buckle if she jumped even the short distance. Even though her heart was beating in her throat, she felt dreadfully tired. Her eyes wanted to droop. Was that adrenaline exhaustion or hypothermia beginning to set in?

Their captor was still shouting. She had close-cropped blonde hair and wild blue eyes. Those eyes flicked between Amelia and Jasper. Neither of them had a functioning weapon, but the woman didn't know that, and she was outnumbered.

They must present quite a sight. Her, dressed in the remains of an evening gown stained with river muck. Jasper, standing in a tuxedo that looked like it had been used as a bath towel for circus animals.

The black-clad woman stood well away from them, her back to the catwalk's railing. Frothy brown water gushed below. She was too far away for a lunge. If they tried to charge her and wrestle the weapon away, she would certainly shoot one and probably both of them. Given the reception they'd received so far, Amelia strongly suspected they would both be disposed of in short order anyway. But the vampire hunters still wanted Armstrong and interrogating her and Jasper would produce some information as to where he escaped.

Somewhere in the distance, Amelia could hear more voices shouting. Backup would arrive in a couple of minutes, and then they would be bundled off back to the hunters' barge.

Something stirred in the water behind the female vampire hunter.

At first, Amelia thought it was one of the legendary alligators of the city's sewer system. It was about the right size for a baby alligator, maybe a foot long.

Then another surfaced. And another.

They weren't alligators.

Both Jasper and Amelia watched as the creatures slipped through the current up to the edge of the catwalk. There were hundreds of them. The woman was still ordering them to do…something, probably put their hands up; she couldn't see the things gathering behind her.

One of them slithered up the brickwork to the maintenance pathway. It looked like a massive caterpillar with a drug addiction. The giant grub had skin so pale that Amelia could actually see the outline of its innards. There were no eyes to speak of. A haphazard series of bristles poked from its segmented body. The bristles were too thick to be hairs, but too thin to be quills. They still looked like they could poke somebody's eye out, though. The mouth end and the butt end looked much the same, except the mouth was ringed with little fishing hook graspers and pointed protrusions that weren't quite teeth and weren't quite mandibles.

Raising its "head," the creature seemed to sniff the air. Then, with hideous speed, it bore directly into the back of the blonde woman's calf. Fabric and flesh split as the creature latched onto her leg.

She screamed, an entirely different sound from the shouted orders of a moment before. Kicking, she jumped in a frantic little jig, but the worm-thing was latched on tight. Its mouth parts anchored it on like a giant leech.

Moving in a swarm, the other creatures scaled their way onto the catwalk and attacked the woman. Amelia was already moving up the ladder as the second wave of miniature monsters stormed the beaches. Jasper followed suit as the ground became thick with writhing bodies.

They attacked in a great, rolling wave of maggot flesh. Fighting for space, they latched onto the woman's body and began sucking the blood out of her body. Amelia watched as their transparent bodies grew red.

The woman stomped on one of them with her boots. The creature exploded like an overstuffed sausage, leaving a smear of greasy, red fluid. More immediately replaced their fallen comrade. Many more.

Amelia couldn't even begin to count the creatures frothing out of the water. Instead, she focused on launching herself up the ladder. Her feet threatened to slip with each step up, but she finally reached the manhole cover.

Below, the bizarre creatures had swarmed all over the vampire huntress. She swatted at them, trying to brush them off her legs, but more of them simply attached themselves to her hands. She stomped on them, squashing half a dozen. Blood and streamers of guts shot across the floor. The creatures' innards prolapsed out from either end of their bodies and spattered against the ground. Moving to stomp on another creature, the woman slipped on a slick of sputum and went down hard.

Pushing with her shoulder, Amelia wedged the manhole cover up and off its tracks as their would-be captor writhed under a mass of squirming bodies. She had to hunch herself up directly beneath the heavy lid and use the strength in her upper body and legs to shift it. She pushed the steel cover all the way out and crawled onto the street.

She looked up just in time to see a set of headlights bearing down on her. The sharp beams of light filled her world, blinding her. With a lurch, she rolled out of the shaft and lay in the gutter. Rainwater pounded down on her upturned face, but she could barely even feel it.

God, she was tired, so very tired. All she wanted to do was go to sleep, right here on the asphalt.

Jasper crawled out of the hole next, beaching himself like some sort of primitive creature crawling out of the primordial ooze for the first time and flopping blindly onto the land.

The vehicle that had almost hit her screeched to a halt a few feet past the open manhole cover. It was a bright yellow taxi, one of the thousands patrolling the streets of New York twenty-four hours a day.

Scrambling out of the vehicle, the cabbie gawped at them. "Hey, you two all right?" His English was accented with a heavy pinch of Latin seasoning.

No.

Jasper came over in a hunched walk, moving like he was at least double his actual age. He helped Amelia to her knees, then looked the cabbie over. "We need a ride," he said, giving Laramie Resweber's address.

Screams echoed echoed from out of the open manhole.

The cab driver's eyes were wide and staring, obviously trying to decide if he should break and run.

"Please, we need your help," Amelia said in Spanish. Her words were slow and muddled, but he understood them. Hearing the words spoken in a more familiar language finally convinced him not to get back in his taxi and take off at full speed.

Breathing a litany of curses, he scampered over and took both their hands. He half-led, half-dragged them over to his cab and shoved them into the back seat. He looked back over his shoulder at the open manhole.

Below, the screaming had stopped, cutting off in a gurgle. The cabbie started to walk over to see if anyone else needed help, and Amelia warned him off. She didn't need to, though.

Two male voices began shouting in some Slavic language. The first vampire hunter's backup arrived, far too late to help. The shouts transformed into screams followed by the dull crump of explosives detonating underground. Grenades, probably.

Without waiting to see what emerged from the hole next, the cabbie raced back to his taxi and flung himself into the driver's seat. The engine buzzed to life, and the vehicle sped off.

A few minutes later, they were in front of Laramie Resweber's apartment. Even in the rain, this was probably a record run for this particular taxi. Amelia didn't think the man's foot ever came off the accelerator.

Jasper pulled his wallet out of his pocket. Water squelched out as he opened it up. His fingers were too numb to pull out individual bills, so he clawed out a wad worth about three times the fare and dropped the sodden money in the cabbie's hand.

"*Gracias*," Amelia mumbled as she fumbled her way out of the cab. The driver stared at them both as if he thought they might grow horns and fangs. They slouched into the apartment building's lobby, barely able to push through the revolving door.

The same smiling clerk they met yesterday was still working at the counter. His mask of helpfulness faltered and cracked as he saw the two of them.

"Excuse me," he cleared his throat. "Excuse me, but you can't stay here. There's a shelter down the way. We can't have you here."

"We're here to see Mister Resweber, you sack of dog dicks," Amelia tried to say.

"Ungh mefereser," she actually said. She and Jasper gave a stare that implied the clerk better not try to hold them up unless he wanted to spend the remainder of the night stuffed into one of his desk drawers. He decided to back down, wisely ignoring them as they moved toward the elevators.

A minute later, they knocked on Laramie Resweber's front door. Amelia heard shuffling movement behind the door. Finally, the locks came undone one by one with a series of grating, sliding noises.

Resweber's nurse stood in front of them, a robe thrown over her night clothes. Her blonde hair was mussed with sleep, and she stared at them with squinted eyes for a moment before she realized who they were.

"You two...are the detectives?"

"W-w-we got c-caught in the r-r-rain." Jasper's teeth were chattering so badly he could barely speak.

"Maybe we c-could t-talk to Mister Resweber," Amelia sputtered.

"Of course. I'll wake him. Come in. Come in. You two look like hell. How long were you out there? You need to warm up or you'll catch your death."

"A h-hot shower would be n-nice," Jasper said.

Chapter 15
Attican't

Laramie Resweber sat in his wheelchair staring at a spot somewhere to Jasper's left. Jasper was wearing some of the man's spare clothes. His tuxedo was a soaked lump on the bathroom tile. The clothes didn't fit particularly well. Jasper was a half foot taller than Resweber, but at least the clothes were dry. Amelia borrowed some of the nurse's clothes.

Jasper felt much better than he did half an hour ago. His skin prickled as warmth spread back through his limbs. His hands and feet hurt slightly as warm blood tried to force its way back into his frozen extremities. Resweber's nurse had brewed a pot of coffee, and Jasper had a mug in his hands. He wasn't actually drinking it. He was just savoring the sensation against his fingertips.

Amelia sipped at her coffee. Her hair hung in wet strands, but the warm shower water had rejuvenated both of them. She seemed to have something on her mind as Jasper explained the night's activities to their employer. He gave a truncated version to Resweber. The man's face remained very still as Jasper told him about visiting the Yersinia building's charity ball and the invasion of odd attackers and ensuing fireball.

Even now, Jasper could see a faint glow out of Resweber's window in the direction of the former Yersinia headquarters. It might take days for the last embers to burn themselves out.

It took longer to explain exactly what had happened after that because Jasper still didn't have all the pieces himself yet. He talked as best he could about Armstrong's kidnappers, the vampire hunters.

Finally, Resweber interrupted him. "So, let me get this straight, O'Malley. You rescued Armstrong from these people?"

"More or less. This goes a lot deeper than just Armstrong. There's something in the tunnels beneath the city, and he knows what it is." Jasper thought back to the maggot-like creatures swarming over the woman in the tunnel. He thought back to the shape that killed those two Yersinia guards. There was definitely *something* down there, all right.

"With all due respect, I don't care how much deeper this goes. I'm not paying you to dig a hole to China. This doesn't need to be deep at all. I want Armstrong's head on a pike. Ideally, I want him in the electric chair so he can know what it's like. Riding into the great rodeo in the sky on Ol' Sparky would certainly serve him right, but I don't necessarily care about the details. If this other group wants him dead, get out of their way. Maybe I should be paying them, not you."

"And with all due respect to you, we aren't some sort of round-about hit squad. Our job isn't to get Ray killed, even if that's the likely outcome of our work. We're here to connect him to the Horvath murder. Although I blew one of his hands off, if that makes you feel any better."

"It's a start," Resweber said.

"Well, it certainly made me feel better at the time," Amelia said. A mark had formed on her throat where Armstrong had been strangling her.

"All right, then." Resweber leaned forward in his wheelchair. He still wasn't looking quite at either of them. His blind eyes looked like the hard-boiled eggs of chickens fed on a diet of mangled corpses and amphetamines. Jasper shifted on the couch so that Resweber at least wasn't accidentally staring at nothing anymore. "Tell me what you have on Doctor Horvath's death. Any connections to Armstrong?"

"Ray admitted his involvement to us."

"Well, isn't that dandy? I already knew about his involvement. I was there, remember? And you already knew about it because I told you. What does that actually do for me?"

"Not a whole lot," Jasper had to admit. If Ray was in police custody right now, it might be a plenty useful little nugget. However, Ray was out on the streets somewhere, loose and untrackable. No doubt he had gone to some illegal back-alley doctor to have his hand cared for. He wouldn't risk showing up in a hospital record anywhere. Jasper would not be at all surprised if black-clad figures were waiting outside the city's emergency rooms right now.

"Great," Resweber said. His face contorted into a frown, threatening to crack again. The fragile layer of roasted skin covering his face held up, though.

"The police will be looking for whoever burned down the Yersinia building. That will get the ball rolling, hopefully."

"Again, that would have happened without your involvement. If this group of vigilantes has declared war on Armstrong, I have no problem with that. If they draw the police into the fray, all the better."

"I don't think they're vigilantes, exactly. They're certainly paramilitary in their equipment and structure, but they claim to be vampire hunters." Jasper had specifically declined to mention what he'd seen in the sewers. He'd read his Bram Stoker, and he was not under the impression that Count Dracula was a horde of blood-hungry worms.

Frankly, he had no explanation for what he'd seen. Just as he had no explanation for whatever killed the Yersinia guards in the subway tunnel. That certainly wasn't worms either; it had been big, much bigger. Roughly man-sized.

"I don't care if it's Santa Claus and his elves. They want Armstrong dead. I want Armstrong dead. The only thing standing between our mutual goals seems to be you, Mister O'Malley."

"He might be right, Jasper," Amelia said.

Jasper's head whipped around in surprise. With a sigh, he said, "There's a lot more going on here than just Ray Armstrong. I would be fine if the man stopped breathing as well. However, this is bigger than all our personal vendettas. Whatever's going on down there needs to be stopped. I can't even begin to explain the things we saw. Armstrong actually knows what's going on down there because it's all connected to Yersinia."

Resweber shook his head. "Someone else can take care of that problem. Let the police handle it. That's their job. Or somebody's job. I'm not paying you to shine my shoes here, and I'm definitely not paying you to chase whatever wild hare roared up your ass. *Capisce?* Now, get out there. Find Armstrong. Hand him over to the police. Or feed him to the dogs hunting him. Nosferatu's Flying Circus or whoever they are."

There was a knock on the door before Jasper could respond. His hand reached down and plucked the FN pistol off the table. He'd cleaned it, and it was in top shape again. Amelia had done likewise. The smell of gun oil suddenly seemed much stronger.

The nurse started toward the door. Jasper waved her off and crept forward himself. Most likely, it was just the night clerk following up on a note from his cowed counterpart. Some of the faces that would want to track them down to this apartment weren't friendly, though.

He stuck his eye to the peephole and gazed out into the hallway. He didn't like what he saw, but he began disengaging the locks anyway.

No sooner had he opened the door than Iris strolled through, her hands wedged in her coat pockets. Her flowing red hair was tied back and tucked under a scarf. "Whoo, it's chilly out there," she said by way of greeting.

"How did you find us here?" Jasper's voice cut through with a cold the thermometer couldn't measure.

"Please, Jasper. This is my town. Your movements weren't exactly subtle after the ball fizzled. Sounds like you made quite a splash at the after party, too."

Jasper calculated their movements after their adventure in the New York City sewer system and figured out who might have laid eyes on them. It wasn't a very long list. Cripes! How far did Iris's reach extend?

"I see you thinking, Jasper. I know that expression," Iris said. "Don't worry. Nobody else has my connections. Ralitza Petkova and her vampire hunters aren't likely to find you here. Anyway, they had to return to their lair after causing such a big fuss around town,."

"What do you want, Iris?"

"I want to help. Helping you helps me. You get Armstrong out of the way, and I get my talons into Yersinia's good stuff."

"I don't think Yersinia is much of a going concern for anybody right now."

"True. They just lost a lot of their corporate infrastructure, but they're a multinational corporation. Cutting off the head hardly kills the beast. They didn't lose much they can't replace. Even right here in New York, they have other holdings. Bank accounts. Warehouses. Personnel. Most of it's untouched. Their headquarters was mostly just a hood ornament, something big and shiny to impress investors with and someplace for the board of directors to thrash out decisions. They'll probably attract a lot of sympathy business over this. They'll probably thrive, actually. They're a legal entity. So long as they still have their holdings and intellectual property, they can continue to exist out of a tent on Coney Island."

"So why are you gracing us with your presence this evening?"

"Always with the suspicion. This is why you don't have friends, Jasper."

"Enough," Laramie Resweber all but shouted from the main room. "Who are you? If you have something to add, add it."

"I'm helping Jasper track down Ray Armstrong," Iris said, striding over. She sat down next to Amelia, occupying Jasper's spot on the couch. She reached into her expensive-looking, fur-lined jacket and removed a plain file folder. She laid it on the table and flipped it open.

"What's that?" Amelia looked at the collection of photographs and typed papers collected in the folder.

"Honestly, not much," Iris responded. "It's everything I have on your intrepid friends, the vampire hunters. They're led by a woman named Ralitza Petkova. I don't have much on her, but the group is old. They're basically folk heroes in large parts of the old Austro-Hungarian Empire and the Balkans."

"They actually hunt, err, vampires then?" The nurse stood nearby, looking uncomfortable.

Iris shrugged and lit up a cigarette. "That's their line. They do a lot of traveling these days, heading to the sites of supposed vampire outbreaks and tracking them down. Ralitza Petkova is wanted in Panama for shoving stakes through the hearts of a couple of their diplomats. She removed their heads and filled their mouths with garlic, too. She's thorough."

"And they think the incidents occurring underground are the work of vampires in New York, then?"

"You got a better explanation?" Iris cast her green eyes on Jasper.

"Can't say I do," Jasper half-lied. He thought back to the oversized, fluke-like creatures that attacked the hunter in the sewer. He wasn't about to let his sister in on that though, at least not until he could explain what he'd seen.

"We saw something in the tunnels," Amelia said. Jasper's head shot around. "Something attacked one of the hunters. It was like a swarm of caterpillars, though."

"Caterpillars?"

"More like maggots, maybe. Big ones. They killed at least one of the hunters."

Jasper started to interrupt. "Amelia, maybe we should wait until—"

"Let her speak, Jasper," Iris interrupted. "I'd like to know what's going on just as much as you. So you think the vampire hunters have been misled? I don't really picture caterpillars when people start talking about vampires."

"I don't really know," Amelia said. "I just know what we saw. Armstrong said Yersinia had released a bunch of experimental fleas into the city's underworks as part of an experiment. That seems to be what caused all this and why the vampire hunters are after him and Yersinia. They want to destroy all the materials and people related to the project. Ray said it started out as a project to fight Spanish Flu."

"Hmph. Good. It's a start at least. Spanish Flu research would be valuable for my business. Something a little more…exotic would be worth quite a bit more."

"Don't even think about it, Iris. Whatever this is, it's too dangerous. It's killed several people already and probably quite a few more we don't know about yet." Jasper thought back to all those red X's on Armstrong's map. Some of the pieces were starting to come together for him, but he didn't have everything yet. Netting Ray would give him the answers he needed and allow the state authorities to jump on this with both feet. He couldn't go in with what he had now, though. No one would believe it.

Jasper tried to fit things together in his head to see if he was just chasing his own tail. Dr. Horvath had been the point man for the vampire hunters here in New York City. The professor of Old Church Slavonic had probably read enough dusty documents and parchment to know what to look for and report it back to Europe. Really, what else would anyone do with a doctorate in the topic other than work for a monster-hunting organization? Somehow he caught wind of the blood-drained corpses and disappearances underneath the city and connected Yersinia to the outbreak's origin. Maybe he reached out to Ray. Maybe Ray's security apparatus found him first. Either way, Horvath agreed to a meeting with Armstrong, the contact engineered by Laramie Resweber. Ray then killed Horvath and left Resweber to take the fall, but Horvath's death attracted the attention of his superiors. Ray must have hoped it would silence the flow of information about Yersinia's secret inoculation project, or at least delay the arrival of Ralitza Petkova's army of stake-wielding hunters.

None of that seemed to fit with what Jasper had seen underground, though. Something half-seen and big had killed a pair of Yersinia security guards, and a bunch of giant maggots killed some vampire hunters.

He mashed his brains together trying to figure out how to find a connection, if there even was a connection. First, he needed to get his hands on Ray again. Then he needed to keep Iris out of the loop as much as possible because she would just sell the information he dug up, no matter how dangerous. Preferably, he needed to prevent Ralitza Petkova from burning down half of New York in the meantime.

"We had a deal, Jasper," Iris said, apparently reading his thoughts. "In exchange for my help, you were supposed to pass along any information you found. Clearly, you've been holding back. Thank you for telling me about the sewer creatures, Amelia. As you've already seen, Jasper isn't always forthcoming with information when it doesn't suit him. You should think carefully about working with him."

Jasper gritted his teeth. Maybe he was in over his head. Maybe the situation had become too personal and he needed to pull his hands off the live wires. Maybe it was time to go back to Chicago with Amelia. The Atticans had a local office. He could turn the mess over to them.

No, he couldn't do that. There was too much unfinished business with Ray. Armstrong would want him dead after tonight, anyway. More than that, though, no one was safe while this was happening. The things in the sewer would continue to kill, and the vampire hunters would chew a bloody swathe through New York in the meantime. No, he had to see this through. He couldn't allow this situation to fester any longer.

"I...I'd like to work for you," Amelia said to Iris. "Is that offer of employment still good?"

"Wait, wait, wait." Jasper held up a hand. A sudden stab of fear clenched his heart. Amelia was one of the few people he counted as a friend. He didn't want to go back out into the cold, neon-lit world by himself again. What was more, he didn't want to lose her to his sister, who was damn dangerous in her own right. "You don't know what you're getting into here."

"Jasper, I didn't know what I was getting into when I started working for the Atticans, either. I certainly didn't expect *this*. How many times did we almost die tonight? How many *ways* did we almost die tonight? This isn't our fight."

"Something needs to be done about the situation. The information brokerage doesn't do good work. At least we try to fix things with the information we have. They either leave things as they are or break them further for the right price."

"We already had this conversation," Iris said. "Everything is worth what people are willing to pay. We merely redistribute information based on the value people attach to it. I might also point out that not one single person has tried to assassinate me tonight. It doesn't matter how much good you do if you're dead, Jasper darling."

"Yeah. That," Amelia said. "I wasn't exactly working inside the law when we met. I worked for a Detroit mob boss because it's what I was good at. Hell, you ignore the law when it suits your needs. Who was it that got thrown in jail less than a week ago for releasing a toxic opium cloud over half of Illinois?"

"Ah, so that was you. Smooth move, big brother," Iris said.

Jasper waved his sister away and looked Amelia straight in the eyes. "Look. It's a long story. This isn't about the law. It's about doing what needs to be done. We're partners."

"Some things aren't worth it, Jasper. You're one of the few people I trust. Maybe the only person I trust, but this is insane. We can't go up against these sorts of odds for very long. The dice won't keep coming up in our favor forever. We're both lucky we're not twenty flavors of dead tonight. If you can't drop the issue, I need to leave."

"You do have a way of tearing through the partners, Jasper," Iris added. "You've only ever had the three that I know of. Percy's dead, and you blew Ray's hand off with a pistol tonight. It's not exactly a record that instills a lot of confidence."

Jasper leaned forward, ignoring Iris. "Amelia, we have to do this. People are dying. We need to at least gather enough information that we can pass along to someone better equipped to deal with the situation."

Iris leaned forward, too. "Someone, like, I don't know, actual vampire hunters. You're just impeding things out of your own pig-headedness. See, you could gather some information, sell it to Miz Pet-kova, make a tidy profit, and then sit back and let the problem take care of itself. That's what I intend to do. I'll make some money, and no one is going to gun me down in the process. Everybody's happy."

"Amelia, I need you for this. For my own sanity, I should finish things with Ray, but this is bigger than that. A lot of people could die if we don't wrap this up."

"I can't, Jasper. I just can't. We're going to get killed over something we have no stake in. You can't solve all the world's problems, and you won't help anyone if you die trying." Amelia got up from the couch and headed for the door. Iris followed her. She flashed a big, toothy grin at Jasper.

"Wait," Jasper said.

Amelia didn't wait. The door banged shut. Outside, thunder rattled the windows as the storm grew worse.

Chapter 16
Ten Hours Remaining

Jasper sat on a stool in the cramped, little dinner. It wasn't light out yet, but he didn't feel much like sleeping. He just needed a dark, anonymous corner to sit and think for a while. He stirred his eggs around with a fork whenever the waitress, a plump brunette, walked past. Frankly, he didn't feel much like eating.

A dull ache sat in his stomach like an angry fist. It was the sort of sensation that made you want to curl up into a little ball, but that wouldn't work, so then you'd try stretching out flat, but that wouldn't work either, so then you'd just try to move as little as possible.

There were only a couple of other patrons sitting on the stools and in the booths lining the eatery. Most of them had a steaming mug of coffee in one hand and dark circles under their eyes. Jasper fit right in.

Outside, the storm lashed the building's exterior. Occasionally, a car slogged through the streets. Jasper watched a city work truck go by, rooster tails of water fanning up from its tires. The truck's bed was loaded down with fallen tree branches and broken equipment, including a street sign some yokel had run over.

He hoped the city wasn't sending anyone into the sewers or subway tonight. Forget whatever was down there. They might very well drown if this kept up much longer. Everything had to be running on overflow at this point. Jasper's fingers still ached where the feeling had come back to them. Resting his chin on his palm, he stirred at his eggs some more.

As a general rule, he didn't get on well with people. Some of it was his personality. Some of it was things he'd seen. Some of it was things he'd done. Amelia had been an exception to that rule, and now she was gone. He felt like he'd been eating lemons all day.

He didn't like to listen to Iris because she was too blithe at laying some of his own fears out in the open. She could vivisect his feelings, pull their guts out, and wave them in front of his eyes when she wanted to.

His old wounds from losing Armstrong and Percy as partners had scabbed over, but they had never fully healed. He had screwed up handling the situation with Ray. It had blindsided him, and he'd played his hand poorly. Jasper wasn't one to stay up at night and agonize over bad moments, but those memories had a way of crawling into his head when he least expected it.

There was never much warning over the matter. Some part of his brain would seize on even banal details and flashbulbs of memory would burst to life in his mind. It was hard not to cringe when he remembered that moment confronting Ray in the bank.

Things hadn't gone well with a lot of the other people he'd worked with over the years. His brother, Percy, was one of them. One of the old Attican couriers, a fellow named Tycho Vedel, was another. They'd both died in incidents relating to cases he'd been working on.

Iris was right. He didn't really have friends anymore. But that was largely intentional. He could do things his way and not have to worry about anyone else. He'd worked alone for years after Percy died, and he'd gotten set in his ways.

Then, he'd brought Amelia into the organization. He'd actively avoided thinking of her as his protégé, beaten those thoughts back whenever they reared their heads. But now he realized he had never completely banished his pride in how she was doing. Those feelings had just sunk into the quicksand of his subconscious, buried, just waiting to rise to the surface.

And now she was gone. He'd lost a third partner. It did not feel good. Watching her leave for his sister's organization was an even bigger gut punch. And perhaps the worst part was that he understood why she left. They were in a bind, and he'd put them there. There was no reason they couldn't do the task assigned to them and leave except for his own damn stubbornness. It had almost gotten them both killed, and it brought all hell down upon them.

That didn't mean he intended to stop. As he saw it, he still needed to figure out a way to end whatever was going on beneath the city before more people died. All it meant was he understood why Amelia had left for greener pastures. His pastures were brown, parched, and littered with cow flops.

The waitress made another pass, and he stirred his eggs some more. For now, the plan was to sit in this diner and feel sorry for himself for a few hours. It wasn't a great plan.

He gazed out the windows. The neon sign outside buzzed and cast pink reflections off the slick sidewalk. New York might be the city that never slept, but that didn't mean it didn't trundle along at the edge of consciousness sometimes.

Someone braved the storm and scampered across the street toward the dinner. His boots splashed in the water. At one point he stepped in a sunken pothole and nearly pitched head over heels, his foot sinking up to the ankle. The man pulled his leg up, muttering something, no doubt admiring of the city's road crews and helpful suggestions as to where they could park their work trucks. Hopping to the curb, he stripped his boot off and poured out the water that had flooded in and soaked his sock.

The man had a crew cut and big flapping jowls that looked like they could be unfurled into a cape. He had the sort of face that looked like it was behind on its scowling quota and needed to work extra hard to keep up. He scowled at his wet sock, scowled at the diner, and then looked back and scowled at the hidden pothole for good measure.

Popping the boot back on with a grimace, he breezed into the diner and sat down on a stool, the leather covering of which had been repaired with several layers of tape. The waitress walked up to him, and he ordered something. Jasper had gone back to stirring his eggs, but still kept an eye on the newcomer.

The stranger glanced over, saw Jasper, then quickly turned his gaze down to the counter and began an intense study of its surface. A few minutes later, the waitress came back with a stack of hotcakes.

The stranger looked at the hotcakes, up at the waitress, over at Jasper, down at the hotcakes, and up at the waitress again.

There were posters up at the warehouse Yersinia's security department was using. Posters describing a lanky man with fine features. A lanky man missing part of one ear.

A lot of people were looking for that man.

"Help you with something, honey?" The waitress gestured with a half-full carafe of coffee.

"This joint got a telephone I can use?"

"Yeah. In the back. But it'll cost ya'." The man was already up and moving toward the rear of the diner.

Crewcut's mouth managed to crease itself into a smile before flopping back down into its usual position like someone trying to do one too many sit-ups.

Jasper made a noise down in his throat. Maybe it was better Amelia left before he got her killed, too. Everything had gone to pot here.

He stared at his eggs and started scraping them into a big mound to push around some more. They had long gone cold, and now they looked a bit like something a dog had choked up. Once the breakfast rush arrived, he would slip out. Actually, he'd probably be kicked out for taking up valuable seat space.

Eventually, he needed to find some way to convince the authorities that they needed to close off the underground. Maybe send in the National Guard. What did he have now, though? Connections to the destruction of Yersinia's world headquarters and a major car chase through the city streets. The police would be more interested in arresting him than listening to him jabber about monsters under the city.

That thought simply reminded him that he wouldn't have Amelia to bail him out of jail this time. He'd just stick to himself from now on. Working with people brought too many complications to a case. Things fell apart just when he needed them most.

Behind him, the bell over the diner's front door jingled. A gust of cold air rustled through the little restaurant. A pair of thick, heavy boots clomped on the cheap linoleum flooring. Then another pair, and another, and a fourth. The scowling man got up from his stool at the other end of the counter.

"You boys seat yourselves wherever you want," the waitress called from the kitchen as she hefted a plate of hash browns.

After a pause, all five sets of boots strode in Jasper's direction. The footsteps all fell in together, unconsciously turning into a march. Normal footsteps didn't all come together like that, but it was common among men who had all been in the military. It didn't take them long to reach Jasper's stool, where they fanned out behind him.

Jasper had split the pile of eggs into two smaller piles using his fork, and now he was working on making four piles. Breakfast mitosis. He didn't look up from his efforts as someone behind him cracked their knuckles one at a time.

He could see their reflections on the stainless steel surface of a nearby fryer. They all wore matching jackets. Could just be part of a late night shift getting off work, looking for a place to rest their heels.

"Jasper O'Malley?" one of them growled. Another reached into his jacket, and Jasper caught the gleam of something metallic. Nope. Definitely not industrial workers clearing the graveyard shift.

Swiveling off his stool in one swift motion, Jasper took his fork and jabbed the prongs in the first man's thigh. With a howl, the man tried to pull the gun the rest of the way out of his jacket pocket, but it was too late. Jasper swung his plate of eggs around with his other hand and broadsided the man's face.

Fluffy yellow eggs sprayed across the room, along with shards of porcelain as the plate exploded. Some of the jagged pieces scrapped across the man's face, tearing the skin off and raking across one of his eyeballs. He yowled and stumbled backward into one of his friends before dropping to the floor in a kicking mess.

The fellow next to him was trying to pull a sawed-off shotgun out of his jacket. Definitely not legal to be carrying around. The other patrons and the waitress all scrambled for cover amid startled grunts and screams.

Jasper recognized the man. They'd seen each other rather recently, actually. The first time they met, the man was wearing a janitor's uniform with the name Ernest Hives sewn on the breast. They'd seen each other a second time last night when Jasper saved him from choking on some prawns. His face was puffy, and he had a mouse under one eye that had swollen it half shut. His mouth was open in a snarl, and Jasper could see some gaps that were supposed to house teeth.

Grabbing the first thing at hand, Jasper swung a glass ketchup bottle around and brained Ernest. The heavy glass bottle struck him just above the right temple and exploded in a splash of crimson. It looked like the man's head exploded. The blow would probably need stitches, but most of the red was just ketchup. Glop smeared across Ernest's face, covering his mouth, nose, and eyes, even splattering into his ears. He wheeled away, grasping for the counter, his shotgun clattering to the floor.

Jasper kicked him in the back of the knee, and he went down. A second later, the remains of the second ketchup bottle crashed down on top of his skull. Ernest flopped down on his face, out cold.

Two more men came at him in the crowded space between the booths and the counter. Dropping his shoulder, the closer man heaved a punch at him. Jasper stepped into the blow, deflected it with his off arm, and drove a knee directly into the man's open crotch. The air whooped out of his opponent. His descendants would feel that one for several generations.

Jasper shoved the wailing thug into a booth before he went after the last man. Raw panic in his eyes, the goon looked at his downed comrades and scooped a steak knife off the nearest table. He lunged toward Jasper, thrusting the knife forward.

Jasper took a step back and grabbed a weapon of his own, a pot of coffee, simmering on the burner. The man was bearing down for another thrust when the pot of scalding coffee splashed into his face. He screamed and clawed at his skin. Pawing at his eyes, he shrieked again.

The hot coffee would leave second-degree burns across most of his face. The liquid that seeped into his clothes and down the collar of his jacket would create additional burns and painful blisters if he couldn't strip out of his clothing in time.

Picking up the dropped steak knife, Jasper turned to the man he'd kneed in the groin. The schmuck was struggling to pull himself into a sitting position in the booth, clutching himself the whole time. Jasper took the knife in one hand and drove the blade straight into the leather seat half an inch from the man's groin.

"Talk or I start cutting," he said, in no mood for niceties.

A high-pitched, wavering whine issued from the man's throat.

Suddenly, something smacked against the back of Jasper's head. Bright lights flashed across his vision before a little black void opened up, and he fell straight in. Jasper slumped to the ground with a grunt. His hands automatically reached out to steady himself, grabbing onto the edge of the table.

Before he could regain his senses, a second blow crashed down on top of his head. He fell to the floor next to a smear of ketchup.

The scowling man with the crew cut tucked the blackjack back into his pocket, right next to his Yersinia security badge. God, that never got old. His mouth reluctantly stretched into something that might be a smile.

"Alvin, get up, you worthless slob," he said to the supine man in the booth. "Get the truck. We've got a little prize for Mister Armstrong."

Chapter 17
Keep Your Spirits Up and Your Enemies Down

Amelia woke up with a sick feeling in her stomach. It was the sort of feeling that made her want to curl up in a little ball, but that didn't help, so she tried to stretch out as far as she could, but that didn't help either, so she eventually just tried remaining very still.

There had been an admission ceremony of sorts at the information brokerage, mostly consisting of bubbly liquids. Even late at night, plenty of Iris's employees were around to meet her and show her around. She'd enjoyed herself plenty, but the feeling in her stomach didn't have anything to do with the drinks.

Heaving the blankets off herself, she made her way out of bed, washed, and headed for the waterfront. The brokerage looked much the same as it had the night before. From the outside, it was a dismal warehouse that looked ready to collapse if the rain fell any harder. Even the seabirds sitting on the pier looked especially miserable and skeevy.

The interior was still impressive as hell, though. She found herself walking with extra caution across the reinforced glass floor, expecting each step to send her plunging into the tank. A few fish came over and investigated the soles of her shoes as she walked until a shark frightened them off.

She didn't regret leaving Jasper behind. Not exactly, anyway. At the rate they were going, it was only a matter of time before somebody punched both their tickets. However, that didn't mean she felt good about it. Jasper had been one of the few constants in her life of late.

He was also one of the few people who had opinions she listened to. Maybe not about everything, but she could tell when she wasn't living up to one of his expectations, and she tried to do better next time.

Iris O'Malley was…an interesting character, but Amelia wasn't sure she would ever care much what the woman thought of her. Her goals weren't noble, and that didn't bother Amelia, but she knew she was being played as a pawn to wound Jasper. Their needs were temporarily aligned, but there was no kinetic fission, no connection, no sense that she was really *needed*. She was a trophy and a useful tool here.

Jasper had his own peculiar drive, damn him, and Amelia had never completely figured it out. If she had to, she could jump ship from the information brokerage in a few months. It wouldn't be the first time she'd picked up roots. Maybe she'd even go back to Detroit and start a little one-woman detective agency herself.

Pushing open the door to Iris's office, she saw her new boss in her chair. Folders were arranged across the desk in a vast array, and Iris was pouring through them, making notes in big, looping letters. One of the open folders had a grainy photograph of a naked body, the head missing. The corpse was too badly mutilated to tell if it was a man or a woman.

Iris noticed the direction of Amelia's gaze. "Ah, one of our ex-clients. Didn't know we were gathering information on them when they were selling us information. Pissed off some of the wrong people, including some slick bastard from Tennessee who was willing to pay a bundle for our information."

"Sounds like a peach."

"Oh, you meet all types in this business. Don't worry. Everybody knows better than to mess with my people, though. Here, it's as important to keep your spirits up as it is to keep your enemies down. That's what I always say." Iris reached into a drawer in her desk and pulled out a glass and a bottle of amber-colored fluid that looked like it was worth a small apartment in a middling section of town.

Amelia waved off the bottle. She didn't feel like drinking.

"Overdid it last night, eh?" Iris poured a dash into the glass and began working on it herself. "I suppose you'd like to know what your first job is."

"The thought had crossed my mind."

"I like you, kid." Iris finished her drink with a gulp and tossed her hair over her shoulder. "You've made the right choice in coming here. Here's what we're going to do. I still need information about what's going on under the city. Ralitza Petkova and her band of misfits have declared war on Yersinia, and on Ray in particular. I'm very much interested in seeing how this all plays out."

"I left the Atticans to avoid getting in the middle of that fight. If you're just going to throw me back in, we have no business together."

"Hold your horses. I'm not asking you to do anything I wouldn't expect from the rest of my people. You have the inside track, though. I'm not throwing you to the dogs. I just want to assign you to the matter broadly. Consider it a trial run. You've got a leg up on everyone already. Get me what you can, and I'll evaluate how you've done once the dust clears. I don't expect you to get in the center of it all. Play it how you want. Make googly eyes at one of the police investigators until he spills his guts. Find Jasper and trick him into thinking you're working together again. I don't care. Just get me the final tally, any of Yersinia's good stuff, and all the dirt you can gather. Easy as pie."

"I can do that," Amelia said. She had some ideas about what she could do. Tricking Jasper wasn't one of them. The look in Iris's eyes implied this was a little more serious than a simple test, though. Amelia looked back down at the picture of the dismembered corpse on the desk. *Out of the frying pan…*

"Good girl," Iris said.

Amelia frowned and stepped out of the office to chase down some leads. The rain spattered her trench coat as she stepped outside into the mist.

Chapter 18
The Hammer

When Jasper opened his eyes, the first thing he saw was his arm in an oversized medical brace. His hand was resting on a cheap wooden table, but he couldn't move his arm. The medical brace had been chained to the arm of a chair, effectively locking him in place.

His head throbbed like his brain was ready to hatch. The mere effort of coming awake almost made him throw up. Jasper sat very still for a few moments, gathering his wits and tamping down on the churning flow of nausea.

He tried to reach over with his other hand and discovered that it was handcuffed to the chair's other arm. Looking down, he recognized his own set of handcuffs. But the last time he saw those, they were still attached to…

Oh, balls.

The chair creaked as he shifted his weight. His legs were tied down, too. This was not good.

"Well, well, well. Look who's waking up." Ernest Hives stepped into his field of vision. A patch of his hair was shaved from his head, exposing an ugly zigzag of stitches that crossed halfway across his skull, sealing the wound left from the ketchup bottle. "Looks like we got ourselves some entertainment, boys. How's it going, Sleeping Beauty? Remember me?" Ernest grinned, showing his missing teeth.

"It would be hard to forget a face like that," Jasper said. He tried to clear some of the cobwebs from his mind. Ernest kicked him in the shin hard enough to make him cringe. The pain shot up his leg before subsiding to a dull throb. The sensation actually helped him gather his wits a little more and put his thoughts in order.

He was in a storage warehouse of some sort. The skylights above told him the sun had finally poked its head over the horizon, though not very far yet. Rain still pattered against the roof, but a little natural light was filtering in now. All told, he'd been out for maybe an hour. His eyes kept wanting to fall shut again, but he forced them open until some of the gears in his brain could start turning again. His head felt like a car left out in the cold too long, struggling to fire its engine.

Crates were stacked high around the walls. Most of them were stamped with the Yersinia logo. That explained where the brace on his arm had come from. These crates were probably waiting to be shipped out to some disaster area or remote part of the world.

Most of the warehouse space was taken up by metal canisters, though. They weren't barrels; they were the sort of cylindrical containers used to hold gas, not so different from the helium tubes that might fill a child's balloon at the county fair. Well, actually, there was at least one major difference with these canisters. They were all marked with a skull and a set of crossbones. Great. Skeleton gas.

He squinted, trying to see the label more clearly as his vision stabilized. Most of the canisters were labeled "Prussic Acid." Then under that, in smaller type, it read, "Hydrogen Cyanide."

Jasper knew a little about prussic acid. The Allies used it against the Central Powers as a chemical weapon during the Great War, and he'd read field manuals on what to do in case the Germans decided to come up with their own supplies.

It could be loaded into modified artillery shells and sent roaring toward enemy trenches. The shells would burst and spray deadly gas toward hunkered-down troops. In theory at least. The stuff was much more finicky than chlorine or other gases. The main reason it was used in the first place was because it could be readily obtained. It was used as a pesticide and a precursor to chemical compounds across a lot of industries, including pharmaceuticals. Manufacturers produced tons of the stuff for all sorts of uses. Yersinia must have it as a compound for some of their experiments.

The stuff was powerful, too. Whalers sometimes dipped their harpoons in prussic acid to kill their massive prey. No one had ever lobbed any of it at Jasper during the war, and for that, he was grateful. It was bad news.

Gas masks hung from the wall in case one of the canisters somehow ruptured. The masks might save the workers in the warehouse, but anyone within a one-block radius of the structure would die if the warehouse caught fire or suffered some other disaster that released all the gas.

Ernest strutted back into Jasper's field of vision like a preening game rooster. "We've got a little something special in store for you. I think you're going to like it." His words were slightly mushy around his newly missing teeth and puffed cheeks.

"Is it a pony?" Jasper tried pulling his legs against their restraints to see if there was any give. The chair creaked, but there wasn't much he could do. Further down the warehouse, he could see that his things had been piled on top of a crate and inventoried. His lock picks, pistol, and assorted tools lay tantalizingly close, but too far for him to reach. They might as well have been on the moon. It seemed that Ernest had learned something since the last time he'd taken Jasper into custody. Always search the captives.

"I'm afraid not, ol' buddy, ol' pal." Ray Armstrong himself stepped around into Jasper's field of vision. His right hand had been replaced with a prosthetic grasper made of metal, part hook, part clamp. In places, the metal was tarnished and gouged. Clearly, the appendage was not new. It had probably been attached in the back of some dirty clinic by someone who almost certainly didn't have a valid medical license.

"Where did you get the new equipment?" Jasper nodded toward Ray's hand. Mostly, he was just trying to buy time to think up a plan of some sort. Right now, he had nothing. Whatever was coming next was sure to be unpleasant, though.

"From the pawn shop, actually. Somebody actually pawned their hand. Can you believe that? I'm not sure what kind of straits you need to be in before that seems like a good idea. It's mine now, though. I'll replace it eventually, I suppose, but I kind of like it. Great for bippy pinching. Field tested it myself on that front. Plus, there's a certain charm to walking around with somebody else's hand, wondering where the thing's been, why its original owner gave it up, that sort of thing. This is strictly last generation. They created some fancy new ones after demand skyrocketed from the war. Fake fingers. The whole nine yards."

"Fancy."

"You bet. Like I said, I like this one, though. It's got a sort of piratical flair. The fit is a little off, but I can get that adjusted later. Part of that's because my wrist hasn't quite healed up yet. Which reminds me. As much fun as my new hand is, I really preferred the original. Which also reminds me. You shot my goddamn hand off, you asshole."

"Oh, yeah. That."

"Yeah. That. Now, don't get me wrong. I probably would have done the same thing in your position. Actually, scratch that. I'd have popped a couple of lead pills in your skull first because you might get pissed and decide to exact excruciating revenge. You know, if you were in my position. But I respect your decision to let me live. I strongly endorse it, actually. Doesn't mean there won't be all hell to pay for shooting off my hand, but hey, we can't all be winners, after all. That's just not how this game is played, you know?"

"I think I see the point you're trying to make."

"Well, in this case, it's less of a point and more of a blunt object. We can work our way up to pointy things over the next few hours, but I'd like to demonstrate something first. So, you've obviously noticed that medical brace on your left arm. It's got you pretty much locked into place, right? Good. Good. That'll keep your arm still and your hand glued right on that table. We don't want it squirming around."

"I don't like the sound of this."

"Ernest, hand me that hammer. No, the big one, you imbecile. What do I pay you for? Come on. Work with me here, people." Ernest handed Ray a large claw hammer. The metal head gleamed in the early morning light filtering down from overhead. Ray held it up and examined it. He tapped the claw with his metal pincer hand, and it made a dense *chink, chink* sound.

"Ray, I would really feel a lot more comfortable if you put that down."

"See, Jasper, here's the thing. The nub of my gist. The cut of my gib. I really liked my hand. It was my second favorite hand. Now, I've never been one to turn the other cheek. If you get bit on the ass, why would you just offer the other cheek? That's what I've always wondered. I made an exception for you once. I let you leave New York all those years ago. You were my friend, even if you always were a bit of a prig."

"Yeah, those pre-homicidal salad days."

"The thing is, I let you go once. You were willing to leave, and I had the business to myself. Most of the people were willing to stay on. No lasting damage. With you out of the picture, it was all coming up swell. But I figured I might see you again someday, and boy was I right. You always were a dogged son of a bitch, I'll give you that. Made life difficult for a lot of people, turning up like a bad penny the way you did. Remember when you walked in on old Mister Curtis, stuffing his wife's head into that bowling ball bag? The look on his face was just classic. Still cracks me up sometimes. He thought he'd thrown you off the trail but good."

"I heard they gave him the chair."

"Yes indeedy. Fried him up something good. Of course, Missus Curtis was the one supposed to be paying us, so it didn't do us much good just finding her head, but it gave us a lot of credibility with the police. They were always throwing things our way after that."

"It was good work."

"It was busy work. The pay was crap. The hours were crap. The clients were crap. The only thing it had going was the steadiness. Lots of people looking to settle scores. You turned a lot of them down, as I recall."

"I don't do other people's dirty work."

"But you took this case for Laramie Resweber. Yeah, I still have the resources to find out who you've been working for. I forgot about the man, actually. I just assumed they'd roasted him over at Sing Sing already. No such luck, I guess. That sounds like doing somebody else's dirty work to me."

"Mostly, it's my dirty work that I'm cleaning up. Resweber is just willing to pay for something I should have done a long time ago myself."

"Uh-huh. Now, see, that gets me back to my main point here. We're supposed to turn the other cheek and all, but neither one of us is really the forgiving type, right? I know I was always more of an eye-for-an-eye, tooth-for-a-tooth kind of guy myself. Now, there's still this matter of my hand. Obviously, I owe you for everything else, too, but I think we can settle tabs on the hand right now. What do you say, buddy?"

Ray raised the hammer high above his head and brought it down on Jasper's hand at the first knuckle of his index finger. A loud popping noise filled the warehouse as the metal hammer crushed the joint like a reluctant walnut. The bones crunched and shattered, pulverized under the force of the blow.

Jasper shouted. It wasn't a voluntary noise. The sudden lightning bolt of pain simply ripped the sound from of his lungs. His finger twitched spastically, like a berserk telegraph machine after someone tampered with one of the wires.

Armstrong lifted the hammer; some of Jasper's skin was stuck to its head. Jasper's hand instantly began to swell and turn an angry reddish-purple, the color of a diseased beet. Jasper found that he couldn't stop screaming. He bit down on the noise, but the best he could do was muffle it. It seethed through his teeth and filled the storage room.

He automatically tried to pull his injured hand back and cradle it, but the medical brace prevented him from even moving it off the table. His other hand also strained against the handcuffs, with an equal lack of success. Both his feet tapped a frantic little tattoo against the concrete floor.

Blood welled across the back of his hand where the skin had broken, and Jasper could see the ragged edge of a piece of bone poking through. His entire hand was angled in an unnatural bend.

"Now, what I'm going to do here is just pound the hell out of your hand until it's just a sack of blood and bone fragments. I'm not going to cut it off entirely, like what happened with mine. I guess it might fall off on its own if I do this right, though. Say, what exactly happened to my hand? The last I saw, your gal pal was using it to flip me the bird. I hear she's working for Iris now. Ain't that a bitch when you can't trust your friends?"

Ray slammed the hammer down again on the first knuckle of Jasper's middle finger. His hand crunched and contorted like a beetle being stepped by a boot. Jasper made a series of sharp inhalations that weren't quite a scream or a gasp.

Tears formed in his eyes as he tried to maintain some control over his thoughts. The pain clawed at his rational mind like a tiger scratching at the door to a rundown shack. He knew if he let it in, or if it simply smashed down the door to the rest of his mind, it would romp around and leave him a quivering, useless blob.

Jasper had known pain before. Most of his left ear had been ripped off at one point, and he was missing a chunk of one foot from a separate incident, but this was uniquely awful. He could feel the bones grating together under his skin like icebergs colliding against each other. Parts of his hand didn't so much move as flow.

"But seriously. Did you guys keep my hand? Because I'd kind of like it back. I'm under no illusion that they'll be able to sew it back on. Well, certainly not the sort of doctors I'll be visiting. A real doctor would ask too many questions. I mean, sure, they could Frankenstein it back on, but I don't think it would work properly anymore. Especially seeing as it's been off for a while now."

Jasper took big, gasping breaths, trying to keep his breathing under control. He was making a high-pitched keening noise deep in his throat and couldn't stop.

"Mostly, I just want it as a trophy of sorts. I could keep it in a jar of formaldehyde on the shelf in my office. Once I get a new office, anyway. Maybe even keep it positioned in the single finger salute. I'm hoping you guys kept it. If you threw it out, some stray dog is probably chewing on it, or a street vendor found it, brushed it off, stuck it in his grinder, and it's in a couple dozen hotdogs right now. I've never known what's in those things. Some of them definitely taste like loose gutter hands. I mean, I've never just bit into a hand I found lying around in the street, but I imagine that's what they taste like."

Armstrong brought the hammer down again on top of Jasper's ring finger. His aim was slightly off this time, and he missed the knuckle. It didn't really matter though. The bone between Jasper's hand and the first joint of his finger crunched beneath the hammer's weight.

Jagged lumps of bone protruded out on the palm side of his hand where the hammer had smashed the finger flat and ruptured the skin. Blood began to pool on the table and leak off the edge in individual drips.

Jasper thought he was ready this time, but he couldn't control the scream that bubbled out of his throat. When it finally ended, more because he ran out of breath than because the pain subsided, his voice was thick and hoarse. He breathed in wet, rasping gasps, gulping down air. A bubble of mucus blew in and out of his right nostril with each gasp as he tried not to simply descend into a burbling mess. For a moment, he wondered what was making the high-pitched mewling noises that filled the warehouse, and then he realized that it was him.

He tried to move his hand, but it just flopped around like someone had run an electrical current through road kill. His hand felt like someone had filled it with ground glass. Everything grated together and crunched in places it had no business crunching. Even the simple attempt to move his hand nearly sent him into another scream of apoplexy.

Right now, he needed a plan. If he couldn't think of something, Ray would kill him. Probably only after a great deal of unpleasantness. His brain strained to think of something, his thoughts fighting for processing space with the electric waves of pain crawling up his nerves.

Unfortunately, he came up with a plan. It wasn't a good plan. It wasn't even very likely to succeed.

And it was going to hurt like hell.

A big, dopey grin sat on Ray's face. "How ya doing there, Jasper? Looks like you've gone a little pale. Don't worry. I guess you could always get a new hand after this. Second-hand hands are pretty cheap.

"Of course, we've already got a quiet little corner of the landfill all picked out to dump your body once we dismember it and remove any distinguishing characteristics, so it's kind of a moot point, I suppose. We're going to have to dump your head and hands in the harbor. No fingerprints or dental records that way. Did you guys remember to put that on the To-Do list? We can swing by the docks after I stop and get some more painkillers from that quack down the way."

"Boss?"

"Yeah, Ernest?"

"Mind if I have a crack with that hammer? I got a score to settle after what he did to my face."

"You had a score to settle with your mother from what your face looked like before, but yeah, sure. Why not? We're all friends here. Everybody can have a turn. Where are my manners? Hogging all the fun. Here. Have at it." Ray handed the hammer to Ernest. Bits of flesh clung to it, and its metal surface was beaded with blood.

Ernest looked Jasper directly in the eye. His face looked like Dr. Frankenstein had been practicing on it. Stitches and bruising made him almost unrecognizable from when Jasper had first encountered him in the Yersinia lobby.

"Oh, I'm going to enjoy this," Ernest said. The expression on his face told Jasper that he was already savoring the moment. He cradled the hammer, admiring it. "This little piggy went to market."

He hefted the hammer around and pointed to the crooked remains of Jasper's index finger. "This little piggy went home."

Setting the head of the hammer on the table near Jasper's middle finger, he drew little circles across the table's surface. "This little piggy had roast beef."

The hammer left little trails of blood as Ernest dragged it across the table's surface. He moved it closer to Jasper's ring finger. "This little piggy had none."

Ernest paused. The hammer moved closer to Jasper's little finger, the only one still intact on his hand. He lifted the hammer high over his head. "And this little piggy went wee, wee, wee all the way home."

Jasper wanted to look away as the hammer came down, but he couldn't. It was impossible to tear his gaze from the tool as it arced downward. The hammer seemed to move with excruciating slowness. If he hadn't been tied down, Jasper could have knocked it out of the man's grip half a dozen different ways.

But he was tied down. He instinctually tried to drag his hand out of the way, but there was nothing he could do. The medical brace held him firmly in place. His entire arm might as well have been glued to the chair.

After what seemed like a full minute, or maybe an hour, the hammer came down on his little finger. The universe exploded back to its normal speed in a burst of fluorescent pain. Jasper's vision went white for a split second as the receptors in his brain went berserk from the sensory overload coming from his hand.

Agony washed over him like a tide dragging him out to sea. His entire arm rippled with pain, the muscles twitching and contracting and writhing in place. It felt like someone had injected tiny jackals into his bloodstream, and they were chewing their way through his veins and working their way toward the bone. More sick, hitching noises came from his throat.

He could feel his heartbeat in his hand. It was swelling up to a monstrous size, and each flutter of his heart sent more blood coursing down to the area. Each throb pressed against his broken bones, seemingly squeezing them in a vice. His mouth flooded with stringy saliva as his gut tried to throw up again.

"I thought that rhyme was for toes," Ray said.

"Yeah, well, it seemed kind of appropriate, you know?"

Jasper ignored Ray and Ernest. His plan wouldn't work if his hand became too swollen. It probably wouldn't work at all, but he had to try something.

The medical brace fit around his arm like a stiff sleeve. It was narrowest at the wrist, preventing him from pulling his hand out backward, like a monkey with its fist caught in a jar refusing to relinquish whatever prize it had found. If he could just get past that...

His captors were distracted, and his hand would only swell more. It was now or never. He took a few deep breaths, readying himself for what he had to do.

He closed his eyes.

And he immediately snapped them back open as someone kicked open the door at the far end of the warehouse. His first thought was that Amelia had come to rescue him.

It wasn't Amelia.

A bullet cracked over his head as the first of Ralitza Petkova's vampire hunters charged into the building and took cover behind a stack of crates. Several more vampire hunters poured in, firing at Ray's men. The Yersinia guard standing behind Jasper went down, a spray of hot blood spattering across the back of Jasper's neck.

Weapons were unholstered. Curses were unleashed. Ray's men scampered for cover, leaving Jasper unguarded. The warehouse became a two-way freeway of hot lead.

Jasper closed his eyes again. It was now or never. He tensed his left arm and pulled straight back. Previously, his hand had been trapped in place by the narrow wrist portion of the medical brace.

His shattered hand folded like a wilting flower and came clear at the wrist. Jasper's vision contracted to a tiny pinprick of light surrounded by swirling darkness. His teeth gritted together so hard they threatened to crack. His other hand and his feet vibrated in agony. No one even heard his scream over the roar of gunfire filling the warehouse.

He took a second to gather his wits together and gasp down some air. With great reluctance, the swirling blackness retreated from the edges of his vision. Looking down, his hand looked like it had been caught in industrial equipment and then chewed on by Rottweilers. Even if a doctor could put the bones back together again, it would probably never work quite the same.

There wasn't much he could do with just the one broken hand free, but his chair wasn't bolted to the ground. Jasper shifted his weight and hopped a couple of inches off the ground, shoving himself away from the table.

Each pushing, scraping effort rattled his arm. His face felt far too warm for the November weather, and sweat built up on his forehead. He felt light-headed. The pain and exertion nibbled at his consciousness, threatening him with a blackout if he pushed too hard.

Never before had he been so aware of how all the parts of his body were connected. If he shifted his foot, it sent tiny vibrations up to his arm, which sent a flurry of unhappy signals to his brain. Just breathing, the rise and fall of his chest, caused his shoulders to shift ever so slightly, and his hand was acutely aware of each little movement. His fingers screamed bloody murder if he so much as moved his eyeballs to look at them. All this was laid over the constant, pulsating ruckus of pain when he sat perfectly still. There was an entire orchestra of agony playing through his body, all directed by a mad maestro to a syncopated tempo. He didn't have a choice but to continue on, though.

One of the vampire hunters poked his head above a crate, and a bullet smacked through his skull just above the eyebrows. His brains leaped out the back of his head and painted the rear wall, and he disappeared out of sight.

Jasper scooted and hopped his way toward the crate with his equipment laid on top. Each movement brought new agonies, but he continued onward. Finally, he reached the crate and panted like a mad dog in the summer heat. His good hand was trembling in its restraint.

He reached out with his free hand. There was no way he could use his fingers to pick anything up, but Ray and Ernest hadn't smashed his thumb yet. That didn't mean his thumb wanted to cooperate, though. Most of the machinery it was attached to was smashed to oblivion and back, and just extending the digit out set things grinding against each other in horrific friction.

Using his thumb, Jasper managed to clamp one of his lockpicks against the palm of his hand. Using his broken claw of a hand, he transferred the tool up to his mouth and held it with his teeth. He bent over and worked the cuff on his right hand, using his thumb to handle the torsion. Magicians might be able to work a lock with their teeth, but Jasper had never done it before, and he didn't have a stagehand to help in case he dropped the pick.

A machine gun burst chewed the wall nearby, punching holes in the cheap corrugated tin. Houdini didn't have to put up with gunfire, either.

The lock sprang free after what felt like an eternity. His right hand jumped out of the cuffs and snatched the pick from his teeth. He bent down and freed his feet in a couple of seconds.

Lurching up, he staggered halfway to his feet. He remained in a half-crouch to minimize the chance of catching a stray bullet. The vampire hunters hadn't come in force. Apparently, they didn't think the warehouse would be occupied when they dispatched their people to ransack it or burn it or whatever their mission here was. Ralitza Petkova's peasant militia was more or less evenly matched against Ray's small cadre of security agents.

Jasper snatched up his equipment and shoved it into his pockets. No one had noticed he was free yet, but if either side gained an advantage over the other, that would change in a hurry. He picked up his FN Model 1922 pistol and checked the chamber.

Sooner or later, the police would get here. People would have already cleared the area once the gunfire started, probably assuming it was a gangland turf battle. He couldn't rely on the police to get here in time, though.

Cradling his broken hand, he slid over to the wall. What he needed was a distraction to make his getaway. Well, he could create one of those.

Grabbing a gas mask off its hook, he strapped it over his face and checked to make sure the filters were working. Adjusting the clasps was difficult with only one hand, but he managed. The little glass eyeholes restricted his vision, and his breathing sounded loud and hollow in his own ears, like the sound of some great bellows working a hungry furnace.

He remembered training with gas masks during the war. It wasn't fun then, and it wasn't fun now. The rubber and plastic clung to his face like a desperate lover, but there was no way he could fight his way through both Ray's men and the vampire hunters. He moved further down the wall and wrenched one of the prussic acid canisters out of its storage slot. The slots were designed so that the tanks couldn't tip over and risk a breach.

He kicked the canister over so that the spout pointed toward him and the tube's blunt end was directed at the exit. The canister made an enormous racket as it bounced against the ground.

One of Ray's men, the one with the scowl and crew cut, glanced back to find the source of the noise. His eyes widened in surprise and his mouth opened to shout a warning to the rest of the Yersinia security men.

Jasper leveled his pistol and fired off a single round. The bullet roared out of the muzzle and blew the nozzle off the top of the canister.

The contents of the tank had been compressed under enormous pressure. With the top blown off, all the gas tried to escape at once, not unlike a giant bullet riding a wave of expanding gases out of its barrel. The canister shot across the floor faster than Jasper's eyes could track, farting noxious fumes as it went. Blasting across the floor like a torpedo, the tank smashed straight through a wooden crate and roared toward the scowling man.

It missed him by less than a foot. If the canister had connected, it would have smashed his ankles to bloody gumbo. Instead, it continued on its trajectory toward the exit. A vapor trail of prussic acid sprayed out in its wake. Everyone looked down as the low-flying rocket smashed its way through the battle lines and crashed straight through the corrugated tin wall near the door.

Crew Cut looked down at his feet in horror and yelled, "GAS!" He threw an arm over his mouth and tried to wade through the deadly vapor toward the gas masks hanging on the walls. Tears started to stream from his eyes.

Under normal circumstances, the prussic acid was colorless and odorless, so its makers added a chemical eye irritant to warn people in case there was a leak. This was quite a bit more than a leak. So much poison had been released so quickly that it hung in the air in clouds. The choking mist could crop dust half of Nebraska, and it was all confined to this single warehouse.

Taking another wobbly step, Crew Cut collapsed into the roiling vapor. His body stirred up the smoke as it went into its dying convulsions. Most likely, he was already unconscious, and he'd be dead in seconds. It might take his body a minute to figure that out, though, as it thrashed at the spreading mist.

At the far end of the warehouse, the vampire hunter closest to the canister's exit point caught a whiff of the mixture and gagged. He threw up on himself and curled into a quivering ball before seizures wracked his body. The black-clad man arced backward so hard Jasper thought he might snap in half.

Both the vampire hunters and the Yersinia team cleared out of the building in a hurry. Ray, Ernest, and a couple more of Yersinia's security team blew out the back door while the vampire hunters lunged out the side exits. More gunfire sounded from outside, but stopped in a hurry as both sides fled the warehouse. Jasper scurried out, too, the sound of sirens building in the distance.

He grabbed the nearest clump of gas masks and threw them outside for the investigators who would stumble onto the scene in a few minutes. It would be a few hours before the cloud of poison fully dissipated from the structure. He didn't want anyone accidentally dying after inhaling the fumes.

An inventory clipboard hung from a peg on the wall, a pencil on a string dangling below it. He grabbed the clipboard and scrawled a message on the first sheet. "Poison Gas. Sorry." He tossed the note on top of the pile of gas masks and lurched off to find a back-alley doctor to fix his hand.

If it could be fixed.

Chapter 19
Home Invasion

Amelia walked up the home's driveway, moving casually. This was the place all right. The grounds were small, but well-kept, and surrounded by a low stone wall. A wide-open gate allowed access to the driveway. Not much of a security feature if they didn't bother to lock it.

The residence at the end of the driveway was more than a house, but it was a couple of foyers short of being a mansion. Lace curtains covered the windows, and ivy hung from the brickwork in a picture of tranquility. A Model T sat in front of the garage, a converted stable. How perfectly idyllic.

The worst of the storm had passed, but the sky was still gray and a light rain continued to fall. Water dripped off the brim of Amelia's hat as she walked, and her combat boots splashed in puddles as she made her way up the drive.

It struck her as a bit odd that a house such as this would have a basic Model T parked in front as opposed to something a bit ritzier. Some people preferred them, though. She rather liked them herself, actually. They were nice and anonymous.

Finding Leonard Rasmussen hadn't been hard. The head of Yersinia's Medical Research and Development seemed like a good place to start her inquest. Iris wanted information on the company's doings and how it connected to whatever was happening underground. She and Jasper had found the memo regarding the inoculation project on

Rasmussen's desk before the whole building went up in flames, so he clearly knew something.

The chaos surrounding the destruction of Yersinia's corporate headquarters actually gave her an opportunity. Rasmussen couldn't confirm that she wasn't one of Armstrong's internal security people checking in on any information breaches. All the employment records had gone up in smoke, and she knew just enough to bluff her way past any initial questions.

She was here from Yersinia to bring any sensitive corporate documents to a secure location outside the city. No need to worry; Mr. Armstrong sent her. Yes, of course, she knew about the inoculation project. She had clearance. Holding anything back would put Rasmussen under scrutiny for involvement with the group that destroyed the corporate headquarters and would result in his immediate termination. Maybe a little eye batting.

Classic carrot and stick.

If the R&D head kept anything at his home, and given the state his office had been in, Amelia suspected he was disorganized enough to bring things back here, he would hand it over. Amelia would then truck everything back to the information brokerage and separate the wheat from the chaff. Hopefully, there was something worthwhile she could bring to Iris and get herself reassigned to something else as quickly as possible.

She just wanted to be done with whatever was happening beneath the city. It was somebody else's problem. Probably the National Guard's. Too many dangerous people were already involved for her to want to kick that hornet's nest. Add in whatever it was that was living down there, and she was doubly convinced to stay away.

Things didn't add up down there. First of all, she didn't believe in vampires. She'd seen some things in Detroit. Bad things. However, that didn't mean she had to throw all sense to the wind and believe that undead monsters had taken over the sewer system, even if Ralitza Petkova certainly seemed to think that was exactly what had happened. Amelia still wasn't sure if the vampire hunters were legitimate. Maybe they were just a criminal group with an elaborate cover story. There were problems with the scenario, though.

Blood-drained corpses left strewn about New York's tunnel system also seemed to point in the direction of something else, and something nasty had picked off those two Yersinia men in the subway tunnel.

Armstrong had all but admitted that the fleas from the inoculation program had released something bad into the tunnels.

But vampires? This was New York City, not some ruined castle on the ass end of rural Romania. And what about those worm things? They'd killed that woman, and the vampire hunters didn't seem prepared for them. Had the hunters heard rumors of blood-sucking fiends under the city and set off without knowing what was responsible?

But that just left Amelia right back where she started. If it wasn't vampires, then what the hell was leaving corpses in the tunnels?

She wondered if Jasper was making any progress from his side. He was in a lot of trouble with a lot of people already. Hopefully, he was okay.

Amelia shook off the thought. She had her own matters to deal with.

One of the lace curtains twitched. Amelia watched to see if it would move again, but the house remained still. Someone was inside. Hopefully, it was Leonard Rasmussen himself. Things might become more difficult if she had to work her way through a wife or butler.

Stepping up to the front entrance, she raised her hand to knock when she noticed the door was ajar. She thought about that twitch in the curtain again, and her hand dropped to her Luger.

She lunged to the side just as a shotgun blast tore the door halfway off its hinges. Wood splinters sprayed the porch in an arc as the door shattered open.

A figure stood in the open doorway, peering out. The black-clad man obviously expected a shredded carcass on the porch. He'd unloaded both barrels of his shotgun in a single apocalyptic blast.

Amelia squeezed the Luger's trigger and placed two rounds in the man's center of mass. He fell backward into the house, and Amelia stepped over him.

Glancing around inside the house, Amelia didn't like what she saw. Rasmussen lay on the living room carpet. At least, she assumed it was Rasmussen. The man's head had been bashed in, and it now looked like red pumpkin guts. His teeth were spread across the carpet. A stake had been shoved through his heart just for good measure.

Another body, probably Mrs. Rasmussen, sat on the couch. Her hands were neatly folded in her lap. But for the fact that her head was missing, she would look very peaceful. Someone had rammed a stake through her chest as well, pinning her to the cushions.

The house stank of gasoline, and Amelia saw several empty jerry cans sitting in the corner. She glanced around, looking for more threats.

Jesus, the vampire hunters were really determined to clean up shop. They must have everyone in Yersinia's upper echelons on their hit list if they wanted to eradicate all traces of the inoculation project. They were doing their damnedest to cut the head off the snake, and it looked like they were succeeding.

They were targeting all of Yersinia's infrastructure and high-ranking personnel. Scorched earth. No traces. Amelia had seen gangland murders in Detroit. Most of them weren't nearly so feral, and none of them showed the same verve for completionism on display here. Gangsters murdered to intimidate or gain an advantage. They didn't try to exterminate the entire leadership or a rival organization. There were rules.

Of course, Ralitza Petkova's vampire hunters were playing by a different set of rules entirely. They weren't trying to muscle in on someone else's territory. As far as they were concerned, this was about wiping out some unholy scourge and to hell with anyone standing in the way. That hadn't really sunk in until she saw the headless corpse of Mrs. Rasmussen propped up on the couch.

One way or another, somebody had to put an end to this. This was insane. Cripes, she was thinking like Jasper.

She shook off the thought and did a quick sweep of the house. Nobody else jumped out and tried to kill her, but she didn't see anything of use relating to Yersinia, either.

There was still upstairs to search. She debated bailing, but ultimately decided to give a quick glance in each room. Someone must have heard the shots, and the police would show up sooner or later. Still, she needed something for her efforts.

Mounting the stairs, she started opening doors and searching for anything promising. The door to the master bedroom already stood open. Drawers had been pulled from the dressers. The mattress was shredded. Clothes and hatboxes had been ripped out of the closet and thrown on the floor.

However, the real prize was clearly the safe embedded in the wall. A painting, the canvas shredded, sat on the floor nearby next to an array of mechanical tools. Drills, braces, and pneumatic plungers all lay on the floor. There were also jerry cans of gasoline scattered around. Someone had come prepared.

The safe's door hung open, its lock mechanism torn out and its guts hanging from a hole where the dial used to be. It didn't look as if anything had been stolen. A pile of papers and a small lockbox filled the tiny space.

Amelia stepped closer and examined the lockbox first. It contained jewelry and a couple of expensive-looking watches. A few miscellaneous insurance documents and certificates of ownership sat in the bottom of the box. These were the assorted personal effects of the Rasmussens, not that they had much use for anything in there now.

The stack of papers looked more interesting. Several of them had the Yersinia letterhead across the top and appeared to be private correspondence between Leonard Rasmussen, members of the research department, and Ray Armstrong.

Apparently, the vampire hunters hadn't actually read any of the papers. They had no interest in taking them either. They simply busted open the safe to ensure that its contents didn't survive once they burned down the house.

She picked up the stack and flipped through them. Her eyes got wide as she scanned the sheets. Most of the papers were related to Yersinia's inoculation project. Apparently, the whole thing had been performed off the books, and for good reason. The project wasn't about inoculations at all. It was a weapon. She thought back to Armstrong explaining how fleas spread the plague across Europe, causing the Black Death and costing millions of lives.

This was Yersinia's attempt to recreate that as a biological weapon. During the Great War, soldiers lived together in cramped conditions, sometimes unable to even change clothes under the constant shelling barrages. Lice and flea infestations spread from person to person at a lightning rate.

Instead of giving the fleas a weaker version of a disease to grant immunity, Yersinia souped-up an even nastier version of Spanish Flu that was best transmitted through blood contact. The perfect delivery vehicle for such a virulent strain was the ubiquitous pests that surrounded soldiers in the trenches.

They'd improved the fleas, too. A steady supply of hormones and light doses of insecticides created large, more resilient fleas. If they were released over enemy trenches, they'd be almost impossible to exterminate, and soldiers would carry them back home on leave.

Yersinia had been planning to sell the project to the United States government when it entered the war, but the armistice came before the project could be perfected. Rather than abandoning the idea, Yersinia continued to tinker with it, concocting ever more deadly formulas from the very diseases they vaccinated against. Another war would come, and the project would become viable again. At least, that had been the plan. Amelia flipped through page after page of scientific data, graphs, contagion rates, fatalities, and comparisons of various species of fleas. Apparently, fleas hunted their prey by tracking body heat and sniffing out the carbon dioxide their prey exhaled while breathing. Those two signals allowed them to unerringly home in on living creatures and latch on, part of the reason they were such successful parasites and so hard to eliminate in the first place.

Amelia kept waiting to find a sheet explaining where Yersinia came by a sample of vampire virus or whatever they used to make the monsters in the tunnels. She didn't see anything. It was all just pages of data on the best mixture of chemicals and biological refuse to raise the disease carriers on.

Then she found it.

Oh, this was not good. This was not good at all.

Everything suddenly made a lot more sense. A lot of people were very wrong about what was happening in the tunnels beneath New York. Ray was the only one who had all the pieces of the puzzle, and he'd gamed everyone else.

She looked down at the papers in her hands. All the notes were there, all the evidence. It was perfectly damning, and Iris would absolutely love it. Someone would pay a lot of money, a metric shit ton of money to be precise, to either keep the information buried or to buy it for themselves. But the information was also extremely dangerous. She didn't even like holding it in her hands. If the wrong eyes caught sight of this, a lot of people could die. A lot of people had already died. Between Ray trying to cover his employer's tracks, the vampire hunters themselves, and the monsters under the city, this was a huge mess.

Amelia heard a noise from downstairs.

Creak.

Oh bloody hell!

She'd been so absorbed in what she was reading that she forgot where she was. It was time to get out of Dodge. She folded the papers like a newspaper and stuffed them in one of her coat pockets. There would be time to figure out what to do with them later.

She pulled her Luger back out and walked with silent footsteps toward the door. Maybe she could get the jump on whoever was downstairs.

Suddenly, she heard a new sound. *Fwoosh!*

The room instantly grew ten degrees hotter as whoever was downstairs ignited the gasoline down there. Through the open doorway, the hallway suddenly lit up bright orange. Crackling flames shot up from the floor below, engulfing furniture and bodies alike. The little lace curtains went up like flash paper, and the fire began crawling up the walls.

Smoke filtered up the stairs, first in little puffs, and then in roiling clouds. Sweat broke out on Amelia's forehead; her eyes stung and were leaking tears. She tried to swat the smoke away, but it clung to her like a shroud, thickening all the while.

Below, the crackle of flames had turned into an angry growl, becoming louder and louder. There was no way out downstairs. The gasoline had turned the entire first floor into a burning hellscape.

Keeping her wits, Amelia turned to the bedroom's window. She smashed out the glass and clambered out onto the roof. Taking a deep breath of the outside air, she looked around for a way down. Flames billowed out of the downstairs window and through the open front door.

Amelia had just enough time to see the Model T she saw parked earlier peel down the driveway and tear out through the open gate. The vehicle didn't belong to Leonard Rasmussen at all, and that gate wasn't supposed to be open. She cursed her earlier lack of attention and scrambled over to an old tree near the western corner of the house.

Jumping onto one of the overhanging branches, she shimmied her way down to the ground and ran out through the front gate toward her waiting vehicle. The papers in her jacket pocket felt like they weighed a ton as she sped away from the burning building and headed toward the old waterfront.

Chapter 20
Speak of the Devil

Navigating the streets was a nightmare. A lot of roads were still flooded, and drivers were forced to detour onto a small number of side streets. The situation was exacerbated by the fact that the subway was closed. Some of the tunnels had flooded during the storm and couldn't be flushed out yet. The whole system was shut down and closed off until the water could be pumped out. Amelia didn't know how they were going to do it, given the tunnels' inhabitants.

She finally made it to the docks and parked the vehicle in an old industrial building also owned by the information brokerage. She sat in the car for a moment and removed the papers from her coat. Looking down at them, she wondered if maybe she should just burn them herself and finish the job the vampire hunters had started. Nothing good could possibly come from the information contained on those pages.

Swallowing hard, she stuffed the documents back in her coat. She would dump them somewhere later, toss them in a furnace and be done with it. She was hardly some moral crusader, but she didn't want to be involved with disseminating the plans for illicit biological weapons, either. Especially not something like this. The laws of nature were not meant to handle something like this.

In a way, the vampire hunters were right. The current state of affairs couldn't be allowed to spread. If the tunnel denizens branched out to new areas, they'd be almost impossible to contain.

She planted her forehead against the rim of the steering wheel. For everything she'd tried to do to avoid it, she was only getting sucked further and further down this rabbit hole. The more she knew about it, the worse it seemed to get.

Sighing, she got out of the car and walked across the dock to the information brokerage. The building's interior was still just as impressive as ever, but she no longer expected to fall through the floor into the aquarium below every time she took a step. She was sorely tempted to make a detour over to the wet bar along the far wall and pour herself something stiff to put some steel in her nerves. She continued towards Iris's office without stopping, though. If she was going to do this, she needed to make sure her tongue would keep to its script.

Always mix as much of the truth in with the lies as possible. That was something else she'd learned from Jasper. It meant there were fewer falsehoods to remember and fewer places to poke holes in the story.

Pushing open the door to Iris's office, she stepped inside. As usual, the information brokerage's head honcho sat in her chair, an array of files and clippings spread out in front of her.

Iris looked up from her collection of data to glance at Amelia. "Hello there, Dearie. I assume you've seen the news?" She lifted an afternoon edition of the New York Times up from beneath a pile of folders.

Third Yersinia Executive Murdered, the front page headline screamed. Amelia hadn't known about the first two, but it made a certain amount of sense. The vampire hunters were striking as many places as they could, wiping out anyone who might be able to replicate the experiments. The fire at Yersinia's headquarters had been first-page news in and of itself. The fact that some mysterious organization was now systematically wiping out the company's leadership had sent the press corps into a howling frenzy. She could practically sense the editors salivating over every new dispatch regarding the frazzled police response.

She glanced at the picture under the headline. It showed a car parked in an empty lot, a shadowed figure slumped over the wheel. In the foreground, a line of bulky police officers blocked access to the lot.

"Yeah, I knew about a little of this. When was this edition published?"

"A few hours ago."

"It's old news, then. Leonard Rasmussen, Yersinia's top Research and Development man, is dead, too. They pegged his wife as well."

"Who exactly is 'they' in this case?"

"Ralitza Petkova and her vampire hunters. Stakes through the heart. The whole shebang."

"Hmph. A pity. Leonard bought information from time to time. It gave Yersinia the jump on filing a few patents. He always paid for any information on what Yersinia's competitors were working on. Steroid manufacturing techniques. New ways of creating purified adrenaline. Nothing world-shaking, but it made the company a lot of money. Always bought up anything his own employees leaked as well. How did you find this out?"

"I went to his house. There's not much left of it except some cinders. A couple of Petkova's people were there, and they had just set the place on fire when I arrived."

"What else did you discover?"

"Not much. I got there too late," Amelia lied. "I shot one of them, but the other got away. There was nothing I could do."

Iris sighed and rubbed at her temple. Her long hair spilled over her fingers. "So you weren't able to find anything related to Yersinia at Rasmussen's place?"

"Nope. He was already dead by the time I got there, and the place was on fire not long after that. I booked it out of there because I didn't really want to explain to the cops how I came to be at the scene of a double homicide and arson."

Iris made another noise. "You know, you're a lot like my brother. A lot. I can recognize his tells. I don't have to know yours because he's given you some of his. You were something of his pet project. I could tell from the way he looked at you. Maybe a sort of redemption after what happened to Percy. It was one of the reasons I wanted you, but now I think I made a mistake. I can practically smell his influence on you."

"And what exactly are you implying?" Amelia asked. Her voice went smooth and icy.

"I'm not implying a thing. You're new, and Jasper's had his claws in you ever since you joined the Atticans. You abandoned ship once already to join my organization. You're not exactly the most trustworthy person in my employment."

"Miz O'Malley, you steal secrets for a living and re-sell them. That's fine. I don't have a problem with that. But I don't think you're the best judge of trustworthiness." Amelia had almost said, *But you wouldn't recognize trustworthiness if it bit you on the ass.* She'd learned a tiny modicum of discretion from Jasper, too.

Iris rolled her eyes so hard Amelia thought she'd get dizzy and fall out of her chair. She reached down and pulled out something else from under the pile where she'd pulled the newspaper. It was a stack of black and white photographs, blurry but recognizable.

They showed Amelia stuck on the roof of the burning house, looking around like a cat that had found itself precariously high up a tree and was unsure how to get down. A sheath of papers poked out of her pocket. The next photo showed her bustling across the lawn, the Rasmussen house wreathed in flames behind her.

"Fresh off the presses, Dearie. These sure make it look like you found something. I had you followed. Discreetly, of course."

"Yeah. Of course," Amelia said. Her mouth tasted sour. This was not going as she'd planned. Iris O'Malley struck her as a particularly dangerous woman to cross swords with. She had thought she was in good with the information brokerage, but clearly the bottom was about to fall out.

"So, I know you have something for me."

"I threw it away. It was worthless. Old tax files. I thought it might be worth something when I picked it up, but I was wrong. They were from before the war. Nothing of use," Amelia said.

Iris clucked her tongue. "Rocky, be a darling and give me a hand, won't you?"

Amelia started to spin around when a pair of massive hands fell on her and locked her in her chair. Rocky's arms were like big swamp snakes, latching on and threatening to crush her. She never even heard the giant enter the room. How long had he been behind her?

"Search her."

Rocky's big, calloused hands ran over her frame without lingering, quick and professional-like. He reached into her jacket and pulled out the Yersinia documents.

"Oh, those. I forgot about those."

Iris didn't say anything as Rocky handed her the collection of papers. Smoothing them out with her long, delicate fingers, Iris began to read the documents. A red-painted fingernail traced along the words as she read. She flipped through the pages one at a time, taking no more than a few seconds on each. Occasionally, she made small noises of interest. As she approached the end, one of her eyebrows crawled up her forehead, but her expression otherwise remained unchanged.

"So this is why Yersinia wanted to hire Ray out from the information brokerage. No wonder. This would blow their whole goodly world benefactor façade out of the water. A lot of people would frown on testing biological weapons right here in New York City. Looks like things got out of hand, too. I guess that explains why Ray has been sending his security teams down there. They're trying to mop up their mess. And now the vampire hunters have gotten themselves involved. My, my, my. Add my brother into the mix, and that is a volatile mixture of people."

"That's one way to put it," Amelia said.

"I couldn't have hoped for anything better when I brought you two into this. This is exactly what I was hoping for. I'll have to thank Laramie. Delightful," Iris purred.

"Wait, what do you mean? Laramie Resweber hired us for this job."

"Yes, well, where do you think he came first? He wanted information. Believe me, I had plenty that could put Ray's butt in a sling, but that wouldn't get me what I wanted. It's not exactly common knowledge that Ray and Jasper used to work together. How did you think Mister Resweber knew to contact you, specifically? I knew Jasper wouldn't be able to resist a chance to go tilting after this particular windmill, try to right some of his past mistakes. You'd both end up in my court eventually, so I pointed your client in your direction."

"You set this whole thing up so you could get what Yersinia hired Ray to guard?"

"I wouldn't say I set the whole thing up. Mister Resweber simply triggered the idea, and I sat back and waited to see what would happen. It wasn't particularly hard. Besides, there were some wild cards involved. The vampire hunters weren't at all expected, but it played to my advantage."

"Well, bully for you."

"Indeed. Of course, now that I find out you've been hiding things from me, I can't help but wonder if there's more. Amelia, trust is a very important thing in this business. Our clients have to trust in the reliability of our information. Everyone here has to trust everyone else in the organization. It's a sacred bond, and you breached it. Now, I have no choice but to believe there's more you're not telling me."

"That's it. I've got nothing left. You even had one of your boys shadow me, so you know I didn't take any detours and pick up more information elsewhere."

"Ah, but I don't. There are so many opportunities to pick up information. I never got anyone into the Rasmussen house myself, so I have no way of verifying what you've told me. Do you simply expect me to believe you after your duplicity? Hold her down please, Rocky."

"My duplicity? You were the one just talking about manipulating this whole situation to your benefit."

Iris didn't respond. Instead, she cleared off a section of her desk. Stacking the files neatly to either side, she left a nice, bare patch of wood. She went back behind her desk and removed a bottle and a small glass. Pouring herself a stiffener, she looked Amelia square in the eyes. Her green eyes met Amelia's brown ones.

"When I was younger, I looked at Ray as a sort of mentor figure. He was a few years older, knew all the right tricks, and was very handsome. I might have even been in love with him a little bit, although I think he was the only person in the group who wasn't aware of that fact. He was dangerous and charismatic, and he had vision where Jasper had none. It was a very striking combination on an impressionable young girl."

"Cute. Did you leave him notes with all the i's dotted with little hearts?"

"Of course, that was all before I found out he was a sick bastard. Very good at what he did, but maybe not entirely stable. He always had nitroglycerin running through his veins. I learned a lot from him, though. It made me who I am today. Sometimes I wonder if I shouldn't have turned him in, or at least left with Jasper and Percy. But he had a lot of tricks I couldn't learn anywhere else." Iris sipped her drink.

Taking another sip from the glass, she placed the bottle back inside her desk. "Now, see, this is not how I like to do performance reviews. Most bosses are more into constructive criticism. Maybe withhold a bonus. That sort of thing." Her hand re-emerged wrapped around the shaft of a hammer.

"Hey, hold on here a minute."

"Hold her hand on the table, Rocky," Iris said.

Amelia tried to struggle, but she was stuck in the chair. Rocky's crushing grip prevented her from doing anything more than squirm. She tried to scratch at him, but he was out of reach behind her. Her hand simply flapped at the converted mast he used as a shirt. Tensing up her muscles, Amelia tried to prevent her hand from being laid on the surface of the table, but it was like she was a ventriloquist dummy; she couldn't control her own movements. Rocky guided her forearm over the desk and placed her hand on its surface as if she weren't resisting at all, and there he held it. "Real sorry about this, Miss Rio, but Iris knows best in this sort of thing."

In response, Amelia kicked her feet, trying to shove the chair backward into him. It didn't move so much as an inch. It was bolted to the floor.

"So, you've been bad, Amelia. You didn't tell me the truth. My business is the truth, no matter how ugly or obscure. Such things are very important to me. My job might be the only one where the unalloyed truth is so important. Lawyers have to spin their web around facts. Newspaper reporters sensationalize everything to move more product. But I need the unvarnished truth, as complete a picture as possible, to do my work. It's my job, and I find it very hurtful when someone tries to obscure the facts or, worse yet, actively lie to me.

"That's why I have ways of making non-compliance very hurtful for them. I find it gets my point across quite readily, and people tend to fess up to what they've left out. Confession of these things is very important to the healing process."

Iris raised the hammer high, and Amelia squeezed her eyes shut. She couldn't free herself; Rocky's grip on her was like a vise.

Even as she prepared herself for the explosion of pain she knew was coming, it struck her that Jasper and Iris talked the same way when they were angry. Deliberately polite and formal. If Iris could tell she had been learning some of Jasper's techniques, she could see a few strands of shared influence between siblings as well.

"Not to interrupt, but I need to speak with Amelia for a moment," a voice said from behind them. Amelia's eyes cracked open again. She recognized that voice.

"Jasper," Iris said, her face twisting into a grimace.

"Speak of the devil, and he shall appear. By the way, Rocky, I do hate to be rude, but I have a nine-millimeter pistol pointed at the back of your head at the moment. Just thought you might want to know. Nothing personal."

"Hi, Jasper," Rocky said.

"It looks like you had a run in with Ray, judging from that cast," Iris said.

"You might say that. Remember old Doc Festus? The ex-veterinarian who runs the deli with all the weird meats? He still runs his little back-room clinic out of the upstairs office. I had him patch me up. Practically had to beat him back with a stick to stop him from doping me up with morphine, though. I told him I needed my mind sharp."

"Must be painful," Iris said, sounding not in the least bit sympathetic.

"Aspirin only goes so far, I must admit. I have some business to attend to, though. Rocky, would you mind letting Amelia go?"

"Sure thing, Jasper." The iron grip on Amelia eased off, and Rocky took a step away. Amelia stood up from the chair and stepped away. She wanted to be well out of reach of Rocky's wingspan. He could probably snap her neck with two fingers.

She turned around and saw Jasper. He still had his pistol leveled squarely at Rocky's head with one hand. His other hand was trapped in a cast. His fingers stuck out at uncomfortable-looking angles. An angry reddish-purple tone had darkened his fingers from blood trapped under the surface of the skin. The hand had been scrubbed clean where the cast was applied, but she could see the dark rims of coagulated blood under his nails.

Even without the cast, Jasper looked like hell. Dark circles hung under his eyes, and he was even paler than usual. He hummed with unhealthy, feverish energy, practically vibrating. His gray suit was rumpled and marred by a couple of stains that looked like blood.

"Here's the deal. I'm having a bit of a bad day. I could use some help. There's only one person in New York that I actually trust. That's you, Amelia. Plus, it doesn't look like your first twenty-four hours in your new job are going quite the way you hoped."

"You're doing a really good job of not saying 'I told you so.'"

"I figured you could draw that line for yourself. I could use a hand."

"Was that a pun?" Amelia asked.

"I don't suppose you could point that thing somewhere else?" Rocky was looking straight down the barrel of Jasper's FN Model 1922.

"Somewhere else? Sure thing." Jasper shifted his aim so the weapon pointed directly at Rocky's groin instead of his face.

"Funny, I was just about to tender my resignation here, and I was looking for a job," Amelia said. "I'm not sure I can give you many references right now." She gestured toward Iris.

"That's okay. Welcome back to the Attican Detective Agency.

The pay is crap, people tend to shoot at you, and sometimes your clients try to double cross you. Other than that, it's good work."

"Whew. Thank goodness. I was really starting to get nervous about my prospects. The job market is harsh out there."

"Oh, how cute," Iris said.

Jasper flicked his eyes toward his sister. "Things have gotten out of control, Iris. Ray doesn't have a handle on the situation. He never even had control of it, but everything's gone off the rails now. His base of operations got burned to the ground, a lot of his people are dead, he can't protect all the Yersinia executives who are being gunned down, and he has the equivalent to an angry mob of villagers with pitchforks and torches trying to hunt him down. People are dying."

"And you plan to bring everybody together and have them all shake hands? You were hired to bring Ray down, and he knows it. He's not going to cooperate with any plans you have."

"No, but I can moot the underlying problem. At least, I hope so. After that, Ralitza Petkova can have Ray's head on a platter. But things are untenable as they are. I hate to say this, but I could use your help, too, Iris."

"And why would I want to do that?"

"Because you know as much about the situation as anyone, and you have the spare manpower to help do something about it. It might save a lot of lives."

"You know I don't do anything for free, Jasper. You're right, though. I do know more about the situation than just about anyone else, including you. Tell him about the inoculation project, Amelia. Tell him about those vampires Ralitza Petkova is hunting."

Amelia told him.

Jasper blinked once, then twice, as Amelia told him what she had found in Leonard Rasmussen's home before it went up in flames.

He sighed. "Well, if you won't help out for good reasons, maybe I can speak your language a little more clearly. You might want to help out of pure self-interest. Doc Festus isn't the only contact in New York I still know," Jasper said, gesturing toward the cast on his arm. "I know people who can deliver a message, and if they haven't already, a little bird is about to tell Ralitza Petkova that you've known about this situation for quite some time. She's just zealous enough that she'll come after the information brokerage, too."

"You *what?*"

"I helped build this place, albeit not into its current form, and I'll help burn it down if I have to. No skin off my teeth. The vampire hunters aren't invested in the brokerage like some of your other enemies are. They don't care if you have anything to divulge on them, and they'll tear the studs out from under this place if they think it'll prevent the spread of vampirism."

"But they're not even right about the vampires. They're just jumped-up hicks from Transylvania fighting the boogeyman. I have the documents that prove what's really happening down there with the fleas. I can just deliver those."

"And you think they'll believe you? They're a centuries-old order hell-bent on stamping out the spread of those vampires. I have no idea what they've been hunting all these centuries, but they certainly believe they know what they're doing. I don't think they'll be inclined to take you at your word."

"Oh, you bastard."

"Does that mean you'll lend me some help in clearing out the underground?"

"I'll think about it."

"Think fast. I doubt you'll have much time. We will be leaving now. I would recommend that you stay very still as we walk out that door."

They walked backward out of Iris's office. Amelia had her Luger in her hand, but kept it pointed casually toward the floor. Moving briskly, they exited the information brokerage. Both of them kept their weapons in hand, but no one emerged to follow them.

The Peerless was parked on the street. "You drive. I'm having a little trouble with just the one hand," Jasper said.

"What happened?" Amelia looked at the cast.

"The same thing that was about to happen to you. I had an encounter with Ray. He was in a bad mood about the fact that I blew his hand off, not willing to let bygones be bygones. Iris was trying to pump you for information and punish you for holding out."

"Jasper, I'm...I'm sorry I wasn't there to help."

"No, I'm sorry, too. I don't always treat you as an equal in this thing. I tend to override your opinion sometimes, even when you have a valid point. I've worked alone for so long, it's hard for me to get used to taking other people's opinions into consideration."

Amelia opened the door and sat down in the car's sleek interior.

It felt familiar and good. "It's okay. You know I've taken some bad hits in the past. I don't trust people very easily. But you were right. Things have gotten out of hand. It was a mistake to leave, and somebody needs to do something about the situation down there. We've got Armstrong, your sister, and the vampire hunters, and those problems aren't going to go away without dealing with the tunnels first. What did you have in mind?"

"The subways are still closed due to the storm, which is good because we're going to need to steal a train."

Chapter 21
Eyes

Ernest Hives watched the cream-colored sports car glide away from the curb. Even from his position a few blocks away, he could hear its engine rumble like a wild animal. He watched it pull out into the damp street, slipping away into traffic.

A few seconds later, several armed men burst out of the information brokerage, led by a woman with long red hair. She was shouting at the men, one of whom was a small giant. The woman cuffed one of her companions upside the head, knocking his hat off into a puddle. He rubbed his head and fished up his drenched hat.

Dames, man.

Ernest kicked his own vehicle to life. Its old engine sputtered and wheezed as he pulled into traffic. The Peerless had already surged forward, and he had to speed up to keep it in his sights. Staying well back, he observed from a distance, keeping just close enough that he could see where the car was going. Any closer would risk being spotted.

The Peerless wasn't hard to keep track of, even from a distance. It slid through the rest of the traffic like a shark cruising through coastal waves. The woman behind the wheel drove aggressively enough to cow even some of the seasoned New York drivers. Normally that required a natural disaster or some other act of God. If the asphalt split open and the fiery, gaping maw of hell appeared in the middle of the street amid geysers of fire, a lot of drivers would just view it as a particularly bad pothole and keep moving.

Ray wanted either O'Malley or the woman he worked with. Ernest figured he could snatch the woman by staking out the information brokerage. They were all going to have to disappear after this anyway. It wouldn't matter if they pissed off Ray's old partner.

Finding the two of them was both a positive and a negative. On the plus side, he could kill two birds with one stone. Ray would be pleased to get both the detectives at once. On the down side, Ernest was not about to attempt to deal with both of them at once by himself. His face still felt like it might slough off from the other times he'd tried to deal with those two. Well, they would get theirs. For now, though, he would simply follow and keep track of their movements. An opportunity would arise to call his colleagues and settle the matter more permanently, preferably without having his face bashed in again in the meantime.

He settled into a pattern, staying a block and a half back, always watching. Waiting. The opportunity would come. So long as those Euro-freaks didn't show up, this would simply be a matter of patience.

Chapter 22
Watching the Watchmen

Istvan de Vojnich stroked the crucifix hanging from his neck as he watched the battered American car pull away from the curb, the Yersinia security man at the wheel. He wasn't aware of his hands as they continued to stroke the crucifix.

In a past life, what seemed like eons ago, he had been a captain in a mountaineering brigade in the Austro-Hungarian military. Even now, part of him was still trapped in that dark mountain pass, the Italian army camped across the ridge, both sides slaughtering each other to advance a few hundred meters at most. The same scraps of land were fought over again and again, blasting the landscape to hot gravel, spraying snow in every direction and causing avalanches. He still remembered the red snow, frozen limbs sticking out of the packed sleet like they were trying to crawl their way out from their icy graves.

Some things never left him. If he thought about it too long, he could still feel that same deathly chill, the cutting wind that passed through the ravines. Sometimes, he didn't even need to think about it at all; suddenly he was back amidst the crashing artillery and roaring machine guns, desperately hoping that the small campfire wouldn't give away his position to a sniper or mortar team.

Perhaps the memory most likely to prey on his mind in the night, to keep him awake until the rise of dawn, was the thing from the mountain. He didn't know if it ever visited the Italian troops further down the slope. He never saw it close up, but he saw the footsteps in the snow around the freshly slain bodies. He saw the soldiers with their throats ripped out and the bloody claw marks. Some nights, and only at night, he heard the screams, and in the morning, one or more of their number would be missing.

That was the worst. Sleep was sometimes their one reprieve from the fighting, and it was often denied for days at a time when another offensive bogged down in the sweep of machine gun fire and the mounds of bodies. It was supposed to be a cherished requiem, but no one slept easily once the killings started. Not when they knew sleep only made them vulnerable to the depredations of the beast of the mountain.

Sometimes they saw something higher up the mountain, scrabbling up the sheer rock faces like a huge, pale spider. It didn't move like anything human. Nothing human could move up those walls of rock. Even with binoculars, it wasn't much more than a skittering smudge near the summit.

He'd been the one to suggest they send a team up there. Of course, he'd pitched it to the higher-ups as a scouting mission to reconnoiter the Italian positions and investigate the feasibility of using some of the higher passes to sneak troops closer. So long as he let them steal credit for the idea when they pitched it to the top brass in the area, there was enough enthusiasm to scrape together a twenty-man team.

They went out, often for days at a time, looking for the beast's lair. The rest of the troops knew what they were really doing up there, and it was enough to make them the most popular men along that section of the front. Everybody wanted to share an extra portion of their rations or give away an extra pair of warm socks sent by loved ones at home.

Many phrases spun through the camp. *Wampyr. Dracul. Vampire.* Before the war, he would have written off the mumblings as the fears of superstitious peasants. Surely a cave bear or some sort of Highlands cat was a more likely culprit.

Of course, he never would have believed that thousands of men would die in great, invariant heaps fighting over the same quarter mile of useless land over and over and over again. The war had changed his perspective on many things, and so he led the expedition up the mountain.

Fritz was killed when his tether line snapped. Bogdan got separated and froze to death during a storm. The going was hard, but after almost two months, they found the thing's nest. It was unmistakable. The entrance was a fissure cut into the rock and ice of the slope. Bodies lay strewn everywhere. Some had their heads ripped away; others had been torn to pieces no larger than a baby's fist. The icy temperatures had preserved all of them remarkably well. A few of the corpses even looked like they predated the war, unfortunate mountaineers exploring the edges of the Alps and discovering things best left undiscovered.

Some of the clothing scraps and gear looked like they were very old indeed, maybe even centuries old. A chipped sword blade looked like it might have come from one of the Ottonian Empire's invasions of northern Italy almost a millennium ago.

None of the team had known exactly what to expect, but this was ghastly beyond their wildest imaginings. It was a frozen charnel house.

Each of them came with a small supply of explosives. They laid the satchel charges just inside the entrance to the cave when they saw the trail of carnage led deeper into the darkness. There were also more artefacts. A row of coins from the Byzantine Empire, long since washed into the seas of history, left a little pathway into the shadows. It almost looked as if the little lumps of gold had been purposefully arranged to lure the avaricious and foolhardy deeper into the gloom. Seeing that, they wasted no time readying the timers.

He didn't know exactly what happened after that. There was a shriek from inside the mountain, a high-pitched noise like an engine tearing itself apart under enormous mechanical strain. The noise echoed and re-echoed down into the depths of the mountain. Then suddenly, there was a flash of movement and pale, leathery flesh as something burst out of the fissure. He remembered being sprayed with hot blood as the man to his left was cleaved apart in the blink of an eye. He was knocked back by a force that broke two of his ribs and sent him sailing over the ledge. The snow caught him some thirty feet down, and he must have been knocked unconscious and rolled further down the side of the crevasse. He never even heard the explosives go off.

When he came to, the section of the mountain above him was no more than loose boulders and cratered ice. He wandered for hours, but couldn't find any sign that the rest of his team survived. He found a foot that he was pretty sure belonged to Josef, but anyone who survived the initial attack was now under several tons of rock and snow.

The fissure entrance had simply ceased to exist. The satchel charges collapsed the tunnel and turned everything around it into a mélange of snow and fractured stone.

He still wondered if that thing was down there, beneath the rock. Given enough time, and every indication he'd seen implied it had plenty, it could probably scrape its way free. Over years and years, wind and running water could sculpt rock into all manner of shapes. Claws could very well do the same thing, and one day, it might very well scratch its way out of its wintery tomb. If nothing else, the mountain would one day erode to dust.

Hopefully, the explosion killed it, tore it apart in its fiery embrace. If not the explosion, then perhaps a rock fell and crushed it, smashing it to a pulpy red goo. These were the things he told himself late at night when sleep would not come, but some part of his brain was quite sure that the thing was trapped down there, merely biding its time until it was free once more. It would chip away at its rocky confines a little more each day, a little more each year, and then it would be free to cause havoc once again.

When he climbed back down the mountain, he discovered that the war was almost at an end. Austria-Hungary was on the verge of collapse, and even Germany would soon be forced to sign a peace treaty. In two weeks, their position in the mountains, a place thousands died defending, would be abandoned. In short order, the entire Empire broke apart into various smaller entities.

It wasn't long after that he received a letter from Ralitza Petkova. He'd already been mustered out of the military and had returned to his hometown near the Romanian border. Somehow, she'd gotten ahold of his final report. He had no idea how. The military's central command had been broken up when the Empire imploded. Not even he knew where his report finally ended up or if anyone had bothered to read it. He'd assumed it was probably thrown away, or maybe just used as kindling.

But Ralitza said she knew what the thing in the mountains was. She said her group had been dealing with them for hundreds of years. She said she might be able to help him put his mind to some sort of rest if he at least knew how to defend himself against such *ur*-predators in the future.

With nothing better to do, he jumped at the chance. Her group was mostly comprised of people who had survived encounters with such creatures and been scarred in one way or another. Grown orphans who couldn't even remember the night their parents were swallowed by the night. Veterans like himself who saw things best left unseen at the far edges of the front. Widows and widowers. Failed seminary students and ex-military chaplains. It was a strange concoction of people, but they did good work. Very good work indeed. Everyone there had experienced some variation of what he saw up on that mountain, and that made the group closer to him than anyone else on earth.

He couldn't talk to his old friends anymore. Some part of his spirit had gone dead. It was like when he was a little boy learning about death for the first time, discovering that someday he and everyone he knew would die. There was no going back to the same innocence of youth after that realization dawned on him. Being with people who knew the things he knew, who shared the same purpose, that was the only normalcy he knew now. He was forever separate and apart from his old life.

New York was a strange destination for fate to take him, but it made a certain sense. The shadows were deep indeed here, and prey was abundant.

There were many who would not be missed in this gigantic, concrete feeding pen. He had seen the corpses, their bodies drained of fluid. Their quarry was here. All the signs were present. Everything fit into place.

What he could not comprehend, though, was why anyone would tamper with these abominations? Yersinia's scientists had created something in their labs, and it had escaped into the tunnels beneath the city. The hubris to try to harness something so unnatural, so profane!

The exact purpose of their experiments, he could not say. He knew nothing of what went on in that dark dungeon of a testing space, but he possessed the knowledge that what was spawned could not be allowed to spread. Creating one of these monstrosities put untold lives in danger.

Unpleasant though it was, the genie needed to be stuffed back in the bottle. Those responsible needed to be dealt with. There were some realms in which man was not meant to tinker, where information could not be used safely or responsibly. The things loose in the sewer system only proved that point. Yersinia and its top people needed to be laid low. Clearing the tunnels would come later. It would be difficult, but they had the equipment and the experience to deal with this scourge.

First, the knowledge of how to make more of these creatures needed to be scrubbed from mankind's consciousness, and that meant eliminating those with the knowledge. Ralitza Petkova would need

Ray Armstrong to ensure they discovered everyone involved with the project, for he knew all Yersinia's secrets.

As Armstrong's man drove away from the curb, Istvan started his own engine. At some point, the dog would need to return to the master. If these two detectives who had bumbled into the situation led his own target to the goal, so be it. They would die, too, for their interference. He and his brothers and sisters would wipe the slate clean.

He placed his foot on the accelerator and gently threaded his way through the New York traffic, just another drop of steel blood flowing along the city's asphalt arteries. The Yersinia guard never even checked his mirrors to see if anyone was behind him.

Chapter 23
It's a Gas

"Hyunk arrie ossifer," Jasper said through his gas mask. He handed the clipboard to the police officer standing outside the warehouse.

"What?" the beefy sergeant asked. He wore a rain poncho that barely covered his bulging belly. A decade ago, there had probably been a lot of muscle under that girth. Time had swapped it out for fat, though, one of the many cruel tricks of aging.

Jasper gestured to Amelia, also wearing protective clothing and a gas mask. Wearing the heavy rubber gloves and work cowl, she was completely sexless. The mask obscured her face as well. To the best of Jasper's knowledge, there weren't any women who worked in the toxic waste disposal field. Undue questions might arise if the sergeant new Amelia was a she.

Next, Jasper pointed to the heavy duty flatbed truck they'd arrived in. Twenty dollars to a factory foreman was enough to rent the vehicle and the safety equipment for a day. He needed the items, and he would just mark it down as an expense, leaving Laramie Resweber to reimburse him.

He waggled the clipboard again. It was a standard waste pick-up form from an industrial complex not three blocks down. Several of the boxes were already checked, indicating the most dangerous chemicals and extreme precautions. An elaborate scribble worked as a signature, "authorizing" them to secure dangerous chemicals.

In this case, prussic acid.

Jasper thrust the clipboard into the sergeant's hands again. He handed the man a pen and pointed to a line below the first scribble. "Urr eir tuh hick uh huh gas hannisters." *We're here to pick up the gas canisters.*

The sergeant eyeballed the document. After a moment, he added an equally indecipherable squiggle beneath the first. "Right. I figured they'd send somebody out to pick this stuff up. The gas has pretty much dissipated from inside the building. It's clear enough that we were able to send in some of our boys and clear out the bodies. You're going to need to mind where you step, though. There's still some blood caked onto the floor."

"Uht happen'd?" Jasper's mask amplified his breathing in his own ears and cut off half the sound from outside. He could barely hear the cop explain.

"Some sort of gang attacked the Yersinia warehouse. Some of the security guards were inside when it happened. A couple of them caught a hot one and went down easy. At least one wasn't so fortunate. Gas got him. We're still trying to figure out who these freaks are, but they really have it in for Yersinia. Same guys who burned their headquarters to the ground, we reckon. Been raising hell all over the city. We've put our own men on Yersinia property and around their remaining people, but it's stretching us thin. They didn't finish the job here, though. A stray bullet must have popped one of the canisters and filled the whole place up gas. A couple of the attackers died, too. The whole thing's a goddamn mess."

Jasper nodded at this sage observation.

"I know it's pretty safe in there now, but just between you and me, I'm glad they're not making us go in there to clean things up. Some of those chemicals will stick to a surface. You touch the wrong thing with your bare hand and *BAM!*, the next thing you know, your balls fall off."

Well, actually, a deadly cocktail of cyanide bonded with your cells at a molecular level, shutting down cellular respiration and resulting in a writhing, frantic struggle before the brain ceased functioning and death took hold. Jasper decided to keep the advice in mind and keep his gloves on the entire time, anyway. He wouldn't leave any fingerprints that way, either.

Together, he and Amelia loaded the truck as quickly as they could. They moved fast in case an actual clean-up service or, worse yet, Ray

Armstrong himself showed up and demanded to know what in the blue blazes they were doing.

Jasper could only carry the canisters with one hand and needed Amelia's help loading them into the truck. It took extra time to strap everything down as well. It wouldn't do to accidentally spill dozens of tanks of prussic acid onto the streets of New York.

Sweat poured down Jasper's face and stuck to the inside of his mask as he worked. Even though it was early November and the clouds were beginning to spit rain again, the work was hard even without a broken hand, and he was trapped in the warm, rubberized confines of his safety gear. He could hear Amelia panting, too, as they filled the truck to overflowing.

Finally, they dared not place any more canisters in the vehicle. Its bed sagged dangerously under the load of deadly cyanide compounds.

Waving to the policeman, Jasper hopped into the truck's cabin, and Amelia climbed behind the driver's seat. With a rumble, the engine started up, and the truck snorted away from the warehouse.

Instead of traveling deeper into the industrial district, the truck turned and moved toward Manhattan's more cosmopolitan heart. Jasper couldn't help but be painfully aware that if something happened, if the truck somehow overturned, they would very likely kill everyone nearby. It would be worse than a sustained chemical attack on the wartime trenches. But Amelia drove cautiously, following the flow of traffic. It was only a short distance to the first subway entrance. A big orange sign warned that the subway was closed due to flooding. Jasper slid out of the passenger seat as Amelia parked the truck outside the subway's entrance.

He pulled off his protective gear, leaving the gas mask dangling around his neck just in case. Underneath, he was wearing the orange vest of an anonymous maintenance worker. Digging into a pocket, he pulled out a bottle of aspirin and munched on a couple of tablets. His hand throbbed with a dull ache just sitting in his lap. Every time he jostled it, the pain screamed at him.

Amelia ripped off her sweaty protective gear as well and grabbed a brimless cloth cap from out of the truck's cabin. From a distance, they'd look like a couple of city workers trying to get the subway up and running after the flooding from the storm.

Jasper walked over to the subway entrance, careful to move down the stairs without disturbing his hand too badly. The entrance was closed, blocked by a roll down steel cage that latched into the ground. Nothing bigger than a mouse could fit through the cross-hatched bars. However, the latch was secured by a simple lock. Dozens of copies of the key that opened the gate probably existed across the city, a few for police and emergency services, a few for the subway workers themselves, a few for the maintenance teams. A variety of parties needed access to the tunnels. Unfortunately, Jasper had no idea where to locate any of those copies, but he didn't need to, though. Bending down, a lockpick sprang into his hand. The lock fell open in his palm, and he pushed the cage up. It rattled upward, and Amelia dragged the first of the canisters down the stairs.

Maybe Yersinia kept the prussic acid on hand for this very purpose, in case their little experiment truly got out of control. It would be useful in a variety of other scientific contexts as well, but the quantities here were enormous. Jasper turned around and began to lug a canister down into the darkness himself.

Two blocks away, a car pulled to a halt in front of a fire hydrant. A man with a battered face killed the engine and watched the two distant figures haul the metal canisters down the stairs into the subway.

After a few minutes, he stepped out of his vehicle and walked into a nearby restaurant. After a couple of minutes spent haggling with the waiter, he pushed his way into the back room and made a series of phone calls. Satisfied, he walked back out to his car and sat inside, smoking a cigarette. He blew smoke rings out the open window, waiting for backup to arrive.

Two blocks behind Ernest Hives, Istvan de Vojnich pulled into an alley and parked his vehicle behind a dumpster. Glancing around, he emerged on the sidewalk and strolled into the nearest apartment building. For a dollar, he found the floor man amenable to the use of the manager's phone. With a password, his call was redirected and, with another password, redirected again before reaching its ultimate destination.

He relayed the information and snuck back to his car. Leaning on the hood, he stayed far enough back in the shadows that he could watch the Yersinia man without being seen himself. He lit a cigarette and waited, the only sign of his presence from outside the alley was the hot glow of an ember and the cool glitter of his eyes.

Two blocks further back, a Rolls Royce Silver Ghost pulled to a stop in front of a small office. The hulking figure behind the wheel stepped out. Rocky hopped up onto the curb.

The office was closed for the evening, its door shut tight. A little placard sat in the window, giving the building's hours. Without even slowing down, Rocky gripped the knob in his hand and shoved. The wood around the lock splintered apart, and the door swung open.

Shutting the door gently behind him, Rocky moved through the dark straight to the front desk. Papers and documents were spread across the surface, detailing schedules, order numbers, and a reminder that someone named Henry would be out for the week with pneumonia.

Rocky ignored the paperwork and lifted the phone sitting on the desk. After the operator connected him, the phone rang exactly twice before being answered. He could hear the smile in Iris's voice as she thanked him for tracking the vehicles. He shuddered at the implications of that smile.

After hanging the phone up, he grabbed a pen off the desk and the note about Henry's pneumonia. "Sorry about the door," he scribbled. Satisfied, he left the note on the desk and walked back out to the Rolls Royce.

From all over New York City, vehicles began to converge.

Chapter 24
Loco-Motive

Jasper had the train up and running. The tunnel ahead was clear and free of water. No one else was in the tunnel system. The flooding had closed all the entrances and driven everyone to higher ground.

That was perfect, though. Anyone caught in the tunnels today would be in deep trouble. He and Amelia were going to take care of the problem down here.

Amelia had found a control panel in the station's office and closed off all the subway vents to the surface. She'd also mapped out a route that covered the whole of the subway system, terminating in Grand Central Station.

Jasper flipped on the overhead arc lights from a control booth, but the subway still felt eerily empty when it was devoid of people. The darkness seemed to seep in from the tunnels. His every footstep clopped on the cement like he was wearing hooves.

Distorted sounds boomed in from further down the tunnels. He was fairly certain that it was the sound of heavy trucks passing overhead and the occasional rat scuttling through some garbage, but it was still enough to send his heart into duple meter when he could hear noises from deeper down.

The train chuffed and hummed, warming up. They'd loaded the canisters on board.

Really, it was a simple plan. Once the train started moving, they would take the longest, most roundabout route possible. By breaking into the station's control center, they could reroute some of the track switches for a better path. They couldn't hit every tunnel, but they could travel down a lot of them. As they went, they would release the prussic acid from the tanks, killing everything in the tunnels. Bottled up underground, the gas would reach sufficiently deadly concentrations to wipe out everything that moved down here.

Amelia stood in front of a large control panel, staring at a map of the tunnel system. She glanced over at Jasper.

"I think we should hit these tunnels over here," she said, jabbing at the map. "There's a whole section where they excavated out extra space for an expansion that never happened. Looks like it connects a few different tunnels."

Jasper looked at the map. There was a section with grayed out tunnels running parallel to the main tracks. The extra tunnel ended as suddenly as it began on the map, marking the exact point when funding ran out.

The unused section of the tunnel would make a good hiding place. Once upon a time, there had probably been a vagrant camp set up in the abandoned space. Now, something else had probably found the area and claimed it.

"Good thinking," Jasper said. "That whole area is almost certainly a nest. We should make sure we saturate it."

Amelia flipped a couple of switches on the station's control panel. A series of lights flipped from green to red. The train would no longer follow its usual, designated route. They were covering a much larger, more winding path.

Once they'd poured poison all along the system's perimeter, they would pull into the heart of the hub, Grand Central Station, and release the remainder of the prussic acid. From there, it could spread down dozens of tunnels and saturate the underground in curling mists of powerful insecticide.

By the time the gas escaped, through little cracks and out grates, it would be too dissipated to harm anyone on the surface. That was one reason prussic acid was never as popular as chlorine or certain irritants during the war. It didn't linger on the open fields, and a wisp of breeze could render it useless.

There was a certain beauty in the plan, too. They were using Yersinia supplies to exterminate Yersinia monsters. This wasn't going to be subtle. The police would notice in a hurry, but their first suspicions would fall on Yersinia personnel like Ray. Once they discovered the inhuman corpses in the tunnels, more Yersinia connections would come to the surface, and Jasper would be there to shovel dirt over Yersinia's name.

The safety of anyone who might be in the tunnels had to come first, though. Jasper walked back to the control booth, its lock busted out. There were supplies, schedules, tunnel maps, and all manner of other utilitarian accoutrements in the booth. Jasper ignored them in favor of the intercom unit mounted into the wall.

It had several settings, one for just this station, one for alerts along this line, and one for the entire system. Jasper flicked the switch over to address everyone in the subway tunnels. The creatures seemed to have wiped out most of the transient population that sometimes slept in the dark warmth down here, but there might be a few left here and there.

"Your attention, please," he said. Feedback squealed at him. "Your attention, please. If you can hear this, we're about to release a large quantity of poisonous gas into the tunnels. We strongly advise that you exit to the surface now. Thank you."

Amelia walked up behind him. "May I see that for a minute?" She pointed at the intercom speaker.

"Sure."

She lifted it to her mouth. "Listen up. If you're down here, you have three minutes to get out before we wreck this place. Get while the getting is good, and you'll live. Stay, and you die. Your choice."

Putting the receiver back on its cradle, she looked at Jasper. "Sometimes you can't pretty up the language. No pleases or thank yous. Better to just crack them over the head with an order when you really want to get a point across. A reason and a request will get some people moving, but there's always a couple who need to hear the whip cracking over their heads."

"Noted."

Walking back to the train, Jasper climbed in the rear passenger compartment. Gas canisters lay across the seats and piled on the floor. Like the station, the train looked empty and foreign, something from a dream. The people, the crowds, were such an integral part of the city that it felt somehow wrong to see normally bustling areas sterile and devoid of human activity. It suddenly struck him that this is what New

York would look like if the things in the tunnels decided to come to the surface. If they spread, they would clear out large swathes of the city. It was like being visited by the ghost of Christmas future, a grim preview of what might be.

He shuddered as the train strained and began to move. Amelia was up front, working the controls. She had no experience with trains, but she could operate damn near anything else with an engine. This didn't need to be complicated. They just needed to keep moving and switch tracks every once in a while. She had a map of the subway system up with her, with the connectors to the city's sewer system circled in red ink.

Jasper slipped his gas mask back over his head as the train began to pick up speed. The back door to the cabin was propped open, and he lugged the first canister over and began to unscrew the nozzle. A blast of poisonous fumes spewed from the top of the tank with a hissing noise. The tank rattled in his hand under the force of the escaping gas, but it didn't shoot away from him. He directed the spray out of the train, filling the tunnel with an aerosol haze.

Behind the train, the station grew more distant. Through the spray of gas, it was simply an island of light in an ocean of darkness. Jasper watched it grow farther away like a medieval sailor watching the shore grow more and more distant at the start of a long journey.

"Here there be monsters," he muttered to himself.

A noise echoed down the tunnel. He tried to pinpoint its origin. Down here amid the echoes and noise of the train, it was nearly impossible, but he thought it was coming from the direction of the station. It almost sounded like…

A pair of headlights bounced down the station's staircase and slid onto the platform itself. Jasper saw the bright lights flash at him like the eyes of some jungle creature screaming out of the darkness. They drew closer to the rear of the train and Jasper could hear the sound of tires beating the ground. With a roar, the driver accelerated, and the car screamed over the edge onto the tracks.

The headlights bounced madly as they rattled over the tracks. Tires *thump-thump-thumped* over the crossties. In the darkness, Jasper could only see the lights bearing down on him like a pair of hungry eyes. There was no way to see who was driving from that distance.

He stood up and tried to wave them off. Unless they brought protective gear, they would die in a cloud of noxious gas spilling out of the train. Flailing his arms, he tried to motion for them to stop. For all he knew, they were a pair of metro police feeling a little over-zealous with their car.

A bullet whipped past Jasper's head and cracked against the interior of the train. Definitely not metro cops.

He saw the muzzle flash of the second shot as it went high and buried itself in the tunnel's cement ceiling. Someone was leaning out the car's passenger window with a pistol. The car was bouncing too violently for the passenger to get a clear shot, but that didn't stop him from trying. The split-second strobe effect of the muzzle flash revealed that the shooter was wearing a gas mask.

They had come prepared. That meant they knew about the prussic acid and must have been keeping an eye on them for some time. Not good.

He heard the sound of another car crashing down the stairs and careening onto the tracks. A second later, it pulled up behind its companion. Jasper watched through the rear window before unholstering his pistol and unloading a few rounds at the first car, punching out one of its headlights. A third car pounced out of the station and began rumbling over the crossbeams toward them. Oh, this was not good at all.

This was turning into a regular convoy. Whoever had been following them had brought all their rowdy friends. Jasper had a pretty good idea of who it was, too. They'd raided the Yersinia stockpile, and that gave Ray and his friends plenty of time to observe and organize.

The driver stuck his hand out his window, and Jasper caught a glimpse of gunmetal. He dropped to the floor as a volley of submachine gun fire cut through the toxic mist and peppered the train. Several of the windows behind Jasper shattered as bullets smashed into them. The hot brass projectiles cut through the mist of poisonous gas like angry hornets defending their nest.

Through the cataclysmic blasts, Jasper caught sight of the driver of the vehicle. It was Ernest Hives. Jasper could only see the men in the vehicle when the light was perfect, usually in the reflected blast of gun-fire. He, on the other hand, was perfectly silhouetted against the interior lights of the train. His only advantage was the smoother ride the train provided him compared to the rattling, bouncing cars. Even so, the rolling motion of the train interfered with his own ability to aim. It was less like a gunfight and more like blindfolded children all whacking at a piñata. Hitting anything was difficult. Hitting a target the size of a man was primarily a matter of luck.

Jasper fired off the rest of his magazine as the vehicle surged closer for a better shot. At least two of the shots sparked off the vehicle, but he couldn't tell where the others went. The entire tunnel was a kaleidoscope of flashing lights and harsh noise.

Beneath him, the train's wheels shrieked and entered a turn. Wires and cables hung from the cement walls and chipped masonry to either side. Arc lights created little pools of light, fighting a losing battle against the omnipresent darkness. As the train sailed past them, the lights dwindled into the distance, seemingly as far away as the cold stars in the night sky.

The Yersinia car stayed right on the train's caboose, riding along behind it like a wolf running down a much larger creature. The other two Yersinia cars were fast approaching.

Amelia had no doubt heard the commotion at the rear of the train, but she needed to work the controls. Jasper was outgunned in terms of both numbers and firepower. Sooner or later, one of their pursuers would get lucky and send a slug into the space he was occupying.

The train hit the first switch in the tracks, and it shifted off its designated course and onto the route Amelia had designed. The tight confines of the tunnel opened up on one side, revealing a side-tunnel large enough to run a second train. Unfortunately, it also gave the pursuing vehicles more room to maneuver.

He reloaded, a laborious process with only one working hand. Racking a shell into the chamber, he skittered over to a nearby prussic acid canister. He had set them all up so the nozzles would point toward the back of the train, allowing the gas to escape most easily out into the tunnels.

With a kick, he sent the canister spinning around so the nozzle now faced the interior of the cabin. The blunt end of the tank was pointed out the door.

Leveling the end of his pistol so it was touching the nozzle, he pulled the trigger. A blast of gas shot out at and threatened to rip his clothes off his body and tear the gas mask off his face. For a split second, he was trapped in the winds of a poisonous hurricane. He stumbled backward and clutched at his mask to keep it tight on his face. Behind him, the damaged nozzle buzzed into the train's interior wall and stuck there like a mysterious, industrial-age shuriken.

The deadly wind broke as the canister shot off out the open door.

As it moved, the gas made a sort of grotesque gurgling noise as it all struggled to explode out of the tiny opening at once. It sounded like someone had opened a giant bottle of beer and was pouring it out.

Behind the train, Ernest Hives's passenger had leaned out the window to fire off another shot at the interior of the train. The canister streaked through the air like an oblong artillery shell, shooting straight ahead amid a rocket flare of poisonous gas.

Moving like a bat out of hell, the impromptu projectile that sailed off the back of the train arced directly through the battered car's windshield. Jagged shards of glass exploded into the interior of the vehicle, spraying Ernest and slicing at his flesh.

His partner wasn't so lucky. The metal tube entered the windshield on the passenger side like a battering ram. It struck the Yersinia security guard in the chest and kept going. His ribs collapsed inward in a rapid-fire series of snaps and crackles. The canister pulverized his lungs to hot jam and simultaneously released a massive cloudburst of poison directly into his body cavity.

Burrowing deeper, like a carrion bird stuffing its head into a body to fish out the tenderest sweetmeats, the canister punched through the man's spinal column, severing it. The canister only stopped its relentless march forward when it smashed into the upholstery and springs of the seat behind the passenger. Had the man's body not cushioned the blow, the tank might have shot through the entire car.

However, it was now wedged firmly in the interior of the vehicle. The passenger flailed his arms in grotesque death spasms, the gun falling from his unfeeling fingers. Bloody foam erupted from his mouth and nostrils as his innards were violently compressed out of the way of the canister sticking out of his chest. His eyes rolled up into their sockets even before the last of the bloody sputum leaked out of his mouth.

Mr. Hives was not so lucky. Behind the glare of headlights, Jasper could see the outline of Ernest flailing at his face. His hands came off the steering wheel as he tugged at his gas mask, and the vehicle drifted to one side. The spray of glass had sliced open his skin, leaving exposed wounds, and shredded his gas mask.

From the passenger seat beside him, a white stream of high-pressure prussic acid erupted out of the hole in the canister. The stream sprayed into the car in a directed gust, like an out-of-control blowtorch.

In a matter of seconds, the entire vehicle was filled with a deadly haze, angry wisps leaking out of the open windows.

Ernest slammed on the brakes. His mask was breached. He had open cuts all over his upper body. The gas was in his blood, coursing through his veins and shutting down his body's ability to process oxygen.

He stopped the car and threw open the door, stumbling out of the deadly hotbox. His eyes bulged in their sockets as he clawed at the slashed seals on his mask.

The other two Yersinia cars darted into the side-tunnel and raced around their stalled comrade, nearly running Ernest down in the process. That might have been a mercy. He was already dead on his feet. Making horrible noises deep in his throat, he fell down to his knees.

Jasper was already preparing another canister when more headlights rounded the bend and appeared behind the train.

Cripes. How many men did Ray even have left? Were the entire remnants of the Yersinia force down here?

Then he realized that these headlights were different. They were higher off the ground, meaning bigger vehicles. The first of the new vehicles passed by one of the sputtering arc lights, and Jasper saw that it was much larger than the sedans the Yersinia men were using. It was boxy and painted black. In fact, they all were.

Jasper would recognize those outlines anywhere. They were black war-era ambulances.

Oh hell.

Upon catching sight of the train, the first ambulance surged forward, its heavy engine roaring even above the clatter of the train. It came to the stopped Yersinia vehicle and passed on its left.

It smashed directly into Ernest Hive's kneeling form with a dull thump. His head left a sizable dent in the front grillwork, but the ambulance kept moving as if nothing had happened. The ambulances moved forward in coordinated single file, like the Grim Reaper and his posse late to a swinging funeral party.

Seeing the glimmer of headlights in their mirrors, the two Yersinia cars realized that they had unfriendly company. The tunnel grew wider as multiple tracks converged and ran parallel to each other, a junction where several lines met. The Yersinia cars sped up and sped through a gap in the heavy beams separating the tracks, moving to either side of the train.

One was slower than the other and struggled to catch up. Its motor strained and farted, accelerating much slower than its cousin. The faster vehicle sped past, and Jasper caught a glimpse of Ray Armstrong in the passenger seat glancing out the window behind him.

He looked up, and their eyes met for a second. Time froze, and Jasper felt an electric tingle as his old partner's eyes bore into his. Even behind the gas mask, Jasper recognized his old friend.

Over the years, he had often wondered how he never saw the sickness hidden inside Ray. Was he really such a poor judge of people? Or was there something that crawled inside peoples' thoughts and changed them to monsters?

Staring into Ray's glittering eyes behind his mask, Jasper decided he had his answer, or at least part of it. What overtook Ray wasn't some invasive force that took over his mind. It was a sickness from within.

He thought back to his memories of his youth and the charming, witty friend he'd shared his goals with. That clear-eyed man was dead, broken by his constant need for something, anything bigger and better. Ray could never be content, and it hatched into an unscratchable itch.

And for that, Jasper pitied him.

As the car sped past, Ray raised his claw up to his mouth, apparently forgetting he didn't have a hand to cup anymore. He shouted something. The wind whipped most of the statement away, but Jasper was pretty sure it was, "Asshole!"

The first canister Jasper had opened fizzled out, the last of its contents escaping in a little puff. Jasper shoved it out the back of the train. It bounced on the tracks, and the slower Yersinia car had to swerve around it to avoid crashing into the obstacle. The ambulances, still gaining, mirrored the moved and dodged around the tank as it came to rest on the tracks.

He spun the nozzle on a fresh tank, and a new stream of poison gas began drifting out the back of the train. He needed to keep the gas flowing if he wanted to scrub the tunnels free of the menace that had taken up residence in them. There couldn't be too many pockets of fresh air.

Just as he finished uncapping the new supply of gas, the ambulances pulled up beside the slower Yersinia car. The huge black vehicle loomed over the sedan.

A hand reached out from the passenger window of the ambulance and pointed something directly down at the driver's side of the smaller car. The tunnel burned brightly for a brief instant as the sawed-off shotgun went off, unloading both barrels.

The effect was instantaneous. Pellets whizzed out in a wicked spread, buzz-sawing through the sedan's thin roof. The blast smeared the Yersinia driver across the interior of the vehicle. He didn't so much slump as splash across his partner in the passenger seat.

Without a driver, the Yersinia car began to wobble on its course. Not bothering to slow down, the ambulance swerved to the side and sideswiped the Yersinia car.

Out of control, the smaller car flipped over onto its side and grated over the tracks. A gap in its shredded roof caught the protective sheathing that covered the third rail and tore it away as metal crumpled and oil flew.

The chassis of the chair came into contact with the electrified third rail, and a massive blast of energy surged through the vehicle. Tumbling unrestrained through the interior of the car, the passenger shrieked as the electricity surged into the vehicle's metal frame.

Both his clothing and the upholstery burst into blue flame, and his body danced a crazed mambo as more power surged through it. In a matter of seconds, a massive fireball devoured the vehicle whole. The crackling fire illuminated the entire tunnel as the ambulances continued past the wrecked, burning vehicle.

Jasper watched as the convoy of vampire hunters accelerated toward the train. This was not going to be pretty.

Chapter 25
Tickets, Please

Jasper kicked another canister into place as the ambulances lined up behind the train. There were no fewer than ten vehicles in the group, all of them storming forward at full speed. He grimaced.

Ralitza Petkova and her people wanted to stop Ray, too. The enemy of his enemy should have been his friend. Unfortunately, life was rarely so simple. If their actions involved at least some color of the law, they might have been allies, but Ralitza and her men had only one goal: exterminate the creatures and everyone associated with them.

He was fully behind the first part. In fact, that was what he was trying to do right now. However, the chaos the vampire hunters had caused was too much. People died when they raided the Yersinia charity ball, and they'd murdered a substantial portion of the company's upper echelons in cold blood.

Jasper only operated according to the law when it was convenient to him, but that didn't mean he murdered his way out of a problem. There were institutions much better equipped to administer justice than a bunch of vigilantes with stakes.

He sighed to himself. They'd already crossed paths once before, and it hadn't gone well. These people were well-equipped, well-trained, utterly fanatical, and very, very wrong about what was happening here. Oh, and they wanted to kill him.

May the flaming bridges behind him light his way forward.

He pulled the trigger on his FN Model 1922 pistol just as he saw a hand emerge from the passenger window of the lead ambulance again, both bores of the sawed-off shotgun aimed directly at the rear of the train and Jasper.

One of Jasper's bullets ripped the nozzle off another canister and sent it sailing out the back of the train like a torpedo.

The ambulance was both larger and farther back than a Yersinia sedan, so the tube couldn't go through its windshield, but there was no time for the big vehicle to swerve. The gigantic metal lozenge shot straight out and buried itself in the front grill of the truck, just above the dent Ernest Hives's skull had made. The tube tore straight through the thin metal protecting the front of the vehicle and pierced the engine compartment.

The canister smashed through the fan and struck the engine block itself. Metal crashed and howled like Vulcan's forge on overdrive. Striking the engine, the blunt end of the tube was pushed inward until it crumpled and ruptured.

Breached at both ends, the canister lost all structural integrity and the enormous pressure locked inside caused it to explode. Flanged metal shot through the engine block, spraying oil and coolant and shearing off pistons. The shrapnel wasn't contained to just the engine compartment, either. It pierced through into the passenger area like a hungry whirlwind. The strips of metal sheared off flesh and punctured organs. The two vampire hunters virtually melted under the spall.

All of this happened faster than Jasper's eyes could blink. One second the ambulance was accelerating toward him. The next, the entire front portion of the vehicle was a cratered mass of jagged metal and shattered internal mechanisms. Blood and oil leaked to the ground as the unmanned vehicle slouched off to one side and ground up against brickwork of the wall.

The other drivers saw what happened and fanned out into the side-tunnel to avoid a similar fate. That still left nine vehicles full of angry monster hunters to deal with, though.

Swerving around their downed comrade, the vehicles moved up to flank the train. Surely they weren't going to try what he thought they were about to try. Oh, surely not.

But it looked like that was exactly what they were about to try. The ambulances accelerated in two columns moving to either side of the train as it screamed down the tracks.

At his feet, the second canister of prussic acid breathed its last. A final puff of gas wheezed out of the open nozzle, leaving only a residual amount of poison left in the container. Jasper kicked the empty out of the back of the train and watched it bounce into the darkness. It clanged off the tracks and disappeared.

He ran over and grabbed another just as the first ambulance pulled even with the train car. Submachine gun fire chewed a hole through the wall of the train, and Jasper threw himself onto the floor.

A stray bullet struck one of the canisters lying on a seat. The bullet punctured the metal, and the tube took off at a crazy angle, corkscrewing across the aisle and knocking several more canisters onto the floor. It careened over Jasper's head, crop dusting him with the powerful insecticide contained within, and then it shot straight through the opposite wall, ripping a hole large enough to throw a medium-sized dog through.

He was going to owe a hefty IOU to the city of New York by the time this was over. Assuming he survived, of course, which didn't look particularly likely if things kept up at this pace. Hopefully, the city had some heavy-duty insurance.

Taking the canister he'd grabbed, he pivoted it around to the side. He'd intended to release the gas at a normal rate out the rear of the train, but screw it. Through the windows, he could see the ambulance pull even with him, the passenger handing the driver a fresh drum magazine for his Tommy gun. Not three feet of space separated Jasper from the man behind the wheel.

He propped the tube up on the seat and fired his pistol at the nozzle. With an angry rush, the canister shot off and tore through the wall of the train car like a fist through cheap drywall. It crashed through the driver's side door of the ambulance, too, smashing it inward in a way the hinges were never designed to go.

The tube struck the driver just above the hip with enough force to pulp his liver and instantly cause massive, irreparable internal damage. He was carried out of his seat like a mouse snatched off the ground by a hawk.

Colliding against his partner in the passenger seat with bone-snapping force, the canister propelled them both to the side. Both of the men collided against the door with enough force to blast it off the vehicle's frame. They shot outside and smashed against the tunnel wall like a pair of bugs hitting a windshield. The ambulance slewed to the left and crashed into the side wall, screeching to a halt amid a spray of sparks and grinding noises.

The other drivers weren't stupid. They saw what was happening and decided not to linger as they moved past on either side. No one tried to shoot at Jasper and risk having another salvo of makeshift artillery directed at them. All eight ambulances zoomed by, four on either side.

Jasper didn't waste the opportunity. He lugged another cylinder to the rear exit and unscrewed the nozzle. Another steady stream of fumes began to emit from the tube. He slammed a new clip into his pistol and began moving toward the front of the train.

There would only be a minute to prepare for what was about to happen, so he knew he had to think of something. He opened the door leading to the next car.

Further up, the first ambulance pulled even with a gap between the cars two up. The vehicle's rear doors flew open. The area that would normally be used for stretchers and medical equipment was filled with five black-clad vampire hunters.

One by one, they made the short leap onto the train, boarding like modern-day pirates running down a merchant vessel. Jasper cursed to himself as he saw what was happening. The vampire hunters fanned out and began moving toward the rear of the train. They moved in distinct groups, three advancing and two staying behind the train's seats to cover before the groups leapfrogged each other. One group would advance while the next provided cover fire. It was a solid tactic meant to corner him and flush him out.

They advanced quickly, checking behind seats to see where he was hiding. Jasper wriggled into a hiding spot, holding his fire. He was going to need to time this just right if he wanted to make it through this alive. He was outnumbered and injured, and they were trained and precise, a bad combination if there ever was one.

Finally, they reached the last car, where Jasper was lurking in wait. The gas canister hissed like a furious serpent at the rear of the train. Sweat beaded up on Jasper's forehead and dribbled down the inside of his mask as he watched through the eyeholes.

The first three vampire hunters eased up to the door separating the last car from the rest. They'd just cleared all the forward cars except for the engine. They knew he was in there.

Their leader counted with his fingers. On three, they threw the door open and stormed in. Simultaneously, the two rear vampire hunters moved into the position their comrades had just vacated.

The three inside the rear car looked around in confusion. Jasper wasn't in the final car.

He swung down off the roof of the last car, from directly above the two rear hunters. They looked up in surprise as a gray streak swooped down on them like a vengeful phantom.

Jasper directed his swing to the side, gripping the overhang with one hand. Using all his momentum and weight, he slammed his feet into the chest of the first vampire hunter, a woman with dark eyes. Her gun went off as he shoved her backward over the waist-high rail. The bullet punched into the ceiling and through the spot Jasper had occupied on top of the train a second before. She gave a startled squawk and then disappeared over the rail.

Whipping around, Jasper pulled out his pistol and fired off three quick shots. There was no time to take cover from the three surprised vampire hunters in the rear car. They'd been moving under the assumption that their backs were covered, that any attack would come from the front, not the back. They went down in short order, sprawled in triplicate.

The last hunter had the most time to react. He raised his Tommy gun from a distance of no greater than two feet. Jasper didn't have time to swing his gun around the full ninety degrees he needed to draw on the man.

He lurched forward, stepping nose-to-nose with the hunter, stepping inside the arc of the Tommy gun's barrel. The man squeezed the trigger and unleashed a blaze of bullets, but it was already too late. He couldn't pull the gun back far enough to bring it to bear on Jasper. They stood as close as lovers performing a sensual tango.

Jasper was too close to use his own gun as well, so he dropped it to free up his good hand. He reached up, grabbed a fistful of the man's gas mask, and tipped backward. The straps holding the mask in place snapped like old rubber bands, and the protective gear came free.

The man gasped in surprise, and his eyes went wide. After launching several gas cylinder missiles from the rear car, the air inside the train was just as toxic as anywhere else in the tunnels. Dropping his gun, the hunter clawed at Jasper, but it was too late. It only took a few seconds for the poison to work its way into his system, digging its claws deep into his body at the cellular level.

His knees gave out, and he collapsed in shuddering convulsions. Foaming spittle welled up around his lips, but he was already unconscious. The noxious atmosphere down here would kill just about anything in a matter of seconds. At least Jasper hoped so. If not, this entire exercise was pointless.

The man had a German potato masher grenade tied to his vest. Jasper grabbed it and tucked the handle into his belt. He snatched up his pistol, too.

A second ambulance pulled even with a gap further up between the cars, and another five vampire hunters jumped aboard. Their ride peeled off so another could take its place and unload more hunters. He had to move fast or he'd be overwhelmed. If the odds jumped to ten to one, he was in very deep kimchee.

This group had a better plan than the last. Rather than advancing toward Jasper and risking being attacked from close range in the confines of one of the train cars, they stayed in place in the gap between cars. Three of the hunters took turns sending potshots down the length of the train, forcing Jasper to take cover. The other two began working at the floor grating, prying it up.

Jasper suddenly realized what they were going to do. With him pinned in the rear car, they were going to decouple the train. The engine would continue forward of its own power, but the rear cars would slowly coast to a halt. Then he'd be stranded, like a naval disaster survivor stuck in a lifeboat as the sharks slowly circled. There were a lot more vampire hunters than there were of him. If they caused the train to stop, they could put his car under siege and pump the entire cabin full of lead.

He poked his head up from behind a seat to fire off a shot at the two working at the coupling, but a bullet nearly parted his hair. Ducking back down, Jasper counted his options. He only had a few seconds before the second ambulance pulled up and disgorged more of Ralitza Petkova's people. He might have even less time before the ones already on board found the release lever and sent him sliding to a deadly halt.

Taking a deep breath, he readied himself to spring up and vault the row of seats. He would have to fire as he went, hopefully hitting a couple of the vampire hunters and at least scaring the rest into taking cover for a second. Maybe he could lob the grenade at them, too, really scatter them. It was a crap plan, as likely to get him killed as anything else, and there was no way he could take out all five of the men before he had to slip back into cover. But that was the only option he had left.

His legs trembling from excitement and the adrenaline of being shot at, he bolted upright. A cascade of gunfire echoed down the train car, shots coming in rapid order.

The two men lifting the grate went down in dual sprays of blood. Jasper saw the head of the man on the left suddenly deform to one side as a round entered his skull and smacked against the interior of his braincase on the other side without exiting. In the span of less than a second, the three hiding behind the edges of the door to the car went down like bowling pins, their legs falling out from under them.

Amelia stood in the next car behind them, smoke billowing from the end of her Luger. Jasper stood dumbly in the aisle, his unfired pis-tol in his hand. Another ambulance was pulling close but hadn't seen Amelia yet.

She flicked her wrist to the side and fired her remaining rounds into the ambulance's windshield. Star-shaped holes bloomed to life in front of the driver's seat, and a delicate spider web of cracks spread across the glass. The vehicle continued straight for a second before it slewed to the right and crashed into the side of the train.

The impact wasn't hard enough to break through the train's outer wall and into the passenger compartment, but it did cause the entire wall to wobble and bulge for a second. The impact with the train sent the ambulance bouncing back the other way, where it crashed directly into a steel support beam. Trying to grab the steering wheel out of his colleague's dead fingers, the passenger was catapulted straight through the damaged windshield. Anchored into the ground and roof, the steel beam acted almost like a huge straight razor blade, almost shearing the ambulance in half.

"Don't you need to be at the controls?" Jasper asked.

"Yeah. You're welcome. It sounded like you needed a hand. Re-lax, Tex. We're not going to derail. This area's straight enough that so long as I leave the speed steady, we should be fine." Amelia reloaded her gun with a single, smooth movement.

Jasper plucked the grenade out of his waistband. "Here, I got you something special."

"Oh, you shouldn't have." Amelia took the explosive and checked the pin.

"I need to keep the gas flowing. You keep this area clear. I'll be back in a minute." Jasper took off toward the rearmost car. The open canister was starting to fade, its steady hiss pitching higher as more and more of its contents escaped.

He threw another cylinder down on the floor and uncorked it like an oversized bottle of champagne. The hissing noise redoubled. Jasper kicked the empty out the back of the train and watched it clatter back into the darkness.

Suddenly, his eyes picked up stray movement where there should have been nothing. The train passed by another of the arc lights unevenly spaced through the tunnels, and he caught a better look at the area behind the train.

He stopped breathing for a second.

He was staring directly at what should not have been. Even knowing exactly what he was looking at, he couldn't quite believe it. A shiver climbed up his spine.

The inhuman figure, pale and awful, stepped into the light. Jasper gripped his pistol, not at all sure it would do any good against the dreadful thing. Speeding away, the train put distance between Jasper and the figure.

This was definitely the thing he caught a glimpse of in the tunnels before, when it killed the two Yersinia guards. Perhaps not the exact same one, but another of the same kind. There was no mistaking the alien way it moved. Everything about it put Jasper's hackles up, some deep-rooted instinct bristling to life.

The creature tensed its legs and leaped forward. Jasper didn't even have time to react. The leap took the creature straightforward almost one hundred feet. It soared through the air as smoothly as if it had been shot out of a cannon. When it landed on the tracks, its feet cracked one of the wooden crossbeams in half.

He tried to draw a bead on the monster, but it moved too fast. With impossible speed, it shot forward again, seemingly blinking from location to location. The thing moved like death itself, a pale streak in the darkness.

The prussic acid was supposed to kill these things. Jasper looked down at the hissing tube by his feet. Gas rippled out of its nozzle and faded into the tunnel, but it didn't seem to be doing any good. The creature tensed up, and Jasper knew what was coming next.

Blasting forward again, it reappeared not twenty feet behind the train, directly in front of Jasper. Before he came to collect the canisters from the Yersinia depot, Jasper had gone to the New York State Library and done a little research in some of their dustier tomes. What he'd found hadn't been good, but nothing had prepared him for *this*.

Another leap and the creature would be on him. Its claws were already stretched out to receive him, its beady eyes locked onto his.

Jasper leveled his pistol and fired while the beast was stopped. He pulled the trigger as quickly as he could. Shells dropped to the ground as the gun fired its last round and slapped dry.

The inhuman monstrosity gave no indication that it had even been hit. It didn't stagger or reel backward the way a man would upon absorbing an entire fusillade of bullets. Jasper was sure he'd hit it, absolutely sure, but there was no sign to prove it.

Not good. Not good at all.

He started to reload as he saw the creature's legs tense up for another leap. This one would certainly land it on the train, directly in front of Jasper. Those claws would latch onto him, pin him in place, and then it would be all over.

He tried to maneuver the gun and reach for a clip at the same time, but it was difficult with only one hand. His hot fingertips touched the cool metal of a fresh clip and started to pull it out of his pocket, but it slipped on a bead of sweat. The clip tumbled to the floor and landed with a clatter. Bullets spilled out and rolled under the nearest seat.

Jasper looked up, fully expecting to see the thing pop into existence directly in front of him like some sort of nightmarish jack in the box.

Instead, it took a wobbly half-step forward and performed an awkward jump that only took it about ten feet, well short of the receding train. On landing, the monster's legs collapsed under it, and it fell to the ground in a kicking, struggling heap.

The gas! The gas worked after all. It simply took a while to take effect. As the train continued forward, Jasper watched the monster's leg continue to kick mindlessly in a death spasm. Finally, as the creature receded completely into the darkness, Jasper watched the legs go still and curl up to the figure's abdomen in a crude fetal position.

Opening a fresh container of prussic acid, Jasper darted back up toward the front of the train as more gunfire erupted from the cars further up. He pulled out a new magazine and slapped it in place as he dashed away.

He arrived just in time to see two ambulances trying to unload their cargo on the train at the same time. They were getting smart, trying to board multiple parties at once, hoping to overwhelm the two detectives, but they were running short on men. The narrowness of the tracks and high rate of speed made it difficult to launch a coordinated attack. If everyone could get on the train at once, he and Amelia would have already been dead.

The rear doors of the vehicle closest to Amelia opened up, and a crew of vampire hunters appeared, all guns and crucifixes. Almost as soon as the doors opened, something landed inside the ambulance's rear bay at the hunters' feet.

While Amelia ducked and tossed away the grenade's pin, all eyes turned to the metal device rolling across the floor of the ambulance. One of the vampire hunters reached out to grab the grenade and throw it back when the entire tunnel suddenly bloomed bright yellow and orange.

Jasper threw himself inside the alcove between two cars as the ambulance tore itself apart in a twisted wad of flames. The rear of the vehicle blew apart like an oversized firecracker, the vehicle's walls first expanding, then disintegrating as they failed to contain the explosion and ensuing compression blast. Metal snowflakes tore through the tunnel, shredding everything around them as the fuel tank ignited and sprayed burning gasoline against the walls and side of the train.

Almost immediately, the fire started to lick at the train's wooden paneling. Pieces of flaming metal tore through the walls and spread the flames into the train's interior as well. Jasper looked around but didn't see anything to extinguish the flames. If they didn't act fast, the entire train might catch fire.

Unfortunately, they didn't have time to put out the fire. The ambulance that had sped ahead threw its doors open, and three vampire hunters jumped into the next car.

There was another problem, though. Most of the vehicles seemed to have five hunters in them. This one only had three boarders because there was something else taking up the additional space. Another hunter stood behind a shiny new Maxim machine gun mounted on a swivel.

This was shaping up to be a really bad day.

Jasper and Amelia both went to the ground as the machine gun unleashed a hail of bullets. Brass cartridges spilled out the rear of the ambulance as bullets chewed the train car to pieces. The windows shattered and sprayed glass across the interior of the cabin. Chips of wood flew in every direction as the weapon crossed back and forth down the length of the car.

Bullets stitched their way across the wall a foot above Jasper's head. Beside him, Amelia cursed loudly in Spanish. Jasper wasn't sure what she was saying, but it sounded like it would turn a sailor's hair white.

The machine gun made a noise like a giant length of sailcloth tearing before it fell silent. The operator needed to load a new belt into the weapon.

"I got one," Jasper said.

"One what?"

"One of the creatures. The poison gas killed it."

"Good job, Van Helsing. You got any ideas about this?"

Jasper looked up and down the length of the car. It had been chewed to bits. It looked like a hurricane had swept through and torn the place apart. Smoke rose from where the fire was beginning to take hold. He couldn't smell it through his gas mask, but it clouded his vision, and he could feel the heat.

Options. He needed options. He could go back to the rear of the train and grab another cylinder of prussic acid to use as a missile.

The three vampire hunters who had hopped aboard appeared in the doorway to the next car. Jasper and Amelia rolled to opposite sides of the aisle as another burst of hot lead zipped toward them.

Jasper's broken hand screamed at him as he rolled over it. The stiff cast prevented any serious damage, but the sudden pressure sent the jagged bone edges shearing against each other. He gritted his teeth as little yellow spots exploded to life in front of his eyes. Taking a deep breath, he beat back the pain and steadied himself. Amelia returned fire and forced the vampire hunters to jump back while he paused to gather his wits again.

Getting a tank of gas from the rear car was out. He'd be ripped to shreds trying to move down that long, straight aisle all the way back. It might as well be a shooting gallery.

Another blast of machine gun fire tore into the train. The shooter couldn't see them to pinpoint where they were in the train, and the ambulance was bouncing like a bucking bronco over the crossties. The weapon's operator was working off the assumption that if he poured enough bullets into the train, he'd get lucky eventually. Jasper didn't think the man was wrong.

The flames grew hotter as they spread. Jasper watched as it started to burn through the wall in one place. The movement of the train fed it a steady supply of oxygen, encouraging its growth. If they didn't do something, it would engulf the entire car and then the entire train.

"I hate to say it, but we're going to run out of straight track soon," Amelia said. "I'll need to get back up to the controls to regulate our speed. If we hit a bad patch going too fast, we might derail."

"I think I have a plan," Jasper said. He explained what she needed to do. Amelia started swearing in Spanish again.

Chapter 26
All Aboard

Amelia dashed back to the second car as Jasper popped up and fired a few rounds at the vampire hunters aboard the train. The hunters danced back and took cover. Jasper disappeared again as the Maxim machine gun opened up again and unleashed another wave of devastation on the interior of the train.

She scrambled up the ladder on the side of the train and shimmied onto the roof. There wasn't enough room to stand; there was barely enough room to crouch. Remaining on her stomach, she crawled forward.

From below, she could feel the growing heat of the fire starting to spread through the car below. It was hot against her palms and stomach. Smoke billowed past her, obscuring her view as she slid forward, pushing with her feet. Arc lights whizzed past in staccato bursts of brightness.

Moving as quietly as she could, she dragged herself toward the opposite side of the car. She felt like a piece of meat on a barbeque as the fire built up below. The roof of the tunnel was only a couple feet above her head, and sometimes low-hanging cables threatened to snag her and rip her from her precarious perch. At this speed, the cables might very well decapitate her.

As she reached the third quarter of her journey, gunfire broke out below. A stray bullet punched through the thin roof three feet to her right. As she stared at the tiny hole, jagged splinters poking up from its edges, the Maxim machine gun opened up again with a roar like the end of the world but louder and opened up a hole right next to her. Inside the compressed space of the tunnel, the noise was gargantuan, well above the threshold of pain. Trapped in the ambulance's compartment, the gunner and driver would probably be deaf for days.

She wanted to clamp her hands over her ears, but she was afraid she might start to sizzle if she stopped moving. Her mask protected her from the acrid fumes all around, but it made the heat even worse. The mask's rubber stuck to her skin. Sweaty strands of hair plastered her forehead.

Directly ahead of her, a gasmask-decked face appeared. Behind the glass lenses, the man's eyes widened as he caught sight of Amelia. Either the vampire hunters had figured out what she was doing, or they had the same idea and were sending one of their people across the top of the train in an ambush of their own.

The man tried to hang onto the ladder with one hand and bring his submachine gun to bear with the other. In the tight space between cars, the weapon's barrel caught on a rung, and he had to wrench it free.

That was all the time Amelia needed. Her pistol barked in her hands, and one of the lenses on the man's gas mask blew out. A red hole gazed out at Amelia where the eye had been a moment ago, and the man slipped off the ladder. There was a *thud* and a shout from below.

Time to move. Amelia rolled to the side as a bullet typhoon crashed through the roof of the train, tearing gashes in the wood and tin large enough for her to stick her fist through. Her shot had given away her position, spoiling the ambush.

She paused for a second at the edge of the train and looked at the ground rushing by below. Then she turned and saw the roof of the train bucking up and down as holes blasted through it. Flames licked through some of the holes.

She wouldn't survive if she tried to stay on top of the train. There was no choice. She plunged over the side of the car and landed on top of the black ambulance pacing the train, exactly as planned. She thudded gracelessly onto the top of its converted machine gun bay. Before the gunner inside could react, Amelia scrambled forward onto the roof of the cab like a spider on a skillet. A second later, machine gun fire peeled the roof off the top of the ambulance.

She jumped onto the hood. Behind the windshield, the ambulance driver stared at her in slack-jawed amazement. Amelia raised her gun to blow out the glass, but the driver recovered from his surprise and twisted the wheel hard to the left.

Amelia had to use both hands to hang onto the hood as the driver twisted the wheel back and forth. She grabbed onto the windshield wipers to steady herself as the driver tried to throw her off.

That lasted for all of a second. One of the wipers snapped off in her hands as the driver sent the ambulance careening across the tracks. With a crash, he sideswiped the train. Black paint scraped off the side of the ambulance to reveal the original drab military colors beneath.

The collision sent Amelia sliding, flipping her onto her back. She came half off the edge of the hood as the remaining wiper blade bent in her hand.

Pulling herself back to the center of the hood, she reached out and tried to grab the side mirror. It came off the vehicle as she pulled it, nearly spilling her onto the tracks, but she managed to keep hold of the mirror. She brought it down on the front window, using the hard frame to smash a hole in the windshield. Sparkling shards of glass spilled into the ambulance's interior as she bashed away more of the windshield and found a grip on the vehicle's frame. The driver reached for a pistol on the dashboard, but Amelia threw herself headfirst through the gaping hole in the glass. Jagged pieces of glass tugged at her clothes as she scratched at the driver, her legs dangling through the shattered windshield.

He punched and thrashed at her, trying to shove her away. With his other hand, he reached for the gun again. Amelia swept it onto the floor, but the move left her wide open. The driver punched her on the side of the neck as she tried to twist away.

No longer under anyone's control, the ambulance drifted over the tracks like a rogue comet, streaking this way and that as the wheel was jostled and shoved during the struggle. The interior of the ambulance was a maelstrom of awkwardly aimed blows and counter-blows as its occupants fought like two feral cats trapped in a sack.

The driver tried to bring both hands up and get them around Amelia's throat. Instead of warding off the hands moving toward her, Amelia reached past them. She grabbed a fistful of the hunter's shirt just below the neckline as his own hands settled around her neck.

She gave a sharp yank with all her might, jerking the man toward her and pulling herself forward at the same time. His mask crunched inward, breaking his nose.

Yowling, he released his hands from around Amelia's throat and threw them to his face. His nose was broken underneath his gas mask. A few specks of blood smeared the inside of the eyeholes. In a few seconds, the blood would gush out and completely stop up the inside of his mask, making it difficult to breathe.

The other ambulances were slowing down and dropping away. She looked over her shoulder and saw why. Up ahead, the tunnel narrowed as one of the tracks split off onto a new route. There wasn't enough room for a vehicle to run beside the train anymore.

The driver ducked down and fished for his gun near the accelerator pedal. Unpleasant sniffling noises filled the passenger compartment as blood filled his mask and interfered with his breathing.

Amelia grabbed him by the back of the collar and wrenched him back. He shoved at her, and she slammed his head against the steering wheel. Stunned, he tried to take a swing at her. She deflected the blow and punched him hard enough to force him up against the door.

Shifting her legs up, Amelia twisted around and lashed out with a foot. She put her entire body into it, booting the driver square in the ribs. He made a noise somewhere between a gasp and a scream as the kick smashed him against the door.

With a snap, the door's latch broke, and the door swung open. The vampire hunter tumbled out of the speeding vehicle and was swallowed by the abyss. Amelia shifted into the driver's seat and brought her foot down on the gas pedal. Her heart pounded against her ribs, and as she rubbed her neck, could feel the faint impression of the man's calloused, cracked hands on her throat.

The ambulance humped its way forward, struggling to pick up any speed against the train. She had almost reached the branch in the tunnel. If she didn't brake and move behind the train, the ambulance would be crushed like a walnut in a vice. But if she hit the brakes, she'd be stuck behind the train, unable to get back on board, which would leave Jasper alone to deal with the vampire hunters already on the train.

Behind her, a slot opened up between the driver's section and the rear compartment. The gunner started to ask a question in what sounded like Greek only to realize that his driver was no longer aboard. The slot slammed shut.

Amelia pulled up even with the gap between train cars and glanced over. Right next to her, the remaining two vampire hunters on board the train had taken cover to either side of the doorway. They were less than two feet away.

One of them looked over at the ambulance and realized who was driving it. He was frantically signaling to his partner when Amelia dropped both of them with a pistol from the passenger seat. Propping the door open, she stepped over the short gap and boosted herself up onto the train.

Behind her, the ambulance started to slow with no one at the wheel. It fell back to about a third of the way down the car when the track split off and the tunnel suddenly narrowed. The brickwork rose up like the swell of a tsunami and slammed the ambulance into the side of the train.

Rough brickwork scoured the side of the ambulance, stripping away metal in a fireworks show of sparks. The ambulance screamed like an injured cat. The train's wall bulged inward, straining and groaning.

Squeezed from both sides, the ambulance popped up onto two wheels. Its right-hand wheels thumped along on the sidewall, and its headlights tilted at a crazy angle. The train helped carry it forward, dragging it along at high speed. The vehicle crunched down to half its original size and broke away from the train with a noise like a scrap shearing machine vomiting. Amelia didn't care to think about what had happened to the gunner.

It wasn't so pretty on board the train, either. Everything was on fire, and the flames were about to spread to the adjacent cars. Amelia looked around but couldn't see Jasper anywhere.

Her heart skipped a beat. *Where was he? Surely, he hadn't...*

He popped up on the opposite side of the car. His gray suit was smudged with soot, and there were black burn marks down the length of his cast, but he was standing and alive.

Amelia waved. He waved back. Gesturing, he indicated that he needed to go back and begin spraying with a new gas cylinder. She pointed to indicate that she needed to head back to the train's controls and regulate speed and power. Going too quickly could be dangerous in this section of the tunnels.

Given the roiling flames, there was no way for them to reach each other right now, but Amelia was just glad to see Jasper alive and in more or less one piece. He nodded to her from across the aisle, and then they each dashed off to perform their separate tasks.

Turning away from the fire, Amelia felt the intense heat on her back. Sweat poured down her face and pooled between her mask and her skin. The stale, filtered air felt artificial in her lungs. She would have liked nothing better than to rip off the stifling mask and take a few good, long deep breaths of slightly less stale subway air. At least the vampire hunters had been forced back behind the train, where they could now only follow instead of swarming aboard.

Now that they weren't being shot at, Amelia had time to actually look at the fire. It was spreading at an alarming rate, eating its way through the siding and roof of the train car and leaving nothing but a shell.

At this rate, they weren't going to be able to complete their circuit around the tunnels before the fire consumed the entire train. They had intended to end up at Grand Central Station to release all the gas from a central hub, but they weren't completely positive it would reach every corner of the tunnels that way. That was the purpose of spraying the perimeter first.

They were going to have to cut things short, though. If the train burned up in some obscure corner of the tunnels, the gas definitely wouldn't distribute itself through the whole system. By now, the police had probably gotten wind that there was something strange going on underground. The fumes would keep them out, but she and Jasper weren't going to get a second chance at this if they failed to hit the whole system.

Even if the cops didn't drag them off to jail, which wouldn't be at all unreasonable under the circumstances, the subway would reopen to the public in a few days. Convincing the police that they had stolen a massive quantity of prussic acid, hijacked a train, sparked a gunfight, and left a miles-long trail of destruction to exterminate sewer monsters would be a losing battle. Unless they got results, not even their Attican contacts would get them out of this one.

Amelia had taped a map of the tunnels next to the train's controls. Up ahead, there should be a junction that led to Grand Central Station. With everything shut off due to the subway's closure, she would have to stop the train and manually switch the tracks herself.

She was not looking forward to that. The vampire hunters were still behind them, albeit in much-reduced numbers. However, they could see the flames and figure out the implications. They were stalking the train like a pack of jackals trailing a wounded animal. When the train stopped completely, all hell would likely break loose.

Amelia didn't know what had happened to Ray Armstrong and his Yersinia team. They were up ahead somewhere, but she couldn't see them anymore. Maybe they decided to flee when the vampire hunters showed up in higher numbers.

Up ahead, a single red light blinked on and off. That meant the track was already diverted toward Grand Central Station. Had someone forgotten to switch the track back when the tunnels were abandoned? Had that light been flashing in the darkness for days, unattended?

Something pounced in front of the train. It simply appeared, seeming to materialize out of nothing. Amelia jumped backward in surprise.

The thing was pale and horrid. It was hairless except for some thick, inhuman bristles. Intellectually, Amelia knew what it was. She knew from the Yersinia papers she'd found at Rasmussen's house. She'd been in the tunnels when one killed those two Yersinia guards. Jasper told her he killed one with the gas. Ralitza Petkova and her vampire hunters wouldn't even be in New York City, let alone pursuing her, if not for this thing and its ilk.

But she'd never completely believed that the things existed. Her brain just couldn't bring itself to accept their existence. Something like this shouldn't have been possible, yet here it was. Yersinia had done it. The crazy sons of bitches had really done it, damn them.

Cold, dead eyes stared at Amelia through the glass, displaying no emotion, no empathy, nothing remotely human. The eyes were pure black, with no visible iris or cornea, like shark eyes.

The creature had made a mistake, though. Apparently attracted by the flickering movement and warmth of the fire, it hadn't realized that the approaching light show was actually an incoming train.

There was a saying about curiosity and cats. The train slammed into the creature at full speed. Amelia felt a small tremor in the train's movement as it ran down the monstrosity and ground it against the undercarriage. Blood and some yellowish ichor Amelia couldn't identify splashed against the train's front window. The fluids beaded and dripped away.

"Oh, *good one*, Dracula," Amelia muttered to herself. Masters of cunning these things weren't. It made her feel safer knowing that, even if these things were unnatural abominations, and their existence rattled her perceptions of what existed out there, they, being experimental freaks, might be shit-stupid.

In the end, they were just animals. Huge, swift-moving animals with a penchant for the blood of the living that were almost impossible to kill through conventional methods. No wonder Yersinia thought they could use them as biological weapons. Still, she felt vaguely comforted in a way she couldn't fully articulate. The things could be duped and destroyed, and that was exactly what she and Jasper were going to do.

The train passed the flashing red light and split off into a side tunnel, heading for the heart of the underground labyrinth. All roads led to Rome down here, and they would be at the station in a matter of minutes. On either side, the tunnel narrowed further, reduced to just a single track, further preventing any attempt by the vampire hunters to assault the train.

The flames from the rear portion of the train helped light the way ahead. Amelia could feel the heat at her back. By now the fire must have spread to the adjacent cars. Pretty soon, it would eat through all the hydraulic cables and cause the brakes to malfunction. When she glanced backward, she could see flaming debris fall off the train to the tracks like a trail of fiery bread crumbs.

They were almost to Grand Central Station now, and the tracks widened again as another route converged with their tunnel and ran parallel. She could see a faint glow ahead, the proverbial light at the end of the tunnel. That must be the station. Even though there was now enough room to run beside the train again, the vampire hunters kept their distance. Good.

She suddenly found out where Ray Armstrong had gone. Even outgunned and nearly out of men, he hadn't been chased off.

That flashing red light hadn't been on since the subway closed. It probably hadn't been on for more than fifteen minutes because Ray was the one who had switched the track. When he sped ahead, it wasn't to run away, it was to set up an ambush.

Directly in front of them, the tracks had been blown apart. She could still see the burn marks on the cement where the explosives destroyed the rails. Twisted steel lay all around the large hole where the tracks had once stood.

There was no way for her to stop the train in time. There was barely enough time to grab onto something as the train ground its way along the remains of the track. Amelia's teeth rattled in her skull, and the train wailed like Satan's chorus girls.

The train hit the hole where the tracks were completely gone and thundered onto the bare concrete. For a second, Amelia thought she could ride it out, and the train would simply grind to a halt at the edge of Grand Central Station.

Then the rear cars hit the gap and bunched up like a centipede with scoliosis. Several tons of locomotive bucked and kicked and chewed violent grooves in the floor of the tunnel. Amelia screamed as the entire train began to list and then tipped over completely. Her cry was drowned out by the sound of twisting metal and crunching steel.

Chapter 27
Off the Rails

Jasper was switching his attention back and forth between the approaching flames, the convoy of ambulances stalking them, and the sputtering gas tank at his feet when he heard the scream of tortured metal and the cars in front of his suddenly went crooked. He grabbed onto the overhead passenger rail just as the floor dropped out from under him and the world went topsy-turvy.

His car slammed into the next one. Wood splintered with a sound like a skeleton dropped from a very great height. The gas canisters shot forward, unrestrained. Some of them pitched into the fire, the flames billowing as the car tore itself to kindling.

His arm tried to wrench itself out of its socket as the force of the crash clipped him against a beam. He rocketed into the nearest seat at an awkward angle, catching himself in the ribs.

He tried to protect his bad hand, but it smacked against the edge of the seat. Even wrapped tight in its protective cast, it felt as if his hand exploded as the bones shifted around. The pain bit at his entire arm like he'd been set upon by a pack of vicious dogs.

Before he could even check himself to see if he was okay, the car tipped over and slid around, screeching against the ground. Sparks and embers vomited out of the next car. A length of metal handrail, glowing red hot, shot through the car like a javelin and impaled itself on the wall a foot from Jasper's head.

The prussic acid canisters rattled around like pill bugs stuffed in an excited boy's collection jar. One of them flew over and struck a glancing blow on Jasper's leg. He didn't think anything could pull his attention away from the angry throbbing in his hand, but the gas canister did the trick. He screamed as the heavy metal cylinder did its best to shatter his femur.

At last, the train car crunched to a halt. Jasper lay perfectly still for a moment, not entirely sure that he was still alive. But no, the pain in his hand, and shoulder, and leg—and basically everywhere—told him he was alive. Mostly, at least.

Jasper lay flat on his back on the side of the cabin. His bad hand rested on his chest. It was trembling, and he couldn't make it stop.

With his good hand, he checked the seals on his gas mask. Everything seemed okay, which at least meant he wasn't going to poison himself on top of everything else. He tried to sit up, and his ribs reminded him that they needed some attention, too. His vision spun around and didn't quite track when he moved his head.

Unsure of what else to do, his stomach tried to throw up. He tamped down hard on his gorge. If he puked in the gas mask, he wouldn't be able to breathe; he would have to take it off, and he also wouldn't be able to breathe then, either.

He looked around. Most of the gas canisters had plunged into the fire, and the flames were about to eat those that hadn't. If he tried to grab any of them, the hot metal would cook his palm and leave a grease stain where his skin was supposed to be.

Balls.

Taking a deep breath, he squirmed his way up onto his feet. He had to rely onto the wall, formerly the roof, to keep his balance as the world swam in and out of focus. He felt like he'd been run over. Everything hurt. If this kept up, his bones were going to organize into a union and go on strike for better treatment.

Nearby, he heard the sound of heavy vehicles grind to a halt. The large engines idled as doors opened and slammed closed. Headlights poured through the open windows, and boots tromped across the ground, kicking pieces of debris out of the way.

Jasper staggered over to a large gash in the wall. He poked his head through and glanced about. The rear of the train had tilted and crashed into the tunnel's sidewall so it was flush with the brickwork. None of the vampire hunters had clambered over the wreckage to this side of the train.

That wouldn't last long. Jasper lurched out into the darkness, willing his limbs to cooperate. He moved like a drunkard kicked out of a speakeasy after a nasty bender. To keep his balance, he moved with one shoulder pressed against the wall, forcing his feet along in an awkward, forward-ish direction.

He had to find Amelia. Voices shouted in several different languages from the other side of the train. The vampire hunters were systematically clearing each compartment. He and Amelia had wiped out more than half their force, but at least twenty of them had piled out of the remaining vehicles. He would be no match for one of them in his current state, let alone a platoon of them.

As he moved forward, he slid past the other cars. Fire had completely gutted the original car, leaving little more than a smoldering chassis, but the nearby cars had blossomed into full infernos. The leading edge of the flames was halfway down the rearmost car now, gobbling up the train like a snake swallowing a row of baby ducks. Already light headed, the heat nearly wilted him, but he forced himself forward.

He felt a faint breeze on his skin as the fire sucked in air from deeper in the tunnels. If not for his gas mask, he might have collapsed from smoke inhalation.

As Jasper moved forward, he saw what had caused the derailment. A crater filled the entire floor of the tunnel. Someone had blown up the tracks. That could only have been Ray.

Up ahead, the flames hadn't reached the engine car yet. Jasper hobbled over just as the side door creaked open. Amelia half-stepped, half-fell out of the car. She kept one hand clutched to her side, and she walked like a woman three times her age.

"Jasper?"

"How you doing?"

"Been better. You?"

"Another day in paradise. Let's go. We've got people looking for us," he wheezed.

"Right."

They leaned against each other, a pair of drunks using each other as support. Moving down the line, they found themselves almost to the edge of the tunnel, almost to the bottom floor of Grand Central Station. If they could make it out to the station, they at least had some chance of escaping. But in the end, it didn't really matter. They were undone. This was their one opportunity to deal with the situation, and it was now a flaming wreck behind them. The fires lit up the tunnel in shades of orange.

A bullet cracked over their heads and embedded itself in the ceiling with a puff of dust. They froze as voices shouted at them in languages they didn't understand. The meaning was clear enough, though. It was really amazing how "freeze, or we'll blow your heads off" was understandable in basically any language when shouted by an angry, heavily armed crowd.

Jasper and Amelia turned around slowly. The vampire hunters were moving toward them, weapons raised. There was no chance they'd make it even three feet if they tried to run for it. They could barely even stand properly, let alone dash off down a straight tunnel without cover. The crowd would blast them to chunky-style soup if they tried.

Staring at them in the dark tunnel, it wasn't so hard to imagine the same crowd gathered outside the doors to some decrepit castle in the Carpathians, pitchforks, torches, and muskets clenched in their hands. A lynch mob for the undead. Their patchwork of equipment was hardly state of the art. In fact, it mostly consisted of the hand-me-downs of defunct militaries, but that only seemed to fit better with their historical roots. This was a thoroughly modern mob of angry, superstitious rabble.

Ralitza Petkova stepped to the front of the crowd. Even with a gas mask covering her features, Jasper recognized the tall, dark-haired woman. She carried a trench shotgun in her hands that looked like it could rip a man in half. It probably had at some point.

"How's it hanging?" Amelia asked.

Ralitza brushed off the comment. "We ought to kill the both of you right here and now."

"Kind of surprised you haven't, actually," Jasper said.

"We will get to that," the huntress said.

"Ducky," Amelia grunted.

"First, we need to know who you work for. You are not so much the loose ends as the loose middle. You know far too much, have become too deeply involved, could even be exposed. You cannot be allowed to leave here. However, you are here on behalf of someone else. You are private operatives, freelancers. Your presence here is not for your own self-interest. We will need to eliminate those who hired you as well. Tell us now, and you will die quickly, even if you do not deserve such a favor."

Jasper sighed. "You still don't know what's going on down here, do you? You're trying to protect the city from some rural legend, the undead, but you're wrong."

"No, it is you who is wrong," Ralitza said. "You are trying to stop this scourge with chemicals, to spray them like insects. You cannot kill the vampire with conventional methods. The stake. Holy water. Sunlight. These are the methods that have been handed down to us since time immemorial. Nothing else works. Your misguided attempts will only cause them to disperse to a new lair where they can further their plots."

Jasper felt the weight of his pistol in its shoulder holster but knew it would do him no good. He'd be shot down before he could draw it. "Listen, we don't even have to be enemies. What Yersinia created, that was wrong, but it's not what you think it is."

The flames from the train lit up the tunnel behind the vampire hunters, casting them in apocalyptic silhouettes. "Nothing else on earth leaves its victims drained like that. Nothing else lurks in the shadows of civilization and preys on humanity like that. We have centuries of experience. We know the signs. Yersinia created these monsters, and for that, they will pay. Some knowledge should remain forever unknown. That is why everyone who has come into contact with these blasphemous creatures must be eliminated. The knowledge required to make these creatures in a laboratory is beyond mankind's domain. It must be cleansed, scrubbed clean."

"I'm afraid Mister O'Malley is right, Ralitza," a voice said from behind Jasper. "You don't know jack shit about what's going on here."

Jasper and Amelia whirled around, and the vampire hunters all raised their guns in unison to focus on a new target.

Ray Armstrong stepped into sight from around the edge of the tunnel. He had been lying in wait in Grand Central Station the entire time, waiting for the jaws of his trap to snap shut. He'd brought reinforcements with him, too. About thirty men, all of them extraordinarily well-armed, appeared with Ray. This was most of what remained of Yersinia's security team, Ray's personal band of cutthroats. They outnumbered the vampire hunters, and they were better equipped.

Jasper looked back and forth. On the one side, the vampire hunters wanted to kill everyone here. On the other side, Ray's personal hatchet squad also wanted to kill everyone here. And he and Amelia were caught squarely in the middle.

Ray knew the vampire hunters were down here, too, and he surmised that they'd chase the train like dogs after a rabbit. By switching the tracks to a location of his choosing, he could wipe out both his opponents at once.

Shifting, Jasper and Amelia stood back to back, allowing them to keep their eyes on both parties at once. It wouldn't do much good in the long run. They were caught in No Man's Land, and there was going to be one unholy spray of crossfire once things got hot.

Frankly, Jasper was surprised that Ray hadn't simply opened fire and completed his ambush in one fell swoop, taking everyone unaware. Actually, no, he wasn't. Ray had won. He'd beaten Jasper and Ralitza both, two of his greatest challenges. Ray wouldn't be able to resist gloating. It wasn't in his makeup to let such a triumph go untrumpeted.

Then he would kill them.

"Don't look so surprised over there. The house always wins, didn't you know? But Jasper's right. You've been duped, sister. Bearded. You never even had a clue. Your little holy order of dimwits wouldn't believe the donations that have poured in to Yersinia since you burned down our headquarters. Having you peasants gallivant down here without making a dent in the problem has only proven the success of the experiment. Good job, you shit-sticks."

His imminent death had Jasper in a bad mood. He saw no reason not to poop on Armstrong's little victory parade. "Hey, Ray. How's your hand?"

"Shut up, Jasper. You chose your side when you came back to New York. This has been a long time coming."

Ray held up something in his hand, and he pointed up with his hook. "If you'll look above you, you'll notice the roof of your tunnel is wired with military-grade explosives. Originally, I was just going to use them if things got out of hand. Bury the lot of you quick and easy. However, we need to put that train fire out. Don't need those canisters cooking off and putting an end to the experiment now, do we? Plus, you've given me an idea. I think it's high time you met your 'vampires.' If we block off this tunnel with you on the other side, they'll find you. See how much good your holy water does you, then."

Holding up the object in his hand, Ray looked around with an unpleasant glint in his eye. "This little sumbitch here is a remote detonator. I'm going to count to ten and then push this button. Anybody who's still in the tunnel is going to find themselves in a spot of trouble. Now then. Ten…"

Everyone looked up at the ceiling. Sure enough, there was an arc of explosives strapped up there. Jasper had no reason to believe the man was bluffing. They would have to retreat into the tunnels or be squashed by falling debris. Between the fire and the gunfight, anything alive down here knew their location and was probably homing in right now.

"Nine…" Ray grinned so hard it looked like his face was trying to peel itself apart.

Jasper turned around and started limping deeper into the tunnel. What choice did he have? Even moving at top speed, he didn't think he could make it. His leg was half numb from the impact with the gas cylinder, and what he could feel wasn't pleasant. He wasn't going anywhere fast.

"Eight…"

Jasper glanced back one more time and saw Ray and his men standing near the entrance to the tunnel, grinning like hyenas. There was something else, though. A hulking shape moving through the shadowy interior of Grand Central Station from behind Ray. Jasper squinted.

The Yersinia men were all too distracted by the show in front of them to pay attention, but there were other smaller shapes, too. All of them moving with deliberate stealth toward the guards. Things were about to get very interesting. Not better necessarily, but interesting.

"Seven…"

The huge shape behind the men gradually took shape the closer it came to the light. Rocky. Ray jumped at the sound of a weapon racking behind him. The Yersinia men spun around in surprise.

"We need to have a little talk, Ray," Iris O'Malley's voice drifted from the darkness to Jasper's ears. The Yersinia men split apart, and Jasper saw her standing there. She held a pearl-inlaid revolver in one gloved hand, the gunmetal playing off the milky white grip.

She'd brought her friends, too. More of the information brokerage men had taken up positions around the station, and they meant business. Most of them had submachine guns pointed at the Yersinia men. It did not look like a friendly reception.

Of course, the question was, what did Iris want out of this? There was no guarantee her arrival was a good thing. Quite the contrary, possibly.

"Hi, Ray," Rocky waved. He was carrying a machine gun in his other arm. The kind normally mounted in a nest and carried by two men.

Ray waggled his hook at Rocky. "Uh, hey, Iris. Fancy meeting you here."

"Listen up, you heel. You're going to put that detonator down nice and easy-like. Got it? Then, you're going to have your guys stand down and back off. This is going to end nice and clean because it has gone on too long already."

"Whoa, hold on there, Honey. You got this all wrong." Ray dialed up the smarm to suffocating levels. Prolonged exposure to those levels of smarm could probably render a person sterile or something.

"Don't you dare. Don't you dare 'Honey' me. Those days are over. They never really existed. Only when you thought you'd get something. Those scales fell off my eyes a long time ago, and they're long gone. You spent that nickel."

"I have this situation under control. You're butting in." Ray dropped his unctuous, ingratiating tone and shifted to something flatter, emotionless. It sounded like he was reading lines off cards. He was evaluating the situation, taking it in and analyzing it. He was thinking of a new tact…or waiting for an opportunity.

"You have the situation under control all right. You're about to bury my brother under a couple of tons of loose concrete."

"Well, yeah. But you don't even like your brother."

"Okay, maybe, but I'm still pissed you're trying to blow him up. Family is family. And you don't let people blow up your relatives willy-nilly."

"Thanks, Iris," Jasper called.

"Here's the thing, Ray," Iris ignored him. "Jasper maybe an icy, self-righteous busybody who doesn't have the good sense God gave a lima bean…"

"Thanks, Iris."

"But you're worse, Ray. You're a sack of feral cats shaped into a crude, man-like form. I've known for years that I should have left with Jasper. Or at least I should have turned you in. But I was too stubborn. Even when things went sideways, I was determined to stick to my guns. I gave up on you a long time ago, but I'd made a certain peace with my decisions. This is too far, though."

"What about all the dirt you've gathered on Yersinia?" Ray was trying to grab onto a different rope. "If you let everyone here go, the company collapses. You lose a major investment. I know you've been prying for information for a long time. That's one of the reasons they hired me. You finally have some. Word gets out, your biggest coup goes poof. It turns to fairy dust. It's not worth a thing."

"You're right," Iris pulled the sheath of papers from Rasmussen's house out of a jacket pocket. She folded them up and lobbed them over Ray and Jasper's head. They landed at Ralitza Petkova's feet. The woman picked them up and unfolded them.

"Hey. The hell?" Ray asked.

"They're already worthless, Ray. I called in some favors. Yersinia's government contracts are going to be canceled. I know all the dirty little secrets of half the members of Congress, big and small. I know who has connections with a bootlegging operation. I know who keeps a sixteen-year-old Mexican boy in an apartment in Washington. I know who peed his pants in Mrs. Field's third-grade class. I know it all, and it's all coming out unless they bury Yersinia. I may not particularly care for my brother, but he was right about this. This whole thing needs to be shut down. The things Yersinia's done are insane."

Ray and Iris continued to bicker. Ralitza flipped through the papers in her hands with increasing intensity, beginning to realize what had happened.

Jasper felt preoccupied. He'd never quite gotten over the fact that Iris sided with Ray when he left New York. The feeling had faded with time, healed over, but the scar had always been there. Splitting ways with Ray did a lot to sour his mood on people for a long time, but it stung just as bad to have his own sister abandon him. He'd always felt partially responsible for dragging her into this life, like he'd personally warped her senses somehow.

What she'd said wasn't exactly a ringing endorsement. It certainly wasn't an apology. But it was the closest thing they'd had to a rapprochement since he left New York. He'd resolved himself to being cut off from his family for the rest of his days, but this was an olive branch of sorts. Granted, it was wilted and had hornets living in it and had been sharpened into a point on one end, but it was still a sort of olive branch. It was a place to start.

He felt a certain warmth that wasn't just the flaming wreckage of the passenger train behind him.

Suddenly, Jasper heard a faint clicking noise, almost like sharp footsteps. He snapped out of his thoughts and tapped Amelia. She looked up to see what he was on about, and then she heard it, too. Everyone else was busy in their respective groups, reading Rasmussen's documents or sizing each other up in case things went south. No one else heard it.

Slowly, very slowly, Jasper turned around. The tunnel behind them was packed with smoke and roaring flames, but he could make out a shape moving through the darkness.

No. *Shapes.* Lots of them, moving through the smoke toward the crowd. Jasper drew his pistol as one of them tensed up to take a flying leap into the crowd. Oh hell.

"Watch out," Jasper yelled.

But it was already too late.

Chapter 28
Flea Circus

The creature disappeared, but Jasper knew it was actually moving too quickly for his eyes to track it easily. It was a barely visible pale streak shooting through the air, moving like a shooting star through evil skies.

He and Amelia had gone to the New York State Library to research the monsters. The Entomology department had what they needed, but it wasn't reassuring.

Yersinia had been attempting to use fleas as a vector for ever-more-dangerous diseases, especially weaponized Spanish Flu. Just like during the days of the Black Death, fleas seemed like the perfect carriers, spreading easily through cramped populations and leaving plague in their wake.

However, Yersinia's scientists wanted hardier fleas. Less susceptible to repellents and insecticides. They fed the creatures a cocktail of chemically treated blood, rich in hormones and steroids but also laced with impurities. The strong survived and grew. The weak perished. In short order, the fleas had grown much larger, more aggressive, more insatiable. An inch long and capable of draining a small dog of blood in a matter of minutes, Yersinia released the creatures into the sewer as a test, expecting them to feed on rats and the other small to medium-sized prey.

Instead, to the surprise and delight of Yersinia's Research and Development team, they continued to grow. Like swarms of piranhas, they skittered through the sewers and subways and attacked every-thing in sight. Instead of skeletonizing prey, they drained it of life.

As their size grew, their numbers dwindled. There simply wasn't enough prey in the tunnel system to support first rat-sized and then cat-sized fleas. With each new generation, they grew larger and larger, slaughtering each other when prey grew scarce.

Eventually, they grew to be man-sized, and then their growth faltered. There simply wasn't enough food for them to continue to grow larger. Anything from stray animals to the city's homeless population was fair game, though the creatures preferred the dark confines of the tunnels to the brightness of the train stations or the surface world. The occasional maintenance worker supplemented their diet. Jasper sus-pected that once the food supply became too scarce they would branch out and move to some quiet corner of the surface. Up there, they could expand even further. Entire sections of the city might become unin-habitable in short order.

Jasper had learned from the insect books that fleas hunted by sensing heat and carbon dioxide. Body heat told them they were on some living, warm-blooded creature, or that one was passing nearby. Warmth meant juicy, succulent blood coursing just below the surface, like an oil well waiting to be tapped.

Carbon dioxide was a byproduct of respiration. People and animals breathed in oxygen and exhaled carbon dioxide. If they weren't close enough to feel body heat, fleas could actually track down a puff of the gas to it source like tiny bloodhounds. There was no escape from the little ravagers.

Right now, the flames from the burning train were giving off plenty of heat. The burning wooden frame would be emitting trace amounts of carbon dioxide as well. It was a beacon to every flea in the system, signaling a gigantic buffet. Even if the fleas weren't smart enough to distinguish the fire from actual prey at a distance, it was their lucky day. Everyone was still gathered near the flaming wreckage, open and vulnerable.

Fleas were perfectly suited for life in the tunnels, as well. Laterally flattened, like a fish, they could fit through narrow spaces and navigate without becoming stuck. They had thick, backward-facing bristles that allowed them to feel the environment around them.

Generations in the tunnels had turned these fleas a grotesque pale, the color of unhealthy toenails. Their armored carapaces were semi-translucent but extremely strong. Fleas were built to avoid being crushed when their hosts rolled over or scratched, and their chitinous plating could withstand a lot of damage.

Jasper thought back to the worms that had attacked and killed the hunter in the sewer. They weren't worms, at least, not really. They were more like maggots. They were grotesquely oversized flea larvae. He and Amelia had been half frozen to death when the larvae attacked, which was probably why they homed in on the hunter first. Neither he nor Amelia were giving off enough heat to be their primary interest.

The odd husk Amelia saw, the one she thought might be the dried corpse of a giant sewer spider, was a flea molt. As the fleas grew and grew, they became too large for their exoskeletons. They had to split open their old shells and grow a new one periodically, just like a young child outgrowing its clothes.

They weren't parasites anymore. They were ruthless predators. Perhaps worst of all, they were inhumanly fast. Fleas were some of the best jumpers in the animal kingdom, capable of leaping many times their own body length. A single, tiny flea could jump over a foot laterally, the equivalent of a human being leaping the length of a football field.

As part of their transformation, these fleas walked partially upright, using their front legs only to help support them. They moved in a sort of awkward hunch, like huge, insectile gorillas. Scaled up to their new size, they could move down the tunnels in leaping spurts like the devil's pubic lice.

They were tough, damn near invulnerable to conventional attacks. They were deadly, the apex predators of their dark domain. They were fast, far faster than any human being thanks to their remarkable jumping skills. And now they were here in force. There were at least two dozen shapes moving through the smoke, converging in the hopes of slaking their unspeakable thirst.

The first flea tensed its legs and sprang. It landed amidst Ray's Yersinia team, bowling them over. The creature's clawed front legs lashed out and snatched a man as he tried it scramble away. Six-inch-long tarsal claws sank into his flesh and anchored themselves on the bone, slashing through the meat like it wasn't even there.

He made noises like a dog with its back broken. The flea lifted its head slightly, revealing a jagged, tube-like mouth. Screaming, the man tried to wriggle away, but he was caught as surely as a mouse in an owl's talons.

The mouth feeder plunged into the man's body at the base of his throat, and his scream cut off into a shrill warbling noise. It sounded like somebody strangling a turkey. Jasper watched in cold horror as the flea slurped up blood through the man's makeshift tracheotomy.

However, the struggle soon went out of the man. Jasper could actually hear the force of the suction ripping things loose inside the man's body, almost like a storm ripping the shingles off a roof and whipping them away. The man seemed to age forty years in a couple of seconds. He grew deathly pale, and his skin clung tight to the bones. His eyes sank in their sockets, and his body fell limp as he experienced massive, violent exsanguination. It was the equivalent of bleeding out in the span of time it took to refill a cup of coffee.

Startled gunfire erupted and struck the creature. The flea beast didn't seem to care much either way. Its eyes locked onto the next closest of Ray's goons, and it dropped the husk of the first man. The body crunched to the floor like a broken ventriloquist dummy. He looked like a mistreated mummy tossed out of its sarcophagus.

Taking a step forward, the creature's massive foot claws left little divots in the ground as it moved. Lashing out, it snatched up the next man. He didn't even have time to react before he was impaled on the monster's quivering mouthparts.

A shotgun blast ripped off one of the creature's forelimbs, but it didn't even seem to care. It merely adjusted its grip on its prey as its severed limb fell to the ground.

More of the creatures leaped into the crowd, knocking people to the ground and dragging others into the shadows. Screams filled the tunnels. Jasper saw one of the creatures lift up a squirming vampire hunter and plunge its mouth into the man's belly. Ralitza Petkova pulled out a stake made from hard ash wood and stabbed the creature in the flank. The stake's pick-sharp point shattered against the monster's heavy carapace.

With one of its free appendages, the creature swatted Ralitza away. The woman tumbled backward, landing hard on a wooden crossbeam. She'd come expecting a certain problem, and now she and her followers found themselves woefully unprepared.

Digging into her pocket, she pulled out a vial of what Jasper assumed must be holy water. She threw it at the flea. The glass bottle exploded against the giant insect's side. There was no puff of smoke. No flash of divine light. No sizzle as undead flesh melted.

For all her determination, Ralitza had refused to listen. There had been signs she was on the wrong course, but she stuck to the old ways. But now there was something new under the sun, and the old rules no longer applied.

Maybe if Dr. Horvath had survived, he would have eventually passed on information pointing to the fact that these things weren't actually vampires. Instead, his warnings catalyzed a massive response to exactly the wrong kind of problem. The vampire hunters weren't investigators; they were inquisitors, and they had just inquisited their asses into a sling.

Ralitza reached for her trench shotgun, realizing that her usual methods would be hopeless here. A shadow fell across her from behind. Two shadows, actually.

She spun around just as the first flea grabbed her by the shoulders and lifted her up. The second flea grabbed her hips. The insects fought a brief battle, each pulling in opposite directions with their prize.

Jasper looked away from what happened next, but he could still hear the ripping noise that followed.

"We have to get out of here," he shouted to Amelia above the crackle of gunfire. He could barely hear himself over the shouting and chaos unfolding in the tunnel, but the idea was obvious that it didn't need much explaining.

They bent low to avoid at least some of the stray gunfire bouncing through the tunnels. Everything was smoke and blood. Jasper lurched forward, his heartbeat loud in his ears. His body protested as he tried to move faster.

The various groups were trying to retreat and regroup, but the fleas simply sprang into the midst of any group of people that gathered to put up a firm resistance. It wasn't tactics; the fleas weren't that bright. Groups presented the greatest body heat and were, therefore, the biggest targets.

A stray burst of pistol fire lanced down one of the information brokerage men as he made a dash for the exit. He went down, legs kicking. Scenting the blood, a flea swooped down on him and disappeared a second later. A shoe left on the floor was the only sign the man had ever been there.

Rocky stood and fired his heavy machine gun from the hip, the barrel glowing orange as it heated up. A nearby flea stepped into the line of fire. Chunks of its armor exploded off and scattered across the station. The bipedal insect staggered under the blows, flailing at the air. A couple of its limbs flew off, and glops of pale innards that looked like shredded lobster meat flew against the wall. A final spray of bullets popped the creature's head like a massive zit.

Blood, ichor, and fleshy lumps gushed out of the stump. The monster continued to stand for a second, its remaining limbs flailing around to try to find its missing head. Then it tipped over, and its legs curled up to its chest in the classic dead bug position.

Another flea took the first's place. They moved so quickly they seemed to simply appear in place, popping out of existence for a brief second only to appear across the room.

The flea appeared right next to Rocky and grabbed onto his arm with its claws. Rocky bellowed and tried to spin his weapon around, but he was caught. Instead, he hooked his other arm around and punched the creature in its plated snout. The blow knocked the flea off balance for a second, but it didn't let go.

Regaining its footing, it tried to yank Rocky away, but the man was simply too big to be dragged away. Instead, it ripped his arm off at the shoulder.

Jasper moved as quickly as he could. He felt like he was trapped in some crazed Bosch painting. Figures in gas masks writhed and scattered and died while huge, pale monsters swept out of the tunnels. It was absolute pandemonium. Bedlam in a can shook up and cracked open.

"Jasper," a voice called. His head whipped around. Iris had climbed up onto the platform and was moving toward one of the doors. "C'mon, let's get out of here."

A few of the information brokerage men ran past Iris and bolted for the exit. They were primarily information gatherers. Even if they were capable with a gun, none of them signed on for *this*. They dashed out the doors into the night.

But Iris waited. Even with everything going on all around, she waited. The fleas popped in and out of the crowd left and right, grabbing shrieking figures with near impunity. Panic fire sprayed in every direction. One of Ray's men fired a shotgun, trying to hit a flea in mid-leap. He missed, smearing one of his comrades against a pillar instead. Their enemy might as well have been invisible.

Jasper felt a surge of hope as Iris beckoned him and Amelia forward with frantic movements. It didn't last.

A huge, pale shape blinked into existence behind Iris. She felt the breeze from its arrival and started to turn around, but it was too late. A set of claws like reaper blades latched onto the back of her neck.

Chapter 29
End of the Line

With one swift movement, the flea ripped off Iris's head. The skin split and tore. Muscles and sinew twisted and snapped. Vertebrae crackled. And then Iris's head was off her shoulders.

Her red hair followed her head down to the ground like the tail of a comet. The body continued to stand, held upright in the flea's clawed grip. Blood shot from the ragged stump where Iris's head should have been, fountaining toward the ceiling.

The flea clamped its mouth parts down over the stump like a child who had just bitten the head off a chocolate Easter bunny. It gorged, sucking up as much blood as possible.

Jasper couldn't tell if he was screaming or not. He was pretty sure he was screaming, but he couldn't hear anything over the chaos around him. The world went fuzzy at the edges, then red, then dark. He felt light-headed, and suddenly the room seemed very hot.

This. This hurt worse than having his hand pulverized by a hammer. He'd finally won back some semblance of order to his life after years in the wilderness. Even when they went their separate ways, Iris had always been important to him. He'd helped create what she was, and he bore some responsibility for everything that flowed from that.

For one moment, he'd thought he could make up the lost time. He thought there might be some redemption, a chance to ease back some of the mistakes they'd both made over the last ten years.

All for naught.

He had no idea how his pistol got in his hand. It just appeared there. His finger squirmed over to the trigger and squeezed. The recoil kicked at his arm where he'd twerked his shoulder in the train crash, but he didn't care. The pain kicked the darkness away from the corners of his vision, and the world came rushing back into focus all at once.

The heat he'd felt chilled to a hard, icy shell, like molten lava cooling into impermeable basalt. It felt like a drain had opened up somewhere in the base of his being, and something important had washed out, swirling away.

He flashed back to his brother, Percy, killed while working a job with him. He'd buried himself in work after that incident, and had finally put it behind him after years of effort. Now, he didn't know what he'd do.

His finger pulled back on the trigger again and again. The rounds thudded against the flea's armored head, not even penetrating down to the soft tissue. Everything was moving in slow motion, almost frozen. Jasper felt like he could walk through the entire station, examining each detail like a hobbyist recreating an ancient battle on the table with wooden soldiers.

Instead, Jasper shifted his aim almost imperceptibly, lining up the shot for what felt like hours, maybe days. The pistol barked again, blasting a spear of flame out from its muzzle.

The bullet burst out, straight and true. With a splash of vitreous fluid, the flea's left eye exploded. Squealing, the monster dropped Iris's corpse and swiped its claws at its ruined eye. Disoriented, it spun around to try to face Jasper.

The monster's other eye popped like a gravy-filled balloon. Goopy liquid dribbled down the side of its face. Completely blind, it spun around, clawing at its empty sockets. Panicking, it tried to leap away and crashed directly into a concrete wall. A plume of dust rose up as the flea cratered the wall with its impact. The creature fell to the floor, its head smashed to oozing pulp.

Something pawed at him, and Jasper swung his pistol around to fire again. Amelia stumbled backward as he pointed the pistol at her nose. His finger came off the trigger.

For the first time since he'd known her, she looked genuinely afraid. Her eyes were wide and staring. The fire went out of his blood, replaced with a sick emptiness, and he dropped his weapon to his side.

"Jasper, we need to go," she said. She was right, of course. It was only a matter of time until a flea zeroed in on them. The vampire hunters, closest to the group when they emerged from the tunnel, had been almost completely wiped out. Ray's guards weren't faring much better, but at least they were putting up a fight. Some of the information brokers had escaped, but others were cut off from the ramps up to the surface level.

He looked back to the lifeless body sprawled on the ground. He wanted to do something, anything. But there was nothing he could do. Nothing at all. Often, that was the cruelest path in life.

A fist came out of nowhere and rocketed into Jasper's eye. He reeled into the edge of the platform, his legs nearly going out from under him. Instead, he grabbed the concrete ledge and steadied himself like a boxer leaning on the ropes.

He had just enough time to throw up his arms as a flash of silver came toward him. Ray's hook sliced through the fabric of Jasper's sleeve and tore into his flesh, but it missed scraping across his eyes as intended.

Ray's eyes had an unhealthy shine behind his gas mask. He came at Jasper like a rabid animal, clawing and snarling.

Amelia started to draw her weapon, but Ray swatted her hands away. The Luger skittered away into the middle of a heavy melee between a group of fleas and Yersinia guards. The guards were not winning.

Still sporting the same crazed eyes, Ray jabbed at Jasper again with his fist. The blow caught Jasper just under the ribs. They should have been roughly equal fighters, but Jasper was hurting from head to toe, and on every other level inbetween, and Armstrong had taken him by surprise.

Amelia threw herself on his back and tried to throttle him, revenge for choking her while she'd been driving. Ray roared and threw her off with the strength of the damned. She landed hard on the ground, and he delivered a quick, sharp kick to her back. With Amelia writhing on the tracks, Ray turned his attention back to Jasper.

"We finish this thing right now."

Jasper was more than happy to oblige. Something wild had taken hold of him, some feral part that rarely surfaced from the swamps of the primitive lizard brain part of his mind. It was a cagey, hungry thing that thought in reaction times and opportunities to strike with sharp teeth and flashing claws.

Ray slashed at him again with his hook; Jasper dodged but was too slow. His limbs were shaking and numb. He raised his pistol, but Ray closed in fast and pounded him against the edge of the platform. Jasper tried to push him away, but Ray pistoned a fist into the pit of his stomach.

Doubling over, Jasper fell to the ground. Ray's boot smashed into his ribs with enough force to take his breath away. Jasper gasped, trying to pull air back into his lungs, but it seemed as if his gas mask was choking him. Ray jerked him his knees and then walloped him again, knocking him back to the ground. Jasper tried to raise his pistol, but Ray stomped on his arm with a heavy boot. The weapon dropped out of Jasper's hand and clattered to the floor.

They were like two scorpions trapped in a jar, absolutely determined to fight to the finish regardless of what was going on around them. Both of them were locked in a haze, frenzied beyond thought or reason. But Jasper had come into the fight already hobbled.

Lashing out with his foot, Ray kicked him again and again. The boot smashed into his ribs one, two, three times in quick succession. Jasper reached out and tried to grab Ray's foot, but his attacker drew back and wound up for another blow, this one aimed at Jasper's face. He twisted around so as not to catch it directly in the nose, but he didn't move quickly enough. Ray caught him on the cheek. The inside of his mouth flattened against his teeth, lacerating the soft flesh. His teeth rattled in his skull as the blow knocked him over onto his back. If the blow caught him at the wrong angle, it likely would have snapped his neck.

Jasper tasted blood in his mouth. He wanted to spit, but he couldn't with the mask. Everything felt wobbly, like the earth had tilted off its axis and was starting to spin out of control. He was tired, bone tired, and the strength began to ebb out of his muscles.

Ray could tell he had the upper hand, and he pressed it. He took one step back to give himself room for a shattering kick. Maybe he'd smash Jasper's gas mask and drive the glass eyeholes into his flesh.

Something as pale as Death's horse and a whole lot uglier suddenly appeared behind Ray. Neither Jasper nor Amelia were on their feet, making Ray the most obvious target. He realized something was amiss almost instantly.

The flea snatched up Ray in its claws. Ray screamed and squirmed, bashing at the monster's talons with his prosthetic hand, but he was caught as surely as a worm on a hook. The creature almost seemed to consider Ray for a moment. In a way, Ray was partially responsible for the creature's existence. Without him, it wouldn't be here. The Frankenstein monster sought out its creator in a quest for acknowledgment and meaning. This one just wanted to eat.

Standing between Jasper and Amelia, the flea looked down at the abundance of prey before it. Ray continued to writhe in its grip to no avail. Jasper reached for his pistol and noticed something about where the flea was standing. If it grabbed him, Jasper didn't think he'd be able to shoot it to death, but there might be another option.

Shifting its head, the flea spotted Amelia as she tried to crabwalk away. It transitioned Ray to just its right claw and reached for Amelia. She screamed as she saw the claw groping for her.

No! Jasper had already lost too much today. It was far more than he'd been prepared to give when he came to New York. He wouldn't lose Amelia, too.

He lifted his pistol and fired until the chamber was empty. The bullets struck the flea in its left leg, striking it in the backward-facing "knee" joint. That was where the creature's exoskeleton was the thinnest. Its spindly legs were like giant springs, so they weren't encumbered with the same armor as the rest of its body. The leg snapped, shorn chitin at the joint and shredded the meat within. Unbalanced, the flea dropped to the ground, landing directly on top of the subway's third rail.

Electricity crackled and sputtered as it shot into the flea's body. A noise like lard sizzling on a grill filled the air, and steam shot out from between the beast's armored plates. The flea's limbs flailed in spastic motion. One of its limbs exploded as the meat inside fried, but the expanding heat couldn't escape quickly enough.

Even as it jittered and died, the creature never released its grip on Ray. Electricity conducted straight through the monster into Ray's body. The man jerked like a marionette whose master was having a seizure. His gas mask flew off as he was whipped around in the monster's grip. His lips peeled back, exposing clenched teeth. Hot vapor began to filter out from between his teeth as his organs cooked. Crackling blue arcs shot off Ray's hook in a miniature lightning storm.

Ray's hair caught fire, and the flames quickly engulfed his entire head. His flesh began to melt like wax. Soon, there was nothing but a burning skull staring at Jasper.

Laramie Resweber said he wanted Ray fried for setting him up.

This probably wasn't exactly what he had in mind when he made that request, but it would do.

Jasper looked around. There weren't many other people left alive in the station. The desiccated corpses were piled three high in some places. There were only a few dead fleas to match the carnage they had wreaked on their human prey. One man had backed himself into an alcove and was trying to fend off three fleas at once. They dragged him out and ripped him to shreds. Another darted into a nearby restroom and slammed the door shut behind him. The pursuing flea knocked the door off its hinges and wedged itself inside after him.

Jasper pulled himself to his feet and dragged Amelia up after him. If they didn't leave right now, they were both dead. They moved toward the ramp leading to the higher levels and the exits. The train platform was a death trap.

As much as Jasper would have liked to move at a dead sprint, he couldn't. Neither could Amelia. He felt like his body had been taken apart by a curious toddler and hastily reassembled with string and chewing gum. It felt like things would start falling off if he moved too fast. His breathing was loud and heavy, and each breath bore the coppery taste of blood.

Screams and dwindling gunfire died away behind them as the fleas eliminated the few remaining pockets of resistance. Jasper and Amelia's feet dragged on the ground as they climbed up onto the platform and made for the exit. Everything felt clumsy and slow.

Suddenly, a flea appeared in front of them. One second the path was clear. The next, a slavering, fleet-footed flea beast stood before them. It was like a good magic trick, seemingly impossible but really just the result of speeds too great for the eye to observe.

Jasper and Amelia stumbled to a halt. The monster took a step forward, rising to its full height above them. Its fearsome talons dug into the floor as it moved. Clicking its front claws, it advanced on them.

Raising his pistol, Jasper pulled the trigger. Nothing happened. The gun was dry. He'd used the last of his bullets on the flea clutching Ray. Jasper tried to think of something, anything else he might have, but there was nothing. He was out of ammo and out of ideas. The flea took one last step forward and reached for them. Jasper stared with hollow eyes as the claws moved toward him.

Something exploded behind them, and Jasper got to see the same magic trick of something suddenly appearing before his eyes. In this case, it was a cylinder of prussic acid, firmly embedded in the creature's side. Gas sprayed out from the nozzle in a hot cloud, and the metal glowed a merry red.

The flea made a noise like a truck engine being castrated. Wheeling around, it tried to grab at the cylinder impaling its flank, but its claws merely scraped against the hot metal.

Sizzling and boiling, the contents of the flea's ruptured stomach spilled onto the ground at its feet. Blood, gallons and gallons of blood, splashed out of its belly and spread across the floor. Jasper stared in amazement at the red sea, several lives sucked out and commingled in the vile creature's guts.

Another bang sounded behind them. The flames from the train wreck were causing the gas cylinders to explode, their nozzle's popping open under pressure they were never meant to endure.

It was simple physics. As the gas inside grew hot, it expanded. But it could only expand so far in the closed confines of the metal tubes. With enough heat, though, the internal pressure grew too high. Something had to give, and the structurally weakest part of each canister was the nozzle.

The first explosion seemed to cause a chain reaction, and the canisters began exploding like popcorn, shooting in every direction. Some of them disappeared further down the tunnels, others crashed into the station, embedding themselves in the walls or anything else unfortunate enough to get in their way. The temperature in the station began to rise as superheated toxic gases sprayed across the chamber.

In front of them, the tube-skewered flea fell on its side as the hot cylinder seared its organs to black, shriveled lumps. But the other fleas in the terminal started to collapse as well. They moved with jittery motions, as if they'd been downing coffee instead of blood.

One of them tried to jump toward Jasper and Amelia, but its legs misfired. It smashed into a length of railing instead, collapsing in a tangle of metal and twitching limbs. The fleas collapsed one by one like drunks. Some of them tried to retreat back down the tunnels, but they ended up walking in uneven circles or bumping into each other. One by one they curled up and died.

But the canisters continued to explode inside the remains of the train, tearing apart anything the flames hadn't gutted. Canisters shot out, spraying burning steam in their wake. Clinging to each other, Jasper and Amelia navigated the thick mist of noxious chemicals and hauled themselves up the ramp to the exit.

Already, the fog of chemicals was starting to spread out, drifting into the other tunnels and spreading through the system.

Together, Jasper and Amelia found a door and lurched into the night.

Chapter 30
The Flea's Knees

Jasper leaned against a tree, breathing the cool November air. A fresh rain had swept the skies clear of smokestack emissions and car fumes, and it had made the ground rich and soft. The grass glistened with the moisture.

Amelia stood nearby, her hat brim low over her face to hide the black eye Ray had given her. She was dressed in black. Jasper wore gray, as always. The Peerless sat nearby, ready to ferry them back to Chicago when they were done here.

It had been a week since the incident in Grand Central Station. Jasper and Amelia were both stiff and sore, but their bruises were fading to yellowish-purplish splotches. Jasper's hand was still in a cast, but he'd survive.

Only three people had come to Iris's funeral. Him. Amelia. And Laramie Resweber. Of course, the priest and grave crew had come, too, but they didn't really count, and they were anxious to leave. Most of the people Iris had been close to were dead, and the remaining ones didn't want to be affiliated with her. Given the events that had occurred, the information brokerage was receiving a lot of police scrutiny. People were going to ground, and it seemed there was no room for sentimentality.

The gravesite was a nice one. Jasper liked it. Especially the tree standing over it. Very peaceful. Amelia had helped pick out the location.

It took a few days to get Iris's body. First, it took a while for all the gas to disperse through the subway system to safe levels. Then, the police and medical examiner had to actually sort out what had happened and who was dead and why in God's name there were giant fleas strewn about Grand Central Station.

Identifying the corpses took longer, too. Mostly, they had to use dental records due to the state of the bodies. Actually getting the bodies released was an odyssey of paperwork as well, but Jasper knew how to use the system.

The priest had finished up and driven away, and Jasper had shooed away the funeral assistant. Now it was just the three of them.

"Thanks for coming, Laramie," Jasper said.

"No problem. I've already settled up with the Agency and all, but it didn't seem right just turning you loose." Resweber was no longer in a wheelchair. He'd graduated to a cane, but his nurse still sat in the car. His body was healing, though he'd always have some impressive scars from his ride with Ol' Sparky.

"You heard they positively identified Ray Armstrong last night?" Jasper didn't move as he talked. Even his eyes stayed fixed in place.

"Yeah, and that's just the bee's knees from my perspective. They had to shut down power to the station for an hour to scrape him off the rail, I hear. Listen, I didn't know this was going to turn into… this…when I hired you."

"I know, but that's life, isn't it? I didn't, couldn't, imagine this when I left New York the last time. I don't think I'll be back again."

"Fair enough. You planning to leave for Chicago right after this?"

"Straight off. I need to think about things."

They sat in silence for a minute. Amelia put a hand on Jasper's arm. He didn't shrug it off.

"So, you probably know the police are pretty hot under the collar about this," Resweber finally said.

"I could guess. This shut down the subway system for a week, left a stack of bodies all through the tunnels, and will probably make us look pretty bad when they find out about it."

"That's what I wanted to talk about. You looking bad and all. I still have some contacts. Nothing serious, but I like to keep my ear to the ground. I got surprised once, and I don't want it happening again."

Jasper nodded.

"Well, the thing is, the train company is pretty interested, too.

This is a lot of lost revenue for them, and one of their trains was destroyed. They're real keen on figuring out what happened, so they hired their own investigative team. Turns out it's the New York branch of the Attican Detective Agency. I passed a word along. I don't think you're going to have any trouble with the law because of this. Looks like Ray's the prime suspect for the whole mess. My sources tell me there haven't been any more disappearances reported in the tunnels, even with people crawling all through there. Looks like you took care of business."

"Thanks, Laramie," Jasper said and meant it.

They frittered away their last few minutes together with idle chatter about nothing at all, and then Resweber said his goodbyes and picked his way back to the car. He patted his nurse's hand, and they drove off together.

Jasper stayed a few minutes longer and then strode back to the Peerless. He threw one glance backward and then pulled himself into the car. Amelia sat down in the driver's seat.

"Hey, you okay?" she asked.

"I'll survive," Jasper said.

"I'll help," she responded. For the first time in a week, Jasper's face showed something that might have been a smile.

"C'mon. Let's get back to Chicago."

She turned the key, and the Peerless hummed to life. It tossed up sprays of water as it cruised away from the cemetery and left the city behind.

Chapter 31
Finders Keepers

Paul Nelson moved through the wreckage of Grand Central Station, following the police sergeant. Clean-up crews with mops and hoses were trying to remove the blood stains sprayed across the terminal. So far, the blood stains were winning.

Other crews swept chunks of concrete and other debris into buckets for removal. There was a lot of work to be done yet. A group of Attican detectives stood near the train wreckage being dragged out of the tunnel, arguing with a train company official. The detectives seemed to be getting the better end of the argument.

"We know the stuff dissipated. Obviously, we're walking through here without any protective gear at all, although I'd wash my hands before eating anything if I were you," the police sergeant continued. "But our crew isn't trained for this kind of volume with chemical clean up. We need to know what sort of after effects we might expect, if there might be pockets that didn't clear, that sort of thing. Here, I'll show you where most of the canisters burst."

Nelson headed the Chemical Engineering Department at BioSyn, one of Yersinia's main competitors. Normally, this would be Yersinia business. It was their equipment, after all. Even then, the cops would normally handle the clean-up, but the sheer scale of the mess meant they wanted some outside advice. No one wanted to accidentally poison themselves.

And most of Yersinia's top people were dead. Nelson didn't know the exact details, but it was somehow linked to this chemical spill. The police had been very hush-hush about the whole thing. No one in the press knew exactly what was going on, which made it all the more mysterious.

He was more than happy to help. If nothing else, he was intensely curious about whatever events wiped out his counterparts at Yersinia. The prussic acid should have dissipated fairly quickly, but this would give him a chance to poke around.

The sergeant made his way toward the scorched skeleton of a passenger train. "Watch where you step through here. There's still a lot of blood. And what's this? Hey, Bosman! I found another arm over here! Go get one of those ghouls from the Medical Examiner's office and tell them they missed a whole section over here. Tell them to bring those bags, too. The heavy duty ones. Lots of them."

The smell of death was nearly intolerable in the tunnel. Dried blood and voided bowels and rotting flesh all combined into a potpourri reminiscent of the mouth of hell.

"Hold on," the sergeant said to Nelson. "We have to get this cleaned up. Wait right here." The man trotted off to fetch someone to deal with the errant body parts.

Good God. What happened down here? Nelson considered following the sergeant and simply leaving. They had warned him that it was an active crime scene down here, but this wasn't a crime scene. It was a charnel house.

Across the station, he watched four men lift something up on a stretcher. Whatever it was, they'd placed a blanket over it so no one could see. The shrouded shape was the size of a man, but it was shaped all wrong. Nelson shuddered and pulled his jacket up over his nose to block some of the smell of battlefield slaughter. He'd made up his mind. He was leaving. No amount of morbid curiosity was worth this assault on his senses.

He took a step backward, and his foot crunched on something. He looked down and saw he'd stepped in a cluster of glass shards. They looked like they'd been a vial or beaker of some sort before they exploded into their current form. This didn't look like it belonged here.

And there was something else nearby. It appeared to be a length of carved wood. Obviously, the point had been smashed against something hard, splintering the wood.

Was this part of the train? Nelson didn't know locomotives, but this looked more like an oversized tent stake someone had tried to pound into a rock by mistake. It wasn't burned, so it must have come from somewhere other than the train.

And there. What was that? It looked like a sheaf of papers. They were crinkled and wedged half under some wreckage, but Nelson could still make out the Yersinia logo on the letterhead.

Glancing around, Nelson saw he was the only person in the tunnel. None of the workers paid any attention to him. He reached down and snatched the papers.

There were some splotches of blood on the top sheet, and he almost dropped the papers in disgust. But there was more red on the papers, definitely not blood.

The other red was ink, in the form of a stamp reading *TOP SE-CRET*. Nelson eyed the papers, debating what to do. The first page was an internal memo about some sort of inoculation project Yersinia was working on.

Finally, Nelson decided to peek inside the packet. After all, there might be something relevant to the chemical spill in there, and he should know right away. No time to wait for the policeman to come back. Time could be of the essence and whatnot.

He'd be remiss in some sort of civic duty or something if he didn't allow himself at least a quick glimpse. Thumbing through the pages, he suddenly realized what he was reading. The formulas. The studies. The experiment results. It was all right here. What he was holding in his hands was completely unprecedented, arguably insane, but it made a certain sense in the context of what he could see all around him.

Hot damn.

He could hear the police sergeant approaching again, chewing out one of the poor souls here to remove the human remains. Nelson looked down at the papers in his hands, at the dribbles of blood marring the words on the front page. The sergeant's voice grew louder, nearer.

Nelson folded the papers and tucked them into his pocket. His friends in BioSyn's Research and Development Department would want to see these.

ABOUT THE AUTHOR

Jonah Buck wanted to learn everything there was to know about pale, semi-human creatures that flit across the sunless landscape to terrorize the living, so he became an Oregon attorney. His interests include professional stage magic, history, paleontology, monster movies, and exotic poultry.

Press
Presents

And be sure to check out *Substratum*, the first
entry in the Jasper O'Malley series.

Chapter 1
Hell Hole

June 26, 1925

Hugh Corbett ran for his life. Probably his soul, too. He'd been running for a long time, trapped down here, and he was breathing hard. A stitch pulsed in his side, but he continued onward. It had been a long time since he ran the police department fitness test, and he felt it. His flashlight beam sent crazy shadows jittering in every direction as he ran. His lungs burned, and he slowed down. It was like being trapped in a giant funhouse, facing identical tunnel after identical tunnel. The mine's gritty, white walls bore no distinguishing characteristics. For all Corbett knew, he'd been running in circles the entire time.

He was lost in the Detroit Salt Combine's mining tunnels. Each of the salt mine's shafts looked exactly the same, and he had no idea how he was going to get out of this pit. The mine was laid out as a series of long, straight tunnels radiating out from a center chamber. Cross shafts connected all the main tunnels at regular intervals, creating a nice, circular grid pattern like a spider web. Hell's suburbs. The tunnels were a marvel of the industrial age, a modern day labyrinth even larger than the city they were buried under. Stretching beneath Lake Erie in some places, the massive network of tunnels ran for miles. A man could get lost down here and starve to death before finding a way out. Hugh Corbett was very lost.

That wasn't the bad part, though. Not even half of it. There were things in the darkness. Corbett had seen them, and now he wished to God he hadn't. He wanted to run until he reached daylight, chew his way straight through the rock to the surface if he had to. He didn't want to be trapped down here with those things, but he had to stop and rest. His legs were screaming at him, and his spit tasted sour in his mouth. He was pretty sure he'd lost his pursuers somewhere deeper in the mine anyway.

Each of the tunnels was peppered with alcoves so workers could get out of the way of mechanical borers or other heavy equipment. Corbett slipped into one of the dark corners and stopped. His legs trembled, and he forced back the sudden urge to puke. He leaned over, hands on his thighs, regaining his composure.

Gradually, his ragged breathing leveled off, and he listened. He looked around and tried to shake off the vice grip of panic that had sent him running for miles through this maze. In the subterranean gloom, his flashlight was the only source of light. It allowed him to see, but it also highlighted his location to anyone else in the tunnels. Any*thing* else in the tunnels. He flicked it off, and the darkness descended on him. Corbett strained his ears, ignoring the sound of his own heartbeat hammering like a timpani drum.

The arc lights that normally illuminated this stretch of tunnel were all dead. His fellow police officers cut the power themselves, thinking it would befuddle their quarry and give them the advantage. Now Corbett was the one being hunted.

Corbett knew how to move in darkness. Slipping through Detroit's back alleys at night and staking out speakeasies had taught him how to move confidently in minimal light. He befriended the night years ago, learning to cloak himself in shadow when needed. This was different, though. This wasn't some shadowy alley. This darkness was complete, absolute. It engulfed Corbett, swallowing him whole. He was but a tapeworm in the earth's guts.

At 791 feet high, the Woolworth Building in New York City was the tallest building in the world. Corbett was more than 1,100 feet below the earth's surface. That far underground, there was no light. None at all. Right now, Corbett's eyes could only pick up visual static. Black noise. He was literally in the underworld, gobbled up by the earth. He struggled to remain calm. He was all but suffocating on the blackness. It seemed like it was pouring into him the way water swept into a drowning man's lungs as he went under for the final time.

A monsoon of sweat had sprung up on Corbett's face as he ran, but he still felt a chill that penetrated down to his soul as he thought about what he'd seen deeper inside the mine. Wiping his brow, he tried to concentrate.

Nothing could have followed him, not in this plutonian blackness, but he didn't completely believe that. A particular part of Corbett's brain had risen to the forefront and seized the reigns from his rational mind. It was the part that prehistoric shrews used to avoid being eaten by dinosaurs. It was the part honed in primitive man as he explored caves that might be infested with saber-toothed cats. It was pure survival instinct.

When he was a boy, Corbett had a stuffed rabbit he kept with him under his covers when the darkness in the closet was too terrible to contemplate any longer. Now that he was an adult, he wished he had his service pistol — it offered the same form of comfort — but he'd lost it back in the tunnels when those things killed his partners. Five cops had gone into the tunnels with Corbett, and now he was the only one left.

Somewhere, maybe miles away, machines boomed and squealed. Men shouted to each other and threw salt rock into carts. The collective bustle echoed and re-echoed down the tunnels, creating an eerie blanket of meaningless sound. Clanks and whistles sounded at random intervals, and he jumped each time. Sometimes the mine itself popped or groaned as millions of tons of rock settled. Even under the best of circumstances, Corbett didn't know how the miners kept their sanity. If the mine caved in, they'd be buried alive almost a quarter of a mile underground or, more likely, crushed like screaming wine grapes. Of course, harrowing as they were, those were the best of circumstances. There were much worse dangers in these tunnels now.

He needed to find the central shaft and make his way back to the surface. It was imperative that he get back to the upper world, not just for his own survival, but to warn everyone. He was the only one left who could tell them what he'd seen. They'd have to quarantine the mine tunnels and send in the military. Hell, never mind the military. They should just blast all the mine's support columns and let the tunnels crumble in on themselves, crushing everything down here. The things Corbett had seen could never be allowed to —

What was that?

Corbett stopped breathing. He'd heard something. It was a quiet, stealthy shuffle, almost hidden by the whispers and groans of background mine noise. Something new had just entered the mine's echo-system.

It was a faint *tap*, almost like someone with a hammer was knocking on one of the walls deeper in the tunnels. The sound emanated from the direction he'd just fled from. Anything moving in that section of the tunnels was not going to be friendly.

Even though he couldn't see anything, he automatically reached for his gun. It wasn't there. Of course, it wasn't there. He'd lost it in the hungry darkness. But his sleeve brushed against the rough wall as he reached. The fabric whispered against the rough surface.

Corbett grimaced. In the darkness, the sound of his sleeve rasping against the salt rock sounded as loud as a scream. He remained perfectly still, listening. His teeth bit into his lower lip as he held his breath.

Seconds ticked by. In the cloying gloom, they could have been eons. Corbett thwarted the urge to turn his flashlight back on. No matter what meager comfort it might provide, switching it on would give away his position as surely as if he'd been illuminated with a spotlight. The seconds stretched into minutes. Maybe the minutes stretched into hours. Trapped in the darkness, his senses deprived of input, it was impossible to tell. Nothing else sounded from the tunnels behind him.

Whatever he heard must have been a trick of the mine's acoustics.

His heart spelunked its way back down his throat as he decided the danger had passed. Corbett slumped as he suddenly became aware of how tense his muscles were. God, he was exhausted. The adrenaline keying through his system began to fade, leaving his nerves stripped raw.

He and his fellow police officers had been patrolling the tunnels in one of the Detroit Salt Combine's survey trucks. Half of Detroit's police force was down here doing the exact same thing, running a dragnet. Miners had been disappearing from the tunnels, and the city had dispatched every beat cop it could spare to comb the shafts. At the time, he'd thought it was a fool's errand. The entire state of Michigan didn't have enough cops to thoroughly search the tunnels in a systematic manner. Hundreds of miles of tunnels stretched below Detroit in a subterranean mirror of the road network above. It was like a giant ant nest. They couldn't patrol every single tunnel any more than a doctor could check every single capillary in a sick patient. If they ran into whoever was responsible, it would be purely a matter of luck. Bad luck, as it turned out.

Corbett's squad had been puttering down one of the abandoned sections of the mine, shining a truck-mounted searchlight into every nook and cranny they could find. All six of them were tired after hours of poking their noses into dark corners. The other patrols had fanned out and gone into different parts of the mine, hopelessly separating everyone. The rock walls meant radios were worthless, and nobody could see anyone else. There was simply no way to keep what was supposed to be a cohesive search force organized. It was like sending a gaggle of blind kids out trick or treating without supervision.

Corbett had been an infantryman in the Great War, and he remembered columns of men scrambling out of their trenches for assaults. The formations quickly hit barbed wire, craters, and machinegun fire, and the highly organized mobile armies turned into individual squads of frantic soldiers within thirty yards. All the brilliant planning in the world couldn't fix some boondoggles, and this expedition had not been brilliantly planned.

They'd been maybe four miles out from the mine entrance when they got hit. Murphy had been complaining about how the mine's stale air messed with his sinuses and how the salt grit got into everything. Corbett had been standing in the bed of the truck, swiveling the light into tunnel after tunnel, wishing Murphy would shut up already. The man never seemed to stop complaining.

Suddenly, something had darted past the headlights. Corbett had only caught the briefest glimpse of it, but it had looked like a hunched figure scampering into a side tunnel. Scraps of cloth clung to its frame as if shuffled into the shadows. Nelson, the driver, had slammed on the brakes, nearly throwing Corbett onto the hood of the truck in the process. The searchlight had careened around at a cockeyed angle as Corbett grabbed onto it. Regaining his footing, he had drawn his service revolver. "Freeze!"

Hot metal clicked and pinged as everyone struggled to scramble out of the truck at once. "The hell was that?" Murphy had asked, pulling at his door handle.

As Corbett tried to track the figure they'd seen with the searchlight, he had become aware that they weren't alone in the tunnels. Murphy had finally managed to unfasten his door when a set of claws clamped down on the frame and tore it off the vehicle's chassis. Another set of misshapen talons had reached inside and ripped Murphy himself out of the truck.

Corbett had only seen the thing that did the ripping for a split second, but he knew it was a vision that would live in his nightmares for the rest of his life.

Once upon a time, the creature had clearly been human. Now it was a mass of twisted, organic chaos. It looked like a graveyard had had an abortion. More shapes were moving through the shadows just outside the searchlight's beam. They had come from everywhere. Dozens of them. Each one had looked like something that would send the Frankenstein monster screaming into the night. They seemed to be coming straight out of the damned walls, slithering bonelessly out of every available crevice. The shadows had suddenly become alive with writhing, shambling movement.

The monsters hadn't encircled the back of the truck yet, and Corbett hadn't waited. He'd jumped to the ground and ran for his life as the truck's other doors were being torn open. Something had climbed over Murphy's empty seat and fastened its teeth to the driver's face.

Corbett had fired his revolver a couple of times as he ran. He didn't know if he'd hit anything. The gun had been knocked out of his hand as something tried to grab his arm. Dodging away, he'd sped down the tunnel as fast as he could, the screams of his friends following him as he ran.

Now, all Corbett had was his flashlight and his wits. He needed to get out of the mine. He had no way of contacting any of the other patrols, and he couldn't guarantee his fellow officers would find him before those things did.

There was another *tap* from somewhere else in the mine. Thinking about what he'd seen, Corbett shuddered. He wasn't sure what that noise was, but it was time to get moving.

Some of the mine intersections were fitted with signs to direct the workers. He hadn't stopped to read them while he was running, but they might save his life now. They labeled every cross shaft. Some of them must point to the mine elevators.

His thumb rested on the flashlight's switch. He was going to need to use it if he wanted out of here. Hopefully, its batteries had enough juice to get him to a part of the mine where somebody could help him.

Tap. Tap. Tap.

Corbett's blood turned to ice. There was that noise again, and it was definitely closer. Maybe it was just a natural sound of the rock shifting, but if it wasn't…

Some primal sense told Corbett that things weren't right. The air had changed in the tunnel. It wasn't something he could articulate, but all the hair on his arms suddenly stood at attention. He couldn't see anything, couldn't hear anything, couldn't even smell anything, but alarm bells were ringing in his head. Long-buried instincts were sending up smoke signals to his higher brain. He needed to move.

Taking a deep breath, he flicked on the light. And screamed.

A face stared back at him from only a few feet away. At least, it used to be a face. Now, it was little more than a crater of bone and teeth and split, flaking skin.

The monstrosity had once been a man, but something had gone very wrong with nature's plans. In places, the flesh was pierced with what looked like layers of fingernails growing like scales. The jaws jutted forward where the bone itself had twisted and changed. Hyper-elongated teeth pierced through the cheeks at obscene angles. Dozens of new fangs grew in a jagged row behind the first set. Corbett could see the thing's fleshy tongue through the holes in its cheeks. It was raw and mottled, as if the uppermost layer had sloughed off. Blood blisters pebbled the tongue like a layer of scavenger beetles. However, the worst part of the ruined face was the eyes. The right eye was glossed by some sort of nictitating membrane, a semi-transparent second eyelid streaked through with a riot of veins. Corbett could see the monster's pupil jittering about, constantly moving. The other eye … Well, there was no other eye. It was just a hole, but it wasn't empty. More teeth — little, stumpy canines — rimmed the socket and continued deeper into the skull in neat, concentric orbits. Most of the flesh had peeled away from the socket like yellowing wallpaper, and the underlying bone was split open towards the temple. The flaps of bone opened and closed, snapping mindlessly, creating a secondary mouth on the side of the man's head.

Corbett knew that he'd never forget that little mouth trying to grow out of the side of the man's head. It would be with him when he ate, and when he read the paper, and when he sat on the can. It would be rattling around in his brain, pinballing through his thoughts like a loose ball bearing, for the rest of his life. A little part of his sanity choked on its own vomit and died just then.

The thing that had once been a human being was dressed in the remains of a Detroit Salt Combine miner's uniform. More of the creatures stood in the shadows just outside the reach of Corbett's beam. They'd followed him, tracking him perfectly through the stygian gloom of the mine tunnels. They too were dressed in the shredded remains of mining coveralls.

The miner directly in front of him reached out a scaly claw. Corbett ducked, swinging the flashlight. The metal tube crashed into the creature's ribs with a sickening crunch. Corbett felt something inside the monster's chest snap like old, rotting wood.

Darkness consumed the tunnel again as the flashlight fizzled out, but Corbett was already running. Inhuman hands grasped for him, clawing at his arms and face. He slammed straight into one of the creatures, auguring his shoulder into the monstrosity's center of mass like a football player steamrolling a smaller opponent out of the way. The creature's innards felt spongy, like a sack of rotten cheese.

Corbett heard a strange sound echoing down the tunnel, and he realized he was still screaming. He propelled himself down the passageway at full speed. Completely blind in the blackness, he ran in the first direction his legs took him.

Sometimes divers became disoriented in sea caves and lost track of which direction was up. They might travel in the wrong direction for minutes, thinking they were heading toward the surface. Sometimes they became so confused they ran out of oxygen and died down there before they could find their way out. But Corbett didn't have minutes. He might have a few seconds at most to choose the right direction. He lunged in the general direction the tunnel led, flailing in the darkness.

Tap. Tap. Tap.

That knocking sound came again from somewhere behind Corbett, even louder than before. Whatever was making that noise, it was following him.

Without any warning, Corbett slammed into one of the mine's walls, nearly knocking himself unconscious. His nose snapped like a twig as he met the rocks face first. His teeth rattled in his skull as the air blasted out of his lungs. He bounced off the wall and landed on his butt, cracking his flashlight against the ground as he fell.

Weak, wavering light spat out through the broken lens, blasting Corbett in the face and sending purplish rings across his vision. Blood ran down his face in a warm torrent from his shattered nose, but he put all that out of his mind. He could hear shuffling footsteps behind him.

Struggling to regain his feet, Corbett flipped himself up onto his knees before collapsing again. Running into the wall had knocked him nearly senseless and turned his thoughts fuzzy. He managed to get to his knees again, steadying himself against the wall. He grabbed the flashlight and wrenched himself back onto his feet, nearly falling down again in the process. His mind was sluggish, his limbs uncooperative. It would be so much easier to rest ... just for a minute. He could close his eyes and let the mushiness drain from his mind.

No! He had to get out of this hell hole; he had to escape. A single thought sliced through the stunned cobwebs clinging to his brain: *"RUN!"*

With a supreme effort of will, Corbett stumbled forward, half bent at the waist like a drunk trying to escape a speakeasy raid. He went to his knees again and began to pull himself up when something splattered against the ground next to him.

He glanced down. It was some sort of clear, viscous liquid. Another rope of the syrupy goop dribbled down from the ceiling, landing on his shoulder. More globules began to rain down all around him. The stuff was unpleasantly warm and ... and ...

Corbett suddenly realized what the stuff on his shoulder was: saliva.

Tap.

The knocking sound came again, directly overhead this time. Slowly, almost unwillingly, Corbett raised the flashlight and looked up.

"Oh God," he said, and then he started running as fast as he could. He knew he couldn't outrun the thing on the ceiling, knew it with a cold, bone-hard certainty. He wished he still had his gun. Not that the weapon would offer him the least bit of protection. No, he wanted the gun so he could at least kill himself quickly and cleanly. There was no doubt he was about to die. The only question was how horribly.

His eyes burned when he'd looked at the thing, but that was nothing compared to the inferno raging in his head. It felt like just the mental image of the thing was chewing through his head like acid, soaking into his mind. Hot chills and frozen fire crept up his spine. His brain chafed as strange ideas and images squirmed through his head, clamoring over each other as they overran the ramparts of his sanity. He realized the monster was in his head. He could feel it rummaging through his thoughts, sniffing his memories. Impossible, inhuman thoughts crawled across his cerebellum like electric spiders.

Something huge and powerful slammed into Corbett's back, knocking him to the ground. He landed on his stomach and instantly tried to scramble to his feet. He rose to all fours before an immense weight landed on his back.

The pressure was horrendous, crushing. Corbett wriggled and squirmed, tried to struggle out from under the massive weight of one of the creature's legs. He was pinned by one of the monster's talons, like a prized butterfly on an entomologist's display board. It hurt like hell. He could feel the innards in his midsection compressing, squeezing together as he was pressed into the rocky earth. His spine strained, the vertebrae creaking and grating together. Corbett flailed his arms, desperately seeking purchase to help him crawl out from under his attacker.

Suddenly, the thing pinning him jerked backward, dragging him across the floor feet first. Something new clamped down on each side of Corbett's midsection, just below the ribs, and Corbett screamed again. An entire galaxy of white hot agony blinked into existence behind his eyes. He nearly passed out then and there.

There was a horrible squeezing sensation and a thick ripping noise, and then Corbett was free. The pressure relented. His shirt must have ripped, freeing him from the horrible thing's grasp.

Corbett crawled forward on his elbows commando-style, pulling away from the thing. It must have ripped more than his shirt. His entire torso felt like it was on fire, and hot, wet stickiness coated his sides.

He pushed himself up on his arms to get to his feet again, but he just flopped down on his face. Corbett suddenly realized that he couldn't feel his legs at all. He was paralyzed. Oh shit. Shitshitshit. The creature must have broken his back.

Writhing like a worm on a hook, Corbett tried to push himself onto his feet again. He willed feeling into his legs. The thing on the ceiling hadn't grabbed him again yet. If he was going to escape, this was probably his only chance. Hot tears of frustration and pain rolled down his cheeks as he fell onto his chest again. Flipping himself onto his back, Corbett shined the flashlight back toward his attacker.

As it turned out, he wasn't paralyzed. His legs were just gone. Corbett had been scissored in half just above the navel. The flashlight beam revealed a river of blood where Corbett had crawled away. He was trailing lengths of his own intestines, and his organs were starting to spill out of his ruptured body like groceries out of a ripped sack. Most of the pieces were already partially encrusted with a layer of salt crystals from the mine floor.

Corbett moaned and grabbed some of the warm, sticky viscera, trying to stuff it back inside his body, but it was no use. Touching the ragged flesh around the stump of his torso only caused more of himself to spill onto the ground.

Casting the flashlight madly about, Corbett caught one last sight of his limp legs. A set of gigantic mandibles stuffed the appendages into an equally gigantic mouth. Corbett watched his legs disappear into the huge maw, slurped down like jointed spaghetti.

He was beginning to feel light headed, distant. Even the pain was beginning to recede into a dull throb. More blood jetted out of his wounds onto the floor with each heartbeat, but the pulses were growing further and further apart. Or maybe it just seemed that way. Corbett couldn't tell anymore. Dark fog was beginning to creep into the corners of his vision, and he felt so tired. So very tired. Everything was slowly disappearing into the blackness that was engulfing him.

The thing approached him, little more than a shadowy outline against the midnight devouring Corbett's sight.

Tap.

Corbett's breathing grew increasingly unsteady. Red foam bubbled up his throat from his lungs, and he tried to cough, but only a little dribble of red came out. He stared at the monster hovering over him. Suddenly, it ducked its head, and Corbett felt himself being lifted off the ground in the thing's mouth. He tried to scream one last time.

The mandibles snapped down on Corbett's body, piercing his chest and mashing his lungs to pulp. Without waiting for the man to stop twitching, the mandibles pushed what was left of his body further down its gullet.

The flashlight slipped out of Corbett's limp hand and plummeted through the air. The bulb smashed, and the mine returned to perfect darkness.

Chapter 2
Fitzhugh Gets Served

One week later

Jasper O'Malley stood across the street from the laundromat. As always, bedlam reigned on the streets of Chicago. Traffic cops blew their whistles to little effect as vehicles whizzed past. Street vendors hawked everything from fruit to cigarettes to pulp magazines. The city smelled of factory fumes and hot asphalt. Pedestrians flowed around him like water pushing past an obstinate river rock. A few of them gave him odd looks as he stood perfectly still, waiting, watching. He ignored them. There was business to attend to.

Jasper owned seven suits. He was wearing suit number six. Not that it mattered; all of his suits were an identical slate gray and expertly tailored to his tall, wiry frame. Under the jacket, he wore a plain white shirt and a blue silk tie. A matching gray hat sat perched on his head at a rakish angle. He kept the hat tipped at an angle to conceal the fact that his left ear was missing. His face might have been handsome if he were smiling, but he rarely smiled. A large, aquiline nose, the kind that would have looked good on a Roman emperor, sat in the middle of his face. Two dark green eyes rested above the nose. They moved back and forth like big jungle cats restlessly pacing their circus cages, never stopping to focus on any one thing for too long before sliding on to the next point of interest. They were the sort of eyes that quickly made people uncomfortable. Boyish freckles dappled his face. Despite the warm summer day, Jasper remained buttoned up in his suit.

He watched the crowds milling past the laundromat on the opposite side of the street. His eyes flicked from person to person, assessing
each before moving to the next. Jasper saw a few potential targets,
but none of them went into the laundromat.

He waited.

Ten minutes passed. Then twenty. Jasper continued to stand and
watch the laundromat like a big gray shark watching the beach, waiting for swimmers to splash into the water.

Finally, Jasper spotted someone who matched the description
he'd been given. The man was big and broad shouldered, built like a
boxcar. He was wearing an expensive-looking coat, but it fit poorly
around his massive arms and stumpy neck. He had strong, classical
features. His square jaw was currently thrown open in a laugh as he
put his arm around the shoulders of a short-haired blonde woman.

She was dressed in a green flapper dress and a floppy hat. The
big man's arm practically engulfed her. Jasper noticed she wasn't laughing. Her feet wobbled on a pair of glittery heels.

As he watched, the man opened the laundromat's front door and
stepped inside, not bothering to hold it open for the woman. She had
to grab the handle to keep the door from slamming shut on her face.

Jasper waited. A minute ticked by.

At last he decided he'd given them enough time, and he began
walking toward the laundromat. His polished shoes padded off the
sidewalk and onto the street. A horn honked at him, but he ignored
it.

A length of bells hung on the inside of the laundromat's door,
but they barely made a sound as Jasper opened the door and stepped
inside in one fluid motion. He glanced around the dark room.

Neatly pressed clothes hung from dozens of racks situated all
around the room. Little numbered placards were attached to each
hangar. A counter stood directly in front of him, but there was no one
there to help him. Steam wafted gently through the air like a sauna.
Jasper spied several large cauldrons bubbling like witches' brews and
a set of wringers, but there was no sign of the man and woman he
had tracked in here.

He walked up to the counter, curled his hand into a fist, and
knocked on the wooden surface.

Tap. Tap. Tap.

A door at the back of the room popped open and an elderly

Asian woman appeared. Her hair was streaked gray, and her face was a roadmap of wrinkles. She smiled when she saw him. "Hello. You pick up or drop off?" Her English was heavily accented, but passable.

"Actually, I'm looking for someone," Jasper said.

The elderly woman's face instantly hardened into a mask of suspicion. "Pick up or drop off?" She put her palms on the counter and squared her shoulders, looking unhappy.

"He was a big fellow," Jasper continued, unfazed. "A woman was accompanying him."

"No one like that here," she insisted, her voice cold.

"I saw them walk in here."

"You see wrong."

"My apologies for bothering you then, Ma'am. I guess I'll just pick up my clothes." Jasper's hand crept inside his jacket and grabbed something.

"You have number?" she asked, suspicion in her voice.

"Of course." His hand emerged from his jacket with a ten dollar bill poking out from between his long fingers. "I seem to have lost my stub, but I believe I was number ten."

"I don't think that was your number."

A five appeared beside the ten as if by magic. "You're right. How silly of me. I was number fifteen."

She stared at the two bills for a moment, obviously trying to decide if she should push for more. Then she looked up and saw Jasper's eyes and decided to settle for what she could get. This one could be trouble if he wanted to be.

"Ah, yes. I believe I have your items back here. Follow me and I'll get them for you." She dropped her falsely halting speech and slipped into perfect, Chicago-clipped English. The elderly woman turned around and began walking toward the back of the laundry without waiting to see if he followed.

She approached the litter of hangers lining the back wall. Coats and dresses of every color hung from the racks. Sticking her hands between two suits, the woman spread the clothes like Moses parting the Red Sea.

With the space now cleared, Jasper could see a door behind the clothes. "There's only one rule back there — don't cause trouble. I don't know what your business is, but if it interferes with *my* business, you'll regret it."

"I shall endeavor to keep that in mind." Jasper tipped his hat and opened the door.

"You do that. Welcome to Madame Mai's," she said as Jasper stepped into the secret room behind the laundromat, and the door shut behind him.

The place was a "blind tiger," a type of speakeasy. Prohibition made the manufacture, transportation, and sale of alcohol punishable by law, but it was still perfectly legal to drink the stuff. Or give it away, for that matter. Thus, enterprising criminal minds had come up with a solution of sorts. If patrons bought a ticket to see a performance or an exotic animal, they could be served a "complimentary" beverage. Patrons could buy as many tickets as they liked, receiving a drink each time. Often the "tigers" they were paying to see were mangy alley cats, but no one seemed to mind. A halfway-decent prosecutor could still nail the proprietors for transporting the alcohol and probably any number of other charges, so the illicit bars continued to exist only in the shadows.

The deception, for the most part, was for the customers. They could come in and enjoy themselves without the feeling that they were participating in anything illegal. It was a quaint, little illusion to set people at ease, transforming the illicit business into a secret club. It calmed customers' nerves, and they probably bought more product as a result.

The building's construction was spartan, with large, wooden beams holding up the roof. A banner hung between two of the rough-hewn pillars. "WELCOME TO MADAME MAI'S," it said. "COME SEE AGATHA, THE WONDER CHICKEN. 50¢."

From the outside, the building probably looked like just another rusting warehouse or anonymous storage depot. The interior, though, resembled a posh restaurant. Dozens of small tables lined the high-ceilinged structure like a Parisian café. A phonograph in the corner warbled a jazz set. Reproductions of famous oil paintings lined the walls. A sixty-foot long bar took pride of place along the back wall. Hundreds of bottles lined the shelves behind the bar, some of them of pre-Prohibition vintage. The fifty cent price tag to see Agatha, the Wonder Chicken, might buy a man two of the cheaper, newer drinks, but some of the aged, amber-colored whiskeys would likely require several tickets.

His work took Jasper into speakeasies more often than he liked.

From his experience, most of them were dark, unpleasant holes that stank of desperation and stale vomit. Usually, they were located in abandoned garages or hidden sub-basements, and they were only open at odd hours. After a few years of operation, every available surface, from the stools to the walls, became sticky with cigarette tar. Because the main concern for such structures was usually muffling sound, ventilation was poor. The bottled-up funk of tens of thousands of chain-smoked cigarettes built up until it clung to the structure's very studs. Often, the speakeasies were too primitive for plumbing, so there was sometimes just a trough in a dark corner of the room. Sometimes the trough was directly in front of the bar stools so that the men at the bar didn't have to risk losing their spots by getting up. Most of the drinks themselves were strongly flavored to hide the raw, volatile taste of pure alcohol. Sometimes the drinks were tainted, either with chemicals or some outside effluvia, and the customers would become violently ill.

Of course, there were always exceptions, and Madame Mai's obviously catered to a different type of clientele. All of the customers were well-dressed, dapper-looking chaps and well-groomed dames. Jasper spotted the deputy mayor sitting at one table, slowly working his way to the bottom of a tumbler. Other patrons appeared to be lawyers, bankers, and other professionals from the nearby districts, chatting with their colleagues.

Usually, a successful place like this would be guarded. If the owners weren't already associated with organized crime, mobsters would almost certainly come a-calling to offer protection. Less-prosperous booze barons might employ a few local street toughs to keep tabs paid, fights broken up, and undesirables out. Jasper had once seen someone crush a man's larynx because he owed three dollars. The body had been dragged into a back room, and there was a minute-long pause before everyone went back to the business of drinking. For a ritzy joint like this, the hired muscle would probably quietly lead you to the back alley, club you over the head, and load you into a truck to be anonymously buried in a field outside of town rather than just killing you on the spot. Pure class, that.

Jasper spotted Madame Mai's goons almost as soon as he stepped through the door. They stood out like a couple of turds in a punch bowl. Their matching suits were both cut from the same cheap, black cloth with the same overdone shoulder pads to make them look bigger and more intimidating. One was a squat man built like a fire plug. He was leaning against the nearest pillar, watching the door. The second thug was a big bruiser with a shaved head. He continually swept the room with a sour gaze. Whereas most of the customers were wearing pointed wingtips, the guards wore heavy, blunt ankle boots. Boots like that had many utilitarian functions, chief among them, kicking the crap out of people.

Jasper continued looking. He was searching for the big man he'd seen enter Madame Mai's laundromat. Sawing his eyes back and forth over the tables, Jasper began to stalk through the room. There was no one matching the big man's size. The bouncers were the only ones who even came close.

One of the patrons locked eyes with Jasper and raised a friendly glass. Jasper nodded to Tycho Vedel, but didn't bother to stop or further acknowledge his presence. There was business to be done.

The big man was not at any of the tables, nor was he at the bar. Jasper eyed a doorway at the back of the speakeasy. A sign hung over the door: "AGATHA, THE WONDER CHICKEN. 50¢."

A pretty girl stood next to the door selling cigarettes from a tray. She smiled as he approached. "How many tickets to the show, sweetheart?"

"Just one." Jasper did not return the smile. He reached into his pocket and removed five dimes, dropping them into the girl's hand one at a time. Once they were all in her outstretched palm, she counted them again.

"Thanks for visiting, hon. Once you're done, you can redeem your ticket for something special over there." She pointed in the direction of the bar, but Jasper was already through the door, hunting.

The small room was dimly lit. More for form's sake than anything else, hard, uncomfortable-looking benches lined three sides of the room, providing ample viewing space for the star attraction. A small cage stood atop a simple podium, but Jasper's focus was on the two people standing to either side of the pedestal. The big man and the woman were peering into the cage.

Blonde locks bouncing around her face, the woman tittered as she watched the big man. He had stuck his fingers through the bars of the cage and was pinching Agatha, the Wonder Chicken's tail feathers. Agatha was struggling to get away, but her feet just scrabbled uselessly against the floor of her cage. She made undignified noises as she ran in place.

"But Edwin, they're *so damn adorable*. Are you sure I can't have one?" The blonde's voice was high pitched and grating. She took a drag on a long, thin cigarette and exhaled a stream of fragrant smoke into the cage.

"Beulah, you wouldn't know how to take care of a chicken if they came with instruction manuals."

Agatha finally managed to break free of Edwin's grasp, losing a couple of tail feathers in the process. The blonde pouted.

"C'mon, I didn't bring us here to play with chickens. Let's go get those drinks," Edwin said.

The blonde immediately brightened. "Okie-dokie," Beulah said, and giggled again. Jasper noticed that her eyes weren't quite focused, and the pupils were dilated. She was unsteady on her feet, at risk of toppling right out of her sparkly heels. She was more than just drunk. On laudanum, maybe.

She seemed unsure what to do with her exhausted cigarette, so she stuffed it through the wires of Agatha's cage. Edwin grabbed her hand and started to lead her out of the room.

"'Scuse me, Bub." The big man attempted to shove his way through the door.

Jasper moved out of the way and let them pass, then walked over to the cage and examined a small plaque glued to the side of the podium.

> *Behold the rare Mongolian Steppe Chicken. These chickens were carried by Genghis Khan as his endless hordes of barbarian horsemen swept across Asia. Easily transported over a long distance, the chickens were valued for their meat, eggs, and plumage. Often, the chickens roamed free after a battle and were known to peck flesh off the bodies the Mongols left in their wake. Agatha is the only example of Mongolian Steppe Chicken in the Western Hemisphere, a true marvel of the mysterious Orient.*

It was a good story, but Jasper recognized the small chicken as a Bearded d'Uccle, a Belgian breed. She had creamy tan feathers accented with points of blue-grey. A big muff of feathers under her beak gave her an exotic appearance. She sat in the middle of the cage, unhappily preening her tail. A clutch of tiny, peeping heads poked out from under her wings, chattering incessantly. One of the fluffy chicks, resembling a small, yellow cotton ball, escaped out from under Agatha and ran over to investigate the cigarette smoldering in the bottom of the cage. Curious, it poked at the embers.

A small padlock latched the cage's door. Jasper dipped his fingers into the cuff of his jacket and pulled out a lock pick. Within a few seconds, the padlock snicked open, and Jasper reached into the cage.

Peeping frantically, the chick scampered back under the warm, safe confines of its mother's feathers. Jasper snagged the smoldering butt. A hint of bright red lipstick lined the cigarette's base.

He flicked the cigarette onto the ground and relocked the cage. They were beautiful chickens, and the cage was much too small for them.

Jasper turned around and walked out of the room. Back to business.

The job sounded simple. All he had to do was serve Edwin Bartholomew Fitzhugh III with divorce papers. But no one came to the Attican Detective Agency with simple problems.

Normally, it would be a task for a certified court courier. Someone would deliver the papers, hand them to Fitzhugh, and leave. That was all the law required. Simple. Easy-peasy. Applesauce. But that was before three couriers in a row "lost" their deliveries in transit. Fitzhugh came from old money. His grandfather expanded into Chicago's slaughterhouse business early in the city's growth and made great heaps of money in the process. Granddaddy Fitzhugh's stockyards provided countless rations of tinned meat to Union soldiers during the Civil War.

As the scion of a meat-packing family, Fitzhugh had cash to spare and friends in every corner of Chicago. Jasper had done research on the man, trailing him for the better part of a week to learn his habits. Madame Mai's was his favorite hangout, and he visited nearly every day, a different girl slung across his hairy arms each time. All Jasper needed to do to find his quarry was stakeout the speakeasy's laundromat front.

Fitzhugh was built like a tyrannosaurus with a growth condition, and he had the personality to match. He was a hedonistic, boorish playboy prone to fits of extreme anger. As near as Jasper could tell, the man's favorite, and possibly only, hobby consisted of betting on dog fights.

The Fitzhughs virtually shanghaied Edwin into a marriage with Georgina Whittacker, the daughter of a prominent railroad family. Maybe the family thought marriage would settle Edwin down. Maybe it was just a cynical attempt to forge a permanent alliance in an industry that could transport meat products to all corners of the nation. Jasper didn't know, and it wasn't his job to care.

Georgina Fitzhugh contacted the Attican Detective Agency ten days ago, asking if one of their operatives could serve her husband with divorce papers. After two years, she'd had enough of Fitzhugh's abuse and philandering. She wanted out, and she needed someone who wouldn't be intimidated or bribed into ditching the papers.

Fitzhugh didn't give an eighth of a damn about the marriage. He probably didn't even care about the potential business aspects. The slaughterhouses could churn out meat products under the command of a board of directors indefinitely. No, Fitzhugh refused to grant the divorce because it would be a black stain on his social standing. He was a vain creature, and he knew higher circles would talk about it behind his back if he allowed the marriage to dissolve.

Georgina feared that if she couldn't get rid of Fitzhugh legally, he might use his connections to get rid of her. Legally or not. It was much easier to walk among Chicago's elite as a widower than a divorcee. And if Fitzhugh wasn't served the divorce papers, the process couldn't begin.

Jasper turned around and walked back out the door. He spotted Fitzhugh immediately, perched on one of the barstools with Beulah by his side. One of the barkeeps was pouring something expensive-looking for the pair. The stool looked like it was about to snap in half under Fitzhugh's girth.

At six feet, Jasper was taller than most of the men in the speakeasy, but he was primarily composed of ropy sinew and tough gristle, like a jackal. Fitzhugh, on the other hand, was built like a gorilla. He had at least four inches of height on Jasper and a chest like a steam boiler. His shirt was of an expensive cut, but tight, clearly chosen to show off his muscular physique rather than for any fashion qualities. The man looked like he could probably snap a yak in half if he wanted to.

Treading across the floor on silent feet, Jasper watched Fitzhugh slug back an entire glass of fiery liquid. Fitzhugh raised a finger, and the barkeep began to prepare another drink. Fitzhugh slid a ticket across the counter in payment. Jasper tapped him on the shoulder.

"Edwin Bartholomew Fitzhugh III?"

Edwin Bartholomew Fitzhugh III spun around on his stool. "Yeah? What's it to you?"

"Necessary for identification. I'm glad I found the correct man. Allow me to introduce myself; I'm Jasper O'Malley, with the Attican Detective Agency." A badge appeared in Jasper's hand, was flashed at Fitzhugh, and then disappeared just as quickly.

The barkeep finished Fitzhugh's drink and left it on the counter. Beulah twisted around to look at Jasper. She would have been pretty if she hadn't been plastered out of her mind. Her eyes were round and glassy. One of the straps of her dress had slipped, and the already low neckline sagged considerably.

"Can I help you, Detective, or are you just here to waste my time? If you know my name, you must recognize that I'm a very busy man." Fitzhugh flashed a big, carnivorous smile.

"Of course. This won't take but a moment." Jasper reached out and fixed the strap of Beulah's dress, slipping it back over her shoulder. The barkeep, who had been enjoying the view, moved on to serve a new customer. Jasper then reached into his jacket and removed a large, manila envelope. "I have some documents from your wife. I am hereby serving you with —"

"Oh, Christ. Not this again," Fitzhugh reached into his back pocket and removed a thick leather wallet. Without looking, he reached into the billfold and peeled off a wad of bills. "Listen, Sport, my wife isn't well. She's in the hospital; it's her nerves, you see? Just take this and scram. For the inconvenience she's put you through and all. Once she's better, I'm sure she'll agree that she's being silly."

Eighty dollars dangled in front of Jasper's nose. He brushed Fitzhugh's hand out of his face using the back of his fingers. "I am aware that Georgina is in the hospital. I visited her. Her nerves seemed just fine. Her primary ailment appeared to be that her legs were broken, an injury not inconsistent with being picked up and tossed out a third-story window. If the hospital told you the problem was her nerves, perhaps you should take that money and hire some competent doctors."

"Hey, pipsqueak, this doesn't concern you, okay? It's a purely private matter. I don't care who you are. I'm not accepting those papers."

"Drat. It would seem that we're at an impasse. I was hired to ensure that you accept these papers." Jasper held the envelope out again.

Fitzhugh irked him. Time to try a different tact. "Out of curiosity, does Fitzhugh Meat Packing have a specialty item? I'm guessing you deliver quite a bit of horse's ass. You seem to have a lot of it on hand."

"Here," Fitzhugh snatched the papers out of Jasper's hand. Jasper didn't try to grab them back. Fitzhugh ripped open the top of the envelope and pulled the papers out. He crumpled them in one massive fist without looking at them. His face was beginning to turn an unhealthy shade of red.

Technically, Fitzhugh had just accepted the papers. In the eyes of the law, he was officially on notice. Mission accomplished. Nevertheless, the man had put Jasper's hackles up.

Fitzhugh took the wad of papers and tossed them at Jasper. They bounced off the lapel of his suit and fell to the ground. "Stick it where the sun don't shine, pal." Fitzhugh turned back to the counter, ready to quaff down his drink.

"That can be arranged," Jasper said, picking up the wad of papers. He tapped Fitzhugh on the shoulder.

The big man swiveled around on his stool again. That was a mistake. He should have stood up immediately, using his height and weight to their maximum advantage. Sitting down, he was shorter than Jasper, and precariously balanced on the too-small stool.

"Get out of my face, or *GLUARG!*" Jasper jammed the wad of court papers in Fitzhugh's mouth. Fitzhugh's eyes went wide in disbelief. He grabbed for Jasper, but missed as the wiry detective stepped backward.

Beulah snorted high-pitched laughter. Fitzhugh swung his arm around the full length of his body and delivered a vicious backhand to Beulah's face. The blow knocked her clean off her stool, and she fell backward with a squawk.

Fitzhugh spat the papers out onto the floor. He didn't look at Beulah, who was on the floor squalling.

"You," he snarled. "You're a dead man."

And don't miss out on these exciting releases!

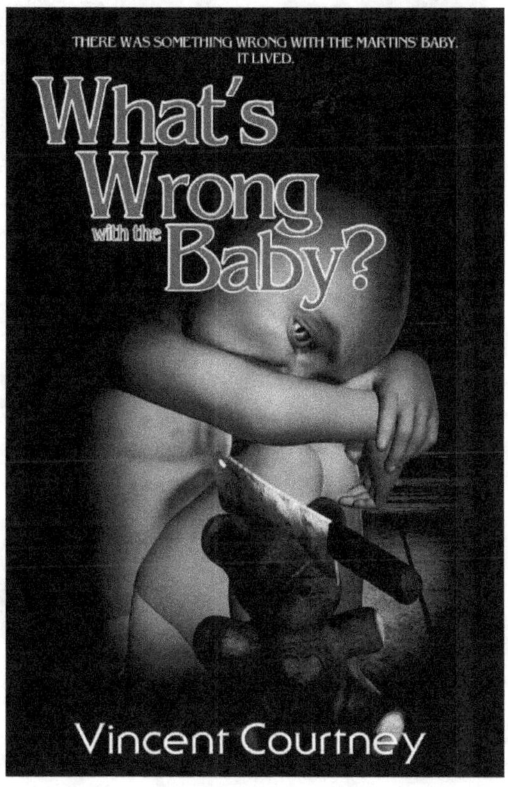

Some children are just born evil. Nobody knows
this better than Marty Martin.
He's seen his baby brother do things no infant is capable of
doing, but nobody believes him. Will Marty be able to convince
his parents that there's something wrong with the baby before
the body count gets to high?

Find out in Vincent Courtney's
What's Wrong With the Baby?

They call it *Isla do Los Perdidos*.
Island of the Lost.
According to legend, all those who venture
onto its shores never return.

Valarie DeNola and her sister have chosen to ignore
the warnings and proceed to lead a film crew
to the cursed island.

Will they suffer the same fate as those who've gone before,
ot will they be the first to reveal the secrets concealed
upon the island?

Find out in *Infernal* by Cheryl Low!